Lindsey

by

Lane McFarland

Please visit Lane McFarland's website at

http://romancingtheeras.com/

to learn more about her and her books.

Lane McFarland

LINDSEY

The Daughters of Alastair MacDougall ~ Book III

Published by Amazon KDP

Seattle, WA

Electronic KDP Edition: June 2014

Lindsey

TABLE OF CONTENTS

Lane McFarland

TABLE OF CONTENTS

Lindsey

Dedication

This book is dedicated to my husband, Ken, and

my son, Kenneth. I thank you for love, patience,

and encouragement to reach for my dream.

You are my heroes.

As always, I give a special thanks to Tessy,

for her confidence in me and her sweet,

nurturing spirit. I have truly been blessed

with her friendship!

I am so grateful to Helen, my kindred spirit

at One More Time Editing!

Thank you for your patience,

guidance, and wonderful suggestions.

Many thanks to HHRW Critters Renee,

Barbara, Wendy, Sam, Kathleen, and Joan,

and my critique partners in

Lane McFarland

Celtic Hearts for their invaluable
comments and tremendous support.

Chapter One

Northumberland, England
August 1299

Lindsey MacDougall descended into the dark pit of hell. The stench of excrement and death struck her, but she resisted the urge to gag on the wretched fumes of brutality. Fearful tremors racked her body. She had made it thus far and prayed she could continue.

She glanced over her shoulder at the enemy soldiers standing guard on either side of the door she'd just passed through. Swords strapped to their sides, they watched her every move with steely eyes. Few outsiders were allowed in Collins's dungeon. The men would not hesitate to sound the alarm if they grew suspicious of her and the reason for her visit.

Howls of anguish and despair drifted from below, and she envisioned Satan himself wielding instruments of torture. She gripped the worn stair railing with one hand, her large healer's basket in the other, and eased her foot onto the next step, then the next. Cold air swirled up from the dark cavernous hole. Flames sputtered from torches secured in brackets lining the dank dungeon, monstrous shadows dancing up from the black abyss.

Nerves stretched taut, sweat dribbled down her temples. She prayed the moisture didn't cause the ash-paste that disguised her face to slide onto the bodice of her scratchy woolen gown. However uncomfortable, she wanted the soldiers to be put off by her ungainly appearance.

She peered over the railing and let her eyes adjust to the dim light at the bottom of the stairs. Ominous looking corridors ran in four directions like spokes of a wheel, with three English soldiers positioned in the center, huddled around a wooden crate.

One guard threw down several cards on the makeshift table and roared while slapping the soldier next to him on the back.

Another tossed his cards on the discarded pile. "I'm out."

A high-pitched scream followed by agonized moans sent chills slithering down her spine. What evils did the darkened corridors hold? An urge to run back up the stairs and escape the nightmarish scene nearly overcame her. Instead, she inhaled a fortifying breath and took another step down.

She could do this.

As a messenger who routinely delivered missives behind enemy lines for the rebellion, she should be used to danger, but she rarely found herself in such an unsavory position. Aye, she could outrun and outmaneuver any man on horseback, but this assignment was different. Hamish, a rebel leader, had given explicit orders to convey a message to the Scots' commander and leave, but she had not counted upon learning of Logan's capture.

Her friend needed her.

Swallowing hard, she continued her plunge into purgatory. Upon reaching the bottom step, she hunched her shoulders and shuffled toward the menacing group. Grit crunched beneath her feet and stagnant water soaked the hem of her overly large gown. More tormented howls reverberated through the thick dungeon walls. Her body quaked as she fought to retain composure and pretend the wails did not affect her.

The enemy soldiers straightened, their attention focused on her. A burly guard advanced, his dark eyes narrowing. "Who the hell are you? Where's Cora?"

Another man circled her. He stroked her mud-crusted hair, then squeezed the padding on her bottom. She inwardly flinched and moved out of his reach. *Dirty cur.*

"Och, the old healer be feelin' poorly," Lindsey answered. "I'm 'ere to fix up the master's prisoners fer 'er. Hear tell they be taking them to stand trial, and Master Collins wants 'em looking guid, their injuries healed."

She faced the groping man and offered her basket to him while struggling with the overwhelming urge to slam it into his filthy face.

He snatched it from her fingers and rummaged through the contents, extracted clay jars and strips of cloth, then tossed them onto the crate. He'd not find any weapons; she'd concealed a single blade against her thigh.

"Careful!" Her head tilted toward the woven container. "Them salves is all I got to patch up the prisoners afore their trip."

The man shoved the basket at her and grabbed a thick key ring off a rusty peg in the wall. He glanced over his shoulder at the gaming soldiers and barked, "Don't start without me. I aim to win back my coin."

The men laughed and returned to their sport, no longer concerned with Lindsey's presence.

Heart hammering, she stuffed the supplies back into her basket and followed the lumbering man down one of the passageways. The overpowering stench of feces and urine gagged her. Cells lined the dirt aisle. Battered men filled the cramped area. Their clothes were mere rags; little protection against the damp air seeping through the walls.

As she and the guard approached, an eerie silence fell over the prisoners. With widened eyes, they cringed and shuffled from the bars. Lindsey's gaze shot across the men, taking note of the number housed in Collins's torture chamber. She would report these horrid conditions to Hamish. The rebel leader and her brethren Scots would not stand for their fellow countrymen to suffer such savagery.

Rats scurried along the wall. With a curse, the guard kicked one from his path. It squealed and landed against the bars with a thud. Water dripped from the ceiling, causing the flame of the man's torch to hiss as he turned a corner. She ducked under cobwebs and followed him farther into the bowels of the pit. Cold, damp air circled her shoulders, and she gave thanks for the disguise's heavy padding.

Finally the soldier stopped in front of a thick worn door with a small square grate open at eye level. He rattled the key into the padlock. The hinges creaked as the door swung and banged against the wall. As he touched the flame of his torch to one secured in a wall bracket, she stepped into the rank cell. Fire blazed and sputtered, lighting the dark chamber.

More than a dozen men huddled on the floor. They squinted, their hands raised to block the light. Bloodied and torn clothes hung on their haggard frames. Dirt and muck blackened their skin, while festering cuts and discolored bruises lined their arms and legs.

Compassion over the savagery these men had suffered swept through her soul, and she struggled to control the crippling emotion.

The beefy guard waved his torch toward the back of the room. "Them's the beggars goin' to trial."

Twisted shapes of four men, their wrists shackled to the wall and their feet barely touching the floor, came into sight. Her chest tightened as if bands squeezed the life from her. "They'll have to be cut down, sweets. They cannae eat or git fixed up hanging on the wall."

The man swung his head toward her. His lip curled.

Her pulse pounded in her ears, and she trembled with rage. She wanted to pounce on him, grab his blade, and sink it into his gut. Straining to gain composure, she turned her back on the men and set her basket on the floor. Her hand trembled as she inhaled the putrid air and struggled to calm her nerves. She must maintain her heartless pretense, appear untouched by the savagery. Biting the side of her lip, she rummaged through the jars and extracted the healing salves.

Chains rattled behind her. Thumps of dead weight and groans indicated the guard had freed the men. As he marched from the cell, he cast a look at Lindsey and slammed the door. The lock clunked, and his booted footsteps grew quieter as he strode away.

Several men rushed from the huddled group to aid their fallen companions. Lindsey hurried to the first man and knelt beside him. She pushed his hair to the side and grimaced.

Logan.

Cora's little bandits were correct.

His swollen face was blackened, and blood caked the back of his head. "Logan, can ye hear me? It's Lindsey."

His eyes fluttered. Moans of the injured men wafted around her. She jerked the basket to her side and brought out a flask of water, a soft cloth, and a jar of salve. "Look in my basket for more water skins," she called over her shoulder to the other prisoners.

Logan's friends, Adam, Thom, and Colyne lay unmoving. Dark dried blood and dirt smeared the men's swollen, beaten faces. Their listless bodies attested to abuse and neglect.

"The commander takes delight in torturing them."

Lindsey's head snapped to the man who stooped beside her.

"Seems to hold a real interest in them." He grabbed her basket and passed out containers to several others. They crowded around, snatching the bandages, salves, and potions she'd brought.

"Why?" she whispered. "What's so special about them?"

The man squinted and indicated Logan with his head. "Collins couldn't break him. I think that about drove the commander over the brink. He wanted to deliver information on the rebels' stronghold to the king. Infuriated him that he failed to do so."

The man bent over Adam and helped him sit.

While supporting Logan's head, Lindsey held a flask to his parched, cracked lips and dribbled the liquid into his mouth. He sputtered, gulping at the water.

"Easy," she said, giving him sips while she studied his disfigured face. "I'm here to help ye."

One eye was swollen shut, the other barely open. His brown hair hung in filthy strands across his forehead, and a red irritated gash crossed his grimy cheek. She sat on the nasty hard floor and cradled his head in her lap. The medicinal salves would do little to heal him, but she had to try.

Her heart clenched. When she'd last seen him, the days spent with the fear of English hostilities and devastation as constant companions had not yet arrived. The soldiers had not yet destroyed her carefree way of life. They had not been concerned with the next raid or protecting the clan from enemy invasion. Instead, Lindsey and Logan enjoyed each other's company, held the same love for horses, and had become fast friends.

He groaned. "Lindsey?"

"Aye, it's me." Her voice caught as she answered.

His good eye narrowed, and he grasped her wrist, his grip surprisingly strong for someone so battered. "What the hell are ye doing here? This is no place for ye, lass."

"The *Sassenachs* are taking ye and yer men to the east coast in two days." She spoke softly to him while dabbing his grimy forehead and bearded cheeks. "Yer caravan will not make it to the ship. Have faith. Stay strong. I have a plan."

~~~

Lindsey

Cold seeped through the slatted floor of the dark, dank cell as Logan Ross sagged against the wall. His body trembled uncontrollably, and he couldn't manage to stay awake. Dreams of Lindsey wafted through his sluggish mind. Was she really in this Godforsaken pit yesterday? The idea caused his stomach to churn. Surely he'd imagined it, but her gentle caress and soothing voice had drifted over him. Peace had enveloped him, but when the dream ended, the agony of her absence penetrated his soul.

Pain radiated through his ribs. Tattered and blood-soaked clothes stuck to his lacerated back, and filthy hair hung across his face. He moved his shoulder. The cloth tugged at the raw gaping ridges of his skin. The familiar burn coursed down the flayed furrows Collins's whip had forged.

A frigid breeze swirled, fluttering the wall torch's flame. Although one eye was swollen shut, he managed to peer through the other at his men huddled on the floor. They suffered similar injuries from the brutality of their host, *Arnold Collins*.

How Logan would relish getting his hands on Bernard, one of the men who'd joined Logan's group some weeks earlier. A black patch covering one eye, the traitor had stood behind Collins, sneering as enemy soldiers bound the Scots. Logan's vow to get revenge on the one-eyed bastard kept him alive; helped him endure Collins's barbaric inquisition.

The door to the cell crashed against the wall. Two guards marched over to Logan and hauled him to his feet, pulling his arms tight. Excruciating pain shot through his torso, and he struggled to breathe. One of the guards grabbed his hair and wrenched his head up.

Arnold Collins stormed into the room. He held a cloth to his nose and strode over to Logan, a dagger clenched in his fist. He lowered the fabric from his face, and a sinister smile spread. "It's unfortunate you have been so stubborn."

Light glinted off the blade as he twisted it between his grubby fingers. The cur advanced to stand within inches of Logan and placed the sharp tip just below his eye. He pressed the blade into Logan's skin. At the sting, a trickle of blood escaped and dribbled down his cheek. Collins's gaze followed it, and he eased off the pressure.

"We received word you're to stand trial and be put to death. I will rejoice when I hear they've severed your head."

He placed the linen against his nose again, rotated on his heels, and stalked from the cell. The guards dropped Logan. He crumpled onto the cold wet floor and unrelenting pain shot through his battered body. The cell door slammed shut, and the lock grated into place.

Logan coughed. A metallic taste filled his mouth. His head pounded as he wiped bloody spittle from his chin with the back of his grimy hand and leaned against the damp wall. How would he get himself and his men out of this fine mess? Days without food had drained his strength and left his limbs weighty. He struggled to stay conscious and formulate a plan.

Agony spread through his chest with every breath. His vision narrowed as if he looked through a tunnel, and his mind slipped into welcoming darkness.

~~~

A brisk breeze rustled through the tree where Lindsey hid, and her arms pebbled with goose bumps. She peered through the dry leaves and craned her neck to see down the dusty road. What was taking so long? They should have been here by now. Hamish's helper, Cora, felt certain the guards would take this route. Lindsey prayed the woman was right.

When Lindsey had met Cora at the inn west of Northumberland, she'd expected to receive instructions on her next mission. She had not counted on Cora's man, Charles, delivering information of the English caravan transporting prisoners. Under false pretenses of a fair and just trial for the defiant Scots—Logan, Adam, Colyne, and Thom—King Edward ordered the men to London. With any luck, she would thwart the tyrant's scheme.

From her vantage point, the pathway was clear for a good hundred paces. She positioned herself to see the first soldier who would clear the thick forest and exit onto the road. She fingered the bow that rested on her thigh as she watched and listened for sounds of movement.

Dressed in brown trews and a cream-color tunic, her hair concealed in a dark scarf, she appeared as nothing more than a slim warrior. Not the daughter of a former Scottish laird. Her clansmen, Travis and David, crouched on thick branches higher in the tree, and Cora's band remained concealed amongst boulders and thick shrubbery across the pathway. As agreed, no one would make a move until Lindsey issued the order to attack.

The overcast weather added to the chill and with nerves heightened, she fought to control shivers racking her body. Her gaze darted through the trees. Squirrels and birds quieted, and the air seemed to still. She closed her eyes and listened for sounds of the English procession.

Images of Logan's broken body flashed through her mind. Collins's reputation for extracting information was well known. The man stopped at nothing to get what he wanted. The fact that Logan remained alive attested to her friend's strength and the king's desire that he stay alive for his form of questioning.

Logan's life was at stake. They had to stop this procession before the Sassenachs reached the North Sea's low flat landscape. The idea of what the English would do to Logan and his men caused her to cringe every time she thought about it. Hailed as a hero for stopping major battle plans from reaching the wrong hands on many occasions, Logan was a wanted man—wanted by a most feared king.

A soft, short bird call warned of the approaching enemy.

Lindsey's heart leapt.

It was time.

She eased her feet onto the branch below, the leaves trembling as she stood on shaky legs. Travis and David got into position above her.

The thud of heavy hooves grew close. The squeaking of the wooden prisoners' cart became louder, and a gleam reflected off an armor-clad soldier riding a large black destrier as he emerged on the road.

Lindsey slid an arrow from the quiver on her back and nocked it, then aimed the barb at the lead man. "Hold," she whispered.

Massive warhorses carrying heavily clad soldiers surrounded the wagon and blocked her view of the prisoners. She held her breath as they advanced beneath the tree.

"Now," she ordered loud enough for Cora's men to hear. She loosened her grip. Her arrow whistled through the air and sank into the leader's neck. With a grunt, he grasped the shaft as he toppled from his mount. Her fingers snatched another barb. She nocked it and shot it into the next guard as Travis's and David's arrows rained upon the procession.

Shouting, the unsuspecting enemy broke apart, frantic to find cover, but Cora's band swooped upon the retreating fiends. The soldiers' desperate screams and the sounds of battle died as quickly as they had begun.

Lindsey scrambled down the tree, the rough bark scraping her palms. She sucked on the side of her stinging hand and sprinted toward the wagon. Logan and his men lay in the bed, the light of day revealing their ghostly pale faces and broken bodies. She grabbed the iron bars and jerked on the large rusty padlock, but it held tight. Determination welled through her as she raised her sword and slammed the pommel against the lock. It clanged and rattled.

"Mistress," Travis said. "Let me…"

Ignoring him, she hit it again and again. Finally, it fell to the ground. She jerked the gate open, climbed into the wagon, and knelt beside Logan. He was so cold and still. Her chest squeezed as she sat and tugged his head onto her lap. Tears dribbled down her cheeks.

Women from Cora's group settled beside Logan's men. As if in a fog, she heard Travis and David shouting orders to dispose of the English bodies. The cart lurched forward, jostling all who were in it, and they raced for the safety of the woods banking the River Till.

Chapter Two

River Breamish, England

Three small boats silently navigated the tree-lined waterway of upper River Till. They eased into an inlet hidden from sight by large boulders and lush green shrubs. Deep hues of red streaked the evening sky, and a gentle breeze drifted off the water.

Lindsey rode in the first craft, propped against the side of the skiff with Logan's body limp against hers. He was so weak. He'd hardly been conscious since they'd stopped the caravan this morning. She stroked his brown hair, stiff with filth, and prayed he would survive.

A woman from Cora's group, draped in a tan cloak, sat next to her and supported Logan's comrade Adam. He did not appear in much better shape than Logan, and Lindsey's heart tugged at the brutality these men had endured.

Something rustled the bushes lining the water's edge.

She jumped and grasped the dagger at her side. Her pulse pounded through her ears.

It darted out. Wings fluttered as it flew past their boat.

Just a bird.

She took a deep breath and willed the tension in her muscles to ease. Hauling that wagon across the backwoods' rough terrain this morning had prolonged their trip. They had been exposed too long, and her body trembled in anticipation of arriving at Cora's camp.

Lindsey settled back against the side of the boat. Just a bit farther…

Charles stood at the stern, stocky legs braced apart. Dark shaggy hair brushed his broad shoulders, and his bearded face was smeared with grime. In a methodical rhythm, his strong arms stabbed a wooden pole into the river. He leaned over the water, and his shirtsleeves tightened over his large arms as he propelled the boat forward. He traversed the calm waters with skilled grace, gliding the craft farther into the dense shelter.

They rounded a copse of trees, and a man emerged from the thick foliage with Cora close behind. Leaning on a walking cane, she hobbled onto the beach and down to the shore. Frizzled grey hair surrounded her weathered face, and a blue cloak hung from her shoulders, covering her ample frame. She clutched the wrap at her neck and paused. Worry etched lines in her forehead.

Lindsey raised her hand in greeting, and a welcoming expression broke across the woman's face. She could almost feel Cora's relief. The mission had been successful. They had rescued Logan and his men.

The boat slid onto shore and tilted to the side. Two more muscular men sporting scruffy beards and dark clothing stood beside several horses. The men ran from behind Cora and tugged the craft higher on the beach. The bottom scraped across the rocky shore, and the vessel jerked to a stop.

"Lassie, ye're a pleasing sight fer me tired eyes."

"As are ye, Cora." Lindsey eased from underneath Logan and stood on wobbly legs. "The men will need to be carried. They're badly injured."

"Bruce will help." Cora stepped back and let her man pass. He leaned down, grabbed Logan, and hoisted him over his shoulder. Logan moaned and scrunched his eyes tight. Even in the dim light, the paleness of his face appeared stark against Bruce's dark cloak.

"Careful!" Lindsey admonished, but she knew Bruce had no other option. They must get the prisoners secreted away as quickly as possible.

The boat shifted. She lost her balance and grasped the rough side of the wooden vessel.

Cora leaned to the right and peered at the two other skiffs easing onto shore. "Where are yer men?"

As another helper lifted Adam, Lindsey snatched her satchel from the bottom of the boat and scrambled from the craft. "Travis and David are bringing the horses around the western bend to throw off the soldiers. They should arrive in a day or two."

The old woman nodded. "Verrae well, I'll have someone watch for them."

Bruce marched toward a horse. Surely he did not intend to deposit Logan over the saddle?

Lindsey rushed forward and grasped the man's arm. "Logan can't be transported draped over the horse. It'll cause him more harm."

Cora's strong fingers grasped Lindsey's shoulder, her eyes stern. "Being gentle will be for naught if the Sassenachs uncover our trail."

The woman was right, but Logan appeared close to death. "Please, we must place him on a litter. The horse's jostle could kill him."

Cora exhaled loudly and turned to the lads standing behind her. "Grab blankets and ropes from the boats and tie them together. We'll use them as a sling."

The boys raced off.

Lindsey rubbed Logan's back and froze. Ridges under his tunic crisscrossed his skin. Her fingers brushed the raised mounds, and she cringed. He had suffered so.

"Here mistress," one of the lads called as he and another hurried back with the makeshift bed.

They spread it on the ground, and Bruce eased Logan onto it. Charles grabbed one end and Bruce the other. Charles nodded, and they lifted Logan between them.

Two other men pulled the third boat higher onto shore and unloaded the last of the injured prisoners. The women who had accompanied them gathered their cloaks, sacks of leftover food, and Cora's large healer's basket.

They rushed up the beach and disappeared into the dense woods at the water's edge.

"Come, we must hurry." Cora motioned and trudged down a narrow footpath leading into the forest. Three of her men jumped into the boats and shoved away from shore. It wasn't long before the crafts were no longer in sight.

Lindsey slung her bow and quiver over her shoulder and fell in line behind Bruce and Charles, who transported Logan. The wind swayed tall pines, the sound normally comforting. But they were on English soil, and the threat of remaining on hostile territory weighed heavy. She would not rest easy until they crossed the Scottish border.

The tang of wet leaves and earthy moss wafted on the breeze as she surveyed the surrounding forest. To her left, dim sunlight filtered between branches and tall shrubs, their shadows long and eerie. She glanced to the right. Massive grey boulders covered in green lichen formed dark overhangs with water trickling over the ledge.

The group journeyed down the pebbled path and descended deeper into the thick forest. The sun disappeared and cast them in darkness. Lindsey squinted and followed the dim trail down a hill and around a bend. A glow of light loomed ahead, and her spirits lifted.

Cora led the way into camp. Torches positioned around the perimeter blazed into the darkness. A dozen or so thatched huts were nestled amongst the trees. Wooden slats formed the walls, straw was stuffed in the gaps, and the roofs were constructed of tightly woven reeds. Thick oak logs braced the corners and secured the structures. To her right, an old wagon sat empty next to a fenced area containing several horses. The animals whinnied, their ears pointing forward and nostrils flaring.

Flames leapt around logs in a large fire-ring positioned in the center of the rustic encampment. Men and women mingling around the yard turned toward the incoming party, then hurried to greet them.

"Take the wounded inside," Cora ordered. "I'll bring my salves to ye shortly." She faced Lindsey as the group dispersed. "We'll care for them until they're able to ride. Then they must be on their way."

"I understand." A stray lock slid onto Lindsey's forehead, and she brushed it from her face. "We thank ye for yer help."

Charles grasped Logan's arms and hoisted him onto his shoulder. Logan groaned, and Lindsey's heart lurched.

Charles studied her, his eyes narrowed as if he expected her to object. "Come with me."

She followed him across the clearing to one of the huts, then hurried ahead, opened the straw door, and stood back to let him pass. The man ducked through the opening.

Lindsey stepped into the musty one-room home. It was small but inviting with a fire blazing in a blackened hearth and a couple of worn benches placed before it. A bed was positioned in the corner with a curtain hanging around it for privacy. A makeshift kitchen occupied the far wall.

Charles deposited Logan on the mattress. Lindsey dropped her belongings on the bench in front of the hearth and knelt on the dirt floor beside the bed.

The large man rubbed the back of his thick neck. "Cora will bring her healing potions."

"Thank ye, Charles."

His sad gaze held hers before he left the hut. A lad rushed through the door, struggling with a bucket of water in each hand. He placed one next to her, then scurried to the fireplace, filled the pot suspended by a swing bar, and grabbed a long stick propped against the hearth. He poked the logs. Flames flickered around the bottom of the pot. The lad peered at her with widened brown eyes, then ran from the hut.

Lindsey

With the exception of the popping and hissing of logs in the hearth, the room fell silent. Shadows danced across Logan's swollen and battered body. His clothes reeked of perspiration, blood, and filth. Angry purple bruises disappeared under his dark beard. Grime covered his face, a long slash marred his forehead, and a crusty scab traversed the wound on his right temple.

He was so still.

His chest barely rose and fell.

Her stomach roiled. The carefree lad from three years ago was gone. His lean, muscular frame no longer resembled the boy she had known. No. The body of a man, battle-honed and hardened, lay before her.

She opened her leather satchel and sifted through the contents. When her fingers wrapped around a soft chemise, she tugged it out and dipped the cloth in the bucket next to the bed. Easing Logan's hair aside, she dabbed the cold wet undergarment on his warm face and gently wiped away streaks of dirt and dried blood.

"Logan, can ye hear me?"

A groan rumbled in his chest.

Relief swept through her. "Rest easy. Ye're safe."

Cora bustled into the hut with a wooden basket hanging on her arm, a bowl and cup in her hands. "I mixed my healing herbs to treat his wounds." She set the container of pasty salve on the small table next to the bed and handed the cup to Lindsey. "He needs to drink this. It will help mask his pain."

Lindsey accepted the brew and slid her hand underneath Logan's damp hair. She lifted his head and tipped the concoction to his mouth as Cora rummaged through her basket.

"Drink," Lindsey whispered. Logan's cracked lips opened, and she dribbled in the contents.

He swallowed and coughed. His face scrunched tight.

"That's it," she said. "Ye got most of it."

She eased him back as a young lass scurried into the hut carrying a pot. Steam rose off the surface as she placed it on the table. "Here's some soup, mistress."

The aroma of vegetables and broth wafted past her nose. "It smells wonderful. Thank ye."

The girl hurried from the room as Cora tossed several blankets and a worn cloth on the end of the bed. "Eat yer fill. We have plenty." She studied Logan. "How many more will Collins torture and kill?"

"I'll inform Hamish of that hellish pit." Lindsey tugged a grey woolen blanket over Logan's legs. "Our warriors will not let the fiends go unpunished."

"That fortress stands behind enemy lines. There's not much the Scots can do." Cora's back stiffened. "I only pray yer scheme to rescue yer young man hasn't brought further wrath upon the unfortunate souls left to suffer Collins's temper."

The hair on Lindsey's neck bristled with the familiar twinge of anger. She stood and faced the woman. "If I were a man, would ye question my actions?"

Cora's brown eyes narrowed. "Nay, I suppose not."

"Then do not question mine."

Cora stared for a moment, then nodded and shuffled from the hut.

She tired of justifying her behavior and would not feel guilt over freeing Logan and his men. Cora had been against Lindsey's plan from the beginning. *It was too dangerous, too risky for a woman to take on such an operation for a handful of men.*

Well, Lindsey was as clever as any man, and she'd grown weary of proving herself. Her ire rose at the injustice of it.

Logan groaned.

She turned to him.

Her young man.

If only that were true. He'd never harbored anything but brotherly affection toward her. Engaged in the rebellion, he'd had little time for Lindsey. Whispers of his reputation for pleasing the servants drifted past her ears on more than one occasion, but he never made advances toward her. She was just one of the stablehands in his eyes.

She knelt beside the bed. Threadbare clothing clung to his body. She flipped her dagger off her belt and slit his shredded tunic. Peeling the blood-crusted shirt from his chest, she wrinkled her nose. Ridding the dirt stuck to his body would not only reveal the extent of his wounds, but help to make him more comfortable.

After wringing out excess water, she rubbed the chemise over his dirty face and grimy neck, and rinsed away the filth. Dark blond hair sprinkled his muscular chest and abdomen, and a thatch disappeared beneath the trews resting low on his narrow hips. The white chemise turned grey as she removed the dregs and foul matter of Collins's dungeon from Logan's torso.

Dropping the chemise into the bucket, she sat back on her heels and swiped an arm over her brow. Dark purplish marks discolored his ribs, and deep cuts and abrasions crisscrossed his chest and stomach. Unshed tears stung the backs of her eyes over the torture he had endured. Her fingers dipped into Cora's salve and smeared the sticky substance along the cuts.

Although his skin was warm, Lindsey gave thanks it did not hold the signs of fever. She wiped her hands on the cloth Cora left and sat back again. Remembering the ridges her fingers had touched earlier, she lifted his shoulder. He groaned as she gently rolled him onto his side.

Large strips of opened wounds covered his back.

Her breath caught.

It appeared as if someone had carved grooves into his skin. Yellow splotches surrounded deep red bruises and festering pockets of infection oozed from the gashes.

She eased him onto his stomach.

"Shite!" he hissed.

"I'm sorry. I didn't mean to hurt ye." How she wished her sister was here to tend him. "I need to treat yer wounds."

"Go easy," he breathed out. "I'm not dead yet."

Biting the side of her lip, Lindsey tried to remember Cameron's healing remedies. It would be best to cleanse the wounds first. After rinsing the dirty chemise, she dribbled cold water over his back, afraid to rub his raw skin.

His muscles clenched.

"Am I hurting ye?"

"It burns."

"I'm trying to be gentle."

After cleaning the area, she smoothed Cora's salve over the deep gashes. Her heart broke as her fingers worked the ridges. He had suffered tremendous brutality. Resolve washed over her. She would ensure the Scots exacted retribution.

~~~

Logan had slept for three days.

Lindsey stood next to his bed. Hands on her lower back, she stretched. She had remained at his side, pausing only long enough to care for her needs. This afternoon, she gave thanks his red aggravated skin appeared lighter, a bit healthier, but still he slept.

The sound of clopping horse hooves drifted from the encampment. She stepped to the straw door and peered through the dry foliage surrounding the hut. Travis and David dismounted, and Cora, Charles, and Bruce stopped in front of them. Long sable-colored hair blew onto David's bearded face as he spoke. Road dust covered his rough woolen jacket.

Cora pointed at Logan's hut.

Travis's head turned in Lindsey's direction. Short disheveled grey hair dipped over deep furrows cut across his forehead. White whiskers lined his grizzled cheeks, and a black cloak hung over his stalwart frame. His dark eyes narrowed.

Lindsey sighed. Her father's men appeared in good health. Both were old enough to be her da, but she worried about them traveling in English infested territory. She stepped from the hut and waved as she strolled toward them. "I'm glad to see ye made it."

Blaze tossed his head and nickered in greeting. "There's my baby." She wrapped her arms around his velvet neck. He nudged her with his large head, and she laughed. "Did ye miss me, lad?"

She patted the horse's dark chest and straightened as she turned to the men. "Did ye have any trouble?"

Travis's shoulders eased. "Nay, we didn't see any soldiers."

"We disposed of the English bodies and brought their horses with us," David added. "When we finished, there were no traces left of the procession."

Relief welled inside her. A rope stretched from Travis's horse to a line of the English's mounts. Several young lads scurried to escort the animals into the makeshift corral. "What an excellent addition to my herd."

David chuckled. "We thought ye'd like that."

"What of Logan?" Travis asked. "How does he fare?"

"He still sleeps, but he and his men are mending."

"If they continue to rest, they should be well enough to travel in a few days," Cora said.

Cora wanted to hurry them off, erase all signs the prisoners had resided in her camp, but Lindsey worried it was too soon. Yet, she knew the risk of discovery. Her chest squeezed. How she prayed the soldiers did not track them to Cora's hideout. She could not bear to cause these good people trouble. But what choice did she have? She had to save Logan and his men. She could not let the English torture and execute them.

Casting those thoughts aside, she addressed her men. "We have plenty of room in the hut. Come with me, and I'll get ye something to eat. I know ye must be hungry and tired."

A young lad dashed over to her. "Mistress? May I take yer horse?"

Lindsey patted Blaze once more and handed over the reins. "Please see he gets a bag of oats."

As the boy led him away, Cora looked at Travis and David. "There's a stream flowing behind the tree line if ye care to wash."

"Thank ye," David said. He and Travis grabbed their satchels and followed Lindsey to the cabin.

She ducked into the dark room and over to Logan's mattress. He lay on his stomach, his back exposed. Her men dropped their belongings on the floor and stepped beside her.

"Shite!" David rubbed his jaw.

Travis shook his head. "What kind of monster would do that?"

"A fiend." Lindsey crossed her arms before her waist. "I know it looks bad, but his wounds are healing."

The men stared at Logan's still form.

"He barely wakes except to drink Cora's brews," she whispered. "She says sleep will help him heal."

David nodded. "Aye, rest will do him good."

Lindsey grabbed two bowls off the bedside table and stepped to the hearth. She stirred a small pot of bubbling stew, dipped the heavy ladle inside, and filled the containers. After placing the meal on the table, she wiped her hands on her trews. "I'll leave ye to freshen up."

When she slipped from the hut, the sun had dropped lower in the sky, throwing streaks of red and orange across the western terrain.

West.

Toward home.

She warred with her duty to deliver Hamish's message and her desire to remain with Logan. Her plans had turned upside down. She should leave him in Cora's care, hand over the missive, and attend the horse race as she had planned. Logan would be safe, but she couldn't bear the thought of leaving him.

A light wind caressed her face as she made her way through the camp. Three men, gathered around an oak table, worked their blades back and forth over a sharpening stone. A woman scrubbed dirty laundry in a caldron while another hung the clothing on a line strung between two posts. A young lass stirred a large pot of stew over the campfire, and a lad hurried by with a wheelbarrow full of soiled straw from the animals' pens.

Lindsey strolled over to the horses. After grabbing a brush off the worn worktable erected next to the corral, she ducked under the rope, and stepped into the pen. She nudged several of the large animals aside and made her way to Blaze.

His nose was deep in a bucket. A dark, full forelock hung below his eyes, covering his white markings. Crunching oats, he tossed his head. His sleek black coat gleamed. What a beauty. She had raised him from the day Bess foaled him. He was her pride and joy.

That was the year before she met Logan. Running the brush over Blaze's withers and along his side, her thoughts turned to that fall day. Over three years ago, dressed in her trews and tunic with her hair stuffed into a cap, she'd bent over a bale of hay, tugging with all her might to move it into the main stable area. Neighboring clans' horses participating in Da's tournament were housed in her barn, and she was readying stalls for more incoming animals. As she backed and pulled, she bumped into something. Looking between her feet, she saw two legs clad in black boots and brown leggings. Straightening, she turned and stared at the most gorgeous man she had ever seen.

Brownish-blond hair hung to his broad shoulders. Piercing grey eyes narrowed, focused on her. A dark mustache and beard surrounded his lips and lined his cheeks. The corners of his mouth tugged up. "Ye're a lass."

How utterly profound. "I beg yer pardon?"

Hands on hips, he smiled. Crinkles lined his mirthful eyes. His gaze dropped to her trews, then traveled to her breasts before once again resting on her face. "I was told I would find the lad who took my horse to the stables. Ye don't look like Blake."

"I'm Lindsey MacDougall." She tugged off her glove and extended her hand.

He quirked a brow. "Laird MacDougall's daughter?"

"Aye."

His warm, strong hand engulfed hers, and he raised it to his lips. Her heart raced at his intense stare. "It is a pleasure to meet ye." He kissed her knuckles, his warm breath caressing her fingers. "I am Logan. Logan Ross."

From that moment, they had become friends. She never let him know her true feelings—how she longed to be near him and missed him when he was not around. Excited dithers fluttered in her stomach. Although she knew he would never look twice at a scrawny, red-headed lass dressed as a lad, she still dreamed of what it would be like to be held in his strong arms.

Heavy footsteps approached, breaking her thoughts. Travis marched toward her. She ran the brush over Blaze's hindquarters and stepped to his other side. "He looks good. Not a scratch on him."

"Aye, we were lucky to escape undetected, but we must be on our way. The Sassenachs will be onto us soon."

"We have a few more days before we have to leave." She flicked loose hairs from Blaze's rump and looked over his back at the man.

Arms crossing his chest, Travis's eyes narrowed. "Ye're going against yer sister's orders and yer own. Have ye forgotten yer rule to deliver the messages and get away? Not become involved with the prisoners?"

"Those prisoners were different. This is Logan. What would ye have me do? Leave him?"

"Aye. Cora and her group will care for him."

"Nay. I'll stay until he recovers."

The man stared at her, unmoving. "Ye executed yer plan, and he's safe. I thought ye wanted to show yer brother-in-law ye could peddle yer horses? That ye didn't need Laird Campbell's men selling them for ye?"

"Nothing has changed. Once I win the race, MacDougall Castle will be brimming with buyers eager to purchase my horses."

"Then we need to leave on the morrow," he insisted.

"There are still three days before the race." Lindsey stepped around Blaze. "That is plenty of time to get to Dumfries. But if ye and David want to leave, go ahead. I managed on my own long before Heather became aware of my missions."

He huffed. "Ye know we won't leave ye."

"Then do not speak of it again."

Chapter Three

Logan woke with a start. He swallowed, but nothing went down. His mouth was dry, his throat as parched as desert sand. He lay on his stomach. He inhaled and a tight wrap around his chest restricted his ribs. Rough fabric chafed his raw skin. His fingers eased over…what? A straw mattress?

Where was he?

The aroma of wood smoke surrounded him and a warm glow caressed his face. Hazy memories filled his mind—pain eased by an angel with auburn tresses. Heavy lids scraped his scratchy eyes as he blinked, then focused on the dim figure before him.

Lindsey.

She slept on a crude chair, her head resting on her right shoulder. Firelight glowed behind her and shadows danced across her face. His gaze traveled down her tan tunic and brown trews, and he smiled. His princess had not changed. She continued to dress as a lad, but her hair was not stuffed in an overly large cap as usual. Instead, the glorious mane shimmered like flames about her slim shoulders.

The fog in his mind dissipated. Why was she here with him? Being thrown into the bottom of a wooden cart bound for the gallows was the last he remembered.

Two men slept on the dirt floor against a far wall, swords at their sides. A fire blazed in the hearth. Its radiating warmth filled the small space. The hut was quiet, save for the popping and hissing of the logs.

His attention returned to Lindsey.

How he had missed her. Seeing her again soothed his wretched soul. Curls caressed her face, and he longed to touch them, feel the softness slip through his fingers. Her pink lips parted on a sigh. What he would give to press his mouth to hers, bury his face in her silky hair, and blot out the horrors he'd suffered in battle and from Collins's hospitality.

He'd fallen in love with her the moment he saw her working in her da's stables. He adored her carefree attitude and admired her spunky, oftentimes fiery temperament.

Pain sliced through his gut. Lindsey was a laird's daughter and he a bastard son.

She could never belong to him.

Well aware of his station, he had attempted to find comfort in willing lasses' arms, only to have thoughts of his princess end the tumble before it began.

Palms flat on the mattress, he pushed himself up. His tight, sore back burned in protest.

Lindsey startled and sat forward. A grey woolen shawl slid from her arms. Her lovely blue eyes widened. "Ye're awake."

He rolled onto his hip. The room spun. His hand shot to the bedding, and he steadied himself. "Aye."

She grasped his shoulders and helped him sit. "Easy, ye don't want yer wounds to bleed again."

The all too familiar burn seared his back. He scrubbed a hand over his eyes. "Where are we?"

"At Cora's hidden camp."

He squinted. "Cora?"

Lindsey sat back on her chair. "She works with Hamish and supports the rebellion. Her group got word of ye being held in Collins's dungeon and helped rescue ye."

The men on the floor stirred. One rose on his elbow as the other stood. Travis stepped to the bed with David behind. Logan hardly recognized the two. Had it really been three years since he last saw them?

"It is good ye're awake, lad," Travis said. "How do ye feel?"

Like shite. "I'm alive."

33

David rubbed his whiskered chin. "If Collins had his way, ye wouldn't be. With yer injuries, I feared he'd succeeded."

Lindsey held up a cup. "Would ye care for a drink?"

"Aye." Logan's hand trembled as he grasped the mug and gulped the contents. The cool liquid spread down his parched throat into his empty belly. He drained the last drop and thrust the mug at her. "More, please..." he rasped.

She dipped the empty container into the water and handed it back to him.

He turned the cup up and swallowed deeply, his eyes closing. *God, it tasted good.*

"Do ye feel up to eating?" she asked. "I have stew warming over the fire."

Logan looked past the cup's rim into her eyes— eyes he thought he'd never see again. Her teeth raked her plump bottom lip. He refrained from pulling her onto his lap and nuzzling her sweetness. "That sounds good."

She hurried to the hearth as he addressed Travis and David. "What of my men?"

Images of their broken bodies hanging limp from the dungeon walls flashed through his mind's eye, their tortured moans echoing in his ears. His muscles tensed.

"They're well," David said. "A might battered and bruised, but they're mending."

"Cora administered healing salves, and her people have cared for them," Lindsey added as she ladled stew into a wooden bowl. "Adam and Colyne were up and about yesterday. I checked on Thom last night, and he appeared in good spirits as well."

They'd survived. Relief poured over him, and the tension in his body eased.

She dropped the ladle back into the pot and slowly turned to him. Her fingers clutched the bowl, steam rising from the surface. The aroma caused his mouth to water, and his belly rumbled.

"Careful, it's hot."

When he reached for the stew, his hands shook again. Days without food, repeated beatings, and frigid temperatures had caused his muscles to lose strength. He was weak as a bairn.

"Let me help ye." Lindsey sat on the edge of her chair. Her soft hand cupped his, steadying the dish.

She couldn't know how that simple act affected him. No one ever touched him with kindness or concern. Lindsey was special. She had always made him feel whole, as if his bastard birth meant nothing. "Thank ye."

She dipped a spoon into the broth then slid the savory stew into his ravenous mouth. He groaned with sheer pleasure.

A broad smile lit her face. "I'm sure this tastes good after having survived on that pig slop Collins fed ye."

"Ye don't know the half of it." If they weren't fighting rats over scraps, they dined on mealy bread that moved with vermin.

"What happened lad?" David asked, hands on hips. "The last we heard, ye had taken out a convoy off the coast of Edinburgh."

"Aye, it was shortly afterward a new member joined our cause." Images of Bernard, a black patch covering one eye and bloodied clothing, materialized. "He suffered wounds he claimed to have received in a skirmish with the English. His story rang true, and with my guard down, I accepted the traitor into our midst."

Travis's bushy grey brows drew together. "He turned on ye?"

The nightmare of that evening replayed in Logan's mind. Sassenachs had stormed into their camp. The soldiers wielded swords with precision, slashing slumbering men on their pallets. His troops never had a chance. Screams of the dying still resounded through his ears. Only four of the dozen rebel warriors were spared.

Spared for Collins's *questioning*.

"Aye." Logan's jaw clenched. Bernard would regret his betrayal.

"Collins is known for infiltrating the rebel camps with his men." David's arms crossed his chest. "Ye're lucky to have survived."

Logan's attention swung to him. "There was a time I would have disagreed with ye."

Silence stretched as Lindsey continued to spoon-feed him. After he devoured the meal, he held up a hand. "That's enough. My stomach has no more room."

"Verrae well." She placed the bowl on the table and sat back in her chair.

Travis rubbed his neck. "I'm relieved ye're awake, but I'm returning to bed."

"Aye, 'twill be daybreak in a few short hours." David stretched.

The men bedded down, and Logan turned to Lindsey. Her fingers fidgeted in her lap. A log rolled in the hearth and an orange glow glimmered in a draft.

"What are ye doing here, Princess?"

~~~

Lindsey's back straightened at Logan's authoritative tone. "I beg yer pardon?"

"Why are ye in Northumberland and not Kilmarnock?"

What about thank ye verrae much for saving my sorry hide? She flicked dust from her trews. "I am here on business."

His head tilted. "What business?"

She raised her gaze to meet his. "That is none of yer concern."

Eyes narrowing, he nodded. "Ye will tell me what ye're doing miles from yer home in enemy territory."

36

Who did he think he was, demanding answers? Would he mock her as so many others had? Would he laugh at her attempts to support the rebellion?

No. She mentally shook herself. If anyone would understand, it would be Logan.

She swallowed past the lump of nerves stuck like gruel in her throat. "I'm on an assignment."

"An assignment?" He shook his head. "For what? For whom?"

Studying his expression, she hoped she wouldn't witness derision when she blurted, "For the rebellion."

"Ye'd best start explaining."

Her chin rose slightly. "I carry messages to the Scots' commanders for Hamish."

"Shite, Lindsey." He stabbed a hand through his hair. "Ye can't be serious."

Defensive anger bubbled up inside of her. She folded her arms. "Why not?"

"Because ye're a lass."

She huffed. "Many women support the cause."

"This is war. What in God's name can *ye* do?"

"As I said, I carry missives to our commanders. While Cora doctors Collins's prisoners, she garners information for our troops. I deliver her reports to various rebel outposts."

Logan's grey eyes turned dark, his intense glare piercing. "Go on."

She clasped her trembling hands in her lap and fought to steady her nerves. "That's about it."

"Ye did not explain how ye came to be here, with me."

She searched his face. His eyes were the same she had grown to love, but his countenance was stern, his boyish charm replaced with steely determination. She had not expected him to question her so.

His brow rose.

She wasn't sure she liked the changes. Before the conflict began in earnest, he had been her confidant, her friend. Now, his irritable expression resembled her quarrelsome brother-in-law, Alec, Logan's cousin.

"I'm waiting."

"Last week I met Cora at an inn west of Northumberland as usual. One of her men, Charles, arrived a few moments after Cora and I settled in for our evening meal. He had just left Collins's fortress with word of four Scottish prisoners to stand trial in London. A mock trial for Adam, Colyne, Thom, and ye. Charles wanted to get word to Hamish, but there was no time."

Logan rubbed his forehead. "Damn it. I thought I had dreamt yer visit."

"I took Cora's place that afternoon. She couldn't be associated with yer rescue and take the chance of being discovered. The English would uncover and destroy her camp, and her aid to the rebels would end. I was the logical choice. I spread filth in my hair, covered my skin in ash-paste, and donned thick padding around my middle. As a homely woman, no one expressed interest in me."

His dark demeanor radiated anger, and she shifted in her chair. "Cora and Charles filled me in on what I needed to know, what to expect, and how to act. Then, what route the guards would take to the North Sea."

"I can't believe what I'm hearing."

David let out a loud snore. The fire popped and a whistle of air hissed from a log.

Lindsey held Logan's gaze and whispered, "I couldn't leave ye. I wanted to assess the situation, let ye know of our plan…give ye hope."

"Ye should have left me." His deep voice rose. "Do ye not have a brain inside that stubborn head of yers? Do ye know what would have happened if the guards had discovered ye were a young lass?"

Her pulse raced. "I knew the dangers I faced."

"What a foolhardy scheme. Cora had no right to send ye to do a man's job."

Pain sliced through her middle. "Ye ungrateful wretch!"

Travis stirred. He coughed and turned over.

"I am not ungrateful." He lowered his voice. "I appreciate yer willingness to help, but not at the risk of yer life. Do ye think I could have lived with myself if something happened to ye?"

"Well, ye wouldn't have had long to fret. King Edward intended to remove yer head once ye reached London." Tremors wracked her body, and her bottom lip quivered. *I thought he would be different, would appreciate and accept my involvement.*

She stormed to her pallet and dropped down. Jerking the thin woolen blanket over her shoulder, she curled on her side with her back to him and faced the fire. After she had rescued him, bathed his filthy body, and treated his festering wounds, he called her stubborn and foolhardy. While she had not expected adoring praise, a simple thank ye would have sufficed.

"Lindsey?"

Heart hammering, she fought to steady her breathing. She would not give him the satisfaction of knowing he had hurt her.

~~~

Early morning light filtered through wooden slats of the one-room hut. Logan rubbed his scratchy eyes. Lindsey's stiff back had kept him awake most the night. His words had hurt her, but by damn, he could not understand her actions. Putting herself into a situation in the midst of danger was just pigheaded.

The rebellion was no game.

A searing pain coursed down his back. His eyes scrunched tight against the agony. Nightmarish images of Collins wielding instruments of torture surfaced. Wails and moans filled with anguish rang through his ears, and a nauseating stench of burnt flesh and putrefying injuries lined his nostrils.

His heart pounded, and eyelids flew open. Those enemy soldiers would have used Lindsey's body unmercifully. She would have begged for death. The risk she took caused his gut to roil. Why did she do such a thing? A laird's daughter should lead a pampered existence, not endanger her life in the wilds of Scotland and sleep on the dirt floors of smoke-filled huts. He thanked God she had not been harmed.

He turned his head toward her empty pallet. She must've left before dawn.

The straw door swung open, and an old woman with frizzled grey hair bustled in. "I heard ye were awake."

She set a wooden basket on the bedside table, leaned over him, and placed her hand on his forehead. "Not a bit warm. 'Tis guid ye'll be ready to leave soon." She straightened, her hands planted on ample hips. "We're taking a big chance with ye and yer men here, and I want ye gone as soon as ye can ride."

She must be Cora. "Understood. I appreciate yer hospitality."

Her gaze raked him from head to toe and back again. "I'll give ye two more days."

She tossed off the top of her basket and rummaged through the contents. Perusing her jars, she extracted an assortment of containers and placed them on the table beside his mattress. "Roll over so I can tend yer wounds."

Logan turned and once again, fire raged across his back. He grimaced as he eased onto his stomach.

Cora cut the fabric binding his ribs and cold air swept across his mangled skin. "The gashes will take time to heal, but Mistress Lindsey did a guid job doctoring them."

"Lindsey treated my wounds?" Hazy memories of her hovering over him, her soothing voice wafting around him surfaced.

"She wouldn't leave yer side." Cora massaged cold salve into the sore furrows. "I offered to sit vigil over ye, but she refused to budge."

Why had he asked? He didn't want to hear how Lindsey had cared for him. It wouldn't take much to lose control, shove prudence aside, and offer her a life with him.

The idea was absurd. Laird MacDougall would never assent to his daughter's union with the likes of a man such as himself. Logan was an outcast, had never belonged. He'd always been on the outside looking in, trying to prove his worth. He should be used to his station, but he balked at the injustice.

"Sit up so I can re-wrap yer ribs." The woman inflicted her own torturous techniques with her rough jerk of the binding. "That'll do ye."

Logan rolled onto his hip as she snatched a cloth hanging from her belt and wiped her hands. She rummaged through the basket, extracted a bundle, and tossed it on the bed. "My husband was about yer size."

Clean clothes. "Thank ye."

"No need to thank me. They were collecting dust." She gathered her jars and cloths, stuffed them into her basket, and ambled across the room.

As she left, a knock sounded on the wooden structure and Adam stuck his head inside. A grin spread over his battered face. "I just heard the good news." He pushed into the room and limped to the foot of Logan's bed. "I worried ye wouldn't make it."

Logan's head bobbed. "I wouldn't have lasted much longer."

Adam's countenance darkened. "Nay, none of us would've."

"How do Colyne and Thom fare?"

"As well as expected. Thom's arm is broken, and both men suffered lashes from Collins's whip, but they're healing."

"If they're fit to travel, we'll head out in a day or two." Not only had Logan promised Cora they'd leave as soon as possible, he was anxious to return home.

"They await yer orders."

Logan scratched his whiskered neck. "We'll escort Lindsey and her men to MacDougall Castle before we travel to Glencara."

Adam's shaggy head cocked to the side. "Ye've conveyed yer plans to her?"

His gut clenched. Nay. He had not told her. He could barely come to grips with leaving her now that he'd found her again. "I'll inform her to be ready to leave the day after tomorrow."

"Ye might receive an undesired reaction," Adam offered. "Seems the lass is bent on an assignment to deliver Cora's messages. I don't believe she intends to journey to Kilmarnock anytime soon."

Anger surged through Logan, and he sat forward. "She is sorely mistaken if she thinks to continue her perilous mission."

Adam scoffed. "The lass fancies herself a rebel warrior. David claims Hamish continues to recruit her because of her excellent riding skills. She's outmaneuvered the enemy on many occasions, and he has confidence in her abilities."

"Hamish can go to hell," Logan barked. "He will answer to me for involving her in this man's war. He has no right to *recruit* her. She is a laird's daughter—a lass—for God's sake."

"Ye're a better man than me if ye can convince her differently." Adam limped across the room. When he reached the door he paused, then turned back to Logan. "Lindsey normally takes the evening meal with her men beside the campfire."

Logan nodded. "I'll join her tonight."

Chapter Four

As dusk descended, Logan swung his legs over the side of the mattress. Dizziness swept over him, and he fought to quell the lightheaded sensation. He stood on shaky limbs and grasped the table beside the bed. Once his addled mind cleared, he donned the worn but clean buckskin trews and tunic.

He had not seen Lindsey all day. Even her belongings were gone. He stepped from the hut, hoping for some sign she hadn't left. An evening breeze drifted around him. A large bonfire blazed in a clearing, highlighting a disarray of auburn curls. Lindsey's slim body huddled next to the fire. She brought a mug to her lips, and he exhaled a breath and paused, his strumming pulse calming. Travis, David, and Logan's men sat to her right, perched on log-hewn benches. His shoulders eased.

Adam stretched toward the flames. He jabbed a stick into the charred wood and sparks swirled into the darkening sky. Colyne chuckled at something Thom said. It was a miracle Logan and his men were alive.

A miracle thanks to Lindsey.

He treaded the perimeter of the compound. Several cabins huddled together, and he wondered about the people living here, away from the protection of a castle. Who were they? Scots? Scottish sympathizers?

Several lads, arms full of firewood, traipsed around the encampment while others brushed and fed horses corralled in a makeshift pen. Logan made his way to the camp's center. Lindsey watched him approach. Her back straightened.

He'd not apologize. He meant what he had said. This was no place for a lass, especially not his princess.

"Good evening, lad," Travis said. "It's good to see ye up."

Logan stepped around a woman dragging a wooden paddle through a black iron caldron placed over the fire. He dropped onto the bench beside Lindsey.

"It's good to be up, Travis." Logan tipped his head at Thom and Colyne. "Ye look a bit better than the last time I laid eyes on ye."

A cloth sling held Thom's left arm against his body. "Aye. Ye as well."

Logan turned to Lindsey. Tension strung tight between them. She didn't acknowledge him. Her fingers clutched a mug as she stared into the flames.

A pretty young woman with dark hair and a friendly expression handed him a tankard. "Would ye care for ale?"

He accepted the drink, then gulped the strong brew.

More men and women joined the group as Cora served food and passed out tankards of ale. Several men pulled out homemade flutes. Bella, a woman with a striking voice, led the party in song. The verses ended, and Lindsey clapped and laughed with the group, her face lit in unfettered joy.

A young lass, no more than three years, ran after the older children. Lindsey leaned out and scooped the wee one into her arms. Making a loud display of tickling the lass, Lindsey nuzzled her chubby cheeks. The bairn squealed, then wiggled to the ground and took off again.

What would it be like for Lindsey to bear and nurture his bairns? Witnessing her affection toward the little lass heightened the emptiness in his soul. He longed to fill the void with a life beside her, watch her belly swell with his children. But fate had cast its cruel destiny. A bastard could not marry a laird's daughter.

While Lindsey interacted with the others, she ignored him. Logan nudged her arm. Her head turned toward him, her face stilted.

"Thank ye, lass."

She glanced away, then to her lap.

"If it weren't for ye, my men and I would be dead."

Her gaze lifted to his. She paused, her eyes assessing. "Ye're welcome."

His hand slid down her arm, and her muscles tensed under his fingers. "I did not intend to sound so ungrateful last night. Ye're a brave woman, and we owe ye our lives."

"I'm thankful ye and yer men are safe."

One of the lasses grabbed Adam's hand. Favoring his injured leg, he limped while she twirled around him in time to the music. He tugged her to him and held her close as they swayed to the melodies. Another woman coaxed Travis from his seat, and the two circled the clearing in each other's arms.

Logan searched Lindsey's face. "Tell me news of home. Do ye still run yer da's stables?"

A strange look came into her eyes. Had he not been watching closely, he would've missed it. "Aye, my herd keeps me busy."

"The last time I saw ye, ye were training a colt."

Her eyes lit. "Blaze. He grew into a beautiful stallion. I brought him with me."

"Ye have him here?"

"Aye." Her head tilted to the right. "Would ye care to see him?"

Finally her rigid stance eased. He could always rely on her passion for horses to bring a smile to her face. "I would."

They left the warmth of the fire and strolled toward the corral. The moon lit the dirt pathway. Treetops swayed in the wind, the familiar sound comforting.

Lindsey's trews stretched tight across her rear. He dropped back and allowed her to walk ahead so he could appreciate the sway of her rounded hips. His body stiffened. How he longed to wrap his arms around her and hold her against him.

Animals nickered. She ducked under the rope, then held it up for him. He bent at the knees. The pain in his ribs and the scabbed lacerations pulled, almost taking him down. Streaks of pain coursed his back. He gasped and with jaw clenched, he straightened and followed her into the pen.

A dark, long-legged horse sporting a white swath across his face nudged Lindsey's shoulder.

"Here he is." The wind blew an auburn curl onto her face. She brushed it aside, her eyes darkening with adoration.

"Ahh, he is a beauty." He patted the horse's strong withers and ran his palm over the firm flank.

Her hand slid to Blaze's leg. "He's the fastest horse I own. The conformation of his legs is perfect for speed and agility."

The subject was an unwelcome reminder of her perilous occupation of thwarting the enemy.

A lad strode past, a wooden bucket in each hand sloshing water. He nodded at Lindsey and Logan, then weaved through the herd.

"Lass, my men and I are departing for Scotland the day after tomorrow. We'll see ye home before we journey to Glencara Castle."

Her body drew back, and her smile disappeared. "While I appreciate yer offer, I'm not traveling home yet."

"Why not?" Damn it, she would not continue her preposterous escapade.

"Logan, contrary to what ye might believe, I do not answer to ye."

He grasped her upper arm. "Ye will not persist in this game ye play."

Her brow scrunched, and her blue eyes sparked. "Game?"

"Ye don't seem to understand the dangers ye delve in to, the risks ye take. Ye're a vulnerable lass."

She jerked her arm from his hold. "I am not an imbecile."

"Then quit acting like one. Someone has to protect ye from yer idiotic decisions. I forbid ye from taking part in this rebellion."

Her eyes narrowed. "How dare ye *forbid* me to do anything? Ye have no say in what I do."

She brushed past him, ducked under the rope, and stormed into the darkness.

By God he would escort her home if he had to tie the red-headed spitfire to the saddle and drag her there.

~~~

Lindsey awoke with a start and bolted upright. Her pulse quickened. It was still dark. The hearth fire burned low, but she had not overslept. She took a deep breath to quell her strumming heart.

It was time to deliver Cora's information, then travel to Dumfries. Although a boulder sat in the pit of her stomach over her confrontation with Logan, she looked forward to the horserace. If Blaze won, her animals would be known across the territory. She would prove to Alec, now laird of her clan, she could peddle her horses. She didn't require her brother-in-law's help. She was perfectly capable of managing her herd.

Ye don't have anything to say about it. If I choose to move the horses, I will.

Alec's distressing words resounded through her ears. From the day he had become laird of her clan, he fought to displace her role as head of Da's stable. She had bred and raised those horses and with a few words, Alec planned to destroy her life, leaving her destitute without her precious animals. Her sisters' lives were complete; Heather had Alec, Cameron had Robert and baby Douglas, and Elsbeth had her work at the abbey. Why could Alec not leave Lindsey's horses alone? She had devoted her life to

48

managing and caring for the MacDougall stable. Resolve bolstered, she was determined to prove herself to him.

She rubbed her puffy eyes. She'd thought staying in another of Cora's huts far away from Logan would help her stop thinking about the man and get a good night's sleep. But if anything, she thought about him more often. Drowsy from a long night of tossing and turning with his harsh words ringing through her ears, she yawned and wiped sleep from her eyes. As she threw the blankets off and slid from the lumpy mattress, chill bumps rose on her skin. She hurriedly splashed water on her face, dressed, and straightened the cabin.

Grabbing her satchel and belongings off the chair before the hearth, she skimmed the area for anything she might have left behind. The small table and chairs sat empty, the bedding lay folded atop the tattered pallet, and charred wood smoldered in the fireplace. With everything in order, she took a deep breath and stepped out-of-doors.

Dawn lightened the dark sky with splashes of red and pink. Cold air swirled around her shoulders, and she clutched her wrap tighter against her neck. Pebbled grit crunched beneath her boots, the sound loud in the quiet morning as she made her way past the other huts and down the worn path.

Travis and David had saddled their mounts and tethered the garnered horses.

Blaze tossed his large head. She dropped her belongings on the ground and stroked his velvety nose. "Good morn. How are ye, lad?"

"Mistress," David greeted her. "We're ready to ride."

She looked over Blaze's back at her men. Travis secured the last of his belongings and turned toward her.

"Verrae well. Let's be on our way." She tied her satchel, bow and quiver of arrows to the saddle. Grasping

Blaze's reins, she led him past the other animals milling around the pen.

Cora untied the knotted rope and held it open. Lindsey guided Blaze from the enclosure. Travis and David mounted and rode through the path, hauling several animals behind them.

Cora retied the rope. "Ye have the message?"

Lindsey stopped beside her and patted the brown leather satchel. "Aye. I'll see the commander receives it."

The old woman tugged Lindsey into her fleshy embrace. "Take care."

"I will." Lindsey straightened. "Thank ye for all ye've done."

Cora's eyes softened. "And ye, child."

"I left mounts for Logan and his men." Lindsey glanced over the woman's shoulder and back to her. "If he asks…" The words caught in her throat.

Cora held up a hand. "I won't give away any information he does not already have."

Sadness washed over Lindsey. Had she imagined the bond she'd shared with Logan?

He was right.

She was a fool.

~~~

The rich forest, plentiful with wild game, came alive with birds chirping and squirrels jumping from branch to branch. Spending the morning hunting helped Logan's spirits to rise. Having second thoughts over his somewhat less than tactful approach with Lindsey last night, he decided to take a different path. Understanding her desire to aid the rebels, he would convince her of other activities she could perform for the cause—safer activities.

He secured the large buck's carcass to the sapling he had stripped. "Are ye ready?"

Adam nodded, and Colyne said, "Aye."

"One…two…three," Logan counted, and his men hoisted the heavy branch onto their shoulders and balanced the deer between them. Humiliated at being reduced to carrying rabbits, Logan led the way down the narrow footpath brimming with green ferns on either side. The burning pain on his back had subsided, but the short hunt had sapped his energy. Taking a deep breath, he pushed himself, determined to restore his strength.

Thom carried another pair of rabbits, the animals long ears clenched in his fist and the men's borrowed bows and arrows slung across his back. Tomorrow they would leave Cora's band. Logan wanted to repay her generosity with fresh meat.

The men marched into the camp's clearing. Women sitting at a long oak table chopped carrots and leeks. Two lads stacked wood next to a black caldron, readying the fire for the evening meal. Logan's gaze wandered through the crowd of women, searching for Lindsey. Having left long before light, he hadn't seen her today and was anxious to make amends.

A horse whinnied, and his head turned toward the sound. A lad scurried between animals in the horses' pen, arms full of hay. Logan's eyes narrowed. Some of the horses were missing.

"Let me help ye with that," Bruce shouted as he jogged toward Adam and Colyne.

Several women hurried behind him, laughing and offering congratulations. "We'll eat guid now," one shouted.

Charles laughed. He and Bruce lifted the sapling and eased it to the ground.

"What's this?" Cora stepped to the group gathered around the men. She looked at the deer and then to Logan.

He tipped his head toward her. "For ye, m'lady. We thank ye for all ye've done for us."

Cora clasped her hands before her chest and glanced from one man to the next. "Ye're most welcome. Clean up while we put a slab over the fire to roast."

Logan strode to the hut, his head turning from side to side as he searched for Lindsey. He weaved between women preparing the evening meal, young lasses carrying crude cooking utensils, and lads stoking the fire.

Where was she?

He stopped and turned in a circle. His eyes narrowed. Travis and David were not amongst the gathered men.

He rotated on his heel and marched to the horses' pen. Blaze and other MacDougall mounts were gone. Anger welled up, and his chest squeezed.

He spun around and stormed into the camp clearing. "Cora?" he shouted.

Stooped over a pot of bubbling water, she stirred in diced vegetables. She straightened, a cloth clutched in her hand.

"Where is she?" His voice rose.

"I beg yer pardon?"

Logan advanced. "Don't play with me. Where is Lindsey?"

Cora turned back to the boiling brew and dumped in a trencher of chopped meat. "She left."

Pressure built in his head, and he strained to control the urge to shake the woman. "What do ye mean? When? Where did she go?"

She faced him, empty trencher in her hand. "She, David, and Travis left at daybreak. I cannot say where they went."

Logan planted his hands on his hips. "Cannot or will not?"

Her head shook imperceptibly. "Lindsey means a great deal to me. She has helped the cause, unselfishly willing to risk her life for our freedom. I do not know where she travels, only that she carries word of a possible strike on Scottish soil."

He fought to restrain his anger. "Ye sent her with such a message? Did ye strap it to her so the Sassenachs would be sure to find it when they attack and rape her?"

Cora's breath caught, and her hand grasped her chest.

He advanced, fists clenched at his sides. "Mistress, do ye know what will happen to her if the English get their hands on her?" Fury billowed through him. "If ye have any idea which way she went, ye had best speak up."

"I heard her talking about a horserace," a wee voice sounded behind him.

Logan whirled around. A lad stepped back, his brown eyes widened.

"What did ye say?" Logan demanded.

Charles placed his hands on the boy's thin shoulders. The lad's fingers fidgeted. "I overheard her talking to her horse. She asked if he was ready for the race."

"What race?"

"There's an annual event in Dumfries tomorrow," Charles said.

"I thought she carried a message?"

"All manner of men will attend the race," Bruce offered. "Perhaps she expects to meet her contact there?"

Why in God's name would she enter a horserace? Had she lost her mind? They didn't let women compete.

Images of her hair stuffed in a cap and her wrinkled tunic and trews flashed through his mind.

His gut plummeted.

What was she getting herself into?

Chapter Five

Dumfries, Scotland

Lindsey reined in Blaze beside Travis and David and surveyed the activities at the base of the grassy knoll. The annual horserace attracted scores from the northern highlands to the south of London. The flag of Scotland, a red lion on the golden standard, flew beside England's red cross. A fitting sight, the brisk wind whipped the banners against wooden posts, the fabric often tangling in a violent dance much like the Scots' and Sassenachs' conflict.

Blue and purple pavilions housing vendors' wares dotted the green pasture lined with thick trees. Tables supporting baked goods, fabrics, and pottery crowded the tents. Shouts rang out from merchants, coaxing men and women who meandered between the traders' stalls to purchase their goods.

Children squealed, and Lindsey turned to the noise. Jugglers circled red and orange balls into the air, their nimble fingers working the objects with ease. Excitement drummed through her as minstrels dressed in colorful costumes played flutes and danced, kicking their legs to either side as they wove through the crowd with a line of lads and lasses following.

The wind shifted and an aroma of freshly baked bread and pastries wafted past. Lindsey closed her eyes and inhaled. It had been a long time since she attended a fair. The smells brought a sense of contentment, memories of her mum and sisters—a time of innocence before the English hostilities encroached.

She turned to Da's men. "Now that we've delivered Cora's message, we're free to enjoy ourselves." She studied the grounds and spotted a number of people crowded around a table under a brown canopy. With her hair stuffed beneath a cap, her breasts bound, and in her bulky tunic and trews, she'd blend in as another Scottish lad. "That looks to be the place to enter the race."

She guided Blaze behind other travelers arriving for the festival. Laughter and giggling children surrounded her as the group crossed a stout wooden bridge over the river Nith. The sun's rays shined through a blue sky dusted with wispy clouds and her spirits rose, the excitement in the air contagious.

Blaze ambled down a dirt path leading to the festivities. Bagpipes' distinctive sound filled the fair. With the instruments strapped to their backs, two men blew into the long reeds as they marched down the field, a line of horsemen following. Stalwart animals pranced, their massive black heads bobbing, their long manes flowing as they led the opening ceremonies.

The bagpipes' poignant sound engulfed her, stirred emotions to bubble forth, and caused a tingle to ripple over her skin. She couldn't believe she was finally here. The exhilarating sights and sounds overwhelmed her, and she breathed deeply to quell her nervous jitters.

A loud commotion of laughter on the far side of the field caught her attention. Sunlight glinted off shiny plated armor. English soldiers clad for battle gathered beneath a stand of trees. Something struck her as familiar. A hulking man lumbered to the side. He slapped another on the back, and images of Collins's dungeon played through her mind. Her chest clenched. Dreams of the hellish scene still caused her to awaken in the night, sweating, heart hammering.

Another soldier sat at a makeshift table closer to the field, helmet to his side. Lads scurried to serve the man. He waved a hand, and the boys scattered. Lindsey's eyes narrowed. Perhaps he was the ruthless commander. Dear Lord, why were they here? Why were they garbed for war?

She looked at the side of the field where the Scots grouped. No armor or defensive shields protected their bodies. No one appeared prepared for aggression or animosities. While the event had been broadcast as a day to put hostilities aside and share in friendly competition and entertainment, she didn't trust Sassenachs to adhere to the agreement.

Increased wariness filled her, and her fingers eased over the sword at her side. Pulse racing, she fought to calm her nerves while remaining vigilant.

Traversing the muddy path, she guided Blaze through the milling crowd. To her right, tables teeming with salt herring, miniature pastries, and beef marrow fritters filled cramped vendor booths. How she and her sisters had loved sampling the pastries when they were children. She smiled remembering Elsbeth's fingers, sticky from honey cakes, and her face powdered with remnants of sugary treats.

"Come git yer rye bread." A hefty woman on her left waved, her toothless grin welcoming. "Fresh baked barley and sweet jellies right here fer ye."

Lindsey dodged the activities and hordes of individuals meandering from stall to stall. Horses' hooves churned clods of dirt and mud as they pulled carts filled with barrels of sloshing ale. Men and women browsed the wares as children ran and played, weaving in and out of the gathered throng.

As they neared the booth for the race entrants, Lindsey dismounted and walked Blaze over to it.

"Name?" a man sitting behind a wooden crate called out. He squinted, and bushy white brows drew together over his dark eyes.

"Lind MacDougall." Her deepened voice resounded as she thrust two gold coins at him.

The man's head cocked to the side. His gaze raked her up and down. He glanced at David and Travis before snatching the money from her fingers.

"Line up over there." His chin jerked to the right. He dropped her coins into a brown leather purse and tightened the drawstring.

Lindsey turned toward the area indicated and swallowed hard. Rich tapestries and adornments draped the backs of massive warhorses. Prosperous, affluent men displayed their bejeweled steeds that signified their wealth.

People journeyed from miles around in hopes of securing the winner's purse, as well as the prestige gained. While a large contingent of well-to-do men attended, there were people participating from all walks of life.

Word of the winner would travel quickly. Lindsey grinned. She would show Alec she could peddle her animals as well as anyone. Once she had proved herself capable of managing the herd, her brother-in-law would not take her horses and hand them over to one of his men. Her life would continue as normal, not be wrenched upside down. Shoulders pinned back and head held high, she led Blaze past the display of finery to the starting gate.

David stepped beside her and dropped his satchel on the ground. He grasped the bridle as she climbed onto the saddle.

Swarthy participants clad in animal skins and Englishmen sporting short tunics over brightly colored woolen stockings mingled amongst Scottish clansmen in the cramped stables.

A ruckus broke out.

The crowd heaved as several men pushed another into the throng. Horses whinnied. Blaze's ears pinned back, and his head jerked up.

"Whoa…" David held onto the bridle and tugged Blaze's head down.

The horse pranced as Lindsey patted his sleek neck. "Easy lad."

Fists crunched bone, angry shouts, and insults were exchanged before a group of men jerked the combatants apart.

"I don't like this." David scanned the participants while cinching the last notch in Blaze's saddle. "Let me ride him for ye. It's not safe, Lindsey."

"No, Blaze knows my touch. We'll be fine if we can just keep up with them at the start. We'll pass the others in the long stretch."

She considered the competition. Warhorses' powerful hindquarters enabled them to spring forward. They would have the advantage out of the gate. Blaze's slight frame appeared small in comparison, but he ran faster than any horse she'd ever ridden.

He quieted, but his tense muscles bunched beneath her legs.

Travis jogged up, out of breath. His weathered forehead scrunched, his brown eyes intense. "We've got company. Collins and a contingent of his men are across the field. I hear the commander entered several of his animals in the race."

So that *was* Collins she had spied. Her stomach churned. Determination spawned from pure hatred billowed up inside her. How she would love to best him.

David clutched her leg. "Ye need to give this up. It's not safe for ye to ride."

And abandon the chance to prove myself to Alec? "Nay. Ye're acting like old women. What can Collins do? He has to abide by the law of peace declared for the day."

"I think ye're making a mistake," Travis said. "Ye don't want to tangle with that brutal fiend."

Lindsey yanked the reins from his fingers. "Keep an eye on him if it makes ye feel better. I've got a race to win."

She squeezed her legs around Blaze, and he trotted toward the starting line. After she positioned him in the queue, the older man who took her coins marched down the horses, counting off sets of ten. "Remember yer number. The winner of each group will advance to the final event."

A horn blared, signaling the start of the long awaited race. The first group of ten lined up. Mounts tossed their heads, some pawing the ground. The riders leaned forward, reins in hand, eyes focused on the flags marking the finish line.

A whistle screeched.

One horse reared and vaulted in the wrong direction, while the others thundered down the field. The ground rumbled under the animals' tremendous weight.

Lindsey stood in the stirrups to observe Collins. The commander jumped from his seat in the crowd, shouting. His face turned red, and he shook his fist in the air as his man crossed first over the finish line. Cheers rang out from the English contingency. Soldiers slapped Collins's back as he victoriously held his tankard in the air.

The next three heats included riders from Collins's stable, and it appeared as though he would have no competition for the desired purse as his mighty warhorses easily overpowered the slighter animals.

"Next," the older man shouted.

Lindsey jumped.

It was time.

Her pulse strummed in her ears. She nudged Blaze to the starting line. The larger horses crowded her. The men laughed, their massive beasts shoving her aside. A loud shriek filled the air, and the animals charged down the field.

Lindsey dug her knees into Blaze. He careened forward.

Powerful hindquarters filled her view and dirt flew into her face from the immense hooves. A gap between the beasts closed. She couldn't maneuver through them. She pulled the reins to the right.

Blaze veered around the side of the group. She lay flat across him and wrapped her arms around his neck. His muscular withers pumped against her chest. The scent of him filled her nostrils, and the pounding of his hooves resounded through her ears.

His long sturdy legs dug into the freshly churned dirt. He caught the mighty horses and passed them. Exhilaration surged through her veins. The wind bit into her face, and a stream of tears streaked from the corners of her eyes. She hugged Blaze tight as he dashed down the field and crossed the finish line.

I won!

Joy burst through her. She straightened, holding her hands over her head, her body rocking in rhythm with Blaze's gallop, his dark mane brushing her trews. She patted his sleek neck. The other horses raced around her, the men eyeing her with dark glowers and questioning stares.

Blaze tossed his head. He knew he was a champion. She inwardly squealed like a bairn. How she wanted to shout her joy! She rubbed his velvety black fur and steered him back up the field where David and Travis ran to meet her.

"Great job, lad," Travis shouted.

She dismounted and shook the men's hands.

Travis slapped her on the back. "I thought they had ye at the start."

"Those men didn't realize Blaze doesn't like a horse to be ahead of him." She laughed. "They were no match for him."

David fell into step beside her as they walked back to the starting line. "I'm happy ye won, but ye've captured Collins's attention. He did not like ye beating his entry."

"Why don't ye give this up now that ye've won one of the heats?" Travis asked. "That alone will give ye the recognition ye need for peddling yer animals. Everyone is already talking about the MacDougall lad."

She rounded on the men. "Ye must jest."

David shook his shaggy head. "Ye did not see the anger in Collins's eyes. I worry his men will have ye in their sights."

"There is nothing the fiend can do," Lindsey shot back. "He cannot wield his wrath on this field."

Travis rubbed the back of his neck. "Ye're taking a big risk."

"A risk I'm willing to chance." Lindsey glared at him, then at David. "If I win the last race, not only will I earn the purse, I will become known across the country. Scores will travel to MacDougall Castle to purchase my horses."

The men remained silent, their eyes assessing.

Her hands balled into fists. "Alec makes plans as we speak to move *my* horses to Glencara where his men can manage and peddle them. He aims to *take them* from me."

Her chest squeezed.

"Please. I need to prove I can do this." She looked from David to Travis. "Are ye with me?"

Travis's shoulders slumped, and he exhaled loudly. "Aye, we're with ye."

~~~

Later that afternoon, the last of the preliminary heats wrapped up, and ten finalists emerged. The old man overseeing the event ambled onto the field and held up a hand. "Line up for the last race."

Roars went up from the gathered merrymakers. Lindsey's body shook. The future of her horses depended on the outcome of this race.

She had to win.

She guided Blaze amidst the enormous horses. The animals backed and shoved her aside.

"Git in line, lad, or git out of the race," a burly man shouted.

She maneuvered Blaze through the confusion and positioned him to the far right. The whistle screeched, and the horses vaulted. Once again, Blaze started from behind. He dipped low to the ground, his legs bounding across the green pasture.

A man on the sidelines hurtled a stone. Lindsey ducked. Whack! The thud resounded and a stinging pain coursed across her side. *Shite!* It barely missed her head.

Three of the larger horses veered off course and headed for her. She steered around them. Blaze spun to the side, and his powerful legs sprinted forward, carrying her out of danger.

She had lost valuable time. When they approached the tail end of the riders, Lindsey panicked. Lying across Blaze's withers, she stroked his neck. "Come on, lad. Ye can do this."

A path opened between the massive beasts, and Blaze darted through. He stretched out in front of the group, crossing the finish line a full horse-length ahead of the others.

Exhilaration soared.

She'd won!

~~~

"The winner of the purse is Lind MacDougall!"
Lindsey?

Logan's gut clenched.

The crowd clamored and rushed toward the finish line. He sprinted through the throng with Adam and Colyne behind him.

"The lad won," a man shouted.

"He's a true Scot fer ye," another yelled. "But he ain't big enough to hold on to that purse."

Logan's pulse pumped through his ears. He had arrived too late to witness the race, but hopefully in time to protect her from dangerous cut throats anxious to claim the hefty prize. As he shoved his way to the front, hordes of men surrounded Lindsey and Blaze. He could hear her disguised, deepened voice singing praises.

"At MacDougall Castle, we breed the finest quality. Our palfreys offer the combination of outstanding conformation and a calm disposition with a smooth natural gait." She stood beside the animal patting his shoulder and neck. "We also provide a horse with longer legs, bred for speed and agility as ye've seen today."

"Maybe we should've had our bairns ride in the race," an enemy soldier shouted. "The kid had an unfair advantage."

Collins's guard.

Logan would recognize the cur anywhere. Bile rose in his throat. What the hell was the scum doing here?

Lindsey's gaze shot to the instigator. David and Travis moved in front of her, shielding her from what was quickly becoming an angry mob.

Logan grabbed Adam's shoulder. "Get Thom and bring the horses to the west bend."

"Aye." Adam nudged Colyne, and the two ran back through the crowd.

When Logan turned, Lindsey had climbed onto Blaze. The agitated horse tossed his head as her da's men attempted to back him from harm's way.

"I say the little beggar don't deserve that purse," another soldier bellowed.

Logan stepped into the middle of the fray and held up a hand. "The lad won the race fair and square. There weren't rules outlining who could or could not participate.

It was up to each of ye to enter yer fastest horse with yer best rider."

The hostile men grumbled, the heated tone rippling throughout the throng.

Logan backed toward Lindsey. He swung up behind her, grabbed the reins, and dug his heels into Blaze's sides. Pain shot through his ribs, and he groaned as the horse bounded from the agitated group.

Surrounding Lindsey with his arms, Logan leaned low, giving Blaze full rein. The robust stallion stretched his muscular legs and dashed down the pasture. Shouts resounded from behind, but Blaze's powerful stride took them away from the mob.

His pounding hooves churned the path. They dashed onto the hard packed dirt road, rounded a curve, and came face to face with Bernard and two of Collins's men.

Logan jerked the reins, and Blaze skidded to a stop. Fury billowed through Logan. How he would relish tearing apart the man who had betrayed him. The dream to one day get his hands on the traitor had kept him alive, helped him endure endless hours of torture.

Lindsey grasped Logan's forearm. His heart slammed in his chest. Damn it! If only she weren't here. He couldn't do anything to bring her harm. Warring emotions pumped through him. He'd be damned if he would be denied justice.

"Well, well," Bernard shouted. "If it ain't the *Lowlander*."

"Bloody hell, Collins'll be mighty pleased to see you," another man chimed in.

Loathsome swine. Logan eased the knife from his boot. He might not be able to squeeze the life out of the churl with his bare hands, but the man would die.

"He's missed yer sorry arse, bloke." Bernard laughed and extended his hand. "He sent us to take that purse and, o'course, that horse."

In one fluid motion, Logan slung his dagger and embedded it into Bernard's chest. Satisfaction flowed through Logan as the traitor stared wide-eyed, his fist clutching the blade. His eyes rolled up, and he toppled off his horse as Logan launched himself at the other two. Although his ribs had been bound, a sharp pain radiated through his torso. He dragged the soldiers to the ground and unsheathed his sword.

Thundering hooves grew loud as the MacDougall men careened around the bend.

Logan lunged. His blade scraped across the steel of the soldier's weapon. The cur's grip faltered. Logan thrust his sword into the man's gut as the MacDougalls dispatched the third guard.

Logan jerked his blade from the man and wiped blood on his trews. Ignoring the agony coursing through his chest, he strode to Lindsey. Worry over her safety, over what could've happened to her turned into anger. He reached up and snatched her off Blaze. "What in the hell were ye thinking?"

David advanced but Logan shot him a menacing look. "Ye'd best stay back."

Lindsey bristled. "I don't answer to ye."

She turned to mount her horse, but he grabbed her shoulder and spun her to face him. "Ye *will* answer me, damn it. What is wrong with ye? Why did ye risk yer life for a godforsaken race?"

Fury sparked from her blue eyes. "I'm establishing a reputation for my horses. Men will know of the MacDougall herd's fine quality."

Logan shook with anger. "Where's yer da? Why does he let ye travel without his escort?"

"My da doesn't know of the race." Her arms crossed her chest. "He believes I am visiting my friend."

"What? He doesn't know where ye are?" *She can't be serious.* "What if ye ran into trouble? How would he help ye?"

"We've always managed to avoid trouble."

"Until those men decided they wanted yer purse and yer horse." His voice rose. "Do ye know what they would have done to ye if they'd discovered ye were a lass?"

She glared at him. "No one asked for yer help. Why don't ye continue on yer way?"

Fury shot through him. He grabbed her upper arm and pulled her within inches of his face. "Ye'd try the patience of a saint, and believe me, I'm no saint. Ye *will* do as I say. More soldiers will be after us, and I need yer cooperation. Do ye understand?"

Her stubborn chin lifted. "Aye."

He glowered at David and Travis. "Round up their weapons and horses, and let's get the hell out of here before more of Collins's men show up."

She climbed onto the horse's back. Logan gathered the reins, and not trusting her to follow his lead, he swung up behind her and pulled her onto his lap. He inwardly groaned when her luscious bottom rubbed his thighs. Although aggravation with Lindsey made him want to shake her, his body responded to her enticing curves. He swallowed the urge to nuzzle her soft hair, kiss her tempting lips, and thrust his aching cock against her.

No.

He could not have her. Desire unlike any he had experienced punched his gut.

Clearing his throat, he wrapped his arms around her slight frame and nudged the horse into a gallop. Her words replayed through his mind. Establishing a reputation for her horses? Was she daft? Women didn't do such things. While he loved her carefree spirit, she had to know her limitations. It was one thing to dress as a lad and traverse the wild moors on the back of a stallion, and quite another to insert herself into a man's position.

Marveling at how her straight back maintained the uncomfortable position away from him, he leaned into her and breathed in her scent. She rolled her shoulder while leveling a stern glower at him. She needed someone with a firm hand to bring her in line. How he longed for that job. He'd give her more than a firm hand.

An hour later, the sun dipped low on the horizon. Streaks of red and gold filled the evening sky. Pounding hooves caught Logan's attention. "Whoa!" he commanded and held up a hand, his posture alert as his mount came to an abrupt halt.

Travis and David guided their horses beside him. Logan squinted through the dim light, his attention focused on three men on horseback who crested the hill. Adam, Colyne, and Thom trotted toward them and Logan's stance eased.

"I'm glad to see ye made it," Logan called. "Ye didn't encounter trouble?"

Adam shook his head, his fist resting on his thigh. "Nay, we ran in the opposite direction of the crowd and managed to skirt around them."

"But not before we heard the Sassenachs planning to hunt ye," Colyne added. "Seems the commander has taken exception to ye thwarting him twice now."

"Aye, we heard as much from his guards." Logan rubbed his whiskered chin. "We'll get farther into Scotland and find a place to bed down where we can make plans of our own."

They continued toward MacDougall Castle. As darkness descended, Logan reined in beside a stream for the night. Thick trees lined the bank and the interspersed grey boulders not only provided shelter, they hid the group.

He jumped to the ground and reached for Lindsey. She'd not uttered a word on the trip, but instead sat stock still. He grabbed her around the waist and lowered her in front of him. Taking her chin between his fingers, he bestowed the sternest scowl he could muster on her. "Do not get any crazy ideas. I'm in no mood to traipse across the country after some simple-minded lass."

"Simple-minded?" Her violet eyes sparked, and her hand pulled back. He grabbed her wrist and jerked her lush body against his. Her woolen cap dislodged, and thick auburn hair spilled around her shoulders. His body hardened instantly. Nostrils flaring, he captured her scent. He held her tight, drowning in the feel of her soft breasts nestled against his chest.

"Ye would do good to remember I would relish turning ye over my knee." He pressed his mouth to her ear and hissed between his teeth. "Give me an excuse."

She jerked away and stalked off, her back stiff.

Damn it!

Once again, he had let his temper get the best of him. He inwardly groaned. Distance grew between them. Her trews hugged her backside, and her hips swayed as she stalked to the campfire. Lord, she would be the death of him.

A stack of wood tumbled from Adam's arms as she approached. "Are ye all right, Mistress Lindsey?

"I'm fine."

He tossed several small sticks into the flames.

"It was a good race, aye?" Her voice sounded deceivingly innocent.

Adam nodded. "Aye, it was a good race."

Shaking his head, Logan turned back to Blaze and jerked the saddle from his back.

What the hell was he going to do with her?

Chapter Six

Deep muffled voices drifted around Lindsey. Cold air swirled against her face, and she tucked her nose under the warm blanket. Hues of red lightened to pink as sunlight emerged through the thick trees.

She rose on her elbow. Rough pebbles pushed into her hip, and her muscles groaned in protest at spending the night on chilly, unforgiving ground. Men mingled around camp, quietly readying the horses to leave. A column of smoke wafted from the charred remains of the recently extinguished fire.

Logan slung a brown leather bag over his horse's back and marched into the clearing. Dark whiskers covered his cheeks and surrounded his mouth. Light brown hair hung to his broad shoulders. A heavy woolen jacket covered his torso, and straps securing several daggers crisscrossed his wide chest.

She found herself staring, but couldn't turn away. His gaze locked with hers, his grey eyes focused. She swallowed hard. With every step, buckskin trews clutched his powerful legs.

"Good morn, princess." He stood at her feet, hands on hips. "Do ye plan to join us? We don't have time for ye to lay abed all day."

Princess.

After their heated exchange yesterday, she didn't know what to expect or where she stood with him. The affectionate tone gave her hope.

"I didn't hear ye rise." She threw back the blanket and scurried up. Grabbing her satchel, she looked past him at the other men. "I need a bit of privacy."

Dimples pressed into his rugged cheeks. "Ye can freshen up at the creek."

"I won't be but a moment." She clutched her pack and hurried toward the water.

Massive boulders covered in green lichen lay interspersed between trees lining the banks. She dashed across a path cushioned in pine-needles and glanced back at camp. The men paid her no mind. Relieved, she eased down the dirt embankment and extracted a cloth, clean tunic, and trews from her satchel.

She slipped off her clothes, stooped next to the creek's edge, and dipped the cloth into the freezing water. Goosebumps rose on her skin, and her body shivered as she rinsed off. She grabbed the long wrap to bind her breasts and paused. Would Logan find her more attractive if she left her bosom unfettered?

He was a man drawn to womanly curves. Certainly her disguise as a lad tamped down any desire he might muster toward her. Tossing the wrap aside, she quickly threw her tunic over her head, stepped into the trews, and stuffed her unruly hair back into the oversized woolen cap.

Images of Logan whisking her away from the angry mob replayed. Indignation filled her when she remembered how he'd treated her like a child, as if she had no sense. She sighed. Somehow her anger had dissipated, seeped away while she fought her attraction to him.

He had been so handsome, so strong. She paused, closed her eyes, and relived his arms surrounding her. Girlish twitters fluttered deep in her belly. How could she reconcile her feelings for him when he acted like other men, not valuing her skills or viewing her as an equal?

"Lindsey? Let's go!" Impatience laced Logan's words.

Humph, how gracious of him to spare five minutes for her ablutions. She grabbed her dirty clothes and jammed them into her satchel as she scrambled up the bank. "I'm ready."

The men, mounted on their horses, waited. Logan faced her, Blaze's reins in his hand. Someone had rolled her bedding and tied it to her saddle.

Why had no one roused her so she would've been prepared to leave when they were? Rather they sat watching her as if she were a woman they had to pamper. Piqued by their lack of regard, she strode to Blaze. "I apologize for oversleeping."

She attempted to secure her satchel, but her fingers fumbled, and the bag dropped to the ground.

Logan retrieved it, looped the leather belt hanging from the saddle through the bag's strap, and fastened the buckle. While he didn't say a word, his actions spoke loudly: *women can't manage without men.* When he turned to her, he extended his hand. "May I help ye up?"

"No thank ye. I can mount perfectly well without yer assistance." She jammed her boot into the stirrup and climbed into the saddle.

Logan chuckled as he sprang onto his horse.

He led the group from the clearing and onto the dirt road. Fog swirled around the animals' hooves, and dew glistened in the sun's warming rays. The brisk morning air circled Lindsey's neck, and she tugged her tunic tighter. Still tired from a night troubled with thoughts of Logan, she inhaled the fresh scent of pine and concentrated on her surroundings. They must remain vigilant. English soldiers could verrae well be tracking them.

The narrow dirt road snaked alongside the Nith River. Cascading water whooshed downstream, its frothy white ripples cutting a wide course through the dense woodland. Lush shrubbery lined the banks, and yellow and white wildflowers swayed in the breeze. The greyish-white trunks of downy birch touted an abundance of rustling green leaves. Mossy ferns filled the forest floor, harboring nestlings and small creatures seeking shelter. Across the Nith, a mountain rose high, its face freckled with autumn's orange and yellow foliage.

Logan turned in the saddle. "We'll follow the Nith to Cumnock, then turn northwest to Kilmarnock."

Thom appeared pale. Tight lines etched the skin around his eyes, and he cringed as he rubbed his broken arm.

Logan's eyes narrowed. "We're too close to the English border and need to hasten our pace."

Thom nodded. "The farther north we travel, the safer we'll be. Let's get the hell out of here."

"Ye will let me know if ye need rest?"

"Aye," Thom replied. "I'll be fine."

The group nudged their mounts, and the beasts didn't slow until the afternoon sun sank low on the horizon.

A rumble shook the ground behind them.

Logan held up a hand and turned his horse around. Eyes narrowed, he cocked his head to the side.

Lindsey twisted in the saddle and scanned the base of the grassy hill they had just climbed.

The rumbling intensified.

Her nerves stretched taut.

A large contingent of armor-clad soldiers entered the road and charged toward them.

"Adam, Colyne, take Thom northeast. David and Travis, head to the eastern shore," Logan shouted. "Lindsey and I will take the northwestern track. We'll meet at MacDougall Castle."

The party broke apart, fleeing in different directions.

She squeezed her thighs tight and leaned over Blaze's neck. The horse sprinted after Logan, dashed off the road, and into the thick forest. Cold wind stung her eyes, and tears streamed across her face as she steered Blaze through the woods. Her body melded to him. He tore through bramble and brush. Large trees loomed ahead but at the last moment, he veered to the right and brushed past. Rough bark scraped her leg, and a burning pain streaked down her calf.

Logan's horse, Sterling, weaved through the dense forest with Blaze on his heels. Wind whistled by her ears. To the left, the river Nith churned whitewater as it carved a chasm through the thicket. A ravine loomed ahead. Cascading water frothed, but Logan didn't pause. In a fluid motion, Sterling leapt across the glen and landed on the other side of the river.

Logan twisted in his saddle. Blaze's haunches dipped low then he lurched forward. Lindsey's breath caught as they sailed across the gorge, her white knuckles evidence of her fingers' tenacious grip. They landed hard on the pine-cushioned ground. Waves of exhilaration mixed with fear rolled through her body. A grin spread across Logan's face before he turned and galloped through the trees.

Angry shouts and thundering hooves sounded behind her.

Pulse racing, Lindsey bolted behind Logan on a dangerous course, bounding ahead, vaulting over fallen limbs and debris. Thorns scraped her arm and caught her tunic as they veered around a bend and made their way up a steep embankment. Blaze jerked forward, his hooves digging into the rough terrain. Small pebbles rolled down the hill, pinging off boulders strewn below.

They had to make it to the top before the soldiers rounded the curve and spotted them. Her legs squeezed tighter. "Hurry, lad."

Logan jumped from Sterling and guided him through a narrow opening between a rocky cliff and overgrown bush. "Duck down," he called.

They squeezed through the crevice, and a dark cave emerged. Musty, damp air surrounded them as she urged Blaze into the cavern alongside Logan. He turned to her, placed his hand on her leg, and held a finger to his mouth.

The animals' sides heaved. Volumes of air surged through the beasts' noses. A moment later, thundering hooves approached. Blaze's head jerked up, his ears pointed, and nostrils flared.

"Easy," she whispered and stroked his neck.

She held her breath and closed her eyes.

Please, Lord, make the Sassenachs pass.

Her pulse pounded in her ears.

Time stood still.

Finally, the thudding of racing horses drifted. Relief poured over her, but tremors shook her body. "That was close."

Logan reached for her, and she slid from Blaze into his embrace. He wrapped his arms around her and held her against him. "Ye're trembling."

His scent engulfed her, and she nuzzled her face against the solid wall of his chest. "I thought they had us."

"It's all right. We're safe." He stroked her back. "At least for the moment."

His cheek rested against the top of her head. Warmth surrounded her, and she closed her eyes, relishing his secure hold. He lowered his head and nuzzled her neck.

Thunder rumbled in the distance, and he stilled. His thick chest expanded, and his breath grazed her shoulder on a sigh. Too soon, he straightened, leaving her bereft of his body's warmth.

He peered at the cave's opening then back to her. Rough fingers tilted her chin, and he gazed into her eyes as his thumb caressed her jaw. "Unpack while I gather wood before the rain starts."

He paused, his scrutiny intense.

Would he kiss her? She raised her lips, but a stilted expression crossed his face. He backed away, then slipped through the entrance.

Shoulders sagging, disappointment seeped into the corner of her heart. She was a fool to think he'd find her attractive. Dressed as a stablehand she portrayed a lad, not a desirable woman. While her appearance rarely concerned her, she longed for a gown that molded to the curves she normally fought to hide.

A deep breath helped quell her tremors, but her legs shook as she guided the horses to the far side of the cave. She tugged off Blaze's saddle and dropped it on the ground. After dragging it to the side, she removed Sterling's.

Blaze tossed his head, and she patted his nose. Sterling nudged her back, and she turned to him and stroked his damp chestnut shoulder. "Rest easy, fellow."

With darkness falling, she prayed the soldiers had lost their trail and given up for the night. She stepped to her satchel, and a stinging pain coursed down her leg. Blaze had rounded one of the trees a bit too close. She winced as she pulled out a soft wrap and draped it around her body.

Her fingers were numb. She blew warm breath on them and studied the cave. Water dripped from the ceiling and plopped into a pool, the echoing noise magnified against the cavern walls. Small sticks and leaves were strewn to the left side of a clearing the size of her bedchamber. Charred wood lay scattered across the floor, and several long logs lined a dark smudge marring the dirt where someone had built a campfire.

She gathered the pieces, stacked them in the center of the cave, and sprinkled dry leaves on top. Rummaging through her bag, her fingers closed around her flint rocks. She grabbed the two steel pieces, and stooping next to the debris, struck them against each other. Sparks fell into the leaves. She smacked the pieces again and again, adding more sparks until a puff of smoke snaked up. While waving her hands, she blew on the leaves and stirred the flames to life.

Lindsey sat back on her heels and tossed in the remaining sticks. The wood crackled and popped. The warm wrap felt good around her shoulders, and she held her cold fingers to the flames. Finally, they no longer shook.

Footsteps neared and Logan ducked into the opening, arms full of wood. A grin spread across his rugged face. "Well, look at ye. Already got the fire blazing."

Her insides clenched at his smile. How could he flip her heart upside down with one look?

He dropped the branches to the side and dusted his hands on his trews. "Would ye search my bag for a brown package? It holds beef jerky and bread."

"That sounds wonderful." She drew the leather bag to her and combed through his clean tunic and trews. *Cora.* What a dear to give her husband's clothes to Logan. Lindsey fingered the coarse fabric, then rifled through the bottom of the bag and found the food.

Logan tossed a branch onto the fire. Sparks swirled in the breeze and flames curled around the wood. She handed him a hunk of bread and a wedge of jerky. He dropped onto one of the logs and stretched his legs before him.

"Why do they chase us this far into Scotland?" she asked. "I felt sure they'd turn back once we reached Sanquhar."

He threw another stick into the flames. "I'm afraid ye've nicked Collins's pride. The pompous arse doesn't take kindly to anyone besting him." He turned his head to her. "Especially a scrawny lad on a puny mount."

"Puny?" Lindsey challenged.

Logan chuckled as his teeth ripped a piece of jerky. Mirth danced in his eyes. "Settle down."

The fire cast light on the fading yellowish bruises covering his face. Although he was on the mend, ragged cuts marred his skin, and images of his mutilated back came to mind. "How are ye feeling?"

He stopped chewing and glanced at her. "I'm better."

She brushed a smudge of dirt on her trews. "That was a hellish place, and I'm glad ye survived it."

Logan stared at the fire and tossed another stick into the blazes. His silence tore a hole in her heart. He had suffered tremendous physical pain, and torment over the brutal slaying of his men.

"I'll see Hamish gets word of the horrid conditions and the Scots housed in Collins' dungeon," she assured him. "He'll alert the rebel leaders, and they'll end the commander's heinous persecution."

Logan remained silent, his jaw taut. He jabbed the fire with another stick and logs rolled, the flames flickering between them.

"If ye ever want to talk about it…"

He turned toward her, and his eyes had darkened. "Those tales are not fit for a lass's ears."

"I'm stronger than ye think." Who was she fooling? Howls of despair and high-pitched screams still echoed through her ears. The smell of feces, images of the prisoners' hopeless gazes and threadbare rags hanging from their gaunt bodies would forever sear her mind.

A shiver ran across her back. She hugged herself and studied the dimly lit cave. The flames cast eerie shadows along the walls. Logan stood and placed his cloak around her shoulders before stepping to the horses.

She snuggled into his warm wrap, his scent surrounding her. The corners of her mouth tugged up as she remembered years ago, dancing across the floor with him. He had laughed and joked, was full of life. Her attention drifted to him as he brushed Blaze.

He was a changed man now, solemn and serious. Watching friends and family cut down in battle, then suffering Collins' brutality would affect anyone. His battle-honed body beckoned her touch. She longed to comfort him, soothe his horrifying memories. She envisioned her fingers running along his arms and chest, exploring his muscular abdomen.

His dark eyes held her gaze. Embarrassed at being caught admiring him, she turned back toward the fire.

~~~

Logan grimaced. Why had Lindsey attempted to console him? He would never divulge the humiliation and savagery he and his men had endured. She might offer her support, but when she realized what had happened, she would regret him enlightening her on the Sassenachs' preferred methods to extract information.

The lass's gaze held more than compassion. The corner of his mouth hitched up in a grin, and his eyebrow rose. She wasn't immune to him. As he fed and secured the horses in the back of the cave, he relived holding her in his arms, her sweet scent encompassing him. She had clung to him as if she needed him, wanted him. How easy it would be to throw customs aside and make love to her. But what would tomorrow hold? Her da would have Logan drawn and quartered for the mere thoughts he harbored for the laird's daughter.

What was wrong with him? Why did he torture himself with dreams of her? Once he deposited her safely at MacDougall Castle, she would resume her life, perhaps marry a well-to-do laird.

Shite.

The thought of Lindsey with another man soured his stomach. He looked over Blaze's back. She held her small hands toward the fire. The light cast a glow in her auburn hair and shimmering waves caressed her face. He longed to run his fingers through the silky masses. How could he leave her at MacDougall Castle and journey to Glencara without her?

She held his heart.

He longed to be near her.

After rubbing down the horses, he extracted the wineskin from his satchel and returned to the campfire. He extended the container to her. "Here, have some. It'll help yer nerves."

"Thank ye."

Her fingers brushed his, and a jolt shot up his arm. He had to tamp down his desire before he gave in to his urges. He dropped beside her as she turned up the ale and took a gulp.

Sputtering and coughing, she straightened and wiped her mouth with the back of her sleeve. "Oh my, that's strong."

"Just what ye needed." He winked. "Fiery spirits'll set ye straight."

Her tinkling laugh made him grin. "Aye, I seem to recall yer fiery spirits at Da's tournament."

"Don't remind me. Yer mum was ready to flay me alive for introducing ye to the dark ale." Visions of the small woman's stern countenance, hands on hips fussing at him as if he was a mere lad, crossed his mind. "How does she fare?"

Lindsey's expression turned wistful, and she faced the flames. "She passed over a year ago."

Damn. He ran his hand down her arm. "I'm sorry, lass. I know it's hard to lose someone ye care about."

Her shoulders shrugged. "I miss her."

"I've no doubt ye do."

She poked the fire with a stick. Logs shifted and settled, the charred wood flickering in an orange glow. "Ye've never spoken of yer mum."

The sore subject still chafed after twenty eight years. He'd never spoken to anyone about his mum, not even to the woman who raised him. "Not much to say."

She turned to him. "Does she still live?"

"Nay. I never knew her." He guzzled the ale. A welcoming burn spread down his throat and into his stomach.

"That must've been hard, growing up without a mother."

He tossed another stick into the flames. "My mum died birthing me, and my uncle, Grant, took me in. He moved me and my mum's maid, Maria, to Glencara. Maria and her daughter, Skena, shared their home with me."

"What of yer da?"

"Never knew the man." He brushed dust from his trews. Grant had provided for him, and as a laird, trained him alongside his son, Alec. He included Logan in the clan's affairs. But every night, Logan left the castle and returned to Maria's home. She treated him as her own, nurtured him and taught him the ways of the world. But as a bastard, he never felt like he belonged anywhere.

Constantly reminded of his lowly status, taunts and jeers from lads had toughened his hide. He had thrown himself into training, reached for perfection, and strived to prove his worth. After years of honing battle skills, none of the beggars could best him. Even though they engaged in mock fights, the curs realized his strength, the unrelenting swing of his sword. One by one he defeated them. Humiliated from the ease in which Logan dispatched them, the public ridicule stopped. However, nothing stopped their scorn.

When he glanced up, Lindsey's eyes held a tenderness he didn't want to see. Her plump lips parted, and his groin tightened. How he would love to pull her into his embrace, erase the lonely memories, and if they couldn't dream of a life together, bask in the passion of the moment.

He needed to distance himself, for both their sakes. He could not take her innocence knowing full well he would not be able to marry her.

He stood abruptly.

Her blue eyes widened.

"Ye need rest," he barked. "We have a long ride ahead of us."

~~~

The next morning, Logan and Lindsey crested the top of the hill. A man could see for miles around. White billowing clouds drifted on the breeze and shadowed rolling mountains that rose on either side of the valley cut by the Nith. Boundless open pastureland spread before them. It had been many years since he viewed this vast landscape.

Lindsey grinned. "Race ye to the bottom!"

Before he knew what she was about, she kicked Blaze into a gallop and soared down the hill. His mount reared off his front legs and bounded forward. Logan leaned low and slapped the reins over the animal's hindquarters, urging him faster.

Lindsey was just ahead, Blaze's hooves flying over the terrain. Her long red hair flowed behind her, her laughter exhilarating.

She was magnificent.

Radiant.

Happiness billowed inside him. A sense of freedom he hadn't experienced in a long time flooded through him. How he loved her carefree spirit.

They thundered into the valley and drew to a stop at the base of the hill. Lindsey turned Blaze toward him. Her cheeks were rosy, her eyes sparkling. "What fun," she breathed out and patted her horse's neck. "I'll never tire of galloping across these hills."

"Blaze is a beautiful animal." Logan eased Sterling alongside her. "It's been a while since I've witnessed such speed and agility."

"I started breeding horses with longer legs several years ago. Their slight frame and powerful limbs outmaneuver the larger warhorses."

As they ambled next to the Nith, she dropped the reins onto Blaze's neck and twisted her hair into a knot. The tunic tightened over her breasts, and Logan's mouth watered. He couldn't pull his gaze from her erect nipples outlined against the fabric. His cock instantly hardened. How he would love to fill his hands with her soft globes.

She stuffed the twined tresses into her oversized cap and he shifted, tugging the crotch of his trews to accommodate his swelling manhood.

Men emerged on the road ahead.

Logan straightened. He shaded his face and squinted against the bright sun. At this distance he couldn't discern who they were, but they weren't soldiers.

Lindsey waved.

"What the hell are ye doing?"

"It's all right," she assured him. "I know these people."

She kicked Blaze and trotted toward the group. Logan fell into step behind her as a hefty man, walking stick in hand, led the strangers toward them.

"Lindsey MacDougall. Wha' a pleasure to see ye in me parish."

"Thank ye, Father Donovan. It's been far too long."

Sparse brown hair fringed the priest's otherwise bald head. Dark whiskers covered his cheeks and jaw. A friendly expression touched the man's pale blue eyes. Logan's stance eased. A half dozen men garbed in similar rough cloaks with a single rope tied at the waist shuffled behind the man and gathered around Lindsey.

Her arm swept in Logan's direction. "Let me introduce ye to my friend, Logan Ross. He is escorting me home."

The men turned to him, and Father Donovan bent at the waist. "Welcome to Kirkconnel parish. We just returned from the village and would be honored if ye'd join us for the noon meal."

"Thank ye," she spoke up.

"Lindsey, we don't have time to…"

"We have to eat, and we'd love to join ye," she added while watching Logan.

Headstrong wench.

Logan followed her and the monks down a narrow path winding through the woods as she chatted amiably with the priest. The wind whistled through the trees, swaying the tall Scots pines. Moss, dampened from the Nith, grew in abundance across grey boulders scattered throughout the forest.

"Brother Martin baked those sweet treats ye like." the priest said. "He'll be pleased ye're here."

"And what of Ashby?"

"Och, the wee scamp 'as grown," he replied. "Ye'll be surprised to see how tall he's become."

The pathway opened into a clearing. Yellow budding wildflowers interspersed between weathered grave markers surrounded a dark stone building perched on top of a hill. Monks milled around the yard. As the group approached, the men straightened and turned toward them while shading their eyes from the midday sun.

A large wiry-haired dog stood alert, his ears pointed. He stepped forward and barked. His shaggy, long tail wagged. He took another step then loped down the hill to greet them.

"Ashby!" Lindsey slid from Blaze and ran to greet the dog.

The mutt bounded to Lindsey and sprang on her. He towered over her head and licked her face as she threw her arms around him. Strangling sounds as if the beast tried to speak poured from the dog's mouth.

"He remembers ye all right," a portly monk said as he ambled toward them.

Ashby dropped and ran to the man.

Lindsey laughed. "Brother Martin, ye've turned him into a giant."

The man's hands clasped his wide girth. "He's been eating everything in sight since ye left him with us."

"But he was such a scrawny pup."

He chuckled. "Come inside, Lindsey MacDougall. The table is prepared, and we are serving yer favorite."

Logan dismounted as she turned to him. An unfettered smile brightened her face. She extended her hand to him, and his heart stumbled. She intertwined her fingers through his, and his groin tightened at her innocent, but intimate gesture.

They strolled up the hill behind the monks and ducked into the dim building. Smoke filled his nostrils from a fire blazing in the massive hearth against the back wall. Two long worn tables surrounded by log-hewn pews packed the cramped space. Lindsey guided him to one of the benches and they sat, hip to hip as brothers filled in around them.

Several lads scurried to set the table with a platter of roasted boar and leeks. Lindsey's leg warmed his. Her every move scraped his side, and he reveled in her closeness. Her warmth poured out to the parish members, and the men regarded her with affection.

Logan stabbed a hunk of roast on his trencher with his dagger and addressed Father Donovan. "Have ye seen soldiers in the area?"

The priest rubbed his whiskered chin. "Nae lately. They rarely travel through our community."

"What news do ye have?" Lindsey asked then spooned leeks into her mouth.

The father leaned forward, elbows on the table. "Rumor has it next month Edward will marry Margaret,

King Philip's daughter, further strengthening his ties to France and freeing him to focus on Scotland."

Logan groaned. "I knew the two kings broke their squabble last spring, but I didn't realize their plans had advanced so far."

"The English prepare Edward's ships to journey to Galloway late spring," a brother at Father Donovan's left added. "We received word last week they make repairs, garner weapons, and ready their vessels."

Shite. With France's support, Edward could storm their shores and take over. "Who have ye spoken to about this?" Logan asked.

"No one." A confused expression crossed the man's face, and he looked at Lindsey. "We normally pass our messages to Mistress MacDougall."

Logan fumed at the reminder of Lindsey's involvement. Even priests used her to carry missives. Was everyone bereft of sense? Why would they place her in grave danger?

She patted the man's hand. "Rest assured my friend is trustworthy, and we'll see the message is transferred."

~~~

Lindsey clutched Father Donovan's wrinkled hand. "Thank ye for yer hospitality."

"Ye're most welcome, child." He turned to Logan. "Keep her safe lad."

Irony struck him, but he kept his confrontational thoughts to himself. "I will." He nudged Lindsey's elbow. "We must leave. We have miles to travel before the sun sets."

Lindsey grasped the leather pouch hanging from her belt. Her fingers rummaged through the bag and extracted several gold pieces. "Blaze won these coins in Dumfries."

She pressed the money into Father Donavan's weathered palm. "I want ye to have them."

His eyes widened, and his shoulders sagged. "Ye're an answered prayer, child. I thank ye."

She hugged the old man. "Until next time."

There will not be a next time if I have anything to do with it. Logan guided her down the hill to Blaze. She turned toward him, and his breath caught at the wistful look in her eyes, her plump lips. His hands circled her small waist, and she clutched his shoulders. He paused, struggling with the overwhelming desire to press his mouth to hers, wrap his arms around her, and hold her against him.

Her lips parted, and he leaned down.

"Safe travels," Father Donovan called.

The innocent words pricked Logan's conscience as if the man threw icy water in his face. He took a deep breath and lifted Lindsey onto Blaze, handed her the reins, and mounted Sterling.

She waved as they trotted onto the worn trail winding through the forest. Afternoon sun filtered through the trees, and the thick branches cast shadows along the needle-cushioned path. Scotland's peaceful surroundings welcomed him home.

Home.

After spending months tromping through English infested lands, hiding and attacking, fleeing and constantly looking over his shoulder, the idea of returning home soothed his soul.

But the farther they pushed north, the sooner his time with Lindsey drew to an end.

Chapter Seven

The sun dipped low on the horizon, and an evening chill crept around Lindsey's neck. She shivered. Fine hairs rose on her arms as she nudged Blaze behind Logan onto a path winding through a copse of trees at the top of a lush pasture. The trail opened into a small hidden clearing. Giant grey boulders surrounded the cavity, providing protection from the wind. The crest overlooked the Nith's churning waters at the base of the hill and afforded a vantage point to view unwanted visitors.

After long hours in the saddle her muscles ached, and she looked forward to resting beside a fire. Kilmarnock was only a short day's ride ahead. They were almost home. She would welcome a hot bath and soft bed, but her heart tugged at thoughts of Logan leaving for Glencara.

Warring emotions plagued her. Over the past few days, she was drawn to him, but more times than she cared to remember, he chastised her part in the rebellion. He treated her as a younger sister. His obvious lack of desire made her feel like a foolish child harboring a crush on an older lad.

She found herself longing for home, for the safety of her stables. How ironic that the security she had always known hung by a raveling thread. If Alec had his way, she would no longer have her horses.

Logan dismounted. "We'll stay here tonight."

The wind blew his sandy brown hair across his forehead. He tugged Sterling's saddle, and the coat draping his broad shoulders tightened across his upper arms.

Lindsey slid to the ground. Blaze clopped behind her across the small clearing, and she looped the reins over a bush. The horse's brush lay in her bag. She grabbed it and ran the wiry bristles over his withers.

Memories of Logan resurfaced. She could still feel his taut muscles bunching beneath her palms, his strong arms holding her against his hard body. His touch evoked a strange fluttering in her belly. She longed for him to look at her as a woman, to feel his lips on hers. Heat crept up her neck and slid across her face. She shouldn't harbor such thoughts, but she couldn't get him off her mind. Images of them racing down the pasture—his smiling face, the admiration in his eyes—constantly invaded her thoughts.

But Logan was like all men, taking control, ordering her about, giving little regard to her abilities and contributions. As much as she loved him, she would never turn her life upside down and bow before any man. After all, Da had promised she and her sisters could live their lives as they desired and have their choice of a husband. She'd rather die a spinster than marry a man who stifled her adventurous nature.

For years she had run MacDougall stables, breeding, raising, and selling horses. The animals were her life, her passion. Immersed in responsibilities, she had gained her clansmen's approval, which was no easy task. Now, no one questioned her role. They accepted and admired her abilities. When the rebellion started in earnest, her success as a runner emboldened her confidence.

However, when Heather married Alec, Lindsey's world teetered. She stood to lose everything she had fought so hard to gain. Not only did he threaten her independence, he planned to take her horses to Glencara. Her brother-in-law was in for a rude awakening if he thought she would relinquish her way of life without a fight.

To that end, she had won the Dumfries race. She'd accomplished what she'd set out to do. She smiled to herself. The MacDougall name would be known across the country. She had advanced her position, and Alec would have to admit she could peddle her horses without his help.

She untied the wineskin from her saddle and took a sip. The cool refreshing liquid slid down her throat. While shoving the cork back into the spout, she studied Logan.

Squatting with one knee on the ground, he leaned toward a pile of sticks and coaxed tentative flames to life. Dry splinters caught fire and before long, a blaze flickered.

Lindsey extracted the roll of jerky and hard bread from her satchel. She strolled past him, perched on the ground beside the fire, and broke off a piece of bread. "Here, have some."

He took the meal and bit into the hunk.

The western horizon was lined with the setting sun's pink brilliance, softly fading into a pale peach. The sound of the Nith's rushing waters drummed in the background. A loud pop emanated from the flames, and sparks shot flaming embers outside the fire ring.

Logan had been quiet since they left the parish. While a night of passion might be out of the question, she longed to spend their last evening in amiable companionship.

"What will ye do when ye return home?" Lindsey asked.

Logan paused, then jabbed a stick in the fire. "Regroup and plan revenge."

She straightened. "On Collins?"

He glanced at her. "Aye."

Why his revelation surprised her, she wasn't sure. Collins had inflicted brutality, and Logan would want retribution. But after his severe injuries, she assumed he would rest at Glencara for a time. "Ye will leave soon?"

He tossed the stick into the flames. "What'd ye expect?" His voice sounded gruff. "I would find a good woman and settle down?"

Her gaze returned to the fire. "Something like that."

He huffed and rubbed his hands while extending his fingers to the heat. "And what of ye? Do ye have a betrothed waiting?"

"Nay, I'm not promised to anyone."

His head snapped toward her, his eyes narrowing. "I'm surprised yer da has not matched ye with one of the border Lairds."

"My da would not do such a thing. He promised Mum I could marry anyone I chose."

Logan's eyebrow quirked. "Anyone?"

"Anyone."

He leaned back on his hands and stared into the flames. "Ye will return to yer da's stables?"

"Aye, I look forward to working in the barn again. It's been several weeks since I left."

Fear of Alec taking her horses resurfaced. Worry gnawed at her and sunk into her chest. She would fight him with everything she had, but she knew it was futile. As laird of her clan, she was at his mercy.

Silence stretched between them. "Logan?"

He turned toward her.

She swallowed hard. "Things are a bit different now than when ye left."

"Different?" His deep voice rumbled in his chest.

"Aye. Bairns have been born. People have wed."

He shrugged. "Ye are telling me this…why?"

She exhaled. "Because yer cousin, Alec, married my sister, Heather, and is now Laird of MacDougall Castle."

His eyes widened. "What? Alec and Heather?"

"Aye."

He stared at her. "What of yer da? Why did Alec take over as laird?"

Her fingers fidgeted in her lap. "My da's aged and…has taken ill. Heather wanted to marry Alec, but she worried for Da. Alec agreed to reside at MacDougall Castle as laird."

"By God's bones." Logan turned up the wineskin and swigged a gulp. He paused. "What of Glencara?"

"I don't know Alec's plans for Glencara…"

His skeptical eyes studied her.

She pulled her gaze from his. Concentrating on the flames, she wrapped her arms around her legs and rested her chin on her knees.

"Why is it I feel there is more to the story, like ye're hiding something?" he asked. "Their marriage shouldn't concern ye."

"I'm not hiding anything." She sat forward again. "And ye're wrong that this doesn't concern me. Yer cousin threatens to destroy my stables."

Logan frowned. "Destroy yer stables? That doesn't sound like Alec."

She squared her shoulders. "He thinks one of his men would best peddle my animals, but I plan to continue breeding and selling the finest horses in the area. I've worked hard to learn about each breed."

He cocked a brow. "*Ye* breed and sell the horses?"

"Aye, I do. I've weeded out weaknesses and enhanced their strengths through my selective breeding practices, and I've sold many of my herd to traveling merchants. Because I provide superior animals, I can demand larger sums, and it's thrilling to hand a weighty purse to Heather with the revenues I've generated for our clan." She smiled. "The Dumfries race has made my name known."

His eyes narrowed, and he nodded. "Now I understand why ye entered that race."

"I had no choice." Her voice rose. "Alec forced me to prove myself. Now men will travel across the country to purchase MacDougall horses."

Logan took another swig of ale. "Ye're one of the best riders I've seen. Those men never stood a chance."

Her chest swelled. "That's why I deliver messages for Hamish. Blaze and I make an unstoppable team."

"Ye need to rethink the wisdom of yer part in the rebellion."

Her back stiffened. "If ye think I will sit by and let it play out around me, ye're mistaken. I fight for our freedom the same as ye."

"This is a man's war. I'm suggesting ye help in other ways. It's too dangerous for a lass to carry missives."

"I will not darn stockings and warm my feet by the fire while my fellow Scots fight the enemy. I can outmaneuver and outride most any man. I want to be involved."

"Aye, ye're smart and have displayed skillful riding." His eyes darkened. "But none of that will matter when soldiers get their hands on ye."

She jumped to her feet. "Ye're just like *all* men— never giving me a chance because I'm female. Do I constantly have to prove myself? What does it take to gain the respect I deserve?"

"I respect sound judgment. Ye act as if ye lack sense."

Anger surged through her. She strode from the clearing, tore around the thicket, and jogged down the hill toward the river. He had a lot of nerve. Who did he think had devised the plan that rescued his sorry neck?

Frigid wind sliced through her tunic. She clutched her woolen cloak at her chest, brushed past thorny shrubs and a stand of boulders. She grew weary battling overbearing men bent on changing her.

Falling water caught her attention. She slipped down an embankment and followed the sound to find a tributary cascading over what must be a thirty foot shelf into a pool surrounded by a rocky wall. The deluge cascaded through a narrow gap and continued rushing down river.

She stooped next to the pond and splashed water on her face. How stupid she had been to think Logan would understand her involvement. She was just as capable as any man. Over the past two years, she had avoided danger and outsmarted her opponents. He had it wrong.

"Well, well," a deep voice sounded behind her.

She straightened and whirled around.

Three men approached. Dirt smudged their bearded faces. Shaggy hair hung to their bulky shoulders, their torsos cloaked in padded doublets. The leader sported a surcoat emblazoned with three golden lions, King Edward's coat of arms.

Water droplets dripped onto her tunic, and she swiped her arm across her face. Her pulse pounded in her ears as her fingers eased over the sword dangling from her belt. With the rock wall at her back, she would have to fight her way from the alcove.

"If it ain't the lad from Dumfries," the leader said. "I told you we were on their bloody trail."

Another stepped forward. He swiped a dirty finger across his bulbous red nose. "Collins'll be pleased to make your acquaintance, boy. You made a mockery of 'im and 'e's anxious to repay you."

The other men chuckled.

She jerked her sword from the sheath, and their laughter died. With both hands grasping the hilt, she pointed the sharp tip at the men.

"Now that's no way to greet us," the third man said as the soldiers clutched their weapons. "Not after we've come all this way to find your bloody arse."

One lunged. She jumped to the left. Her blade deflected the attack.

"Whoa!" another yelled. "You can't let that scrawny bugger best you."

The man turned, his sword aimed at her. A grin spread across his face. "Why you're as purdy as a girl. Hair ain't even broke out on your face."

She charged. Her blade aimed at the man's torso.

His dark beady eyes widened. His foot snagged a rock. He tripped and fell over backward.

Her sharp sword sunk into the man's gut. Elation welled through her. She sprang around while snatching the dagger from her belt. Landing on her feet, knees bent, she fisted the blade, her eyes daring the next to attack.

The soldier on the ground gurgled.

"Why you lil' beggar," one of the soldiers hollered.

The men advanced. They split up, one sliding to her left, the other to her right.

Fear welled and she twisted from one to the other. One jabbed his sword at her face. She ducked, but his blade caught her cap and jerked it from her head. Long hair escaped and cascaded around her shoulders.

The two men straightened, their eyes widening. One laughed, his gaze traveling the length of her and back to her face. "Henry, we've struck it rich. Not only will Collins' reward us for bringing him the *boy*, we'll reward ourselves between *her* thighs."

The other man smirked. "My ballocks are tightening at the thought."

Bile rose in Lindsey's throat. Where was Logan? If she screamed, would she alert more soldiers?

Sfit!

The soldier to her right gasped. His eyes flew open and his mouth worked, but uttered nothing. He fell face first into the pool. An arrow protruded from his back.

The other soldier whirled around.

Sfit!

The man grasped the rod jutting from his chest, then crumpled to the ground.

Logan, bow in hand, jumped from the ledge and sprinted to her. "Are ye all right?"

Her legs wobbled, and he caught her as she stumbled forward. He wrapped his arm around her, and she clung to him. Her breath hitched, and she trembled uncontrollably.

His hand cradled her head against his shoulder, his heart thudding in her ear. He looped the bow over his arm and held her from him. "Ye're not hurt?"

She shook her head. "Nay, I'm fine."

He kissed her forehead then pulled her against him again. She threw her arms around his waist. His rigid muscles contracted beneath her fingertips. Her hands ran over the brawny expanse of his back, and she basked in the safety of his embrace.

When he straightened, anguish filled his eyes. His hands ran up and down her arms. "We need to leave. There might be others."

He turned, jerked her sword from the soldier's belly, and grabbed her hand. "Stay quiet."

"Wait." She reached for her cap and snatched it from the ground.

Logan led her over the slippery rocks and stones. They climbed the embankment and ran up the hill to their campsite. He wiped her sword on his trews and tossed it to her. "Gather yer things."

Nerves jangling, she hurried to Blaze, threw his saddle and her bag over his back, and secured the girth straps. She sheathed her dagger and sword, gathered the food, and stuffed it into her satchel.

Logan kicked dirt into the campfire, then sprang onto Sterling's back. "Let's go."

~~~

Senses heightened, Logan scanned the area for signs of Sassenachs as he led Lindsey into the forest along the river. The banks overflowed and spray drifted off the deluge. A bright moon lit their path. However, the surge of water drowned out sounds, making their trek perilous.

His pulse hammered in his ears. He had let his guard down, thought they were too far north to feel Collins's threat. The sight of Lindsey facing the soldiers had scared the hell out of him. Thoughts of what they would have done to her churned his gut. Nothing mattered but her, keeping her safe. He pressed forward. He needed to get her home as soon as possible, secreted safely inside the castle walls.

Miles ran into each other, and the hour grew late. He glanced over his shoulder at Lindsey hunched in the saddle. She was exhausted. He nudged Sterling alongside her and stopped Blaze.

Lindsey jerked upright, her blue eyes wide. "What is it?"

He wrapped his arms around her, pulled her from the saddle and onto his lap. "'Tis nothing. Ye're tired, and I worry ye'll fall."

"I'm fine," she protested. "I can continue."

"Shhh…get some rest." Her legs dangled over his left thigh. He tucked her head beneath his chin. Her arms circled his waist, and she snuggled against his chest as he pulled his warm cloak around them.

Her body felt so right nestled against him. How he wished he could take her away, make her his. No matter how he tried to push her from his thoughts, he yearned to hold her, listen to her sing her horses' praises, and bask in her warmth, her cheerfulness.

Soft breasts cushioned his torso. He closed his eyes and relived viewing the outline of protruding nipples pressing against her tunic. Would they be rosy pink, the color of her plump lips?

His cock thickened. She shifted and her luscious bottom rubbed his swelling manhood. He inwardly groaned and out of self-preservation, threw his thoughts to revenge.

They continued their slow course into the dead of night. Lightning flashed, the wind swirled around them, and the rumble of thunder followed. He scanned the forest for a dry spot protected from the inclement weather and spied a structure partially hidden amongst craggy boulders. He nudged Sterling around the massive rock. A dilapidated cabin came into view.

Logan paused. The dwelling was quiet, abandoned.

"Lass." He kissed the top of Lindsey's head.

She straightened, and her sleepy eyes blinked. "Where are we?"

"South of Kilmarnock." He tucked an auburn lock behind her ear. "We need to rest the horses."

Logan eased her to the ground then swung off Sterling. He clutched her hand, and they strolled to the cabin.

The busted wooden planks squeaked as he stepped inside the dark cramped area. Lightening lit the room. A blackened, cold hearth filled the wall to his right. A long wooden table turned on its side was propped against the opposite wall. Another flash revealed leaves and debris littering the dirt floor, weeds curling around a broken stool, and vines hugging the wall's shelving. Thunder boomed again, and Lindsey shivered, her fingers tightening around his.

He rubbed his hands up and down her cold arms. "It's not terribly inviting, but it'll provide protection from the weather."

"Aye," she agreed. "It's good to be off the horse as well."

"I'll see to them while ye start a fire."

Logan stepped out-of-doors. An icy breeze picked up, and he blew warm breath on his chapped hands while scanning the area for a place to secure the horses. To the right, a rocky ledge jutting from one of the massive grey boulders blocked the wind. Water trickled from the ridge into shallow pools carved in the stone.

He strode to the animals, grasped the reins, and guided them under the shelter. After freeing them of the heavy saddles, he rubbed their backs and glanced at the cabin. A white puff of smoke seeped from the stone chimney. Lindsey had started a fire.

He grabbed the small sack of grain hanging from his saddle. After pouring liberal amounts on the ground, he dusted his hands on his trews, and scouted the area for a bucket. A bent container, overtaken by weeds, lay against an old well. He grabbed it and dipped it into the pool, then placed the water before the horses. He snatched Lindsey's satchel, her rolled bedding and his bag, and hurried to the cabin.

A bright glow radiated from the hearth, the firelight casting shadows through the shack. Lindsey had moved the broken table closer to the hearth and leaned against it, rubbing her arms. "It'll take some time before we feel its warmth."

He tossed their belongings next to her, and she rummaged through her bag. She held up the last of the ale. "Are ye thirsty?"

Logan dropped beside her. "Aye."

He studied her bent head as she worked the cork from the container. She'd had a close call. What if he had not chased after her? Those men would have used her sweet body, then handed her to Collins.

His stomach churned.

"I hope that episode with the soldiers made ye realize the dangerous game ye play. Ye must drop this preoccupation with the rebellion." The words blurted from his mouth before he thought.

She huffed, and her head turned toward him. "Is that what ye think? I'm preoccupied with playing a game?"

He stared at her. "I worry about ye."

The fire popped and hissed.

Sadness drifted through her blue eyes. "I'm not yer sister, nor do I want yer brotherly affection."

"Brotherly affection?" She couldn't be serious. No brother would have such carnal thoughts for his sister. "My desire for ye threatens to overtake my good sense. I have fought my attraction to ye, steeled my body to resist yer curves."

He allowed his gaze to take in her long legs curled beneath her delightful bottom, her breasts pressing against her tunic. Blood filled his cock. "I want ye."

Her chin wobbled. "Then kiss me, Logan."

His will broke, and he tugged her into his arms. His mouth covered hers. She moaned and desire surged through his veins. He longed to sink into her sweetness, lose himself in her enticing body.

Her lips parted, and he slid his tongue into her warm recesses, his manhood throbbing in anticipation. His hand drifted to her breast, and her nipple pebbled through the fabric of her tunic.

"Logan…"

His name laced with desire rolled off her tongue and shot to his groin. Her soft bosom filled his hand, and he yearned to teach her the act of making love, watch her experience the exhilaration of climax.

She ran her fingers through his hair as he nuzzled her neck, his mouth trailing along her shoulder. His cock pressed against her stomach, and she moaned.

His conscience stabbed him.

What was he doing? He had to gain control.

Heated with desire, his heart pounded in his chest. He leaned his forehead against hers and cupped the side of her face. "I can't do this. I can never have ye."

Tears filled her eyes. "Why not?"

"I'm bastard born. As much as I'd like to have ye, I won't soil ye for…" He couldn't bring himself to utter the words.

"I don't care who yer da is, Logan."

He smiled and stroked her soft skin. "I love yer carefree ways, but ye're the only one my birth would not concern. Some traditions will never change."

"I beg to differ." Her chin rose. "In time, senseless traditions will change."

He doubted he'd live to see that day. "Will ye let me hold ye tonight, lass?"

She nodded.

"Come here." Propped against the table, he pulled her to his chest. Her enticing body curled against him. He nuzzled her silky curls and kissed her cheek, then rested his chin on her head.

How would he leave her and travel to Glencara? The thought of another man having her as a wife caused his chest to ache with a debilitating emptiness.

Several hours later, dawn filtered between the cabin's busted boards. He closed his eyes against the daylight and relished a few more moments with his princess snuggled in his arms. Too soon, they would leave for MacDougall Castle.

Chapter Eight

Kilmarnock, Scotland
September 1299

Lindsey guided Blaze through the dense woods bordering MacDougall Castle with Logan close behind. Twilight filtered through the Scots pines and white willows, casting long shadows on green ferns and autumn flowers lining the path. Wild orchids' spiked petals swayed in the gentle breeze alongside tiny purple blossoms perched at the end of silvery foliage. Their sweet scent filled the air as Blaze's hooves brushed past.

The narrow dirt trail wound between outlying cottages. Smoke curled from the chimneys with the smell of wood fires wafting on the wind. Several scruffy dogs barked and ran toward them.

Blaze's ears laid back. He tossed his head, and Lindsey patted his sleek neck. "Easy, lad."

To the left, Gilda struggled across the clearing with a blackened cauldron. Her blonde hair was secured in a red scarf, and a dark woolen shawl swathed her shoulders and hung to her ample hips. Two young lads ran to her and lifted the container from her arms. She straightened and swiped the back of her hand across her brow. "Welcome home, Mistress Lindsey," she shouted.

Lindsey waved. "Thank ye, Gilda. It is good to be home."

Blaze turned off the path and trotted up the dusty road toward the village at the base of the castle. To her right was a pasture full of her father's grazing cattle. Two men amongst the beasts straightened. One raised a hand in greeting, and Lindsey waved in return. Ducks squawked, their wings spraying water as they ran across the small lake at the back of the field.

Logan nudged Sterling alongside Blaze. After Lindsey had awakened in Logan's arms, he had kissed her, then abruptly announced it was time to leave. Once they were on the road, he became silent, withdrawn.

I can never have ye.

Her heart clenched. As much as she wanted to scream against the injustice, deep down she knew he was right. Regardless of Da's promise, he would not approve of her marrying a man without a proper birthright.

It wasn't fair.

She clutched her wrap tighter around her shoulders and studied Logan. He rode straight and tall in the saddle. His brown cloak draped his broad shoulders and dark whiskers covered his stony face.

She loved him.

Determined to fight the longstanding traditions of politically arranged marriages, she squared her shoulders and faced the castle looming before them. Torches blazed into the evening sky. Solid battlements, secured behind grey stone, ran across the outer gates surrounding the fortress. Alec's guards marched across the ramparts, prepared to defend the castle at a moment's notice.

The horses' hooves clattered on the wooden bridge leading to the bailey. Blaze trotted through the large worn gate and past guardhouses on either side with Sterling close behind. Several men sharpened swords and a loud grating sound echoed against the stone walls. To her left, a lad led a chestnut-colored horse from the barn. The animal pranced, his dark mane bouncing.

"Lindsey?"

She turned to the deep gravelly voice she knew so well.

Da's old captain, Fergus, ambled toward her as stablehands ran to take their horses. His wrinkled hands grasped Blaze's bridle. Dirt smudged his tan tunic and damp, grey hair stuck to his forehead. "Thank God ye're back. Yer sister's been frantic."

"Och, Heather worries too much." Lindsey threw her leg over Blaze and slid to the ground. "Logan escorted me home."

Fergus's gaze swung to Logan. "By God, ye're a sight for me tired eyes, lad."

Logan dismounted and grasped Fergus's outstretched hand. "It's been a long time."

The old captain clasped Logan's shoulder. "Ye're well?"

Logan nodded. "Aye, and happy to be back."

"Alec will be relieved to see ye."

"Let's go inside," Lindsey said, rubbing her arms. "It's chilly, and I'm hungry."

They passed through the worn interior gate and into the inner bailey. A lad with bright red hair hurried past, his arms full of firewood. Several women filled containers at the old well while a number of men stood around the blacksmith forge. Loud hammering and heat emanated from the smithy as the man worked the iron. The distinctive odor hung thick, the whooshing bellows circulating a fog of choking fumes.

"I just heard ye arrived." Heather dashed down the stairs and threw her arms around Lindsey. "I'm so thankful ye're home."

"It's good to be back. I'm dirty and tired."

"Logan?"

Lindsey cringed at the deep resounding voice behind her.

"Alec," Logan responded with the sound of the two men slapping each other's backs.

"By Satan's hairy arse it's good to see ye. Ye had us worried when we didn't hear from ye."

Logan chuckled. "I would've sent word if I'd been able."

Heather straightened and held Lindsey's hands. Blonde brows scrunched over her blue eyes. "I feared the English captured ye."

Lindsey squeezed her sister's fingers. "Logan kept me safe."

"Where the hell have ye been?" Alec boomed.

Lindsey rolled her eyes. She dropped Heather's hands, squared her shoulders, and faced him.

Hands on hips, the Laird of MacDougall stood before her, anger darkening his chiseled face.

She crossed her arms and glared. "Ye verrae well know I delivered a message to our troops."

"When ye were gone so long, we imagined the worst," Heather said.

Alec's forehead creased, and he pointed at Lindsey. "I forbid ye to conduct missions from MacDougall Castle."

She planted her hands firmly on her hips. "Ye can withdraw yer unfounded outrage. No one informed me of *my* home's new rules. I supported the rebellion long before ye showed up, and I see no reason why I should stop now."

Alec grasped her upper arm. She tried to jerk away but his grip tightened, his strong fingers biting into her skin. "Ye will do as I say," he growled.

Logan grabbed Alec's wrist. "Take yer hand off her."

Alec's head snapped to Logan. His grey eyes narrowed.

Lindsey's breath caught. Logan's dark demeanor spoke volumes. He'd defended her, protected her.

"I will not tell ye again," he snarled.

Alec stared at Logan. His fist uncurled, and Lindsey stumbled back. "Ye will not cross my words again."

"Keep yer hands off her and there will be no need," Logan countered.

The two men, equal in stature, squared off, eye to eye.

Lindsey's pulse pounded in her ears.

Heather reached out to Alec, and her hand slid down his arm. "Husband, please."

Seconds passed before he turned and stormed up the keep stairs.

Heather watched him leave. "He's just been worried." She shook her head and started toward the stone staircase, calling over her shoulder, "Please come in and have something to eat. I know ye must be famished."

Lindsey turned to follow, but paused and looked at Logan, the intensity of his eyes piercing. "Thank ye," she whispered.

He winked and butterflies flittered around her stomach. Elation bubbled up inside her as she climbed the steep steps with Logan at her side. They strolled through the large oak door and into the keep's dimly-lit corridor. Torches secured in brackets lined the damp passage, the flames flickering in a cold draft. The sweet smell of burning peat greeted them, the scent evoking wistful memories. A longing for Mum washed over her. How she missed her warmth and tenderness.

Heather lifted the cloak from Lindsey's back. "Make yerselves comfortable at the table in the great hall, and I'll let Da know ye've arrived."

Laughter and cheers rang out. Men and women mingled, some gathered near the warmth of the fire blazing in the hearth, while others lined the trestle tables filling the hall. Serving girls ran into the room, carrying trays laden with smoked boar and cabbage. Two lads placed jugs of ale between bowls and trenchers set about the table.

Logan escorted Lindsey to the dais at the front of the room where Alec already sat and slid in beside her. A serving lass set tankards before them and piled their trenchers with roasted venison and carrots. The aroma of fresh baked bread wafting from a platter before them caused Lindsey's stomach to growl. She bit into a bun and sighed as Rena's warm roll melted in her mouth.

Alec glanced over his mug at Logan. "Yer attacks on the convoys have been hailed across the country. Edward's outraged. He vowed to eradicate our rebel troops so we worried when we didn't hear from ye."

"We made a detour into the bowels of hell for a few weeks." Logan gulped his ale. He set the heavy pewter tankard on the table and wiped his mouth on his sleeve. "We ran into trouble off the coast of Berwick early August. A churl joined our group, and the next thing we knew, we were at the end of a rope, marching to Northumberland."

Alec's forehead creased. "A traitor?"

Logan leaned on his forearms, speared a slice of beef on his trencher, and ran it through the gravy. "An English commander's guard."

"Shite," Alec hissed.

Lindsey spooned a spiced carrot on her trencher and popped it in her mouth as she looked from Logan to Alec.

"Ye were taken to the English fortress in Northumberland?"

"The verrae place."

A lass poured more ale in Alec's tankard.

"How the hell did ye escape?" Alec's eyes fixed on his cousin as he bit a hunk of bread.

Logan placed his hand over hers. "Lindsey rescued me."

Her brother-in-law quit chewing. His gaze shot to her.

She turned to Logan, his warm palm covering her skin. She longed to lace her fingers through his. He smiled, and her shoulders squared, her chest filling with pride.

"My men and I were bound and headed to the gallows. I wouldn't be here if it weren't for her." His thumb rubbed the back of her hand. "We owe her our lives."

Her heart fluttered. How she loved him. Not only did he defend her to Alec, he sang her praises.

Heather and Da entered the main hall. Frame bent, Da shuffled toward the table, his balding head tonsured with sparse white hair. "Daughter," he said, his hand coaxing Lindsey to him.

She scrambled off the bench and ran into his arms. He hugged her and stroked her hair. His familiar musky scent filled her and engulfed her in an old sense of security. How many times as a young lass had his embrace comforted her?

He straightened and held her from him. "Did ye enjoy yer visit?"

Her conscience pinched at the lie she had told. "Aye, but it's always good to be home, Da."

A lass swept into the great room, her arms burdened with a tray.

"Rena baked our favorite sweet cakes," Heather said, as she cleared trenchers from the table.

Fergus lifted a gnarled finger. "I'd like a bun."

"Come, let's have one." Lindsey clutched Da's arm and they headed for the dais.

He sat next to Fergus. His eyes twinkled as he accepted one of the special treats. Lindsey selected a sticky bun off the tray, slid beside Logan, and bit into the honeyed scone. Rena's new cinnamon and ginger spices filled her mouth. She took a deep breath and savored the delicacy.

As Heather passed the buns around, Alec asked Logan, "What news do ye have of the Sassenachs?"

"Ye've heard the rumor of Edward's marriage to Margaret?" Logan asked.

Alec shook his head. "Nay, I thought the two kings were at odds."

"They were last spring, but it appears they've patched up their differences. The union with the French will free Edward to focus on Scotland," Logan added. "His ships journey to Galloway late spring."

"Damn it!" Alec leaned back in his chair.

Logan turned to Lindsey. "Who do ye deliver Father Donovan's messages to?"

She swallowed the remainder of her bun and picked up her tankard. "Hamish."

Heather sat next to Alec, and he placed his arm around her as he glared at Lindsey. "I'll see he gets it."

Her body stiffened. But of course he would since he'd forbidden her to conduct further missions. What was it about the man that set her blood to boil? Perhaps it was his determination to rip her life apart. Not only did he order her to cease involvement in the rebellion, he planned to take her precious horses.

What would be left for her? The hopes of marrying a fat old laird and resolve herself to a life of misery?

~~~

Logan ran his hand down Lindsey's tense back. "It's been a long day, and I know yer tired. Let me escort ye to yer room, lass."

She nodded and stood with him. "Goodnight, Da, sister."

She faced Alec and paused.

Logan clasped her arm and tugged her from the hall before she could issue a scathing comment she might regret. They climbed the long flight of stairs leading to the bedchambers and strolled in silence down the drafty corridor until she stopped before a darkened oak door.

"This is my room."

Third door on the right. How he would love to find his way back here tonight. He traced his finger along her jaw and over her plump bottom lip. She opened her mouth, and her lips surrounded the tip of his finger.

Heat shot straight to his loins. His cock sprang to life. He hissed through clenched teeth, "Lindsey."

He pulled her against him, and his mouth covered hers.

She wrapped her arms around his neck, and he lifted her until her feet dangled above the floor.

Shite! He throbbed with need. What was he doing? Did he lack even the smallest amount of control?

He leaned his forehead against hers. He kissed her eyes, her nose and cheek. "Lass, ye're killing me."

Her teeth nipped his bottom lip.

"Nay, we can't do this." He set her from him and ran a hand through his hair. "I'm sorry. I didn't intend to…"

"Shhh…" Her finger stroked across his mouth. "Don't say it."

His arm dropped. He had to leave while he still could.

She stepped into her bedchamber, disheveled auburn hair falling in ringlets about her shoulders. Her passion-filled eyes had turned violet, and her kiss-swollen lips beckoned him. God, she was beautiful. He wanted to touch her, hold her.

With sheer force of will, he stepped back. "Rest well, princess."

"Goodnight, Logan," she whispered and closed the door.

He stared at the door and again, the anguish of leaving her resurfaced. Pain shot through his chest. He took a deep breath and exhaled. He wanted her beside him. She invaded his thoughts, plagued his nights.

Damn it! His open palm slammed the wall. The sting coursed over his skin. He'd better get control of himself and head home before he made a mistake. He would not hurt her.

He adjusted the front of his tight trews and made his way back downstairs.

Alec and Lindsey's father sat before the fire. Logan dropped beside the men, grabbed the container off the table next to his chair, and poured himself a mug of ale. His body still thrummed with need. Leaning back in his chair, he stretched his tired neck muscles.

"I've decided to remain here and run MacDougall Castle," Alec announced.

Logan looked over his mug at his cousin as he took a swig of ale.

"I'll need a strong hand at Glencara. I'd have ye manage it, if ye're willing." Alec leaned forward and grabbed the container of ale off the table.

What did that mean? He would perform the duties of a laird without the title and privileges it afforded? "Manage the castle?" Logan asked.

"Aye, I sent Eric there in my absence until ye returned." Alec poured more of the drink in his tankard and set the container on the table between them. "With yer help, we'll improve the running of the castles. Both properties need repairs. I want to bring the livestock from Glencara here where the land is better suited to support them and merge the MacDougall horses with those at Glencara. We stand to make revenues through our breeding program, and it'd be beneficial to consolidate those efforts."

Logan swirled the amber liquid around his mug. "I'm ready to be home for a while, but I have unfinished business in Northumberland."

"I understand. I'd like to be in on that business."

Logan nodded.

His cousin spread a map of MacDougall Castle on the table between them and pointed to the keep's perimeter and surrounding structures. "There are areas outside the walls that have been compromised. I'll have the carpenter from Glencara travel here to inspect them. He'll work with the MacDougall's carpenter."

He also indicated several areas at Glencara needing repairs. They talked at length of the best way to manage new construction and the maintenance both castles would require in the future.

"While we're working on the repairs, I want to alter the MacDougall stables." Alec straightened. "Although we recently completed construction on the barn, we'll break down the smaller stalls and open them up for maintaining and breeding cattle and sheep."

Alastair rubbed his whiskered chin. "What will Lindsey say about that idea?"

"When it comes to what's best for the clan, she has little to say," Alec answered.

Protective talons coiled through Logan's belly. He understood as laird, Alec made decisions for the clan, but that didn't mean Logan cared for his lack of concern for Lindsey.

"Glencara has a herd of Highland cattle I'd like to bring here as well as the sheep. MacDougall pastures are far superior. The grazing land is more abundant, and the grass is plentiful." Alec rolled out a sketch of the proposed barn changes and pointed at an area. "We'll section a space for the shearing of wool here."

He continued to go over his designs for the castles. After he finished, he leaned back in his chair and swallowed the contents of his tankard.

Alastair blinked repeatedly, the corners of his mouth downturned. "I don't know about filling the stables with cattle and sheep."

Alec leaned over his knee toward Alastair. "Times are changing. We need to change with them or get left behind. Consolidating our resources so they can be better managed will give us an advantage."

The old laird rubbed the back of his neck and stared at the floor. Silence filled the room. A log rolled in the hearth, and blue and gold flames curled around the wood. Finally, he turned to Alec. "Aye, I agree."

Alec looked to Logan. "Do ye agree to manage Glencara?"

"Aye." Logan swirled the ale in his mug as he looked at Alec, then at Alastair. "But, I'm taking Lindsey with me."

Chapter Nine

"Ye're making a big mistake," Alec ground out.

Nay, Logan knew what he was doing. If he couldn't have Lindsey as his wife, he'd at least keep her close and she'd have her horses.

A perfect plan.

Logan leaned back in the chair and stretched his legs before the solar's hearth. The warmth of the fire matched the contentment in his heart.

Alec shook his head. "I had considered asking her to manage the stables, but after her latest folly, I've thought better of it. I don't want to worry over her running off again."

Logan bristled. "It was because of ye that she ran off. Ye made her feel the necessity to prove herself."

"What?" Alec folded his arms across his chest. "It was *my* fault?"

"Ye gave her the impression ye were taking her horses. When I remove that threat, she won't feel the need to run off." *Even if I have to tie her up, she will not carry out anymore missions.*

Alec leaned forward, his eyes narrowing. "That...*woman* has been a thorn in my side for months. She's a hot headed, opinionated female who has no right to interfere in the decisions I make for the clan."

His cousin's words spoke volumes. When Logan first heard Lindsey's accusations, he thought she must have been mistaken about Alec's intentions, but hearing him now, Logan understood her concern.

Shadows cast about the room, the silence broken only by occasional pops of the firewood. Logan studied Lindsey's father, who sat on the bench to Alec's right. The once stalwart laird hunched over, a worn woolen blanket draping his legs, sparse white hair lining his bald head. His weathered, gnarled fingers rubbed the black and white whiskers dotting his cheeks and chin. Why hadn't he spoken? Surely the man had an opinion of Logan taking his daughter to Glencara.

As if Alec read Logan's thoughts, he turned to Alastair. "What do ye say?"

The old man didn't hesitate. "It would kill my lassie to take her horses from her."

"Verrae well," Alec said with a huff. "At least it'll keep her out of my way." He extended his hand to Logan. "It's decided then. In the next few days, ye'll need to begin the move."

Logan shook Alec's hand as he pictured his princess's flashing violet eyes.

She had to agree.

~~~

The next morning, Logan trotted down the long stairs leading into the bailey as the sun's rays peeked over the horizon. A chill crept inside his tunic, and a shiver traveled down his body. He shoved his arms in his roughhewn cloak and marched along the path, gravel crunching beneath his boots.

Two lads carrying sloshing buckets of milk in their hands, raced past with a tan, shaggy dog loping along behind, his tongue lolling. Ducks and geese squawked and waddled through the yard, and a man coaxed several sheep into the pen at the back of the bailey.

To his left, Fergus led a dapple horse pulling an empty cart toward the kitchen. "Good morn," he shouted.

Logan waved. "And to ye."

The former MacDougall captain smiled and shuffled along.

Logan was anxious to inspect the herd, assess the needs of the animals, and determine which stablehands he'd choose to help Lindsey manage the horses at Glencara.

He rounded the corner of the barn and paused in the wide central doorway. The comforting familiar smells of fresh cut hay and grain mixed with the musty odor of horses welcomed him.

Early morning light filtered through wooden slatted windows and highlighted the sturdy construction. Substantial beams, resting on equally thick supporting logs, crossed the wide expanse of the ceiling. A high-pitched roof soared above. Erected in the center of the building, a straight ladder ran from the ground up to a platform. A large pulley hung over the raised area with ropes strung to each side of the spacious barn. The well-made building appeared new, more up-to-date than most with plenty of stalls and room for storage.

A ruckus toward the back of the stable caught his attention. Men and boys crowded around a pen, some offering opinions while others hung on the fencing and watched. His gaze fell on Lindsey's back. Dressed in lad's trews with her hair stuffed under a tan worsted cap, she straddled the wooden fence, focused on the center of the ring.

Logan walked down the main aisle toward the activity.

A red-faced lad grasped the saddle of a bucking horse. Both hands maintained a death grip on the leather as the animal kicked his hind legs behind him. The boy careened forward. The horse reared and leapt off the ground, throwing the rider across the corral. The animal rose on his back legs, his front hooves pawing the air, his nostrils flaring.

"No, no, no!" Lindsey threw her leg over the fence and dropped into the pen.

Logan rushed forward. What the hell was she thinking jumping into the ring with a wild horse?

Arms held out, she eased over to the disquieted animal. He snorted and tossed his head, his black forelock bouncing between his widened eyes.

"Ye can't bully yer way to making him give ye what ye want." She brought an arm down and offered her palm to him. He let her inch over, and she ran her hand down his side. "Easy. No one will hurt ye."

Logan stopped. He couldn't believe it. His princess had calmed the beast.

The horse's mouth agitatedly worked the metal bit, his frightened eyes trained on her.

She slid her hand down the side of his face to the bridle. Her fingers worked the bit's tie until she loosened the knot, then eased the metal from his mouth. "I wouldn't like this thing between my teeth either."

The horse bowed his head and nudged her torso. Patting his neck, she moved to his side, placed her foot in the stirrup and mounted.

The animal tensed. His head jerked up, held stiff.

Shite! She was taking this too far.

"'Tis all right, lad."

Logan held his breath.

She nudged the horse. He took a step, then another.

"Good fellow," she said, stroking his neck. After guiding him around the ring, she coaxed him to go faster. He trotted across the pen twice before she brought him to the starting point and dropped from his back.

Pent up air poured through Logan's nose. His pulse pounded in his ears. Didn't she realize the danger of breaking a horse? Why were these men standing around watching? One of them should be responsible for the perilous task.

Remembering his heated discussion with Lindsey at Cora's squelched his impulse to take her by the shoulders and shake her. He'd have to find another way to ensure one of the men undertook this job from now on.

She reached inside her tunic, pulled out a slice of apple, and offered it to the horse. His lips nibbled the treat, and she beamed. "Ye're going to be just fine."

Logan's body relaxed, and he clapped. "Well done."

Lindsey turned to him. "Good morn."

"That was quite a feat. Ye should take care when breaking a wild horse."

The gathered men chuckled as the crowd broke apart and resumed their chores. Logan failed to find anything amusing. Perhaps they laughed at the absurd notion Lindsey would take care, but he would ensure she no longer took part in this type of activity.

She scoffed and scratched between the horse's ears. "'Tis nothing new, just one of my duties."

Logan leaned against the fence and shook his head. "Ye're going to spoil him."

Several lads raked hay and saw to the needs of the animals while another pushed a wheelbarrow full of soiled shavings down the central pathway.

"Would ye care to show me yer horses?"

She handed a lad the reins. "Be gentle with him. He's just getting started."

Patting the colt's hindquarters, she stepped around him and started toward the main aisle. "Down this way we have a number of stalls where we section off the sick or injured that need special care."

They stopped before a stall, and she opened the gate. "This is Bess." Lindsey stroked the mare's nose. "She is Blaze's dam."

"Beautiful." Logan patted the mare, ran his hand down her shiny coat and across her rounded belly.

"Bess is due for foaling in another month or so. We brought her in from the north pasture where she'll be warm, and we can keep an eye on how she's doing."

"Ye're hoping for another Blaze?"

She rewarded his tease with a radiant smile. "Perhaps."

Lindsey caressed the side of Bess's face then turned and left the stall. Logan followed.

"We breed three different kinds." She held up her fingers and counted them off as she walked down the dirt path. "Our pleasure horses are small and best known for their gentle nature. We've found a number of well-to-do Englishmen like to purchase them for their wives and daughters."

She turned toward him and grinned. "We also breed race horses, as I'm sure ye're aware. They have good overall balance with slightly longer legs for stride and powerful hindquarters to generate speed."

Lindsey swept her arm to indicate another area of the stables. Majestic black beasts, tall and hefty with muscle, mingled in the pen. "And lastly, we breed work horses that are larger and stouter than most. They're not as massive as the drafts, but their broad backs and mighty hindquarters are characteristic of the breed."

"Verrae impressive." With these animals alongside Glencara's horses, the herd would be substantial.

He trailed her through the knotty pine building while she expounded on the workings and activities of the barn. His princess fascinated him. Not only did her expertise rival any man's, she managed a remarkable operation. Everything had a place, and the lads scurried to do their chores.

They came upon her friend, Blake. He carried a bale of hay into the storage area and tossed it onto the stack against the back wall as Lindsey approached him.

"Blake, ye remember Logan Ross, don't ye?"

The man brushed his forehead with his sleeve as his gaze narrowed on Logan. "Welcome back."

Logan extended his hand. "Thank ye."

As Blake accepted the offered greeting, the two silently assessed each other.

Lindsey continued, "I was just showing him around."

Her friend nodded. "Let me know if ye need anything, but if ye'll excuse me, I have work to do."

He grabbed another bale and strode off.

Logan faced her. "I'm impressed with yer knowledge and obvious love for these animals."

Her blue eyes widened. "Ye're surprised? Did ye think I *played* at this game too?"

He sighed loudly as she tossed his ill-advised words at him. "Settle down, lass. I only meant to give ye a compliment."

Her shoulders sagged, and she shook her head. "I'm sorry. That was uncalled for. I'm just sensitive to my role here. No doubt yer cousin still plots to replace me."

Was now the time to broach the subject of her moving to Glencara? He had hoped for privacy to discuss his ideas. He reached out to her. "Lass…"

"Lindsey?" Fergus shouted from the doorway. "Guests have arrived asking for ye."

She whirled toward him and hurried to the barn's entrance. "Asking for *me*?"

Logan stopped beside her.

Three men dressed in finery waited in the bailey. Rich burgundy tunics hung to their knees, and white stockings disappeared into their well-made leather boots. Expensive looking cloaks draped their shoulders, and hats sporting feather plumes perched atop their heads.

"Aye, they want to see the horses Lind MacDougall's selling." Fergus's bushy eyebrows wriggled. "Seems yer peddling might have paid off."

Lindsey turned to Logan and adjusted her cap. "Did I get it all?"

119

He tucked a stray auburn curl into the woolen covering. "Aye, *lad*."

She rotated on her heel, shoved her hands in gloves, and marched through the barn's wide doorway and into the bailey.

One man nudged another with his elbow and extended his hand to her. "MacDougall, I'm Roger Claremont." He motioned to his companions as he introduced them. "George Tucker and Blaine Whiteside."

Lindsey shook their hands. "Welcome to MacDougall Castle," she said in a deepened voice.

Logan smiled to himself.

"We attended the Dumfries race last week and witnessed your stunning ride," Claremont said. "We'd be interested in taking a look at the horses you have for sale."

"By all means, gentlemen. What type of horse did ye have in mind?" She threw an impish grin over her shoulder at Logan as the party accompanied her into the stables and out of sight.

Alec strode down the keep stairs and crossed the bailey.

Logan chuckled and clapped his shoulder. "She's drummed up business for the horses."

His cousin scowled and started toward the stables.

"Wait. Give her a chance."

Alec threw him an incredulous look. "She's a lass. What can she know about selling horses?"

~~~

The men decided upon three animals and handed Lindsey a hefty sack. She peered inside the grey cloth bag at the gold coins and tugged the drawstring tight. It was all she could do to contain her joy as the stablehands led the horses from the barn.

She wanted to shout, jump up and down with excitement. She wanted to slam the money into Alec's hand. Instead, she used great restraint as she saw the men on their way, then strutted past Logan and Alec.

"I'll just give this to Heather to record." She jogged up the stairs and into the keep. Once she cleared the door out of Alec's sight, she held her arms over her head and danced across the great hall, laughing as she went in search of Heather.

Chapter Ten

Logan took Lindsey's elbow, and under the pretense of needing to speak with her, ushered her from the great hall's dais and into the solar. What did he have to say that could not have been discussed at the evening meal?

She sidled into the inviting room, and Logan shut the door behind them. Her father's study had always been a place of warmth and security. She ambled around the room, stopping behind one of the chairs facing Alec's desk. A warm fire flickered in the hearth, and the smell of peat filled the intimate space.

Logan sat on the edge of the worn desk, and his muscular arms crossed his chest.

She fingered the back of the chair. When he didn't say anything she raised her eyebrow. "Ye had something to tell me?"

"Aye. Alec has asked me to manage Glencara while he runs MacDougall Castle."

He was leaving.

A boulder plummeted to the pit of her gut as if a cockatrice had turned her stomach to stone. She swallowed past a lump as thick as gruel stuck in her throat. "That's wonderful, Logan. Ye should enjoy that."

"There's a good bit of work to be done, and I look forward to staying home for a while." He paused as if considering his next words. "Ye need to understand the changes we're putting into place for the better of both castles."

Changes?

Her horses.

Bands of despair squeezed the breath from her lungs. "Nay. Not ye. I won't let ye take my horses." Panic surged through her, and her pulse pounded in her ears. "Please, Logan, tell me ye're not taking them."

"The decision's been made to combine the herds."

She darted around the chair, her eyes brimming with unshed tears. "But I proved I can peddle them. Those men were just the first to show up. There will be more."

Logan held up a hand. "Give me a chance to explain."

"What's there to explain?" Her chest heaved. She wanted to scream over the injustice. "Alec has been against me from the day he arrived, focused on how his *men* can take over my responsibilities."

"Hold on." He clutched her shoulders. "Ye've got it wrong. I want ye to live at Glencara and manage *all* the horses. With both MacDougall and Glencara animals, we'll have quite a herd, and I need yer help."

Lindsey straightened, her eyes blinking. "Ye want me to live at Glencara?"

"Aye."

"But what of Da? He won't agree…"

"I've already received his consent and Alec's too." His hands slid down her arms.

"*Alec* agreed?"

"He did."

She pulled away and crossed the room to the hearth. Staring into the flames, she wrapped her arms around her waist and digested what she'd just heard.

Logan was giving her a chance to stay with her horses. Her mind raced with excitement as she thought of working with the large herd, not to mention living with Logan. She had been distraught over the thought of him leaving. Perhaps this was the answer to her prayers.

He eased behind her and placed his hands on her shoulders, brushed her hair aside, and nuzzled her neck. "I know it's selfish, but I want ye near me."

Joy soared through her, and she turned to him.

He cupped the side of her face. "Ye will agree?"

She rose on her toes and kissed him. "Aye, I agree."

~~~

Logan's heart slammed against his chest. Her few words set his world on its side. While waves of elation coursed through his body, misgivings over ensconcing her so close wrenched him in the opposite direction.

Tossing those thoughts aside, he clasped her hand. "I'd like ye to train the stablehands at Glencara to be as well organized as the lads here." He turned to the solar desk and grabbed a flask of ale and two mugs. "We'll need to be as efficient as possible."

He filled one of the mugs then held it out to her as she sat in the chair before him. She took the drink and sniffed it before tentatively touching it with her tongue.

Heat shot straight to his loins, and he sucked in a breath. He paused, lost in thought as her wide violet eyes innocently peered over her mug at him.

Stuttering, he grasped for composure. "Wh…what was I saying?"

"The stablehands—ye were asking me to train them."

"Aye, the stablehands." Was he making a mistake placing temptation so near? Could he resist her while working around her day and night? His manhood thickened. How would he steel his body toward her, ignore the overpowering hunger she inflamed?

Determined to give this a chance, he cleared his throat and focused on the subject of managing the herd. He took a swig of ale and leaned against the desk. "In the morning we'll determine what needs to be packed and whom ye feel could best serve Glencara."

Lindsey swilled the ale. She stood, coughing and sputtering as she set the mug on the desk.

Logan patted her back. "Ye have to work up to it, princess."

She faced him, her eyes watering. "I don't think I want to work up to yer fiery spirits."

He took her hand and tugged her to him. He couldn't help himself. Before he knew it, he lowered his head and captured her lips. When she responded, he pulled her against his body and nuzzled her cheek. She inched her fingers around his neck, her soft breasts pressing into his chest.

God, she felt so good.

When he slid his tongue into her mouth, she timidly touched it with hers. Desire raged through him. He eased back from her, kissed the side of her face and down her neck. A fresh scent of lavender wafted from her soft skin. His nostrils flared, and he buried his nose in her thick tresses, heat pooling in his loins.

A loud knock pounded on the solar door.

Lindsey jumped and broke from his embrace. She inched back, smoothing the tunic over her stomach.

His cock stood painfully stiff. Cursing under his breath, he straightened. "Enter."

Alec stuck his head inside the room and looked at Lindsey, then at Logan. "Ye have a minute?"

Logan scowled and nodded curtly.

Lindsey clutched her hands before her waist and approached Alec. "I want to thank ye."

His head tilted to the side. "Thank me?"

"Aye. Thank ye for not replacing me." Her chin rose. "I'll do ye proud."

His cousin smirked and a grin broke across his face. "I have nay doubt."

Her shoulders eased, and she glanced at Logan. "I'll talk to ye in the morning."

She slipped past them and left the room. Logan grabbed the container of ale off the desk and poured more into his mug. How would he work so closely with Lindsey and not compromise her? He rearranged the front of his trews and dropped onto the chair before the fire.

"I didn't mean to interrupt."

The humor in Alec's voice was not appreciated. Logan shot him an irritated look. "What do ye want?"

"A runner just arrived from the Highlands. I thought ye'd want to know." Alec sat on the chair next to him and poured himself a mug of ale. "Brandon McLeod thanks ye for the information on the ships heading to Galloway. He and his men are forming counter attack plans." He paused. "I'd like ye to continue to train and drill the men at Glencara. Ye never know when those skills will be needed."

"I was surprised to hear English patrols have been spotted this far west." Logan scrubbed a hand over his face. "They gain ground every day."

"Over the past year, the Grahams have fought alongside us in ambushes I've led for McLeod. We've struck the Sassenachs hard, done our damndest to push them from our soil, but more soldiers just replace the ones we dispatch."

A loud knock rapped on the door.

"Enter," Alec shouted.

Fergus stuck his head into the solar and addressed Alec. "I hate to bother ye, but the merchant arrived late with the barrels of ale ye ordered. Says he needs to speak to ye."

Alec's palm slapped his thigh, and he stood. "I wondered what had happened to him. Tell him I'll be right there."

Fergus turned and ambled off.

Alec placed his mug on the table, then paused. "Hamish might contact ye with future missions. If he does, let me know, and we'll work together."

He didn't wait for a reply, but strode across the room and shut the door as he left.

The solar fell silent.

Logan stretched his legs toward the fire and savored his ale. Hamish. Logan looked forward to thrashing the man for involving Lindsey in the rebellion. If he thought to have her deliver one more missive, he would be met with great hostility.

Memories of Lindsey racing across the pasture with her thick auburn hair flying behind her ran through his head. He marveled over her spirit and tenacity, her graciousness with Father Donovan and the monks.

His thoughts drifted to her soft rounded breasts pressing into his chest tonight. His cock swelled again, and he groaned. Rubbing his whiskered face, he got up and headed for bed.

Men's voices at the front door caught his attention. Adam.

Relief poured over him. He had begun to worry about his men. He strode into the great hall as a lad, weighted down with the men's heavy cloaks, struggled past.

"I see ye made it," Logan called.

Colyne, Thom, and David turned with Adam and Travis behind them.

"Aye, we lost a day hiding from the Sassenachs," David said.

"Close by?" Logan asked.

Adam stepped forward. "Just south of Barrhill."

"Commander Collins must be furious if he journeyed this far. We need to remain vigilant," Logan said. "The commander has not only been threatened by King Edward for losing his prisoners, he was humiliated by a young lad."

Rena shuffled into the room. "Would ye men care for stew? I have it warming over the kitchen fire."

They offered their thanks, and she scurried to the kitchen while Logan escorted the men to the great hall and informed them of Alec's plans for the castles.

~~~

Lindsey stood before her opened bedchamber window, a cup of spiced cider warming her hands. From her vantage point high in the keep's tower, she had a direct view into the bailey. Torches lined the thick stone walls, their golden flames flaring into the midnight sky. Wind whipped the MacDougall banner, the crisp snap of the fabric loud in the night air.

Logan's words echoed through her mind. He wanted her near him. And Lord knew she wanted the same. Although he resisted making love to her, his resolve was slipping. Remembering his arms around her, his mouth on hers, his kisses trailing across her neck, sent delicious tendrils of desire through her.

A knock sounded on the door. Caught in wanton daydreams, heat spread up her neck and traveled across her face.

Heather peered inside the room. Blonde wisps escaped the blue ribbon securing her thick tresses and caressed her face. "May I come in?"

"Please do."

Her older sister padded across the room and stood next to Lindsey at the window. She leaned forward and looked into the inner bailey. "It's lovely at night when all is quiet and peaceful."

A draft swirled through the room. Lindsey rubbed her arms and tugged her wrap tighter around her shoulders. Fergus and Blake walked from the barn toward the keep. They laughed, and the old captain patted her friend on the shoulder before they disappeared around the corner.

"I'm glad ye're still awake." Heather smoothed her blue linen gown over a rounding stomach. "I haven't had a chance to visit with ye and tell ye my news."

Lindsey's mouth dropped open. "A bairn?"

Her gut twisted. Conflicting emotions of delight for Heather and sorrow over the babe Lindsey would never have with Logan surged through her.

Heather nodded and caressed her swollen abdomen. "I believe we'll have an early spring babe."

Lindsey threw her arms around her sister. "I'm so verrae happy for ye."

"Thank ye." Heather rubbed Lindsey's back, then straightened. "And ye have news as well? Did Logan speak to ye?"

"He did."

"And? Are ye going to keep me guessing?"

Lindsey grinned. "I've decided to go."

"Oh, I'm so relieved ye'll be with yer horses, but I'll miss ye."

Lindsey leaned against the window seal and peered into the empty bailey. "I won't be far, and I'll be with the animals I love." *And the man who holds my heart.*

"Ye have feelings for him."

Lindsey's gaze shot to Heather. "How did ye know?"

She smiled. "It is fairly obvious the two of ye care for each other. I simply guessed it ran a bit deeper than meets the eye."

Turning back to the open window, Lindsey whispered. "It doesn't matter. Nothing will come of it."

"Oh, I don't know. He seems quite taken with ye."

If only she knew how much Lindsey longed to believe those words. "He's convinced we can't marry because of his bastard birth." A lump stuck in her throat. "And we both know he's right."

Her sister rubbed Lindsey's arm. "Is this my baby sister, who fights against injustice, speaking?"

Lindsey searched Heather's face.

"I'm only saying if ye feel he's worth fighting for, don't give up. Sometimes dreams come true."

Chapter Eleven

Kilmarnock, Scotland
October 1299

With plans underway to move the horses, the next few days passed quickly at MacDougall Castle. Logan sent Colyne ahead to prepare Glencara for the new herd. A week later, the horses were harnessed in the bailey and ready to depart.

Lindsey gathered the warm wrap off the chair before the hearth in her bedchamber. Her heart sat heavy in her chest as she ran her hand across the soft bed where she'd spent most every night since she was a small lass.

Excitement over being near Logan caused flutters deep within her belly. She knew the risk she took. If he continued to resist her, living beside him without the sanctity of marriage would have to suffice. However, she'd never know the happiness she would have experienced as his wife. Never have the chance to carry his bairn.

Convinced she could be content to remain at his side whether married or not, she looked forward to moving to Glencara. She'd rather live a life near Logan and die a spinster than bow to an overbearing laird who stifled her adventurous spirit.

Would working alongside him be enough?

It was a start.

Although Logan had kissed her and held her through the night in the crumbling shack, he'd stopped short of making love. His obvious desire had nudged against her hip, but he was a man of principle and honor. He would not compromise her. While she loved him for his consideration, her body craved his touch. He invaded her thoughts and crept into her nightly dreams. She longed to be near him and prayed for a miraculous change of tradition. It wasn't fair. Logan had no control over who his parents were, and his bastard birth should not be held against him.

She picked up her worn leather satchel and slung it over her shoulder. She would miss this place, but it was time to venture away from the safety and security of her home. Thoughts of working with the large herd lightened her steps as she made her way down the steep flight of stairs and into the bailey.

Logan tied a bag to Sterling's saddle. Shaggy hair brushed his broad shoulders. A dark cloak draped his body, falling past the top of his boots. He turned and seared her with an intense stare.

Her breath caught. Heat pooled in her core.

Would he continue to combat the passion strumming between them?

She smiled to herself. She wouldn't make it easy for him. His resistance would wane, and she'd be waiting.

~~~

Lindsey continued to wear a lad's breeks, but she filled them out like no lad ever had. The woolen fabric hugged her trim waist and hips, encased her shapely legs, and disappeared inside her leather boots. Logan's gaze traveled to her breasts. No longer bound, they strained against her tunic.

Shaking his head, he tried to clear his thoughts. He had work to do and she was a distraction. He glanced at Adam to find his friend's attention focused on her as well. Hell, she was a distraction to all the men. They couldn't help but watch her saunter past.

Scowling, Logan mounted Sterling. "Get yer belongings secured. We're heading out."

Alastair held his arms open and she rushed into his embrace. "Ye take care of yerself, lassie. If ye want to come home, I'll come get ye straight away."

She kissed his cheek. "I'm going to miss ye, Da."

Heather clutched Lindsey's arm. "I'm still reluctant about ye traveling to Glencara without a proper guardian. Muire would be happy to accompany ye."

"After all the missions I've run, ye're worried about a guardian?" A corner of Lindsey's mouth tugged up. "And I suppose ye expect Muire to ride alongside the herd and sleep on the cold ground?"

Logan shook a ridiculous image of the old healer astride a horse from his mind. Driving a team was no place for conventional rules or proper customs.

Heather sighed. "Stay in touch."

"I will," she said as Fergus reached for her and kissed the top of her head.

Logan crossed his arms. Good Lord. It wasn't as if she was traveling to the other side of the country.

She wiped away a tear as she smiled at her family, even Alec.

"Better get going," his cousin said as he took her hand in his. "No more running off."

Lindsey nodded, then hurried down the line of horses to speak to Blake, David, and Travis.

A clatter of horses' hooves sounded on the wooden bridge leading into the outer bailey. Logan turned as a burly man mounted on a black destrier led several others into the yard. The men trotted over to the departing group. Cloaked in buckskin breeks and a thick fur cloak, the lead man swung down from his horse. The others dismounted around him, and the leader handed the reins to the one at his right.

"Laird Mangus MacAndrew," Alec said. "Welcome to MacDougall Castle."

The man tugged off his gloves as he met Alec. The two grasped hands and Mangus slapped Alec's back. "'Tis good to see ye, my friend."

"And ye. What brings ye to this part of the country?"

Lindsey jogged back to Blaze, her auburn hair bouncing around her slight shoulders.

Mangus paused and stared at her.

Alec turned and followed MacAndrew's focused attention.

The man left Alec and strode over to Lindsey. He took her hand in his and placed a kiss on the back. "Mistress, it's been far too long."

"Laird MacAndrew, how nice it is to see ye."

The look she bestowed upon him would have a priest questioning his convictions. Who the hell was he?

The cur looked at the gathered animals and back to her. "Are ye moving yer horses?"

"Aye, we're driving them to their new home at Glencara."

He held her hand much longer than was proper. Logan seethed. Who the hell did the man think he was?

MacAndrew turned toward Alec. "Surely she can spare a few moments to visit? It's early in the morning, and we should get reacquainted."

That was it. Logan had heard enough. He threw his leg over the saddle, dropped to the ground, and marched over to Lindsey. Crossing his arms, he glared at MacAndrew. "We can't stay for yer unannounced visit."

The man's head tilted to the side. He raked Logan with a scathing glower.

Alec clapped MacAndrew on the shoulder. "My cousin drives the herd to Glencara and has miles to go. Come inside, Mangus. Rest and tell me news of the highlands."

MacAndrew bent at the waist before Lindsey, and Logan itched to kick his pompous arse.

"I anxiously await the day we meet again," he said, his attention fixed on her.

"Mount up, Lindsey," Logan barked.

She nodded at the man, jammed her foot in the stirrup, and swung on top of Blaze.

Logan sprang onto Sterling's back and seared the laird with a glare. He held up a hand and signaled the procession to begin. The group trotted out of the bailey, across the wooden bridge, and onto the dirt road winding through the village at the base of the castle.

Logan patted the parchment inside his tunic. Alec had given him a document signed by an English commander, Barclay Taylor, affording them safe passage to Glencara. While he hoped to avoid English patrols, he would be thankful for the entitlement if their group encountered the Sassenachs.

Hairs on the back of his neck still stood stiff over the arrival of Laird MacAndrew. His interest in Lindsey, the way he watched her lithe body and practically drooled over her tight tunic, boiled his blood. Why did the man appear unannounced? What purpose did he have at MacDougall Castle? Images of his holding Lindsey's hand irritated him like a barbed thistle jammed inside his boot.

Shoving aside the troubling thoughts, Logan concentrated on the herd. The farther away from MacDougall Castle and Mangus MacAndrew they journeyed, the better.

The caravan progressed slowly. They rode well into the late afternoon, but as the sun dipped low, Logan reined in. "We'll set up camp for the night here."

The group secured the horses in makeshift pens while several lads hurried to collect firewood. Thom unloaded the sacks of food and handed out bread, cheese, and dried venison. Lindsey talked to Blake, David, and Travis as they accounted for the horses.

Logan exhaled and rubbed the back of his neck. His plans had worked well. So far, they managed to move the large herd without incident. They still had another day to go, but he felt more confident in their headway.

Lindsey led Blaze to the pen and corralled him with the others. As she tugged the saddle from his back, Logan took it from her. "Let me help ye."

She grinned, and his insides churned. "Thank ye."

He placed the saddle on the ground and turned back as she bent and rummaged through her leather bag. His gaze dropped to her backside, and his palm itched to cup the firm mounds.

When she straightened, she held a cloth in her hand. "After I rub him down, I've got to get something to eat. I'm hungry."

Logan was hungry too, but not for what Thom offered.

Lindsey ran the cloth across Blaze's back. The horse nickered and tossed his head. "Easy laddie, ye just rest now."

She dropped the cloth back into her bag and snatched her leather satchel off the ground. "I'll just wash up."

She ducked under the rope and slipped from the pen. Her hips swayed as she walked to the stream. God, she had his body standing at attention.

"The horses are secured for the night." Adam broke Logan's thoughts.

"Good. We'll get an early start in the morning."

They walked to the fire discussing plans for the remainder of the trip. Logan grabbed his wine skin and a hunk of bread and tossed a blanket on the ground next to a boulder. He dropped onto it, leaned against the rock, and stretched his tired neck muscles. The campfire's flames leapt into the cold night air casting warmth around the wide perimeter. He took a long swig of wine and delicious heat flooded his body.

"Thank ye," Lindsey said as she accepted bread and cheese from Thom and started toward the fire.

Adam's arm swept to the log beside him. "Mistress Lindsey, would ye care to join me?"

She looked at Logan, then started toward Adam. She sat next to him, her dinner propped in her lap. Adam said something, and she laughed.

Logan's gut clenched.

What was wrong with him? Was he jealous? First MacAndrew and now Adam.

He pushed himself up and stalked out of camp. The cool night air blew across his face, and he tugged his cloak tighter around his neck as he marched past the line of horses to the nearby stream. He stooped, cupped the frigid water, and splashed it on his face.

The icy dousing brought him to his senses. He shook his head and cold droplets slung in all directions. The moon cast light through heavy, ominous-looking clouds. He straightened, and wiping his face, looked back at the large fire ring. He would need to get the group to Glencara before the snow hit and made their travel difficult and dangerous.

Rubbing life into his cold hands, he made his way back to camp. "There's a storm on the way, and I want to get started as early as possible."

Lindsey stood, clutching her satchel to her waist. "We'll be ready."

"We need to pick up the pace. Can ye do that?"

"Aye."

"Good." He glanced at the men already bedded down. "We leave at dawn."

Lindsey eased onto her side and curled in a small bundle beside the fire. Her body shivered under her woolen blanket.

Logan shook his head as he prepared his bedding. Before he could stop himself, he padded over, squatted beside her, and touched her cheek.

"Ye're freezing."

"I'm fine." Her teeth chattered as she scooted farther beneath the blanket.

"Come with me." Logan grasped her wrist and pulled her up.

She rubbed an arm. "Where are we going?"

"Where we'll be warm." He snatched her cover off the ground and led her to his blanket.

Her eyes widened, and her gaze skimmed the men huddled around camp.

"They're not paying us any mind." He tugged her toward him. "Lie down, princess."

She knelt on the blanket. He dropped beside her and pulled her back against his chest. He placed his large heavy cloak over their bodies and heads, providing a cocoon of warmth. His arm wrapped around her lush body, his thighs molding to hers. Her enticing rear wiggled, and he groaned.

God's bones, it would be a long night.

~~~

Logan woke with Lindsey snuggled against him. Her small hand rested over his heart, soft breasts nestled his torso, and shapely legs intertwined with his. He rested his chin on her head, and the familiar whiff of lavender wafted off her silky hair. Inhaling the sweet fragrance, he cherished the last few moments he had with her in his arms before they resumed their journey.

The usual morning hardening could hardly be blamed for his stiff shaft. It had stood rigid and aching against her thigh all night. Taking a deep breath, he disengaged from her limbs.

She stirred then snuggled farther underneath the blanket.

He stooped beside her and tucked his cloak tight around her body. His knuckle trailed across her cheek.

She was beautiful.

Morning dew covered him, the tentacles of winter penetrating his heavy clothing. He rubbed his arms, grabbed his satchel off the boulder next to Lindsey, and strode through camp. His foot bumped Adam and Colyne as he passed. "Get up. Let's get going."

Adam rose on his elbow and rubbed his face. The men stirred. Sounds of their waking, the shuffle of blankets, and lowered voices drifted behind Logan as he marched down the narrow dirt path to the river's edge.

Red tinges of dawn displayed a mass of dark, grey clouds hugging the horizon. A frigid wind tossed leaves and swirled debris from the trail. Logan had left his cloak with Lindsey, and hairs stood stiff on his neck and arms.

The gurgle of water cascading over small rocks greeted him. He dropped his satchel and stooped at the river's edge. Splashing his face, his thoughts turned to Lindsey. What would it be like to wake with her in his arms every morning? To hold her at night, watch her sleep? She invaded his thoughts, hell he even dreamt of her. He prayed he had not made a mistake ensconcing her so close. It would require the strength of Hercules to resist the lure of her lush body.

Clenching his jaw, his teeth ground. He jerked his soiled tunic over his head and grabbed a clean garment from his bag. Light snowflakes bounced off his skin, and chill bumps covered his torso. *Shite.* The foul weather had arrived sooner than he'd expected. After he hurriedly dressed, he snatched his satchel off the ground and marched back to camp.

Lindsey had her men and horses lined up. She never ceased to amaze him. Logan strode to Sterling. His cloak lay across the horse's back. He shoved his arms into the sleeves, then secured his belongings to the saddle. "Mount up. We need to get underway."

He swung onto Sterling's back, and studied the group, ensuring Lindsey and her men controlled the herd. With his signal, they headed out, snow falling lightly around them.

By midday, blizzard-like conditions had replaced the flurries. Logan craned his neck and looked over his shoulder, squinting through icy crystals peppering his face.

Blake led the workhorses. Their massive heads bowed low, their powerful legs cutting a swath through the deepening snow.

Lindsey nudged Blaze alongside David, who struggled with a number of the lighter animals. She grasped several horses' reins. "Follow me," her shout barely heard over the howling wind.

David nodded and tugged several animals into line with her. She positioned Blaze behind the larger horses, their wake making it easier for the smaller animals to maneuver the thick wet snow. Once in the forged grooves, she returned the reins to David and rode to check on the others.

What a woman.

Her tenacious spirit amazed Logan. He faced front again and raised a hand to shelter his eyes from the frigid gusts. As they traveled farther north, deep snowdrifts had formed alongside the banks and the brisk wind swirled frosty crystals in the air. Branches, heavy with ice, bent toward the ground. The fierce wind whistling through the woodland, swaying treetops, pervaded the quiet peacefulness that customarily resulted from a snow covered forest.

Logan's breath, visible in white puffs, caused tiny ice particles to form in his mustache. Although his cloak hung to his boots, a biting chill saturated the thick fabric and seeped into his bones.

They traveled throughout the day and into the darkness. He rode down the line encouraging each team to move forward. "Glencara is a short distance away. We should reach the castle within the hour."

Lindsey caught his attention. She fought to stay in the saddle, her small frame hunched from stinging sleet. Swearing, he nudged Sterling alongside Blaze. He grabbed her reins, and her head jerked up. Her lips were tinged purplish-blue, her teeth chattering.

As he'd done several nights before, his cold-stiffened arms reached to pull her onto his lap.

"Nay, I'm in no worse shape than any of the men." Her words were shaky.

Her constant comparison to men wore thin. She was a woman for God's sake and needed to be protected. "I only thought to hold ye."

She cast him a wistful glance, then shook her head. "Nay, it's not a good idea. The men would think I'm weak."

Stubborn.

Pigheaded.

His shoulders sagged.

Courageous.

His numb fingers untied the bedding from Sterling's saddle, and he draped it across her shoulders. "Hold on, princess. We're almost home."

He nudged Sterling and the procession continued. Disappointment flooded through him. How he would have savored the feel of her next to him. To hold her in his arms, cherish the little time he had alone with her.

What would become of her? Would she be content to remain at his side? A dull pain twisted his gut, and he closed his eyes. He could not ask her to give up the life intended for a Laird's daughter—the lady of a keep with a family and bairns.

The lonely years of his childhood still haunted him. Maria did her best to include him, care for him. But he never felt he belonged. He was an outsider always looking in.

How he longed for a family of his own. A wife to return home to, sons he'd teach hunting and battle skills. Perhaps he'd find a woman he could settle down with, but his heart would forever belong to Lindsey.

Chapter Twelve

Glencara Castle
October 1299

The group trudged through the bitter weather, plodded along slowly, but steadily. Over an hour later, they made their way into the cobblestone bailey at Glencara.

Lindsey's breath caught at first glimpse of her new home.

Torches lined massive grey walls surrounding the interior yard, their flames whipping in the frigid wind. Warriors patrolled the stone ramparts connecting towers at the structure's four corners. Compartments for the blacksmith, barracks for warriors, and various dwellings hugged the sturdy bailey walls. Light shone between slats of shuttered windows, the glow inviting. It was a wondrous sight. Frozen and tired, Lindsey relished being *home*.

Stablehands ran to greet them as Logan led the cold, travel-weary herd into the barn. Three large areas had been sectioned off for the incoming horses.

Still snuggled under Logan's thick blanket, she reined in as Colyne jogged down the main aisle toward them. "Ye made good time. I worried the storm would bog ye down."

"Aye, the snow arrived early this morn." Logan dropped to the ground and reached up to her. "See the animals are rubbed down."

Colyne hurried to help secure the horses.

Lindsey slid into Logan's outstretched arms and stood on shaky legs.

He cupped the sides of her face and brushed the hair from her tired eyes. "Let's get inside where ye can warm up."

Wrapping his arm around her shoulders, he hugged her to his side as they walked out of the stables and into the bailey. She leaned against him, and they climbed the steep stairs leading into the keep. Her back and legs ached, the strain of the trip playing havoc on her tired muscles.

Logan threw open the heavy oak door. Raw air and snow swirled into the main hall.

A young lass hurried to greet them. "Let me take yer cloaks." She stopped short, and her coquettish gaze fell on Logan. "Master Logan." She smiled coyly. "'Tis verrae nice to have ye home."

He handed her his wrap. "Thank ye, Brenna."

The lass's blatant examination raked him from head to toe. "Just let me know if ye need *anything*."

She reached for Lindsey's wrap, and her cheerful expression died instantly. The girl glared and virtually snatched the cloak from Lindsey's hands. *The ill-bred cow.*

Adam and Travis, along with others from the incoming party, stepped into the corridor behind Logan. Another lass dashed into the hall and helped gather the bulky wet cloaks.

Logan clutched Lindsey's elbow, led her through a drafty corridor, and into the grand hall. She paused, marveling at the ornate setting. A high pitched roof soared above, resting on a multitude of wooden beams connected to massive columns that supported the structure. Shadows, cast from candles secured in a large chandelier suspended from the center of the room, danced across intricate carvings of hunting scenes cut into blocks of stone lining the walls. Plush burgundy rugs were scattered over the floor, and light from candelabras positioned throughout the room highlighted robust wooden tables and chairs with overstuffed cushions.

The keep hummed with activity. Men, women, and children filled the busy chamber. Some mingled while others ate at the tables throughout the hall. Chatter and laughter, clinking of utensils, and shouts of merriment rang from the boisterous clan.

Logan guided her down the stairs and into the hall. Lindsey recognized Ainslee, Alec's sister, issuing orders to servants. She turned toward the incoming party. Her eyes widened, and a radiant beam broke across her face. Hiking her skirt, she ran toward Logan, calling over her shoulder, "Maria, look who is home."

A plump, older woman with white hair placed a tray on the table and straightened. She swiped the back of her hand across her forehead and squinted at them. Her expression lit, and her wrinkled hand grasped her chest. "My son."

She ambled around the wooden tables and shuffled toward the entrance of the main hall.

Lindsey stood back as Ainslee threw herself into Logan's outstretched arms. He twirled her in a circle and held her close.

"I've been so worried about ye, cousin." She straightened and punched his shoulder. "Why didn't ye let us know ye were all right? We didn't hear a word."

"Logan," the older woman cried, her hands reaching for him.

He kissed her cheek and wrapped his arms around her as she buried her face in his chest. "Maria, it's good to be home."

She must be the woman who raised Logan.

Ainslee turned to Lindsey. "I've looked forward to yer arrival since Colyne brought us news ye'd be staying here." She clutched Lindsey's hand. Her eyes widened. "Ye poor dear. Ye're frozen to the bone."

She rubbed her hands up and down Lindsey's arms and looked to Logan, who embraced Maria. "Both of ye sit next to the fire and warm up."

Logan shook his head. "I need to get back to the horses." He kissed Maria's temple and as he tugged on his gloves, he addressed Lindsey. "And *ye* need to get out of those wet clothes."

145

He turned and marched from the hall.

Maria stepped forward. She wore her braided hair twisted into a bun and affixed atop her head. Wrinkles furrowed her weathered skin. Her brown eyes were soft, and the warmth of her welcome genuine. The older woman wrapped a plaid cloak around her slumped shoulders and squeezed Lindsey's hand. "Mistress, Lindsey, we're happy to have ye at Glencara."

"I'm verrae pleased to be here."

"I have a bedchamber readied," Ainslee said. "Come take a hot bath to warm ye."

Lindsey weaved through the crowded hall behind Ainslee. They climbed the stone stairs and strolled down a main corridor and into a cozy chamber. A big comfortable-looking bed sat against the wall, furs and pillows piled high. On the opposite side of the room, a fire blazed in the hearth, casting its warmth onto wooden chairs and a side table that held a vase of fresh herbs emitting a spicy fragrance. "The room is wonderful."

"I'm thrilled ye're here," Ainslee said as the door opened and several young men entered with a copper tub and buckets of steaming water. "I'll have someone bring up yer things. Make yerself at home, and let me know if ye need anything."

She slipped from the bedchamber while two more lads struggled in with Lindsey's wooden trunk, their arms stretched tight. One end dropped to the floor, and the young boy cringed. "Beggin' yer pardon, mistress."

Lindsey waved her hand. "Och, 'tis only clothes and such. No need to worry."

Relief eased the lad's stilted face. The two shoved the trunk against the far wall and ran from the chamber.

She thanked the other lads and they left. After shedding her soggy clothes, she stepped into the luxurious water and sank up to her neck in the sweet smelling bath.

Closing her eyes, she leaned her head back and relaxed in the comforting heat.

The room was quiet, except for an occasional popping and hissing of the logs. She lay there for quite some time before she heard a light tap on the door. Straightening, she reached for the drying cloth and stood while wrapping it around her torso. "Uh, just one moment."

The door cracked open, and a young woman with chestnut-colored hair and rosy cheeks stuck her head inside the room. "I'm Skena, m'lady, and I've come to assist ye."

Maria's daughter? "Oh, please come in."

The maid entered the room and shut the door behind her. "Mistress Ainslee asks that ye come down for the evening meal."

Lindsey stepped from the tub. As if on cue, her stomach growled. "That sounds wonderful."

"Let me find something for ye to wear." Skena scurried over to Lindsey's trunk and rifled through it. "Ahh, this is lovely." She extracted a soft blue woolen gown. "And it would be beautiful on ye."

A gown?

What would Logan think? Perhaps he needed a glimpse of her feminine side. Lindsey smiled to herself. "That one will be fine."

The maid draped the gown across the back of the chair before the hearth and smoothed out the skirt.

Lindsey rubbed the drying cloth over her shoulder and down her arm as she watched the lass. "Ye grew up with Logan?"

"Aye, he lived with my mum and me." Skena turned. "I think of him as an older brother."

"We've been friends for a number of years."

"Logan's a good man. He always watched out for me when I was a wee lass, even though I'm sure he would've rather I hadn't tagged along." Skena chuckled as she helped Lindsey into a soft chemise, then tossed the gown over her head.

The material settled around her hips. Lindsey ran her hands over the skirt. The bodice dipped low, and the fabric hugged her waist. Would Logan notice? Nerves caused her belly to quiver, and delicious naughty sensations coursed through her.

"Mistress, why do ye wear yer beautiful hair like this?" Skena unwound the thick auburn knot on Lindsey's head and brushed the tresses until they shined soft and silky. "Now, that's much better."

"I think I'm ready."

Skena picked up the soiled clothing. "I'll have yer chambers prepared by the time ye return."

"Thank ye." Lindsey grabbed a wrap from the back of the chair before the fire, draped the heated cloth around her shoulders, and slipped from the room.

Maria supervised the serving staff placing steaming platters of carrots and warm bread on the long tables in the great hall. Most of the MacDougall men already sat, filling their stomachs with the hardy meal.

"Ainslee," Blake called as he strode into the room.

She turned toward him, and her face lit. "Blake!"

He took her hands in his.

Did Lindsey and Ainslee share the same problem? Being a laird's daughter, an arranged marriage for the good of the clan would be expected of Ainslee.

David and Travis marched across the hall and over to her, scattering her thoughts.

"How are the horses?" she asked.

"They're well taken care of." David shook his head as he rubbed the back of his neck. "Logan left 'em in the stables."

"He's not taking any chances with them, and that's good." She crossed her arms. "I'm sure when the weather clears he'll move them to the pasture."

"Ye look beautiful, m'lady."

Lindsey turned to the deep voice.

The pupils of Adam's eyes darkened as he took her hand and raised it to his lips.

"Why thank ye."

He clutched her elbow, and his arm swept toward a long oak table laden with roasted boar, creamed turnips, and boiled leeks. "Let's have something to eat. Shall we?"

Maria fussed at the serving girls to hurry as hungry men lined the tables.

Lindsey slid onto a bench, and Adam dropped beside her, while Travis and David sat across from them. A lass placed trenchers before them.

"Logan tells me ye'll be managing the stables." Adam helped himself to a slice of venison and ran it around the thick gravy. "That's quite a herd."

She reached for her tankard. "Aye, I'm looking forward to it. The stables here have been heralded as one of the best in the country."

Adam nodded and wiped his mouth. "They are impressive."

"Logan must think highly of yer skills if he expects ye to take on such an operation." Travis broke a piece of bread from the loaf on the table.

She spooned spiced carrots onto her trencher. "I won't be managing the stables by myself. I'll have his help."

Logan strode into the room, water droplets plopping from the ends of his hair. Ice and snow sprinkled his head and covered his boots. Thom tossed him a cloth, and Logan caught it midair then ran it over his head.

The men sitting around the tables raised their ale. "Here's to a successful trek," one shouted.

Others mingling in the crowd joined in cheer as Logan grabbed a tankard from the tray of a passing servant, raised it in a silent toast, and gulped the drink. He wiped his mouth on his sleeve. "Couldn't have done it without ye."

"Hear, hear!" The men shouted and pounded the table. Several slapped each other on the back, contagious merriment permeating the light atmosphere.

Logan faced Lindsey. An excited fluttering careened through her stomach. How she hoped he found her attractive in her blue gown. The corner of his mouth tugged up, but when he looked at Adam, his expression turned to a scowl.

He downed his ale, strode over to the table, and dropped on the bench beside her. "Feel better?"

"Aye, I do. Thank ye."

One of the kitchen girls slipped a steaming trencher of roasted boar before him. "Good evening, Logan," she purred. "'Tis verrae nice to have ye home."

"Githa, it's been a long time."

Lindsey didn't miss the look that passed between them. First Brenna and now Githa. She shouldn't be surprised. After all, rumors of Logan's liaisons had long ago spread to MacDougall Castle. But, it riled her to witness it firsthand.

The woman leaned over him, her ample bosom pressed against his back as she refilled his ale. She whispered in his ear. The lustful expression she bestowed upon him left no doubt as to her intent.

Logan patted her hand on his shoulder.

"Bring that tray, Githa," Maria shouted and waved. "We need it for the venison."

The woman tossed her brunette hair over her shoulder, then sauntered from the main hall and down a corridor.

How would Lindsey stomach women constantly throwing themselves at Logan—warming his bed, while he refused to…to be with her? She had not considered that aspect when she agreed to move to Glencara.

Once they finished the evening meal, Logan stood and extended a hand to her. "Would ye care to join me in the solar?"

Before Lindsey knew what she was about, she answered, "Aye."

Strong fingers curled over hers. His smoky gaze caressed the length of her body. "Ye are verrae bonny in yer gown, lass."

He invoked a yearning she could neither deny nor explain. She smoothed the front of her dress, her hands trembling. "Thank ye."

He escorted her down the dim corridor. Smoke wafted from flickering candles secured in sconces lining the hall, and shadows danced across Logan's face. They reached the solar, and she strolled into the room.

A massive stone hearth, surrounded by ornate timber carved with hunting scenes, filled the back wall. Bulky, dark wooden chairs placed on a thick burgundy rug faced blazing flames dancing up the chimney. The aroma of peat filled the intimate space, and a comforting homey feel permeated the warm room.

She drew her finger along an oversized desk positioned before the fireplace. Ledgers were stacked beside a carafe of wine. Flames from a wrought iron candelabra's four yellowed candles melted the beeswax, the drippings splattering on the desk's surface.

Lindsey slipped into one of the bulky wooden chairs before the hearth.

"Mistress?" A lass stepped before her with a mug in her hand. "Would ye care for spiced cider?"

Mouth watering, Lindsey accepted the drink and took a sip of the hot brew. "Hmmm, that's verrae good."

The girl's head bobbed, and she raced away as Lindsey faced the fire, and blew over the mug. Logan's muscular legs, crossed at the ankles, stretched before them. His foot brushed hers, and she turned to him.

He winked and dimples pressed into his bearded cheeks. "Ye did well moving the horses," he whispered. "But I would've liked to have had more time alone with ye."

Her stomach clenched, and she swallowed hard.

I can never have ye.

His words echoed through her ears. What did he expect her to say?

She turned to the fire. "Perhaps it's best we didn't have time alone."

His thumb stroked her arm.

"Ahh, there ye are," Ainslee said, as she and Blake entered the solar.

Logan stood and pulled a chair forward from against the wall. "Have a seat," he offered his cousin.

The two joined them. Logan poured a mug of ale and handed it to Blake.

"Maria had yer belongings moved to Alec's old room, Logan." Ainslee brushed a spot on her skirt. "She said with ye acting in the laird's place, ye should reside in the laird's chambers."

Logan's eyes narrowed imperceptibly. "Verrae well."

A soft knock sounded on the solar door and Skena stuck her head inside the room. "May I come in?"

"But of course," Ainslee answered.

The maid strolled in, a bundle cradled in her arms.

Lindsey's breath caught at the little face peaking from a light blue blanket. "What a precious bairn."

Logan straightened as Skena stooped beside him. "I thought ye'd want to meet my daughter."

Skena placed the babe in Logan's arms, and he brushed aside the blanket hiding the little one's face. Large hazel eyes surrounded by soft porcelain skin blinked. Tiny hands balled into fists waved in the air. "She looks just like ye."

Lindsey's heart tugged at the angelic scene. How she longed to see him hold their bairn someday.

"Do I know the da?" he asked.

When Skena didn't reply, Logan glanced up. A sad expression crossed her eyes before she whispered, "Nay."

She reached for the bairn, and Logan placed the wee lass in her arms. "It's time to put her down for the night."

"She is precious, Skena," Lindsey said. "Thank ye for letting us meet her."

The maid smiled and padded from the room.

Ainslee and Lindsey chatted while Logan and Blake talked about the trip, the horses, and their plans for the next few days. As the night wore on Lindsey yawned.

Logan bumped her arm. "Let me escort ye to yer room. I know ye're tired."

"Aye, it's been a long day." Just as she stood, a screech reverberated through the room.

A buxom blonde ran into the solar shouting, "No one told me ye had returned. I'd have been 'ere right away if I'd known."

Not another one.

Lindsey stepped back as the woman threw herself onto Logan, wrapped her arms around him, and planted her lips on his mouth.

Logan grasped the woman's shoulders and set her from him. "Jolecia, I was just heading to bed."

She pressed her curvaceous body against him. "That sounds good to me. I'll take care of ye, and ye'll be relaxed for sure."

Lindsey's eyes widened at the blatant offer. Heat crept up her neck and traveled across her cheeks. She had no wish to witness this intimate scene. She'd had enough. Head held high, she started toward the stairs.

"Lindsey?"

She paused and peered over her shoulder as Logan set Jolecia from him again and strode to Lindsey. He took her arm. "I'll see ye to yer room."

"It's not necessary. I know the way."

His hand dropped to his side, and he sighed.

"Good night." Somehow her numb body climbed the stairs. Pride pricked, she vowed she would not become another one of his conquests. Her gaze fell on the blue gown. A lot of good it did. To hell with it. She'd return to wearing her trews in the morning.

Dispirited, she trudged down the long hall that opened into a common area with one staircase going up and another below. She ascended the steps and continued along the damp corridor. Candlelight from the sconces lining the cold stone walls flickered at her passing.

A worn oak door stood ajar. Firelight from the room cast shadows on the hall's stone floor. Lindsey paused and peered around the door jamb.

"Come inside and visit with me, Mistress MacDougall," a raspy, deep voice called from within the chamber.

Surprised at the man using her name, she stepped forward and stuck her head inside the room. An older gentleman sat before the fire. A red blanket covered his legs and shavings of wood lay scattered about his lap and on the floor at his feet. Sparse white hair stood out in tufts around an otherwise bald scalp. His weathered but nimble fingers worked a knife across a piece of wood.

He looked up, and she stopped. Thick bushy eyebrows framed his grey eyes—Logan's eyes.

"Aye, come in, come in."

The man must be Logan's uncle.

"I'm Grant Campbell." The welcoming warmth of his face beckoned her closer. His arm indicated the chair to his left. "Sit."

She eased onto the hard wooden chair. "I'm Lindsey MacDougall."

"Aye, I met ye when ye were just a wee lass." The corners of his mouth rose, and he winked. "We harbored the same love for horses. I arrived to visit yer da at MacDougall Castle shortly after ye had taken control of his stables. Ye were a natural around the beasts."

He couldn't have said anything more pleasing. If his intention was to win her affections, he had succeeded. "That is quite a compliment, sir. I thank ye."

He whittled the wood, and more shavings landed in his lap.

She craned her neck. "What are ye making?"

"Ahhh…another for my herd."

Her forehead scrunched. "I beg yer pardon?"

He tugged the blanket to the side and revealed a table lined with wooden figures.

Her mouth dropped open as she stood and eased around the chairs to his other side. A black rearing horse, his mane flowing behind him and his tail flaring, balanced on his hind legs. A light brown horse stood on three legs, his head majestically bent, and his left front hoof pawing the ground. Several others in various positions and groupings covered the tabletop.

"Oh, my. These are beautiful, Laird Campbell." Her fingers eased over the polished wooden surfaces.

"Grant. Please call me Grant."

She turned to him and smiled. "All right."

"Maria tells me ye're moving here to manage our herd."

What would he think of a lass running the renowned stables? "That's correct. Logan asked for my help."

A brief wistful look passed his features. Had she not have been watching closely, she wouldn't have noticed.

"We are most fortunate to have ye join us." He hesitated. "Might I ask a favor?"

A favor? "Certainly."

He studied the half finished wooden figure in his lap. "It has been many years since I've been able to see the barn and the horses."

Her heart clenched. Memories of his accident resurfaced. She couldn't imagine remaining confined to a chair, sitting before the hearth day after day and never seeing her precious horses. "Why is that?"

His head jerked up. "Because I can't walk."

"Nay, but ye could be helped to the stable."

"And show the clan how weakened I am?" Grant frowned. "No, thank ye."

"Yer people will always regard ye as a strong leader."

He turned to the hearth and stared at the flames.

Silence stretched between them. *Damn.* She had not been here a full day and had already offended the old laird. "I hope I have not spoken out of turn," she whispered.

His shoulders slumped, and he shook his head. "Nay, I admire yer directness. Never could tolerate to be told what someone thought I wanted to hear."

"Ye asked for a boon," she said. "What can I do for ye?"

Grant looked back at her. "Will ye visit me from time to time and tell me about yer work?"

She reached out and touched his shoulder. "I'd be honored to visit ye."

Grant's calloused fingers grasped hers. "I can see we're going to become fast friends, Lindsey MacDougall."

Chapter Thirteen

Lindsey opened her eyes and stared at the glowing red embers. Her bedchamber had chilled, the flames in the hearth dying in the wee hours of the morning. She snuggled farther beneath the thick warm blankets.

Today was her first day at Glencara. After gaining a brief glimpse of the active stable when they arrived last night, she anxiously awaited dawn to venture out and explore her new home.

Her thoughts turned to Logan. Perhaps she had been a bit unfair. Although women clung to him, he hadn't really encouraged them. She sighed. Who was she fooling? He was a virile man…with a man's needs. It wouldn't be long before he made love to a woman, and he'd made it clear, it would not be her.

Ye've made yer bed. Now ye must lie in it.

Her mother's words wafted through her mind. She was right. Lindsey had been given a rare opportunity to work in one of the most outstanding stables in the country with a large herd to manage, and she'd best make the most of it.

Hardening her heart toward Logan would not be easy, but she had to protect herself. When women whispered of his prowess, she'd cover her ears. When they tangled in a lover's embrace, she would look the other way.

Determined to throw herself into learning the workings of the barn, she flung the covers aside and slid from the feathered mattress. Fine hairs rose on her arms and neck. She grabbed the wrap off the end of her bed and tugged it around her shoulders while padding across the floor to the cooling hearth. A draft swirled from the chimney as she tossed a dry brick of peat into the embers. Sparks grew into flickers, and within moments a homey scent wafted into the dim chamber.

Her trunk lay open and she riffled through it, plucked out a clean pair of trews and soft tunic. After washing her face and tussling with her unruly hair, she tugged on her clothes and started across the bedchamber.

She swung the door open, and her breath caught.

Logan leaned against the wall, his arms folded over his chest and legs crossed at the ankles. He smiled and her stomach tightened. "Good morn, princess."

Reminding her traitorous body of her recent vow, she composed herself. "Good morn. What are ye doing lingering outside my chamber?"

He pushed away from the wall and advanced toward her. "I know of yer habit to rise early, and I wanted to be the one to show ye around the stable."

Delight bubbled up inside her belly. So much for her intentions. "Verrae well. I was just heading that way."

His head tilted toward the stairs. "After ye."

He followed her down the stone steps and into the main hall.

Maria bustled around the room, directing the lasses serving the clan. The woman glanced up as Lindsey and Logan entered. When she saw Logan, a grin stretched the lines etched into her weathered cheeks. Although she had not given birth to him, it was clear she loved him as her own.

"May I offer ye something to eat?" she asked.

Logan looked at Lindsey, his brow raised. "She makes a tasty porridge."

She shook her head. "I'm not hungry at the moment. Perhaps, I'll grab a bite later."

Logan winked at the older woman. "She's anxious to see the stable."

Maria waved a hand. "Och, don't ye go too long with nothing in yer stomach. I expect ye both back here shortly."

They walked through the keep's entrance and descended the bailey stairs. Snow crunched under Lindsey's boots, causing shivers to course down her back. Breathing in the crisp morning air, she relished the quiet peacefulness from the storm's aftermath.

Hues of blue interspersed with purple filled the sky and bright white snow covered the bailey yard, like crystals gleaming in the awaking sun. A gust of wind swirled icy particles into the air as the two approached the stable.

Lindsey rounded the central doorway of the barn and paused. She had never seen anything like it. The rafters rose twice as high as the MacDougall stable, the structure three times as large. Rope sectioned off stalls lining the walls. A main aisle cut a path through the middle of the building with passageways veering to the right and left, providing spacious room to exercise and train the horses.

At the front of the building, a door stood ajar, and she peered into the dim room. Shelves stocked with supplies and tools, rope, saddles and bridles filled the space. Barrels and containers crowded the dirt floor.

Logan stepped beside her and shoved one of the barrels next to another. "Ye'll find things in here to tend the horses. We try to keep the area clear, but it has a way of becoming cluttered."

He faced her and swept his arm toward the main aisle.

Lindsey slipped past him and started down the barn's central alley. A large chestnut stallion, sporting a black mane and tail, occupied the first stall.

"He's beautiful," she breathed out.

"Aye, he is. His name is Pegasus." Logan ducked under the rope and held it up for her. She followed, and the horse nickered in greeting, tossing his massive head.

"From Greek mythology?" Lindsey ran her hand over the animal's withers and down his powerful shoulder.

Logan cocked his head to the side. "Ye know about mythology?"

She chuckled. "Well, some of it. Mum requested Brother Martin teach my sisters and me the basics, but he had a way of droning on and on."

"Pegasus is one of my favorites. We've raised draft horses for a number of years. Our farming tenants prefer the breed mainly for hard, heavy labor. And with their fairly docile disposition they're perfect for the job."

Logan patted the horse's sleek neck. He slipped back under the rope to the main aisle, and she fell into step beside him.

Movement in the next stall caught her eye, and she hurried to the roped fence. A honey-colored colt kicked his hind legs into the air as he darted around the roomy pen and over to his mother.

"How adorable!"

"Ahh, our new addition to the herd." Logan stood, hands on hips. "Colyne tells me he was born last week."

The mare nuzzled her little one. The colt began nursing, his short black tail flicking back and forth.

"He'll be ready for training before we know it," she said.

Lindsey turned and caught up to Logan as he marched along, explaining the workings of the stable. A loud squeak sounded from high in the barn. He pointed to the lads tugging a thick course rope. "The pulleys make moving bales of hay and heavy sacks of grain much easier."

A broad-shouldered man with closely cropped blond hair marched over to them. He held his arm out to indicate the pens at his right as he addressed Logan. "We made the changes ye requested—broke up the exercise area into three sections, one for each breed."

"We'll leave them in for a day or two before we release them on the southern pasture." Logan turned to her. "This is Kirk. He was my uncle's captain and now Alec's."

"Welcome to Glencara."

Relief spread through her at his warm reception. She had hoped the men would accept her. After all, not only was she an outsider, she was a woman. "'Tis nice to meet ye."

"Merchants are here," a lad shouted at the barn door, then ran back into the bailey, announcing the traders' arrival.

"I need to meet with Clyde," Logan said. "Kirk, will ye help her get acquainted with the routine?"

The man nodded. "Follow me, m'lady."

Lindsey met the other men and lads responsible for the stable and immersed herself into the scheduled activities. Everyone welcomed her. Spirits lifted, she felt at home.

The day wore on with her working alongside lads cleaning stalls, watering and feeding the horses. When the afternoon sun filtered through the slats in the barn, Lindsey straightened and stretched her tired back.

She'd had enough work for the day.

She glanced around the building. Charcoal sticks and discarded wooden shingles used for marking grain levels lay against the far wall. With thoughts of Grant, she stooped beside them. Several shingles the size of a platter leaned against the bundle. After selecting the cleanest, flattest piece, she scrambled up a stack of hay bales and propped the wood in her lap.

She studied the barn's thick rafters as her hand ran the charcoal stick over the thin timber, etching the structure's image. Stalls filled with horses and a lad leading a mare down the aisle materialized on the surface. Rubbing the charred strokes added shading cast from the afternoon sun on the barn's fencing.

Logan strolled down the dirt path, climbed up beside her, and looked over her shoulder. "What are ye drawing?"

She held up the shingle, balancing the edge on her thighs. "A picture of the stable."

He whistled low. "Verrae nice. Ye've got an eye for detail."

"Mum used to tell me it was a sin to waste my *God given talent*." She ran her fingertips over the shingle. "I haven't sketched anything in quite a while."

His thumb traced circles on the back of her hand. "Yer mum had it right."

She turned to him.

His closeness caused heated tremors to spread through her body. "I've got a few God given talents I'd like to show ye."

The wicked curve of his mouth beckoned her. She longed to lean into him, press her lips to his, and bask in his *talents*.

Why did he affect her so? A glance or simple touch, and she turned to mush. She broke his intense stare and concentrated on her drawing, scratching the charcoal across the wood. "I'm sure ye do."

He chuckled, the deep sound rumbling in his muscular chest. "Over the next few days, I'd like to spend time with ye, decide which of yer best mares we will section off for breeding this spring."

Lindsey's hand paused, and she looked over her shoulder at him.

"We need horses able to withstand the rigors of battle, but also that possess agility to make sudden movements, spins or turns." He paused. "Those we'll keep for the rebellion, but I'd have ye continue to peddle the pleasure horses."

Pride welled in her chest. She couldn't have asked for a finer compliment. He trusted her, wanted her opinion. "Aye, I have some ideas about how to best market them."

Dimples pressed into his bearded cheeks, and he squeezed her hand. "I'm off with Adam and Kirk to ride the southern pasture fencing before we turn the herd loose. It might be late before we return. Ye will be all right while I'm away?"

His concern touched her heart. "Aye, I have everything I need."

~~~

Lindsey hugged the wooden shingle to her middle and knocked on the heavy oak door.

A moment passed before Grant shouted, "Enter."

She opened the door and eased inside the room. "Is now a good time…"

Maria smoothed her skirt and ran a hand over her hair. She appeared flustered, her white braid hung loose, and her mouth tinged red.

Lindsey looked from the woman to Grant. He adjusted the blanket across his lap.

Suddenly feeling as though she had interrupted, Lindsey took a step back. "I…I can visit another time."

Grant straightened and waved, coaxing her farther into the chamber. "Nay, please come in and sit before the fire."

Maria bustled around the chamber. "I'll have yer evening meal sent up shortly." She smiled at Lindsey, then skirted past her and slipped from the room.

Could Maria and Grant be lovers? Aye, they were older, but… The idea almost caused giggles to burst forth, but she showed great restraint. Clamping her lips into a thin line, she strolled to the hearth and dropped in the chair beside him.

"I brought ye a gift."

His eyes widened. "A gift? For me?"

She handed him the wooden shingle, her pulse beating in her ears. Why was she so nervous? It was just a simple drawing, but somehow she longed for his approval.

His mouth opened as he scanned the etching.

"I thought perhaps ye'd like to see the stable and some of the horses housed there."

"Many years have passed since I last laid eyes on the barn. No longer able to ride, I didn't want to return to it." His calloused finger traced one of the animals. "I can still smell the fresh cut hay and grain, hear the whinnying horses. Now I can see it."

When he raised his head, his eyes had misted. "Thank ye, lass."

"Ye're welcome." Her chest constricted as if bands squeezed it tight.

He cleared his throat. "So how was yer first day?"

"Smoother than I expected." She grinned. "I guess mucking out a stall is pretty much the same anywhere."

Rich laughter boomed from him, and he patted his rounding middle.

"Logan has asked for my help in culling the herd for breeding this spring." She plucked stiff strands of hay from her trews and tossed them into the hearth.

"He mentioned producing stalwart but agile animals."

Her head tilted. "He's been by to see ye?"

"Aye, he stopped in last night shortly after yer visit." Grant placed his hand on her arm. "He told me how ye rescued him and his men."

She shrugged. "I didn't do anything he wouldn't have done."

Grant's forehead scrunched. "Ye risked yer life, lass."

"As I say, he would've done the same for me. I couldn't leave him."

The old laird seemed to search her face. Uncomfortable in his scrutiny, she turned from him and held her hands out to the fire. The last thing she wanted to hear was how she was a woman who shouldn't be involved in such activities.

Time to change the subject.

"The stable is quite impressive, filled with majestic horses." She leaned back in the chair. "With the animals we brought from home alongside the horses here, the stable must be one of the largest in Scotland."

He cast a wistful look at the drawing. "A dream I harbored for many years."

Lindsey glanced at his legs. Had it really been four years since she heard of his accident? The thought of him wasting away before the hearth with a blanket draped over his lap caused her to shiver with horror. A cruel existence for one who'd been so active, so full of life.

A thought sparked, and she smiled to herself.

She would see Grant ride once again.

~~~

Logan jogged down the stairs and into the main hall. Men, women, and children filled the benches breaking their fast. As usual, he scanned the group, searching for Lindsey. When he didn't find her, he grabbed an apple off the table and headed out-of-doors.

Pulling his cloak around him, he strode across the bailey and into the stable behind several lads toting water. Blake tugged a rope across the pulley and hauled a heavy bale of hay to one of the stalls while Travis and David carried in buckets of oats.

Logan marched down the main aisle, his gaze skimming the barn.

Where was she?

Frowning, he paused and turned back toward the stable's entrance. The door to the storeroom stood ajar. Perhaps she needed supplies. He tread into the cramped space and found her standing on a ladder, reaching high over her head, her fingers searching a shelf.

Logan glanced behind him. With no one nearby, he eased the door closed and leaned against it to watch her.

Buckskin trews hugged her hips and molded to her bottom. She rose on her toes and leaned forward, affording him a nice view. His gaze rested on firm buttocks before trailing down her shapely limbs. The *lad* between his legs twitched in appreciation.

The ladder wobbled. Dropping the apple, he grasped her hips and steadied her. "Ye'd best be careful."

"Oh, ye startled me." Lindsey turned and faced him.

With her standing on the rung, he had to look up. She placed her hands on his shoulders, and he lifted her from the step, her soft breasts at eye level.

"Logan…"

"Shhh…" He let her body slide down, but he stopped her descent as the sweet juncture of her legs nestled the poor swollen fellow straining against his breeks. His nostrils flared, desire pumping through his veins. Leaning down, he captured her mouth as he canted his hips against her softness.

When her toes touched the floor, a little moan escaped her luscious mouth. How he longed to whisk her to his bedchamber and make love to her luscious body.

Men's voices drifted beyond the closed door, and he reluctantly eased away.

Desire darkened her blue eyes to violet. Her rosy lips were puffy from his whiskered face. His thumb stroked her hand. "Good morn, lass."

"Aye, it is a good morning," she whispered.

He had rattled her, reminded her of the desire raging between them. In his dreams, he stoked that fire, pleasured her, made her his. He exhaled in a huff. "What are ye doing?"

"Looking for nails."

"Nails?"

She bent and retrieved several pieces of wood from the floor. "I'd like to make a seat."

His forehead wrinkled as he took the boards from her. "What kind of seat?"

Her teeth raked her bottom lip. "One that can be attached to a saddle for support, with straps to secure the rider."

What was she talking about? "Whatever for?"

Shoulders squared, her chin rose slightly. "For yer uncle."

"Grant?"

"Aye. Do ye know how long it's been since he rode upon a horse's back?"

His eyes narrowed. "He can no longer ride."

"I don't see why not. We can construct a special seat to support him."

He shook his head. "Lindsey…"

"Please." She grasped his forearm, her eyes intense. "He sits day after day wasting away before the hearth, dreaming of how life used to be. With special care, he could regain some of that life, feel whole again."

Why had he not thought of that? Years had passed since Uncle Grant's accident. Perhaps there was a chance. He turned the wood over in his hand. "Come with me. I'll help ye build it."

The smile she bequeathed upon him wrenched his gut. How could he possibly say no? He grabbed a bucket of nails from the bottom shelf, opened the door, and headed for the workbench at the back of the barn with Lindsey close behind.

Before long, they had fashioned a sturdy frame with thick leather straps fastened to the back and sides. The design would provide support for Grant while securing his legs and torso.

Lindsey clutched her hands before her chest. "It's perfect. I can't wait to see his face."

"Hamish just arrived," Adam shouted to Logan over the noise in the barn.

"Hamish?" Logan snarled. "I wondered when the cur would show up."

~~~

Lindsey's head jerked toward Logan as he dropped the constructed seat on the workbench and grabbed a long metal rod leaning against the worktable's base. His fingers coiled around the bar as he stormed down the aisle, a murderous glare plastered across his face.

What was he going to do?

Lindsey's heart leapt into her throat. She rushed behind him. "Wait!"

He paid her no mind as he marched from the barn and into the bailey.

"Logan, listen to me." She ran to match his purposeful strides. "Hamish did not recruit me. I volunteered to help."

"I don't give a God damn if ye threw yerself at his feet. He had no right to involve ye."

Hamish turned toward them and raised a hand in greeting.

Logan charged like a raging bull. "Who the hell do ye think ye are?"

Confused, the commander stepped back. "I don't have a quarrel with ye."

Men and women working in the inner yard turned at the commotion.

"Aye, ye do," Logan ground out. "The day ye coerced Lindsey to do yer dirty work."

She darted in front of him, holding her hands up, her back to Hamish. "Stop!"

He advanced until her palms shoved against his heaving chest. His nostrils flared, his grey eyes piercing.

"I asked to be involved. I wanted to do my part. If it hadn't been Hamish, I would've worked with another of McLeod's men."

His teeth ground, his firm jaw taut.

"Please, Logan," she whispered. "Don't do this."

"Only ye can save the man."

"What does that mean?"

"I won't beat him senseless if ye promise ye will *never* take on another mission."

Not expecting his demand, she hesitated.

Logan started around her, and she grasped his upper arms. "I promise."

He stilled, stared at her, and his tight muscles flexed beneath her palms.

Pulse pounding, she nodded. "I promise, Logan."

His intense glare shot to Hamish. "Ye will deliver future mission instructions to me—and me only." His menacing eyes narrowed. "If ye even think to go near her, I will kill ye."

Chapter Fourteen

Glencara Castle
November 1299

"My legs won't move," Grant stated emphatically.

"I'm aware of that," Lindsey countered. "They don't need to move. The seat will hold ye onto the saddle."

His gaze swung to Logan, who leaned against the bedchamber wall, arms folded over his chest.

Logan shrugged. "What do ye have to lose?"

His chest puffed out. "My dignity."

Lindsey jammed her hands on her hips. "Och, what kind of dignity do ye have while ye sit here wasting away?"

The old laird reared back as if she'd slapped him, his eyes widening.

Perhaps that's just what he needed. Someone to knock sense into his stubborn head. She stooped beside his chair. "Give it a try. If ye don't like it, ye never have to do it again."

His shoulders sagged, and he looked at Logan. "Ye really intend to carry me to the stable by yerself?"

Delight welled up inside Lindsey, and a grin spread across her face.

"Ye're not so heavy." Logan squatted with his back to Grant. "Wrap yer arms around my neck."

Lindsey helped the old laird scoot to the chair's edge. Logan clasped his hands under Grant's legs and stood, lifting him on his back.

She snatched a woolen wrap off the end of the bed and hurried to lead the way down the stairs and into the grand hall.

Maria placed a tray on the table and straightened, wiping her hands on a cloth. She turned toward them and froze. Her hand clutched her chest. "What are ye doing?"

"Going for a ride," Grant announced.

Lindsey grinned and dashed to the door. She opened it wide, and Logan carried Grant down the bailey stairs and across the yard. Men laid down their tools and followed the three into the barn. Several others stepped from the horses' stalls, craning their necks to see the excitement.

Lindsey had saddled one of her more docile animals, and the horse waited beside a raised platform. She grasped his bridle as Adam and Kirk jogged down the aisle toward them.

Logan carried Grant up the ramp where they were level with the horse's back.

"Let us help ye," Adam offered as he and Kirk gathered on either side of Logan. In one fluid motion, they lifted Grant and hoisted him onto the altered saddle.

Logan grasped his uncle's shoulders while Lindsey tied the leather straps around Grant's torso and across his lifeless legs.

"How does that feel?" she asked and straightened.

Radiance beamed from the old laird's face. He closed his eyes while breathing in the barn's scents.

Her chest squeezed, and her throat clogged with unshed tears.

He opened his eyes and patted the binding. "Good. Let's get going."

Lindsey ran to Blaze as Logan mounted Sterling.

"I'll join ye," Kirk said and climbed onto his horse's saddle.

As the animals trotted into the inner bailey, smiles plastered the gathered clansmen's faces. They clapped, and Grant beamed while raising his face to the sun's rays.

Joy soared through her at his expression.

The group rode past the guardhouses, over the wooden bridge, and down the dirt road leading into the village at the base of the castle. A pine-cushioned path wound between outlying cottages.

A woman stepped from her hut carrying a basket of dirty linens while children chased each other around the yard, dogs barking and nipping at their heels. She paused, holding the laundry against her middle. "Laird?"

"Good morn to ye," Grant shouted, his voice robust.

Lindsey waved and nudged Blaze down a trail lined with Scots pines. Silver birch grew alongside the tall trees. Snow banked the white bark, its characteristic trunk marked with black diamond-shaped patches. A light breeze blew through the woods. Sunlight shone around white puffy clouds, warming small winter flowers peaking through the snow covered forest.

She peered over her shoulder at Grant. He sat high in the saddle, a fist propped on his thigh. His proud stance resembled Logan's. The two shared Campbell traits—the same grey eyes and nose, the same sturdy build.

The trail opened onto a pasture of tall brown grass crusted with icy snow.

Grant reined in beside her at the top of the knoll. "Blaze is quite an animal. I've never seen a horse with such long legs."

"Ye should see him run. He's the fastest I've ridden."

Grant's face lit. "Let me see, lass."

She glanced to her right at Logan and threw down a challenge. "Ye ready to eat some dust?"

Squeezing her legs around Blaze, she crouched low to his neck. The horse shot down the hill, soaring across the meadow. She reveled in the power he possessed. His stride was long and smooth as he galloped through the tall grass.

Pounding hooves sounded behind her, and she spared a glimpse over her shoulder. Logan and Sterling bore down, clods of dirt thrown behind them. The horses careened around a bend. Cold wind cut across her face, and tears streamed from the corners of her eyes. The loch at the base of the hill loomed ahead.

She tugged the reins, and Blaze tossed his head as he trotted to a stop. She patted his sleek neck. "Good lad."

Sterling slowed to a gallop, and Logan reined in beside her. "He's a beautiful horse."

"Aye, he is," she agreed, laughing. The horses' sides heaved, and Sterling snorted.

"Quite an impressive run, lass," Grant called as he trotted down the hill with Kirk close behind. "I want to see more animals like Blaze in our herd."

Pride welled up and spilled forth. "My thoughts exactly."

Logan chuckled and nudged Sterling around the edge of the loch. Sunlight glistened off the sparkling water and a gentle breeze blew ripples over the surface. The group made their way to the southern pasture and stopped before the picturesque hillside dotted with grazing sheep.

"Adam and Colyne will move them to MacDougall pastures next week if the weather holds." Sterling pawed the ground, and Logan patted his neck. "Easy, lad."

"They'll take all of them?" Grant asked.

Logan nodded as he scanned the sheep. "That's the plan. We want to get them settled before the ewes go into lambing season."

The horses ambled through the field. Logan pointed to several thatched huts scattered amongst the trees bordering the meadow. Triangular shaped, the simple shacks provided little protection from the elements. Wooden slats, stacked one over the other, formed the walls. Crude chimneys jutted from structure. The roofs constructed of tightly woven reeds, touched the ground on either side of the hovels, and thick oak logs braced an opening for the single door.

"Men live here during the shearing season. With hundreds of animals, the job often takes several weeks, but their efforts pay off."

"Not only is the wool invaluable, but they cull the herd and slaughter a few dozen," Grant added. "Merchants arrive each month, purchase the meat, and sell it through their travels."

The day wore as they rode over Glencara's vast land. Grant couldn't seem to get enough as he suggested journeying to this field and that loch. He showed them hidden caverns and lamented on his childhood days spent exploring the vast caves. At every turn, he pointed to things he hadn't seen in years, places he hadn't visited. But as the afternoon sun dipped low, he waned.

"Ye've had a long day, uncle. We should head back."

Lindsey's belly growled. "My stomach obviously agrees."

The men laughed and turned the horses toward the castle.

~~~

After the evening meal and settling Grant in his bedchamber, Lindsey wandered down the stairs and into the solar. Ainslee sat before the desk, her brunette head bent over a swath of blue linen, her nimble fingers tugging thread through the fabric.

Lindsey slipped onto the chair beside her. "What are ye making?"

She held up the material. "It's a gown for Alec and Heather's bairn."

A punch slammed into Lindsey's gut. After spending more time with Logan, she longed for the relationship Heather shared with his cousin. It wasn't fair. Logan had nothing to do with his birth, and it shouldn't be held against him.

Ainslee reached into the basket at her feet and pulled out a handful of outfits and a cream-colored blanket. "I've been trying to stitch a few items each week."

Lindsey fingered the soft cover, imagining Logan's babe wrapped in her arms. "They're beautiful."

"Thank ye." Ainslee's head bent over the sewing again. "I hope yer sister will like them."

"She most certainly will. It's verrae kind of ye."

Logan walked into the room.

"How's Da?" Ainslee asked.

"Fast asleep." He leaned on the edge of the desk, and his foot brushed Lindsey's leg. "And ye need to head to bed as well."

She stretched and yawned. "Aye, I'm worn out."

Logan straightened. "I'll see ye to yer room."

Expectations of him holding her, kissing and caressing her caused her pulse to race. She placed her hand in his warm palm. "Goodnight, Ainslee."

She glanced up from the sewing. "Sleep well."

Logan led Lindsey through the dim corridor, up the stairs, and along the hall to her bedchamber. Neither of them spoke and her nerves stood on end. When they arrived at her door, she faced him.

"I can't thank ye enough, lass."

Her head tilted. "For what?"

"Ye've given Uncle Grant a renewed outlook on life." His strong fingers intertwined through hers. "I haven't seen him this happy in a long time."

A warm flush coursed through her. "I think he's been enjoying life a bit more than ye realize."

"In what way?"

A grin spread across her face. "I might be wrong, but I think he and Maria…"

"Ahh, I have often wondered about their *relationship*." He chuckled, and dimples pressed into his cheeks. "I've caught them on a number of occasions in somewhat compromising positions, but they always had an appropriate excuse."

"Well, I think it's wonderful if they can find joy in each other's arms during their later years." She paused. "And I'd like to thank ye for making me feel so welcome."

Logan ran his hand along her jaw, his thumb rubbing her cheek. "Let me show ye just how welcome ye are."

He bent and captured her mouth in a soft kiss. Craving more of him, she clutched his broad shoulders and opening her lips, invited him in. He groaned and tugged her into his embrace as he slid his tongue against hers.

Heated tremors racked her and her body strummed with fierce, pulsing need.

The next thing she knew, he opened her chamber door and backed her into the room as his hot mouth trailed across her cheek. She angled her head, giving him access to her neck. His foot pushed the door closed as his hands delved through her hair, down her back to her bottom.

Breathing in his musky scent, her head reeled. A hard bulge pushed against her stomach. She rubbed against it, delicious, wicked thoughts causing her boldness.

He hissed, "Lass, ye're killing me."

~~~

Logan straightened and tugged the wrap from Lindsey's shoulders. It fluttered to the floor at her feet. Candlelight from wall sconces flickered in a chilly draft, highlighting her passion-filled eyes, her fiery wild tresses.

God, she was stunning.

He fought the overwhelming desire to make her his.

She reached out, took his hand and placed it on her breast.

Shite.

Her soft bosom filled his palm, the pebbled tip straining against her tunic.

"Make love to me, Logan," she whispered.

His thumb stroked her peak. "Ye don't know how much I want to."

Her violet eyes rounded. "Please."

His nostrils filled with her tangy scent, his member aching to plunge into her sweetness. He pulled her into his embrace and kissed her soft pliable mouth. She tasted of spices, enticing his exploration of her warm recesses.

Her hands roamed his chest and around his neck, her breasts brushing his torso. He longed to taste her delightful buds, but he must take it slow. It wouldn't do to frighten her with his raging desire.

He straightened.

Her face was flushed, and her supple lips were swollen. He grasped the hem of her tunic and lifted the garment over her head. Silky auburn hair fell over her shoulders and shift. Pink tips pressed against the fabric, and his mouth watered.

A dainty blue bow rested in her luscious cleavage. He pulled the string, and the bow unraveled, the undergarment falling open. Heart pounding, he eased the sides of the fabric from her breasts.

His breath caught, and his cock throbbed. "Oh, my God. Ye're beautiful, princess."

Cradling her full breasts, he feathered kisses across her ivory skin, his thumbs rolling the erect buds. When his mouth found the peak, he suckled and reveled in her delightful moans.

He knelt before her and worked the ties of her trews. The enclosure opened, and he kissed little goose bumps peppering her flat stomach. Her hands grasped his shoulders as he eased the garment past her hips to pool on the floor beside her discarded wrap. Skimpy linen braes covered her haven. He fought the urge to rip them off and sink into her, bring her pleasure, show her how much he loved her.

His fingers snaked into one of the leg holes and brushed the soft curls covering her womanhood.

She inhaled sharply, her limbs trembling, her hands tightening on his shoulders.

"Ye're so soft," he whispered as he glided her braes lower. Auburn curls peaked out the top. Sitting back, his weight balanced on his heel, he slowly tugged her underclothes down, past her hips, her thighs. With her hidden treasure revealed, he paused and reveled in her glorious beauty. Grasping her hips, he leaned forward. His tongue traced her naval and she shivered, her breath coming in short, fast pants. He trailed his mouth lower, kissed her nether lips.

Her intake of air almost caused him to spiral out of control. Taking a deep breath, he slid her trews to the floor, lifted her leg and eased the underwear off.

She stood before him clad in a shift draping off her shoulders, her thick hair disheveled, her eyes darkened. His gaze traveled over her delicious body and back to her face. He straightened, and his fingers toyed with a nipple. Her breathing quickened, and she leaned into his hand.

"Ye're sure, lass?"

"Aye." She reached for his tunic and lifted it over his head. The top landed on the chair behind him as her palms splayed over his chest. He hated the puckered scars, but she didn't seem to see his marred skin. Instead, she leaned into him and trailed kisses across his torso and down his abdomen while her fingertip traced the outline of his throbbing cock.

It jerked in anticipation and sweat beaded his forehead. He scooped her up, cradling her in his arms. She placed her head against his shoulder as he carried her to the bed.

Settling her on the feathered mattress, he hovered over her. His tongue laved a taut bud as her fingers delved into his hair. He captured the peak in his mouth and suckled. She tasted like nectar, and he couldn't get enough.

"Oh, Logan…" She clutched his head to her breast and heat exploded through him, desire running rampant.

~~~

His mouth trailed from one breast to the other. Moisture pooled between her legs, a throbbing ache tightening. She raised her hips and rubbed herself against his thigh. His hand drifted down, splayed over her flat abdomen and inched lower to the sensitive flesh craving his touch.

"Spread yer legs for me," he whispered.

Shakily, she eased her knees apart. His hand glided between her thighs and opened them farther.

She clutched his arm. "Logan…"

His hot mouth trailed to her neck. "Shhh…just relax. I won't hurt ye or do anything ye don't want me to do."

His finger eased between her folds and ran up and down her slick core. Never having felt anything so exquisite, a moan escaped her throat, and she lifted her hips to meet his touch. He parted her nether lips, and his finger swirled her special nub, swollen and longing for his attention.

Wanting to feel his hard member, she reached for the front of his trews and untied his belt.

He caught her wrist and brought her hand over her head. "Not yet," he whispered against her mouth.

His hand returned to fondle her, and she basked in the sensations he brought to life. A finger eased into her, then another. Her legs grew weak with the start of delicious tremors coursing through her body.

She hit a pinnacle and cried out.

His mouth captured hers again, and his tongue thrust into her mouth. Her muscles contracted around the thick fingers plunging into her moisture. His stroking slowed until the last quiver vibrated through her spent body.

He kissed her gently.

Confused, her brow knit. "But, ye didn't…"

"Shhh…"He wrapped his arms around her and lay back, pulling her into the crook of his arm.

Why didn't he…enter her? Wasn't that what was supposed to happen?

"Logan," she whispered and looked up at him. "I don't understand."

"It's all right, princess." He stroked her arm and gazed into her eyes.

"Don't ye want me?"

His hand paused. "More than ye can know."

"Then, why didn't ye…join with me?"

His knuckle raised her mouth to him, and he kissed her. "Because I can't have ye."

"But I'm here for ye. I want ye."

"Damn it, Lindsey. Ye know I can't take ye. I won't bring another bastard into this world." Logan swung his legs off the bed and snatched his tunic from the floor.

His words sliced through her middle and stabbed her heart as if he'd plunged his blade into her. She rose on her elbow, her body shaking uncontrollably. Digging her fingernails into her palm, she held his intense stare.

He jerked the tunic over his head and shoved his arms into the sleeves. "Ye need to think of yer future. Marry a man with status who can care for ye, provide for ye."

Tears flooded her eyes.

His rigid shoulders eased. He scrubbed a hand over his face and knelt beside her. "Don't cry. If there was any way possible to have ye as my wife…"

He paused and bowed his head, his thumb stroking her hand. Exhaling loudly, he stood, then strode across the room and out the door.

She wrapped the bed's top blanket around her body. Images of Ainslee's baby clothing, of Cameron holding her infant son, of Heather's rounding stomach flashed through her mind. Was it so wrong to want the same?

She loved Logan.

Her breath hitched. She didn't give a fig about ignorant traditions. One way or another, she would have him.

Chapter Fifteen

The clash of steel reverberated against the bailey walls. The midday sun, unusually warm for November, beat upon Logan's back. Sweat dribbled down his temple as he focused his attention on his opponent.

Adam lunged at Logan and thrust his sword.

Logan's shield deflected the blow. He jumped to the side, spun around, and slammed his elbow onto Adam's back.

A roar went up from the men gathered around the pair as Adam stumbled forward. He regained his balance and breathing hard, whirled to face Logan.

The blacksmith and his helpers joined the crowd. Several lads snaked between the men to witness the mock battle.

Hunched and rotating the blade in his hand, Logan studied his rival.

Blood oozed from a cut above Adam's left eye. He swiped at the injury.

Logan took advantage of the weakness and charged. His sword slammed against Adam's shield. Striking right, then left, Logan shouted, "Watch yer opening. Keep yer sword before ye. Don't let it drop."

Exhaustion was evident in Adam's inaccurate blows. Finally, he went down on his knee and held up a hand.

Men cheered. "Well matched!" someone yelled.

Chest heaving, Logan bent, hands on his knees.

"Good job." Kirk clapped Logan's bare back and handed him his tunic.

Logan wiped his face with the garment and turned to the amassed Glencara warriors. After hours of intense training, sweat dripped from their hair and ran down their mud-streaked faces. "Break for the morning."

With the fight over, Logan's men and the boisterous crowd slowly dispersed. One of the lads imitated Logan's sword thrust only to have his enthusiastic lunging ridiculed by laughing and jeering companions. David ruffled the youngster's hair as they resumed their duties.

Logan ran the tunic over his chest and grasped Adam's outstretched hand. "Ye almost had me."

Adam laughed and swiped an arm across his forehead. "I look forward to the day I best ye."

Horses' hooves clattered over the wooden bridge as a group of men trotted into the bailey. Logan recognized the bulky man mounted on the black destrier leading the others into the yard.

Laird Mangus MacAndrew.

What the hell did he want?

Dread washed over Logan. He had a good idea why the cur would show up, and it wasn't because he desired Logan's company.

Cloaked in buckskin breeks and a plush fur cloak, MacAndrew and his men reined in before Logan and dismounted.

Lads ran from the stable to take their horses. Logan held up a hand and the boys stopped, awaiting his orders.

Gaze accessing, MacAndrew slapped the reins in his palm. He tugged off a glove and extended his hand. "Ross."

Logan glared. "What brings ye to Glencara?"

A wry smirk crossed MacAndrew's face. He reached inside his saddlebag, extracted a document, and handed it to Logan.

"What is this?" Logan turned the parchment over. A red splotch of wax with the imprint of Alec's seal secured the message.

MacAndrew's arms crossed his chest. "A missive from yer cousin."

Logan broke the seal.

Laird Mangus MacAndrew has requested
Lindsey's hand in marriage in exchange for
his Highland clan's support.
With the continued harassment from the
English, the alliance
would prove beneficial to the Campbells and
MacDougalls.
I trust ye will ensure the agreement is
secured.

Sterling's kick to Logan's gut couldn't compare to Alec's blow.

"As ye can see, I'm here to collect my bride." The pompous arse smirked again. He glanced around the yard. "She is here, isn't she?"

Logan wanted to knock MacAndrew's teeth down his throat and throttle his neck until his eyes bulged.

The man's brow rose.

"Aye, she's here," Logan answered.

"Ahh, verrae good. Please inform her I've arrived."

Bile roiled in Logan's gut. He motioned to the stablehands, and they took the reins from the incoming party. "Follow me."

Logan turned on his heel and strode across the bailey. He had known someday a titled laird would show up and claim his princess, but he hadn't expected it quite so soon. The thought of her riding off with MacAndrew tore a hole in his heart. He tugged his tunic over his damp hair and shoved his arms into the sleeves as he marched up the stone steps and into the main hall.

Ainslee turned at his approach. She held a green cushion against her waist. She paused, and her head tilted. "Ye don't look well. Are ye all right?"

"Aye," he forced out.

MacAndrew and his men entered the keep. Ainslee looked past Logan's shoulder, questions reflected in her face.

"Laird MacAndrew and his men have arrived for…a visit." Logan's arm swung in the men's direction. "Mangus MacAndrew, this is Alec's sister, Ainslee Campbell."

His cousin beamed. "Welcome to Glencara."

MacAndrew clutched her hand and bent at the waist. He stared in Ainslee's eyes, and she appeared mesmerized.

What the hell was wrong with her?

"Mistress Campbell, 'tis with great pleasure that I make yer acquaintance. Yer brother and I have been friends for many years. I've often heard him speak of his lovely sister, but he could not pay yer beauty justice."

Good Lord. Logan's lip curled, but he refrained from rolling his eyes.

Her cheeks pinkened, and she lowered her lashes demurely. "Please, call me Ainslee."

He kissed the back of her hand. "Verrae well…Ainslee."

"Won't ye rest by the hearth while I have refreshments served?" Her voice sounded breathless.

Christ.

Logan had had enough. He turned, strode around MacAndrew's men and back through the keep's entrance. He marched down the steps and across the bailey to the stable. His gaze skimmed the stalls as he walked down the main aisle. To his left, two lads brushed and curried horses. Kirk led a draft into a paddock at his right. He turned the corner and a mass of auburn curls stood out in a pen at the back of the building. He hadn't seen Lindsey since he'd left her room last night, and he wasn't certain how she would act toward him.

As he drew closer, he realized she worked with a filly. He leaned against the railing and watched her gently coaxing the horse. She turned right while tugging on the reins. The filly trailed along. She turned left and again the animal followed her every move.

"Verrae good, Bel." Lindsey slipped a slice of apple from her tunic and fed the young horse. "I don't want to wear ye out so let's return ye to yer mum."

Lindsey unhooked the rope and started from the pen. Her eyes met Logan's and she froze.

"Good morn, lass."

The filly's bowed head pushed her hip. "Good morn."

"I see ye've started training the young ones."

She rubbed the animal's neck. "Aye, it helps to build a bond with them if ye get them early."

He nodded and stepped before her. "Lass, I need to talk to ye."

Her shoulders sagged. "Logan, if it's about last night…"

"Nay, it's not."

Her blue eyes seemed to search his face.

His gut churned as he handed her Alec's note.

"What's this?" She dropped the reins and read the parchment. Her eyes narrowed; her forehead scrunched.

He exhaled. "MacAndrew is here."

Her head jerked up. "He's here? Now?"

"Aye."

"I refuse to be used as chattel. I don't give a damn what advantageous alliance might be built."

Logan stepped closer and clutched her shoulders. His throat clogged. "I don't see ye have much choice."

~~~

She wrenched away from him. "Mum garnered Da's promise my sisters and I would have our say over who we married."

"What are ye talking about?" Logan asked, hands on hips.

"I told ye once before." Her shoulders squared. "As a young man, Da dallied…outside the marital bed. In recompense for his indiscretions, he consented to Mum's demand for my sisters and me to live as we desire, choose whom we marry."

"Does that still hold true now that Alec is laird?"

Her blood simmered. "He has no right to make such a change."

Logan rubbed the back of his neck. "MacAndrew is waiting in the grand hall."

"Let him damn well wait." She grasped the filly's reins, and the horse's head lurched up. Tossing the parchment to the ground, she added, "I won't be in until after I finish my chores."

What was Logan grinning about? She failed to find anything amusing. No one would force her to marry. She rotated on her heel and marched down the aisle with the little filly in tow. Several lads raking stalls, backed into the pathway. She weaved around them and past Blake, who tugged the pulley rope and hauled a bale of hay across the barn. After returning Bel to the worried mare, Lindsey strode to the stockroom.

Mangus MacAndrew. Last week was the first she'd seen the laird since he had visited MacDougall Castle several years ago with interest in Da's horses. A pleasant enough sort. Handsome and wealthy.

But he was not Logan.

She dropped the rope halter in the bin against the wall and leaned her forehead on a shelf's edge. Memories of Logan's caress floated through her mind. Closing her eyes, she relived his hot mouth teasing her sensitive flesh. Thoughts of his fingers stroking her privates caused a quiver to snake through her and the familiar tightening grew between her legs. Tingly heat crept up her neck and a warm flush spread over her face.

Marry a man with status who can care for ye, provide for ye.

Pain sliced through her chest and unshed tears stung the back of her eyes. She had begged him to make love to her, and he refused. Shame filled her. Did she have no pride? He had made it clear he *could not* marry her, even told her to think of a future with someone else.

How could she when Logan filled her every thought?

Not to mention the matter of her horses. After she had fought so hard to keep them, she would not marry Mangus and simply leave her beloved animals behind. She wiped her watery eyes with her sleeve. Disheartened, she popped off the lid to a grain barrel and grabbed a bucket from the lower shelf. After she fed the animals, she'd check on Bess, due to foal at any moment. With a bucket in each hand, she wandered toward the waiting horses.

The late afternoon sun streamed into the barn, dust particles floating in the rays. Lindsey set the container on the ground and scooped grain into the last horse's trough.

"I was told I might find ye here."

She spun at the deep voice.

Mangus leaned against the wooden fence, his blue eyes fixed on her.

"Laird MacAndrew." She nodded in recognition while clutching the wooden scoop against her waist.

His gaze lazily traveled the length of her and back to her face. "May I help ye finish yer *chores* so we might spend time together?"

She dropped the scoop into the bucket and dusted her hands on her trews. "I thank ye, but I'm almost finished."

"Verrae well." He smiled, lines creasing around his eyes. "I'll tag along with ye."

"Suit yerself." Lindsey grabbed the bucket, ducked under the rope, and started down the aisle. A deep breath helped quell her pounding pulse. She weaved around two lads struggling toward the barn's door with carts of soiled shavings.

Mangus fell in step beside her. Hands laced behind his back, he scanned the building. "Quite a magnificent operation ye're managing."

She placed the bucket outside Bess's stall and slipped into the pen.

Mangus followed.

Lindsey stroked Bess's soft nose then ran her hand over the mare's extended abdomen. "How are ye feeling?"

"What a beauty." Mangus patted Bess's hindquarters and slid his hand to Lindsey's. "She must be about ready."

His fingers moved over hers, and she stilled. He stepped closer and brushed her hair down her back. She faced him, and his finger traced her jaw. "Ye must be ready too."

"I beg yer pardon?"

His hand shifted to her shoulder, his strong grip caressing. "Ready for a family of yer own. When I saw ye a couple of weeks ago, I knew I had to have ye. I want ye as my wife, Lindsey."

She held his stare. "I appreciate yer offer, but I don't even know ye."

"Since when has that mattered?" His hand eased around the back of her neck, and his fingertips traced small circles on her skin. "I promise we will get to know each other verrae well."

He tugged her toward him.

Her palms splayed against his chest as he wrapped his arms around her. "This is highly inappropriate. Please unhand me."

His hot breath brushed her cheek, his lips seeking her mouth.

She struggled against his meaty hold. "Laird MacAndrew!"

When he refused to release her, she stomped on his instep.

He let go of her and jerked his foot up. "Shite, lass!" Hobbling, he massaged the injury. "Why did ye do that?"

She rearranged her tunic. "I asked ye to stop."

His eyes narrowed. "Perhaps ye have not seen Laird Campbell's missive and misunderstand the intent of my visit."

She shook her head. "I've seen it."

"Then ye know of our betrothal."

"There is no betrothal." Her chin rose as she wrapped her arms around her waist. "I have not agreed to a union."

"Agreed?" Mangus reared back.

"That's correct. My da promised I would have the husband of my choice, not be shoved into a loveless marriage for political gains."

Mangus's arms crossed his chest. "So ye're telling me I must court ye if I'm to win yer hand?"

Court her? She searched his face and found earnest affection shinning in his eyes. Logan's words repeated through her ears.

"Aye."

He smiled and tipped his head toward her. "Challenge accepted."

~~~

Logan speared a hunk of venison and ran it through the gravy left on his trencher. Men, women, and children crowded the tables. A dull roar of conversation, utensils clinking, and bairns' cries filled the air as serving girls brought food and drink to the clan's members.

Surrounded by his men, Logan's focus continuously returned to the great hall's entrance. Where were Lindsey and MacAndrew? The man left hours ago in search of her. Perhaps Logan should venture to the barn and ensure she was all right.

Feminine laughter broke his thoughts. Lindsey strolled into the hall, MacAndrew at her side. Clutching her chest, she appeared as though she attempted to control laughter.

MacAndrew chuckled, placed his hand on her elbow, and steered her to Logan's table.

With a smile plastered across her lovely face, Lindsey scooted onto the bench and MacAndrew sidled next to her. He reached across the table and pulled closer a platter of sliced venison. He then proceeded to fill Lindsey's plate as if she couldn't do it herself.

She held up a hand. "That's more than plenty. I'll never be able to eat that much."

He leaned toward her and whispered something in her ear.

What the hell did he have to say that couldn't be stated aloud?

Her cheeks pinkened, and her eyes lowered.

Logan bristled. His fingers coiled into a fist. How he would relish slamming it into MacAndrew's aristocratic nose.

The man straightened, a sloppy grin stretching across his haughty face as he turned to Logan. "My men and I will be staying for a few weeks as Lindsey and I…get better acquainted."

Logan glanced at Lindsey's bent head, her focus on the trencher. Unlike her usual hearty appetite, she picked at her food.

"Is that right?" Logan asked.

Her chin rose in her familiar defensive posture, but she refused to look at him.

MacAndrew glared at Logan. "Aye, that's right."

Get better acquainted? Does she consider his proposal? After her reaction in the stable, Logan assumed she would send MacAndrew on his way. What happened to change her mind?

Githa strolled around the table with a basket of fresh bread, the aroma preceding her. She slid the baked goods on the table before Logan. As she straightened, she kissed the back of his neck. "Keep yer chin up, love."

Were his feelings for Lindsey so obvious? He gripped the tankard, his jaw clenching. His knuckles paled as he fought to control the pain coursing through his blood, blot the tormenting thoughts of her and MacAndrew from his mind.

Ainslee hurried into the room with Blake. Her eyes lit on MacAndrew. She dropped on the bench before him and leaned over the table to the breadbasket. "Laird MacAndrew, did I hear ye'd be staying a while?"

Blake sat beside her and glanced between Ainslee and MacAndrew. His eyes narrowed.

So young Blake didn't care for MacAndrew either. Perhaps Logan had found an ally.

She placed the bread before the man.

He wiped his mouth with a cloth and patted Lindsey's arm. "Aye, with Alec's consent to marry Alastair's daughter, I've been given a precious gift." He stroked her hand. "Lindsey's agreed to our courting, and I look forward to getting to know her *much* better."

Logan took a swig of ale, watching the couple over his tankard.

His gut twisted.

He was losing her.

~~~

"He's a unique horse, Lindsey." Mangus rubbed the animal's neck. "Why the name 'Borak'?"

Lindsey shrugged. "I named him for the legendary, magical horse."

Mangus laughed. "Ah, I see. Well, he is indeed magical."

His relaxed demeanor set Lindsey at ease. As they reached the top of a grassy knoll, they reined in the horses. At the base of the incline, the loch's waters lapped against a lush embankment filled with poplars and pines. While Mangus scanned the countryside, she took the opportunity to study him.

Thick black windswept hair blew over his forehead and short curls flipped up at the base of his neck. Grey wisps spread through his otherwise dark bearded cheeks and mustache. He wore a heavy silver chain that dipped inside his tan tunic. Black tufts peaked through the top of his shirt. Her perusal continued down his wide chest and narrow waist. Buff-colored trews hugged his powerful thighs and disappeared into rugged boots. With his deep blue eyes and a straight nose, Mangus was a striking man.

He turned toward her and caught her ogling him. A knowing grin tugged the corners of his mouth. She quickly averted her gaze and nudged Blaze down the hilly pasture.

As they reached the edge of the loch, the midday sun glistened off the water and a slight breeze blew ripples skittering along the surface. Lindsey followed Mangus across a small stream. "Shall we stop and rest the horses?" he asked over his shoulder.

"It is lovely here." Lindsey reined in Blaze beside Borak.

Mangus dismounted and reached for her.

Nerves tightened, she grasped his broad shoulders and slid down. She started toward the water, but his hands lingered at her waist. When she looked up at him, his eyes had darkened.

Careful not to encourage his amorous attention, she moved away and knelt at the loch's edge. Cupping her hands, she scooped up clear, cool water and took a sip. She closed her eyes and images of Logan drifted through her head—his boyish-grin, his touch, and the gentle way he held her. She could smell his musky scent, feel his comforting embrace.

She mentally shook herself. What good did it do to dream of a man she couldn't have? Her chest squeezed. Determined to consider all her options, she stood, wrapping her arms around her waist, and peered at the lake.

"Alec has a gorgeous place here," Mangus said.

Taking in the landscape, she answered, "Aye, there's nothing like Glencara's hills and valleys."

"Ah, but ye have yet to see MacAndrew land." He bent, picked up several pebbles and tossed one in the water. "Have ye ever been to the Highlands?"

"Many years ago, Mum and Da took our family to visit relatives in Aberdeen." Memories of that innocent carefree time surfaced. "They resided on the banks of the River Dee."

"But that was *southeast* of the Highlands." His teasing tone made her smile. He threw another pebble, and it skipped across the water's surface. "I'd like to take ye to Inverness, show ye my land. We have a large stable, and the River Ness cuts across our pastures."

"That sounds lovely."

"Our property is located close to the Firth of Inverness, and with our family in the trading business, I've spent many days on a ship."

"At sea?" She had dreamed of traveling and what it would be like to live on a boat.

He chuckled. "Aye, mostly on the North Sea, but I have a single-masted vessel I sail to navigate the firth's inlet." He nudged her arm. "Mayhap ye would like to join me sometime?"

"Oh, I would indeed. I've never been on a ship."

"Verrae well, I will see that is one of the first things we do, m'lady."

Pride and enthusiasm shone in his bright eyes. Her chest clenched, and she glanced away. She shouldn't encourage his intentions. It was best to cut them off now. "I appreciate yer gracious offer, Mangus. But, ye have to know I cannot leave Glencara."

His head cocked to the side. "Why is that?"

"I won't give up my horses. They're my life. I raised and trained each one."

"I wouldn't ask ye to give them up, lass." She searched his face as he continued. "I know how much the animals mean to ye. Alec has agreed for ye to take yer choice of a dozen horses to the Highlands."

"He did?" She didn't know whether to rejoice or regret the news her brother-in-law smoothed the way for her unwanted marriage.

He paused and grinned. "Aye, but I do have to forewarn ye. I have a young sister who upon learning of yer love for horses, will latch on to ye. She fancies herself quite a horsewoman."

Lindsey returned his smile. "I'm sure I would enjoy her company."

The afternoon sun dipped lower in the sky. Her stomach growled, and she clutched her middle, anxious to change the subject. "Are ye hungry?"

"I am."

She stepped away from him and retrieved her satchel from Blaze's saddle. When she returned, Mangus had jumped onto a flat boulder jutting over the water.

He reached down. "Give me yer hand."

She placed her fingers in his palm, and he tugged her up beside him. His strong hands clutched her waist to steady her. "Careful."

"Thank ye." Drawing away from him, Lindsey extracted a red woolen blanket from her satchel. She shook it then spread it across the rock and knelt. "I packed bread, cheese, and chicken."

Mangus sat across from her and unhooked the wine skin from his belt. He leaned back against another rock, swigged the drink, and watched while she placed the food on the blanket.

"Help yourself." Lindsey broke off a piece of cheese and turned to the lake. The sun's comforting warmth enveloped her. She leaned her head back on her shoulders, enjoying the spring-like weather.

A squawk announced the presence of geese, their honks breaking the peaceful setting. Large fowl, feet forward and wings spread, skimmed the water. With waves rippling from their path, the birds glided to rest on the surface.

"They're quite the jesters." Mangus propped a forearm on his raised knee. "But I'm afraid the joke is on them. At home, thousands of wintering geese will soon arrive…along with avid hunters."

"Och, poor birds."

He chuckled, and his gaze trailed from her neck to her breasts. He looked back at her face, reached out and plucked the cap from her head. Her locks fell down her back. "Ye have beautiful hair, Lindsey."

His smoldering look caused her pulse to pound in her ears.

He leaned forward and ran his hand through her tresses. "So soft and silky."

His arm snaked out and coiled around her. He looked in her eyes as he lowered his head and gently kissed her.

She waited for the excited flutters Logan evoked. Nothing.

Perhaps she needed him to hold her. She scooted closer, and his arms wrapped around her. Gathering her in his lap, he ran his hand down her side and around her back. While his kiss was pleasant, the excited dithers had yet to start.

Logan holding her, bringing her pleasure, played through her mind—his fingers delving through the curls surrounding her womanhood, slipping in and stroking her core. Her body eased, and Mangus moaned, his embrace tightening.

How would she lie underneath this man night after night while envisioning Logan making love to her?

A hard bulge pressed into her hip. An awakening jolt jarred her. She broke his kiss and moved off his lap. He must think her wanton. Heat slid up her neck and spread over her cheeks.

"Ye're desire shouldn't shame ye." His blue eyes peered at her, and he ran his hand down her arm. "I know ye're innocent, and I look forward to introducing ye to the pleasures between a man and a woman."

Chapter Sixteen

Golden rays streaking through clouds of pinkish-purple hues filled the evening sky as Lindsey and Mangus returned to the castle. Their horses trotted across the wooden draw bridge, past the guardhouses, and drew to a stop in the bailey. A redheaded lad with freckles ran from the stable.

Lindsey dismounted and handed Blaze's reins to the stablehand. "Please water and feed them."

"Aye, m'lady," he answered and reached for Borak's reins.

Lindsey turned to Mangus. "I had a lovely afternoon, but if ye'll excuse me, I'm ready to retire."

"I understand. Ye've had a good bit thrust upon ye."

Mary, carrying a basket of vegetables to the kitchen, sauntered past. "Pleasant evening, Mistress Lindsey. Laird MacAndrew."

"To ye as well, Mary." Lindsey tugged her blue linen wrap around her shoulders and climbed the bailey steps. A brisk gust of air swirled into the front hall as they entered. Mangus closed the heavy oak door and followed her down the dim corridor.

Boisterous conversation, laughter, and children's squeals drifted from the great hall. Avoiding the merriment, she started toward the upper floor stairway. Mangus caught her wrist, and she turned toward him.

"I hope I didn't frighten ye, m'lady." He seemed to search her face, his thumb rubbing her skin.

Frighten her? He'd given her a taste of what to expect.

She shook her head. "Nay, I'm simply tired."

He bent slightly, brought her fingers to his mouth, and kissed them. "Until the morrow then. Sleep well."

"Good evening, Mangus." Her troubled mind raced, and she needed time to think. Trying to control the overwhelming urge to run to her room, she took a deep breath and ascended the stairs.

What was she to do? Mangus appeared to be the perfect mate—charming, considerate and handsome. He made her laugh and shared her love for horses. If they married, he would give her children, and she had no doubt over time, she would grow to care for him.

But he was not Logan.

When Mangus's strong arms surrounded her, her body didn't respond as it should. No butterflies flittered in her stomach. No thumping strummed in her chest.

All she had to do was think of Logan, and her heart fluttered. She searched for him whenever she entered a room, thought of him day and night. Although he made it clear he could not marry her, she had been willing to forgo that dream to be near him. But he refused to lie with her. Instead, she would witness him with other women. Perhaps he'd even marry, have children of his own. Where would that leave her? To grow old and alone, without ever knowing the love of a husband and children?

Her chest ached with agonizing loss. She veered to the left and hurried toward her chamber. Light from Grant's room spilled into the corridor, and Lindsey paused. She could use a bit of cheering up. Hoping he was still awake, she strolled down the hall to his bedchamber.

"Ye need to do the right thing," a woman said. "Please, Grant."

Lindsey knocked on the open door and stuck her head inside. "Am I interrupting?"

Maria turned toward her, eyes wide. They surely must be lovers or the maid would not have addressed him so familiarly. The servant glanced at Logan's uncle and back to Lindsey as she smoothed her hands down the front of her woolen gown.

"Lindsey, come in." Grant waved, coaxing her to the hearth.

She stepped farther into the room. Although Maria smiled, worry lines etched the woman's forehead, her eyes sad. What was wrong? Why did she beg him to do the right thing?

Maria gathered a trencher and tankard and placed them on the tray with other remnants from Grant's evening meal. "Let me know if ye require anything else tonight, Laird."

She picked up the tray and scurried from the room.

Lindsey padded over to him. "I didn't mean to disturb yer meal."

"Ye didn't." He patted the chair beside him. "Have a seat. I'm happy to see ye."

She slid next to him.

His head tilted, and he seemed to study her. "Are ye all right, lass?"

Holding her hands toward the warmth of the fire, she swallowed hard. Were her thoughts so transparent? "I'm fine."

His fingers clutched her forearm. "I sense something has ye worried."

She faced him. His grey eyes reminded her of Logan, and her chest tightened. "What do ye know of Mangus MacAndrew?"

"I know his family. Mangus hails from a long line of MacAndrews. His father passed when Mangus was just a lad. From what I understand, he stepped into the laird's role and earned his clan's respect through fair treatment and natural leadership." Grant paused. "I've always heard good things about him."

Her gaze returned to the red and gold flames. She leaned over, grabbed a metal poker propped against the wall, and shoved a log in the hearth. A loud pop sounded as the wood shifted. "He seems to be a fine man."

A moment of silence passed before Grant spoke again. "Maria informed me of his visit, lass."

Lindsey looked at him, and her shoulders sagged. "I have a big decision to make."

"Aye, ye do. But, I commend yer da for giving ye the choice."

Images of Blake and Ainslee flashed through her mind. "And what of ye, Grant? Do ye offer the same to Ainslee?"

His bushy brows scrunched. "I hadn't given it much thought."

"I would ask ye to consider it." A curl flopped onto her face, and she brushed it aside. "We often outgrow traditions. Some need to be changed accordingly, instead of blindly adhering to them regardless of whether they make sense or not."

A strange look passed through Grant's eyes. He glanced down at his wrinkled hands and nodded. "Sound advice."

"And do ye have advice for me?"

He raised his head, and his eyes softened. "Think long and hard before ye accept young Mangus's proposal."

Well, that wasn't much help. What did he think she was doing?

"I've done things I regret and not done things I wish I had." He paused. "With the rare gift yer da granted ye, don't make a rash decision. Search inside yerself, examine yer wishes, yer desires."

"Oftentimes my wishes go against tradition."

His eyes narrowed. "From what I know of ye, Lindsey MacDougall, that has never stopped ye."

~~~

Logan stood on the castle's grey stone battlements. Arms crossed over his chest, he surveyed the quiet bailey. Lightning lit the night sky and thunder rumbled in the distance. Flames leapt from torches lining the ramparts, the wind-whipped blazes matching the fiery turmoil surging through his veins.

Booted footsteps sounded on the stairs behind him. Logan turned as Colyne stepped through the tower door. "Ye needed to speak with me?"

Logan leaned his shoulder against a rampart. "Aye. I want ye to find out all ye can about Mangus MacAndrew—any untoward actions or suspicious behavior. See if ye can determine where his loyalties lie."

"Ye don't trust him?"

Logan paused. "Lindsey considers his proposal, and I simply want to ensure he is as he appears."

"I'll take care of it."

"Take Thom with ye and leave at first light."

Colyne nodded and left, his descending footsteps echoing through the tower.

Rubbing the back of his neck, Logan followed. Hope flickered in his chest. If his men discovered anything questionable surrounding MacAndrew, perhaps it would sway Lindsey's decision to remain at Glencara.

Thoughts of her leaving ripped through his mind, tortured him. How would he get by without her? He loved her. She accepted him for who he was, not giving a whit about titles. He longed to be near her, work beside her and…watch her stomach grow round with his child.

Logan took the keep's back entrance off the garden and skirted the great hall. The last thing he cared to witness was Mangus hovering around Lindsey. Flames from the wall sconces waved in his path as he stormed down the corridor and into the solar, shutting the door behind him. He grabbed a flask and mug off the side table and dropped onto the desk chair.

The mead smelled strong.

Just what he needed.

After pouring a liberal amount, he downed the drink, the burn spreading through his gut welcome. While wiping his mouth on a sleeve, he filled the mug again.

A rap sounded on the door. Not in the mood for idle conversation, he hesitated. "Enter," he finally ground out.

The door opened and closed. Light footsteps sounded behind him, then soft hands rubbed his shoulders. "I thought ye could use some company."

He huffed. "I'm afraid I'm not verrae good company tonight, Githa."

"Ye've got it bad, don't ye?" She eased before him, her hand sliding over his chest and lower between his legs. "Perhaps I can take yer mind off her."

Logan grasped her wrist. "I wouldn't do ye justice, lass."

She sat on the desk's edge and crossed her arms. Her brunette hair fell to her ample bosom. "Ye knew there was a possibility her da would use her to ensure an alliance with his clan." She shrugged. "It's the way of the world."

"I'm aware of the strategic alliance with the MacAndrews." Elbows resting on the chair arms, he cracked his knuckles on one hand, then the other. It would be a good arrangement for both clans.

"Then I fail to see the problem."

His gaze shot to her face.

Fail to see the problem?

The woman I love is considering marrying another man. Hell, he had advised her to do just that. His gut twisted. How he wished he could take back those words, throw caution aside, and wed her.

But at what cost? Would her father disown her for marrying a bastard who had no title, let alone property of his own?

Childhood taunts resurfaced. Often called a leech for his advantageous position as the laird's nephew, would he now hear similar insults that he took advantage of a laird's daughter?

"She's just another lass, Logan." Githa reached out and stroked his thigh. "Ye have many women waiting in line to warm yer bed."

How he wished a good tumble was all he required, but since Lindsey captured his heart, he couldn't go back to the solitary life he had led, drifting from one warm bed to the next.

Logan prayed Colyne and Thom would uncover a reason for his princess to reconsider.

~~~

A week passed with Mangus consuming all of Lindsey's attention. Every time Logan saw her, the cur hovered nearby. His presence chafed like a bloody blister rubbed raw.

Logan hadn't been afforded the opportunity to speak with her, hear her thoughts about MacAndrew's offer. With the amount of time she spent around the man, she obviously gave his proposal serious consideration.

The midday sun beat upon Logan's back. He slammed a mallet against the metal lining the wagon wheel's felloes, flattening it into place. His jaw clenched as he hoisted the repaired wheel and guided the iron rod through the middle hub securing the spokes.

Adam fastened the rusty bolts. "That should hold it."

Logan shook the mounted wheel. "Aye, 'tis sturdy."

The clatter of horse hooves sounded on the hard packed ground. Logan turned as Eric trotted into the outer bailey.

Why was he here?

The man passed several women drawing water from the central well. His horse slowed and weaved between two young lads hauling a wooden cart and Blake, who carried a sack of grain into the stable. Alec's man dismounted and handed a lad his horse's reins.

Logan wiped his hands on his trews and started toward Eric. "Welcome back."

Eric tugged off a glove and extended his hand. "Logan, Adam."

"What brings ye to Glencara?" Logan asked, hands on hips.

"I've a message from yer cousin."

Logan hoped this message conveyed better news than Alec's last missive. "Step inside where we can talk."

He led the way into the keep with Eric and Adam following. The men marched down the dim corridor and into the great hall. A middle-aged woman, her hair wrapped in a white scarf, bent and sprinkled spicy herbs over rushes scattered about the room. A lad with a bucket of sloshing water clutched in each hand, struggled toward several lasses on their hands and knees, scrubbing the floor.

Logan strode through the room and into the solar. He grasped the flask of mead and two mugs from the side table and placed them on the desk as the men sat before him.

Eric filled one of the mugs. Closing his eyes, he gulped the drink. "Ah," he breathed out and swiped his hand across his mouth. "Thank ye."

Leaning back in the chair, Logan focused his attention on the man.

"Alec sends his regards and regrets he was unable to leave MacDougall Castle. Seems he underestimated how difficult it would be to manage both properties."

Understandable. The castles were located miles apart, requiring at least a two-day journey. "While we welcome his visit, ye can assure him Glencara prospers in his absence."

"He has utmost confidence in ye," Eric said. "With the news ye brought of pending attacks, Brandon McLeod has requested a meeting of the clans. Alec asks ye and MacAndrew to attend."

"When and where?" Logan asked.

"In three days at Graham Castle." Eric crossed his arms over his chest. "McLeod has word King Edward's army will strike several locations, including the Firth of Clyde."

"Shite." Adam rubbed his chin. "That's close."

"Aye," Eric agreed. "But with our brethren Scots lying in wait, McLeod intends to stop the Sassenachs before they venture inland."

Logan addressed Adam. "Ready the men. We leave at day break."

Placing his mug on the desk, Adam stood.

"And tell MacAndrew I need to speak to him."

~~~

Late that afternoon, Logan laid his bow and quiver, sword and daggers across the table in his bedchamber. He threw the last of his clothes into his satchel and buckled the leather straps, his thoughts on Lindsey.

It had been days since they had last spoken.

He missed her—missed being around her, watching her work with her beloved horses. Memories of the two of them soaring down the hill together drifted through his mind. He pictured her smiling face when Uncle Grant rode into the bailey, and her moans when Logan had pleasured her luscious body.

He tossed his satchel on the bed and stormed from the room, down the stairs, and into the great hall. His long strides carried him around men, women, and children gathering for the evening meal. He hurried down the steps and marched across the bailey into the stables.

Logan weaved around two lads who dashed down the main aisle with buckets of oats. As he rounded the corner and started down the wing, he heard Lindsey's voice.

"Bless yer heart, Bess."

He paused when he reached the mare's stall. Lindsey ran her hand across the horse's swollen girth.

"I'm surprised she hasn't foaled yet," he said.

Lindsey whirled toward him, her blue eyes wide. "Logan."

Warmth spread over him, and he stepped closer.

"Ah, ye've come to check on the mare?" Mangus lounged against the railing on Bess's other side. He pushed away from the wooden post.

Logan looked to Lindsey. "I'd like to speak to ye."

"Certainly." She moved toward him.

Mangus followed.

Logan held up a hand, blocking his path. "Alone."

Mangus straightened, and his eyes darkened. He stared at Logan, then looked at Lindsey. "As ye wish."

Mangus brushed past him, his shoulder knocking Logan's. It took every ounce of strength Logan could muster to keep from grabbing the churl and slamming his fist into his pompous face. Instead, he turned to Lindsey.

Two lads scurried into Bess's stall, arms laden with fresh straw.

"Come with me." Logan started down the main aisle, and she fell into step beside him. He dodged a man leading a brown draft horse with a flowing dark mane down the aisle and walked into the storeroom. Once she stepped inside, he pushed the door closed.

Light from the window against the far wall filtered into the room, highlighting her fiery tresses. Logan's pulse raced. He reached out and slid his knuckle along her cheek. "I've missed ye, lass."

She placed her hand over his. "And I've missed ye."

He tugged her closer. His arms wrapped around her, and he pulled her against his body, nuzzling her neck and inhaling the lilac scent in her hair. "Just let me hold ye, princess."

Lindsey shook her head. Her palms splayed across his chest, and she pushed against him. "Nay. Stop."

He released her, and she stepped back, pinned him with a glare. "Ye cannot continue to do this to me, Logan."

Ire rose, and his nostrils flared. "Well, ye sure haven't had any problem stepping into *his* arms."

"How dare ye?" She jammed her hands on her hips. "Ye want me, then ye don't. Ye push me into another man's arms, yet ye still want me in yers. What the hell do ye want from me?"

His chest heaved. He searched her blue eyes, sparking with anger. She had exposed the struggle between his brain and heart, his contradictory, irrational actions.

Damn it!

He sighed. "My apologies."

She stood silent and still.

"Have ye come to a decision then?" Good or bad, he had to know.

She hesitated. "I still need time."

Relief swept through him. At least there was a chance she'd refuse MacAndrew's proposal.

"We travel to Graham Castle in the morning." He crossed his arms over his chest. "I know yer sister would enjoy yer company, and I wanted ye to know ye're welcome join us."

She shook her head. "Nay, not this time."

Disappointment replaced relief. Just when he thought he might be making headway, she dashed his hopes.

~~~

The storeroom door swung open, and a lad hurried inside. Startled, the boy jumped. "Begging yer pardon," he said and backed from the room.

Lindsey remained strong as long as she stayed away from Logan, but the second she heard his voice, she melted. Memories of spending the night snuggled against him under his thick cloak ran through her mind. However, with Mangus accompanying Logan to Graham Castle, there would be little chance of another such encounter.

Images of Cameron cradling her infant son with her husband close by convinced Lindsey to remain at Glencara. Given the situation, she could not stomach witnessing the love and affection Robert bestowed on her sister and their bairn.

Nay, she would use this time to make her decision. She looked up at Logan. "Give Cameron my love."

"I will."

Another lad raced into the storeroom. He stopped short when he saw Logan and Lindsey, his eyes wide.

"Come in," Logan said over his shoulder. He paused, watching her. "Kirk will remain here if there is anything ye need."

"How long do ye expect to be away?"

"I'm not certain. Perhaps a week."

"I will pray for yer safe journey."

His gaze slid over her face, sadness reflected in his eyes. He nodded curtly, then turned and marched from the storeroom.

Pain wrenched her gut as if a dagger protruded from it. Clutching her chest, she leaned forward and grasped a shelf. What was she to do? One look from Logan, and her resolve raveled.

This trip was a godsend, a time to make her choice without the pressure of either man.

The lad slammed the lid to the grain barrel, shaking Lindsey from her thoughts. She straightened her tunic and smoothed her hair as she stepped into the barn and made her way to the back of the building.

"Lass?" A strong hand clutched her arm, and she turned toward Mangus.

He seemed to study her face. "Is everything all right?"

"Aye."

"What did he want?"

She shook her head. "He wanted me to know I was welcome to journey with ye to visit my sister."

His brow rose. "And he could not say that in my presence?"

"Mangus…"

"Obviously, he doesn't understand the serious nature of our relationship." He placed his finger under her chin and tilted her head up. "Ye've had enough time to ponder my proposal. I will have yer answer upon our return."

Chapter Seventeen

Graham Castle
December 1299

Logan's legs gripped Sterling's sides as the black horse trotted down a pine-needled path winding through the dense forest bordering Graham Castle. The evening sun highlighted barren trees. Their skeletal limbs, sprinkled with snow, stood in stark contrast to the green pines. Wind swept through the treetops, tossing icy crystals into the air. The trail opened onto a field of winter grasses with patches of snow and ice scattered in low lying areas.

Logan held up a hand and reined in Sterling. The horse tossed his head and snorted as Eric and Adam stopped beside him.

Graham Castle stood at the top of a steep hill. Large torches blazed bright into the darkening sky. A steady stream of riders, gathering for McLeod's meeting, made their way toward the castle. Solid battlements, secured behind grey stone, ran across outer gates surrounding the fortress. Even at this distance, he spotted a number of guards marching along the ramparts. With many clans congregated in one location, Robert Graham would be extra vigilant.

"Men from all over the country have arrived."

Logan bristled at Mangus's voice. For the past two days, the cur had been a constant irritant. He spurred Sterling up the hill and onto the dirt path winding through the village at the base of the castle. Small thatched huts lined the road with candlelight slipping through the wooden window slats. Two scruffy dogs barked and chased the men into the crowded bailey. Stablehands weaved through the boisterous throng as they led incoming horses into the barn.

Clans, some garbed in red and black kilts, while others sported plaids in hues of blue, green, and gold, filled the cramped space. Others donned thick, brown padding over rugged buckskin trews, leather straps crisscrossing their torsos. All sported swords dangling at their sides and daggers affixed to their belts.

Logan, Eric, and Adam dismounted; Mangus and his men did the same. Two lads hurried to them and took the animals' reins.

"Ye made good time."

Logan turned and tugged off his gloves as Alec strode toward them. "Aye, the weather held better than expected."

"MacAndrew." His cousin tipped his head toward the man. "'Tis good ye were still at Glencara. We need support from the Highlands."

"My clan stands ready," Mangus replied.

"Brandon just arrived, and the meeting will start shortly," Alec said. "Follow me."

The group climbed the bailey stairs and entered the keep. Rambunctious conversation and laughter resounded from the great hall as they marched into the spacious room. Women and lasses scurried amongst the gathered clans, serving ale and setting out platters of fresh baked bread, roasted boar, and venison.

Logan grasped a tankard of mead from a passing servant's tray. The blonde paused and smiled prettily, then offered drinks to Adam and Eric as well.

Taking a swig, Logan glanced over the tankard at Mangus and his men. They sat across the room next to the Cranstoun clan. MacAndrew laughed at something Laird Cranstoun said. He held up a mug as if in a toast, then downed the contents.

Someone clutched Logan's shoulder. "It's been a long time."

He turned to his right. Laird McCarthy extended his hand, and Logan grasped it. "Buford, how are ye?"

"We've suffered our share of grief, but overall the clan does well."

"Robert informed us of the attacks ye've experienced."

Deep furrows creased the old laird's face, and thin greyish-white hair hung in strands to his shoulders. He folded his arms across his chest. "With the castle located on the Firth of Clyde, the Sassenachs tried to overthrow us and use our home to attain a solid foothold into the country. It would've provided an excellent base from which to run their unscrupulous campaign."

Logan rubbed his neck. "I'm relieved to hear they didn't succeed."

"If it hadn't have been for Robert, I'm afraid the outcome would've been different," Buford responded. "We're on constant alert. Just last week, one of my men spotted two of Edward's ships sailing up the coast."

"The cur's determined to overthrow us, grind us under his heel."

"I worry he will, little by little." Buford shook his head. "On our journey here, we came upon a burned out village. I assume it was Edward's soldiers who attacked. We didn't find any survivors to tell us differently. Bloated bodies and charred corpses lay on the road, most unrecognizable. Women had been raped, their throats slit."

Logan's gut roiled. Images of Lindsey, bloodied and bruised, flashed before his mind. He'd left Kirk in charge. The trustworthy man would protect the clan with his life, but even the most skillful warriors could be bested. He shook off the foreboding. Glencara Castle was a solid fortress. Lindsey would be safe behind its stalwart walls.

"Good evening."

The deep voice quieted the crowd.

Arms crossing his chest, Brandon McLeod stood on the dais's raised platform at the front of the room. Creases splayed from the edges of his brown eyes and grey streaked his dark hair. His gaze skimmed the assembled clans, the men's attention focused on him.

"King Edward prepares to invade our homeland." McLeod looked at Logan. "Thanks to Ross, we've uncovered the churl's plans."

MacAndrew glanced over his shoulder and nodded at Logan.

"They amass victuals in the counties between the mouth of the Thames and Berwick. Under the threat of imprisonment in The Tower, King Edward forces Sassenachs to march on our borders." Brandon paused. "We will meet the scum and give them a proper welcome to Scotland."

"Hear, hear!" Men jumped to their feet. Others pounded on the tables. Vehement shouts and loud applause echoed through the hall.

~~~

Later that night, the meeting adjourned. Brandon McLeod had been successful. He'd garnered support from every clan present. With plans in place, assignments made, and preparations underway, the group broke apart. Some chose to spend the evening camped close by while others departed for the long trip home.

Logan leaned back in a chair before the great hall's hearth and stretched his legs. Robert strode through the door with Alec, McLeod, and MacAndrew.

"How are ye, Ross?" Brandon clapped Logan on the shoulder and extended his hand. "It's been far too long since I last laid eyes on yer ugly mug."

Logan chuckled. "I'm well."

Brandon dropped onto a chair. "Can't thank ye enough for the information."

Robert offered Brandon a tankard of mead, and the commander nodded while accepting the drink. Alec and Mangus sat to McLeod's right.

"I was surprised when I heard the English intended to land that far north," Logan said.

The commander rubbed his chin. "I just received word enemy soldiers destroyed a village farther north, near the Highlands. Every man, woman, and child were hung and left for the animals to pick their bones."

Silence filled the room. The fire crackled, and a log rolled in the hearth, sending red and gold sparks swirling up the chimney. Memories of Collins's brutality and possibilities of what he would inflict on small towns flooded Logan's mind.

"Here we are." Cameron glided into the hall with her toddler balanced on her hip. Although dark tresses fell to her waist and green eyes peered at him, similarities to Lindsey once again surfaced. They shared the same smile, the same pert nose.

She slid onto the bench next to Robert. The wee lad climbed onto his da's lap, plopped down, and stuck his thumb in his mouth. Robert placed his arm around Cameron as she brushed the dark hair from baby Douglas's eyes.

Logan's gut clenched. What would it be like to have his son snuggled on his lap with Lindsey curled up beside him?

"How goes the betrothal?" Alec's words had the effect of a good dunking in frigid water.

Mangus glanced up. "As of yet, there is no betrothal."

"What?" Alec's sharp glare cut to Logan.

"We've spent time over the past weeks getting acquainted while she considers my proposal." MacAndrew smirked. "We've enjoyed many hours traversing yer beautiful land, Alec."

Cameron leaned against Robert, and he stroked her arm. "Aye, Da granted my sisters and me the privilege of having the husband of our choice."

"How long does my sister-in-law intend to ponder her decision?" Alec asked.

"I will have her answer upon our return."

Bile roiled in Logan's stomach.

How could he let her walk away?

~~~

After a sleepless night of tossing and turning, Logan threw his legs over the side of the bed and rubbed his whiskered face. If Lindsey decided to leave with MacAndrew, Logan would join forces with McLeod. Perhaps he'd hire out his sword arm and amass enough coin to purchase a plot of land. He'd find a woman to warm his bed, provide him sons, and care for his home.

The plan should offer some comfort. But his chest clenched at the thought of living without his princess; never again seeing her cheerful face, listening to her expound upon her horses, and witnessing her tenacious spirit and courage.

He took a deep breath and strode to a basin on the side table. After washing and dressing, he grabbed his satchel, and started toward the great hall.

"Good morn," Alec called, waiting at the bottom of the stairs.

"Alec." Logan walked down the steps.

"I just received a missive to return to MacDougall Castle straight away, and I need ye to stop there on yer way back to Glencara."

"Why?"

Alec turned, and they headed down the corridor to the main hall. "There's a man at the keep who wants to journey with ye. I'd like ye to see to his safe passage."

Logan's eyes narrowed. "Who the hell is he?"

Alec stopped and faced him. "An English commander in Edward's army."

"Yer joke is not amusing."

"'Tis no joke. He wants to see Skena and has requested safe passage across MacDougall land to Glencara."

Skena? Logan would be damned if an English commander would get anywhere close to her. He jammed his hands on his hips. "How does he know Skena? What the hell does he want with her?"

Alec straightened. "The commander is the father of Skena's child."

A blow to the gut from a battering ram could not have been more powerful. The look on her face when Logan had asked about the bairn's da flashed through his mind. She had a babe with English scum?

Logan frowned. "I can't believe what I'm hearing."

"Believe it. The maid is obviously in love with him, and it's evident he feels the same." Alec glanced around behind him and continued. "In exchange for protection of Skena and their child, the commander has kept English patrols from harassing us. He is to arrive at MacDougall Castle today and will await yer escort to Glencara."

"Ye're asking a lot." Logan's lip curled. "I don't like the idea of traveling with an English convoy."

"Ye have no choice." Alec's eyes darkened. "We have a special arrangement, and our relationship is tenuous at best."

Cameron stepped into the corridor. "Gentlemen, please join us to break yer fast before ye leave."

~~~

"Logan. Laird MacAndrew. Welcome to MacDougall Castle." Heather stepped up to the men as they shed their cloaks and handed them to the lass who greeted them at the door.

"Thank ye, Lady Campbell." MacAndrew nodded at her. "We appreciate yer hospitality."

"Alec just went in to see Commander Taylor. Please join them in the hall and rest before the hearth."

Logan's body stiffened. He couldn't believe Alec had talked him into doing this.

Heather led them down the main corridor and into the great room. She swept her arm toward chairs placed in front of the fireplace as she looked at Logan and MacAndrew. A stern warning reflected in her eyes. "Dinner will be served shortly."

This was the one time he would band with MacAndrew, both men disgruntled at the thought of traveling with English soldiers. They walked into the room, and Alec met them.

"Commander Taylor arrived this afternoon." He turned to the man. "Commander, this is my cousin, Logan Ross, and Laird Mangus MacAndrew, a longtime friend."

Taylor stood and extended his hand. "Call me Barclay."

Logan wanted to sneer and spit on his boots. Instead, he used great restraint as he grasped the man's outstretched hand.

Taylor's arm swung out, indicating the chairs beside him. "Please, sit."

Logan dropped onto a wooden bench and stretched his legs. A lass handed him a large tankard of ale. As he took a swig, he gazed over the rim at Heather. She kissed Alec's cheek and whispered something in his ear.

Witnessing the domestic scene caused thoughts of Lindsey to surface. Shite, when did he not think of her?

"Barclay would like to visit Glencara so yer trip is timely," Alec said.

The commander looked at Logan. "You're returning soon?"

"At first light."

Taylor's brow rose. "That soon?"

"Aye."

"Very well. We'll accompany you in the morning. If you'll excuse me I'll inform my men."

"Heather has prepared a room for ye." Alec straightened. "Let me show ye which one."

The commander placed his empty tankard on the table and marched across the hall with Alec.

Logan watched the man as he climbed the stairs. Had he battled any of the soldiers he would escort? Had any of them tortured him or his men at Northumberland? He balanced his tankard on his thigh and looked at MacAndrew. "Keep yer eyes open. I don't like this."

"Nay, it rubs against the grain." MacAndrew glanced around the hall.

Logan agreed. "Stay close and alert yer men. We won't be caught off guard."

Chapter Eighteen

Glencara Castle

Frigid air swirled around Lindsey's neck as she stepped from the keep. The cold slithered over her body. She shoved her arms into a coarse woolen cloak and blew warm breath on her hands as she trotted down the bailey stairs.

Dawn had yet to break. Flames from torches lining the thick castle walls, whipped into a frenzy by the icy wind, blazed into the dark sky. The gust's lonesome whistle echoed through the empty yard. She wrapped her arms around her middle and hurried into the stables.

Frustrated after suffering a restless night, agonizing over her decision, she had donned her clothes and looked forward to spending time with her cherished horses. She strolled over to Blaze and he whinnied.

"Good morn." He pushed his bowed head against her, and she rubbed between his ears. "Ye like that, don't ye?" Slipping a slice of apple from her tunic, Logan's teasing drifted through her mind, and she inwardly smiled. "Oh Blaze, what am I going to do?"

Sighing, she patted him, ducked under the pen's rope, and strolled down the aisle to the back of the quiet barn. Desperately needing the reprieve work always afforded, she climbed the ladder to the rafters where an area had been sectioned off for storage. A musty smell wafted from stacked hay bales filling the platform. A narrow walkway wound between the bundles of rope, shovels, and rakes leaning against the back wall.

A soft mewling sound caught her attention. She paused, her gaze skimming the area. Upon hearing it again, she squeezed through a small opening in the bales. Just on the other side, a black and tan cat nursing four kittens lay nestled in the hay.

"Well, look at ye." She made her way to the animals. The cat purred and stretched her neck so Lindsey could stroke her head. "Four wee ones. How precious."

She sat beside them and ran her fingers over the soft furry kittens. The humming cadence of contentment rumbled from each as they kneaded the mother with sharp little claws. Lindsey curled up beside them to watch the sweet scene. Her lids grew heavy. Closing her eyes, she thought to rest them for a moment.

She jarred awake at the sound of clashing metal and men shouting. She rubbed her eyes and scooted over to the slats in the barn's wall.

Edward's soldiers stormed the bailey like ants swarming a disturbed mound. An armor-clad assailant plunged his sword into a man's gut. The injured man fell to his knees, and the fiend jerked the blade from his body.

Blood dripped from his weapon as he turned and swung the sharp edge across another's belly. Clanging swords, screams, and yells reverberated through the bailey. Women and children stumbled from the keep. British guards followed and shoved them down the stairs into the yard. Wails and frightened cries filled the air as the group clad in nightclothes, huddled together against the far wall.

Kirk shouted orders and raced through the bailey. A soldier charged him. Kirk swung his sword. He forced the man back, relentlessly slamming his blade against the attacker's shield.

Heart racing, Lindsey squeezed through the straw and darted to the ladder. She grasped the wooden frame.

English soldiers combed the stables below.

Shite! She ducked out of sight. Her pulse pounded in her ears as she scampered back between the hay stacks. Jerking bales together, she closed off the entrance.

Men's voices grew close.

The ladder creaked.

Holding her breath, she pressed her body against the straw.

Heavy footsteps landed on the wooden planks. Hands trembling, she peered through a slight opening. Two soldiers jabbed their swords into the haystacks as they moved across the platform toward her. She frantically searched the area for a place to hide, safe from the sharp blades' thrust.

A loud crash sounded in the bailey. She swung back to the small opening and peeked through. The soldiers leaned over the railing, their attention on the commotion. "Come on, there's nothing up here."

They turned and descended the ladder.

Lindsey collapsed against the hay, her chest heaving. That was close. Too close. She swallowed hard, then took a deep breath and scooted back over to the wall.

The clank of steel clashed to her right. Kirk swung his sword, both hands clutching the hilt. Two men circled him, their blades driving perilously close to his chest. The captain lunged. One of the men slammed his shield on Kirk's arm, causing his sword to clatter to the ground. The soldiers grasped him. He fought against them as they dragged him to the middle of the bailey.

Lindsey sat powerless to help.

The battle ended abruptly. Bodies littered the ground. Crying children huddled next to their mums, their frightened tear-streaked faces smeared with dirt and ash. Old men and young lads had been tied together while the injured were under guard. Acrid smoke filled the air. She turned to the right. Flames leapt around a wagon full of hay, the dry fibers igniting a blaze.

How had this happened? How had the Sassenachs broken through their defenses?

Two soldiers held Kirk at the point of their swords. An English commander riding a black destrier paraded through the main gate toward them. He studied the bailey before dismounting and strolling over to them. The man stared at Kirk, and then turned and scanned the clan members. "Where is he?" he asked, his voice menacing. "Answer me!"

"We didn't find him, sir."

The commander rounded on the man. "What do you mean, you didn't find him?"

The soldier shoved Kirk forward. "This one seems to be in charge."

Lindsey strained to hear.

"Where's Logan Ross?"

She gasped. How does this man know Logan? Who is he?

Kirk reached into his tunic and fished out a parchment. "Glencara's under the protection of Commander Taylor. I demand ye leave at once."

The man snatched the parchment and ripped it into small pieces. The fragments fluttered to the ground. "Does that show you how much your *protection* means?"

He flipped a dagger from his belt and held it to Kirk's throat. "Now ye will tell me. Where are Logan Ross and Linds MacDougall?"

Linds? Lindsey's eyes widened. *He thinks I'm a lad.* She leaned closer to the slats and studied him. She didn't recognize him. How did he know her as Linds?

"They're not here."

Her fingers gripped the wooden boards, her pulse pounding in her ears.

Blood trickled down Kirk's neck.

"Where are they?" the commander yelled, eyes bulging from his red face. "I have it on good authority Ross and the boy reside here."

"They left for Kilmarnock several days ago."

"You had better not be lying."

What English commander would know her and Logan? Thoughts whirled through Lindsey's mind. The

Dumfries horse race. She strained to get a better look at the man. Her breath caught. She jerked away from the slats, her hand clutching her chest.

Collins.

Tentacles of fear snaked through her insides. Had he tracked them all the way from Northumberland? Nightmares of his torturous questioning techniques and terrifying dungeon resurfaced. She couldn't breathe. It was as if the barn's pulleys squeezed the life from her. What torment did this fiend plan for the Glencara clan?

"I want this place searched. Ye will bring Ross and MacDougall to me at once!"

Lindsey eased on her knees and peered down at the crowded bailey. What had happened to Grant, Ainslee, and Maria? She frantically skimmed the crowd. She leaned to the left and searched another group. Where were they? Women and lasses who worked in the kitchen were bunched together, but where was Maria? Could she have escaped with Logan's uncle, Ainslee, and Skena? *Nay.* They wouldn't have been able to carry Grant from the keep.

A stocky soldier marched across the bailey and over to Collins. "Ross and MacDougall will return. We're in good position to catch them when they arrive. The castle is secure. Now we wait."

Collins rotated on his heel and stormed up the stairs. When he disappeared into the keep, Lindsey sagged against the wall, her mind racing. She had to warn Logan and get help, but she couldn't just ride out of here. It would be best to wait until dark.

In the meantime, she needed to secure a weapon. Unlike her bedchamber, the barn didn't contain swords or daggers. But this platform had farming tools. Hope surged through her as she eased through the bales, her gaze searching the area for soldiers. All was clear. She slipped across the planked walkway.

Rakes and shovels leaned against the wall. She picked up a scythe and turned it over. The long handle would be hard to swing in close quarters. She replaced it, and her fingers touched a sickle then a spade, but both were just as unwieldy.

An axe rested in the shadows. Her fingers coiled around the wooden handle. She signed with relief, then glimpsed over the platform's edge. Several soldiers leaned against the door at the front of the barn. She craned her neck, looking throughout the building for others. One stood at the back door. Apparently, the men were stationed to prevent anyone from gaining access to the horses and leaving. If only she could get to Blaze...

Having to wait until darkness would be hard, but she had no other choice. She inched back between the bales and considered her options. Logan and Mangus would return any day now. She had to reach them, warn them, and make plans to rescue the clan members.

Knees drawn to her chest, she wrapped her arms around her legs and prayed God would be with them.

~~~

Darkness finally descended on Glencara Castle. Torchlight from the bailey shined into the dim stable. Clutching the axe, Lindsey studied the man at the barn's back door. Arms folded, he leaned against the wooden frame, his legs crossed at the ankles.

She turned and searched the front of the building. Several men milled around. One clapped another on the shoulder, and they all laughed.

It was time.

Her foot eased onto the rung. The wood creaked. She froze. Her heart hammered, her pulse pounding loudly in her ears. Hands trembling, she turned and grasped the rough ladder. Glancing to the right and left, she descended.

Finally, she stepped onto the ground and ducked into a roped pen. Weaving between horses, she made her way to Blaze. He nickered as she grabbed a bridle from the nail on the side of the stall and slipped it over his ears and tied it under his jaw. Talking softly, she slowly led him through tangle of animals.

"Easy," she whispered and patted horses' hindquarters while slipping to the back of the barn and praying they would not create unwanted attention. As she neared the door, she looped Blaze's reins over a board and eased back under the rope.

Her fist gripped the wooden axe handle. Could she do this? She had never snuck up behind someone and bludgeoned them. Her body trembled.

The soldier's back loomed in front of her. She glanced past him. The alleyway behind the barn was clear.

It was now or never.

Nerves jangling, she crept behind him and swung the axe. The blunted heel slammed into his head, and the soldier crumpled to the ground. Panic-stricken, her eyes darted back and forth. When no one sounded an alarm, she hurried back into the barn, and scrambled onto Blaze's back.

She nudged him out the back door and around the side of the stable where a narrow alleyway ran the length of the bailey's stone wall. If she could make it to the far end, she'd stay hidden from view and only expose herself at the main gate.

Rubbing her sweaty palms, she took a deep breath and urged Blaze forward. Just as they reached the end of the passageway, a voice boomed in the bailey.

Collins.

Crouching low over Blaze, she stroked his neck. "All right, lad. Give me everything ye've got."

She dug her heels into his sides, and he charged around the stable and into the bailey.

Collins's glare met hers, and his eyes narrowed. "What the hell?"

Shite!

"That's Linds!" he shouted.

"Catch him," someone hollered.

She spared a glimpse over her shoulder as Collins and his men ran to their horses.

Lindsey pulled the reins to the right. Blaze veered past the guardhouses, across the wooden bridge, and down the dirt road leading to the village.

The sound of hooves thundered from the bailey.

She laid flat against Blaze and wrapped her arms around his neck, praying they'd escape. The young stallion's powerful hindquarters propelled them forward. The wind bit into her face, and a stream of tears streaked from the corners of her eyes as Blaze dashed off the road, across the field, and into the dense woods.

Angry shouts rang out behind them.

The horse sprinted down the narrow dirt path. A branch loomed ahead. At the last second, he veered to the side. Spiky needles scraped her shoulder as he careened by a tree's low slung branches.

An arrow whistled next to her ear and struck the tree ahead. Another, then another whizzed past. "Don't lose him!"

Stampeding hooves resounded.

They grew closer.

Lindsey slapped Blaze's hindquarters with the reins. "Come on, lad!"

Memories of Grant's outing filtered through her panicked mind. To the left, hidden caverns sunk into the rugged terrain. The thicket marking the cave's entrance was just ahead. She swerved off the path. Blaze lurched up the steep embankment, hooves digging into the rocky surface, pebbles skittering down the hill.

Massive grey boulders hid the tight opening. Blaze slowed, and they squeezed through the passageway. She jerked her legs up, placing her feet on his back before his sides scraped the rocks. They stepped into a vast dark space. Frigid air surrounded them, and Blaze's heaving sides produced foggy plumes wafting on the breeze.

Men's shouts were close.

The sound of sliding rocks grew loud.

Damn! They were just outside.

Blaze's head jerked up, and his ears shot backward.

"Easy." Her body trembled as she patted his sleek neck. "Easy, lad."

She nudged him farther into the cave. He slipped, and she gasped. Gaining his footing, he moved forward a few more feet.

Light from the passageway dimmed.

Someone blocked the path.

She held her breath, her eyes focused on the cave's entrance.

"No, he couldn't have come this way," a man yelled. "The entrance is too small to enter."

Once again, light filtered into the dark space with the sound of retreating hooves.

Shaking, Lindsey swiped her forearm across her face. She now had her chance to get help. Logan said they'd be back within the week and that was any day now. With any luck, she'd meet on their way home.

Taking a deep breath, she nudged Blaze back through the narrow opening. She craned her neck to the left.

All was quiet.

Urging him down the steep hill, Lindsey's gaze shot through the dense woods. Once back on the path, she dug her heels into his sides, and he dashed back towards Glencara, then turned southwest to Graham Castle.

Chapter Nineteen

On the Road to Glencara Castle

Two days traveling alongside Sassenachs made Logan irritable. Dusk had descended, but the group forged ahead with only miles to go before they reached Glencara. It would not be soon enough until he rid himself of the blackguards.

Disbelief over Skena, a woman he cared for as a sister, lying beneath the enemy turned his stomach. Betrayal washed over him.

Riding alongside Barclay Taylor, Logan studied the man who had fathered Skena's child. Back straight, the commander rode high in the saddle. A grey plated helmet shielded his head, flaps on either side brushing his shoulders. Chain mail covered his neck and disappeared beneath a golden tunic, Edward's red lion emblazoned across the torso. Woven metal chinks enveloped his arms, and ties crisscrossed his black leather boots.

Alec considered the man trustworthy. But after enduring torture at the hands of Edward's minions, Logan would never accept anyone who supported the ruthless king.

Animosity simmered in his blood. Flanked by MacAndrew and Taylor, Logan fought to control the hostility coursing through his body. Not only did he suffer the company of his nemesis as each step taken brought them closer to Lindsey's departure, he had to tolerate a dozen Sassenachs cloaked in armor, trailing him.

Movement ahead caught his eye.

A lone rider streaked across the pasture below. The horse's hooves pummeled the hard packed earth. Logan squinted in the darkness, straining to see who rode as if the fires of hell singed their arse.

A thunderous rumble sounded, vibrating the ground.

He held up a hand and stopped the procession. Three men on horses dashed from the dark woods and sprinted after the rider.

As the first rider drew near, a mass of auburn tresses came into view.

His heart slammed against his chest.

"That's Lindsey!" Logan cracked the reins over Sterling's hindquarters and the horse shot forward. The rumble of hooves sounded behind him as he tore down the field.

Lindsey raced toward them. "It's Collins!"

Her words crashed over him. The fiend chased his princess. Burning vengeance coursed through his veins.

"Keep running," Logan yelled as he passed her. He had dreamed of this day, the chance to beat the man senseless and end his miserable life, to avenge fellow Scots who suffered Collins's brutality.

Sterling bore down on the commander.

Collins bellowed a battle cry, his beady eyes glowering.

Still on Sterling, Logan raised his sword over his head and brought it down on Collins's shield, knocking him to the dirt. Sterling slowed, and Logan dropped to the ground. Before Collins could recover, Logan kicked him in the face. The man's helmet flew from his head. "Get up and fight ye worthless cur!"

The fiend rolled to the side and surged to his feet, calling to his men, "Get him!"

The two soldiers charged. Logan could feel a man at his back. Was that MacAndrew fighting with him? Shouts and clashing swords sounded around Logan, but he concentrated on Collins. He would finally have retribution.

The commander sneered. He sprang forward and slashed his sword to the right.

Logan hopped back.

The man lunged, his thrusts wild.

Logan ducked and avoided a swing to his head. He rose up and slammed his blade against Collins's chest. Vibrations rippled down Logan's arms. His grasp on the hilt slipped, but he regained control, swung again and knocked the cur's weapon from his hands.

The commander's sword clattered to the ground as he fell over backward and landed hard. Blood poured from a gash on his head. He struggled to get up, but his weary limbs couldn't lift the weight of his armor.

Hatred filled Logan as he stood over Collins.

Fear flashed in the man's eyes.

Fists clutching the hilt, Logan raised his sword.

"Stop!" Commander Taylor rushed to Logan's side. "You *don't* want to kill an English field marshal."

Memories of Logan's arms stretched between two poles, his toes scraping the floor, and his back bared for Collins's savage beatings surfaced. He could still feel the searing pain from festering pockets of infection, a result of the whip's chinks biting into muscle. Images of his men's raw furrowed skin, bloody and bruised, flashed before his mind. Their pleas for mercy had fallen on deaf ears. Rather, they fueled Collins's barbaric questioning techniques.

"Aye, I do. Although death is too easy an end for this miserable bastard for the torture he inflicted on me, on my men, all the Scots he killed senselessly."

He aimed the sharp tip of his blade at Collins's neck, a weak spot above his chest plate. "How does it feel to be helpless? At my mercy?"

Collins's eyes scrunched, and he cried, "Have mercy."

"Mercy?" Logan repeated. "Did ye acknowledge my men's pleas?"

"The commander's right, don't do this," MacAndrew asserted.

Thoughts of depraved acts the miscreant might have inflicted on Lindsey had the scum caught her flooded his mind. Without looking away from Collins, Logan asked, "What would have happed to Lindsey if this monster had caught her?"

"He didn't," MacAndrew softly said.

It would be so easy to thrust his sword, bury it into the man's black heart. He wanted to, had dreamed of it for months.

Time stood still.

Panic emanated from Collins's eyes.

"Logan?"

Damn, it was Lindsey.

Shite! He couldn't kill the man with her watching. Inwardly he screamed against the injustice, the unfulfilled retribution. How ironic Logan would have to rely on an English Commander to deliver the Scots' vengeance.

"Logan, please."

Her plea struck his stomach, twisted his gut. Chest heaving, he lowered his sword.

Taylor shouted orders to his men. "Bring him to the castle."

The English soldiers dragged Collins to his horse.

Logan straightened and took a deep breath. He glanced around for Lindsey, not knowing from where she'd spoken. She stood beside Blaze with one of Taylor's men protecting her. Their eyes met, and an unspoken empathetic message passed between them.

As Logan turned, he froze.

Adam lay unmoving in the grass.

Oh, God.

He ran to him and knelt at his friend's side. A flap of skin hung from a gash in his scalp, and blood covered his face and chest. Logan touched the pulse point at his neck. Weak and faint, but it beat.

"I need help," Logan shouted.

Two of Taylor's men hurried to Adam. Logan grasped him under the arms, and with the soldiers' help they carried him to his horse. As the men secured Adam for the ride to Glencara, Logan stepped back.

"Ye're all right?" Blood splattered MacAndrew's face and clothes.

The man had fought at Logan's back. "Aye."

As the laird started to move away, Logan extended his hand. "Thank ye."

MacAndrew hesitated, then with a nod, accepted his offer.

Lindsey ran over to them, tears in her eyes. "Ye must hurry."

"What's wrong?" Logan asked.

"Collins attacked Glencara at sunrise. His men control the castle."

"How'd they get in?"

"I don't know." She shook her head. "It was dark...I...I didn't see them until they were inside the walls."

"What about Skena and the babe?" a deep voice demanded.

Lindsey whirled toward Taylor. "Skena?"

"Yes, are she and the child all right?"

A look of horror passed over Lindsey's pale face. "I didn't see them," she whispered.

Taylor's mouth drew into a tight line. He grasped his horse's reins and sprang onto the saddle. "How far to the castle?"

"A few miles." Logan swung onto Sterling's back as Lindsey ran to Blaze. "I need some of yer men to stay with Lindsey outside the castle walls. I won't have her in danger."

Taylor signaled two of his men. "She'll be safe."

"Let's ride."

He spurred Sterling and led the thundering horses from the field. Minutes later, they bolted across the bridge and inside the castle walls. A piercing clang of steel rang out as clashing weapons collided. Shouts and bellows resounded. Red and orange blazes leapt into the sky with dark plumes billowing from the barracks. The small chapel smoldered, and flames flickered around the burnt ruins. A thick acrid stench clogged his nose and burned his eyes.

A burly soldier swung his sword at a scrawny lad. The boy thrust his shield. He blocked the strike but stumbled backward and fell. Barely managing to contain his fury, Logan leapt from his horse and ran to defend the lad. He slammed his blade upon the assailant's arm. The man's weapon skittered across the ground, and Logan sank his sword into the churl's gut.

Another charged. Logan jumped to the side. The man's momentum propelled him forward. Logan hooked the fiend's foot and caused the soldier to lose his balance. Logan turned and brought his elbow down on the attacker's back. The man dropped to his knees.

"Cease!" Taylor stormed into the melee. He grabbed a soldier's shoulder, then another. "Halt. Now!"

The fight ended abruptly.

Breathing heavy, Logan stared at the yard. Injured and dying men moaned. Lifeless bodies lay scattered across the ground. The senseless killing and maiming caused bile to billow into his throat. The clan had depended on his protection, and he'd failed them. A wave of despair crashed over him. Once again Collins struck Logan through the attack on his home, on his people. How he would relish the opportunity to rip the man apart with his bare hands.

Taylor marched over to Collins and jerked him from his horse. Hands tied behind his back, the commander fell to the dirt. "What's the meaning of this?" Taylor yelled. "Who gave you orders to attack this castle?"

Collins sneered as he struggled to sit. "I make my own orders to secure Scotland for Edward!"

Logan's fists clenched. An overpowering urge to beat the fiend surged, and he struggled to suppress it.

Taylor back handed Collins. "This castle and the inhabitants within it are under *my* protection, Field Marshal Collins." His glare skimmed the crowd. "I am Commander Barclay Taylor of Edward's Elite army. Let it be known, I represent King Edward I and through me, these lands receive his protection." He glowered at Collins. "Lock him up!"

Taylor's men grabbed the English cur and dragged him away.

With the castle under control, Lindsey rode Blaze into the bailey behind Taylor's soldiers. Logan stepped to her and helped her dismount. His hands lingered on her waist as he searched her face. "Ye are well?"

"Aye."

MacAndrew joined them. His eyes narrowed with concern. "Ye're sure ye weren't hurt?"

She moved away from Logan and shook her head. "I managed to hide. They never saw me until I bolted."

MacAndrew clutched her shoulder. "I'm verrae relieved to hear it, lass."

Lindsey turned toward the stable. Blake leaned against the central doorframe holding his side. She gasped and ran to him with Logan close behind. Blood soaked his tunic and covered his leg, but he grinned. "We put up a hell of a fight."

"Ye're hurt." Her frantic gaze searched him.

He held up a hand. "'Tis only a few scratches."

"I thought the English controlled the castle?" Logan asked.

Blake nodded. "They did until we rose up against them."

His back slid down the wall, and Logan caught him. "Come on, lad. Let's get ye inside."

Lindsey's eyes filled with worry and dread. "Have ye seen Grant, Ainslee, and Skena? What about Maria?"

Blake winked. "I hid them."

His body sagged. Logan braced his shoulder underneath Blake's arm and clutched his waist. Half carrying him, Logan helped the lad across the bailey. Weaving amongst the injured men and smoldering debris, he trudged through the yard. Lindsey ran ahead of them as they climbed the keep's stairs. They continued to the great hall where Githa issued orders to place pallets and mattresses around the room. No sooner had the young lads toted in a makeshift bed, than an injured clansman dropped onto it.

Lindsey stopped at an empty mattress against the far wall. "Lie down here," she said and reached for her friend.

"Nay." Blake moaned. "I have to get Ainslee. I told her not to move until I came for her."

Logan eased him onto the pallet. "Where did ye hide them?"

Sweat trickled down Blake's temple, and his eyes scrunched. "In the secret room off the solar."

~~~

Relief had poured over Logan upon finding Ainslee, Maria, Skena, and her bairn huddled around his uncle in the cramped, hidden space off the solar. After settling Grant in his bedchamber, Logan marched down the keep's stairs and across the yard filled with wounded men and lads. Women coaxed those who could walk into the keep, while men carried those who could not make it on their own.

He skirted past stablehands who ran with buckets of water toward a multitude of fires blazing throughout the bailey. Two men lugged a wounded clansman between them, the man's listless body covered in blood.

Logan's gut clenched. If only he had been here. If only he had gone after Collins as he had first planned, perhaps his clan would have been spared.

Choking smoke clouded the bailey. He waved the offensive fog from his face and skimmed the area. Nigel, leaning against the well with his legs sprawled before him, held his side and groaned. Logan's chest pinched. The man had grown up with Logan and Alec.

Logan stooped beside his friend. Blood trickled from a cut on the stalwart warrior's forehead, his skin's greyish-pallor worrisome. Sweat covered his face, his breathing labored. Logan clutched the man's shoulder. "Hold on. We'll get ye inside so Maria can treat ye."

Logan whistled and motioned for Kirk to come over.

"Laird MacAndrew has readied an area outside the barracks for the overflow of wounded," Kirk said.

Logan looked over his shoulder at MacAndrew. He carried an injured man and placed him on a pallet. He knelt over the man and clutched his shoulder, then straightened and stormed back to the wounded.

"All right, we'll take him there," Logan said, and the men lifted Nigel. Together, they hauled the hefty man across the yard. Numerous warriors lay on mattresses, some with severe burns, others with sword wounds. Several women scurried between them, administering salves and tonics. Logan and Kirk weaved around the crowded space and found an empty bed. When they laid Nigel down, his face scrunched.

Logan clutched his friend's arm. "I'll ask someone to tend ye, give ye a potion to lessen yer pain."

"Thank ye," Nigel breathed out.

Logan made his way through the throng of wounded, stopping to check on the men as he went. After informing one of the women of Nigel's pain, he strode back into the bailey. Darkness had descended on the men and women trying to aid their clansmen, regroup, and put the castle in order. As Logan marched past the smokehouse, a pair of small boots on the other side of a water barrel caught his eye.

He changed direction and peered around the back of the container. Roderick, a lad of no more than twelve years, lay in the dirt, his legs positioned at an odd angle. A frozen stare held his last moments, his widened brown eyes no longer filled with life. The boy had worked in the stables alongside his grandfather, Harold.

Logan stooped beside Roderick and closed the lad's eyes. His heart broke as he gathered him in his arms and started toward the grandfather's cabin. How would he tell Harold his young grandson had been struck down? With no answers coming to mind, he trudged toward the dreaded duty, struggling with how to console grieving loved ones.

After posting guards to secure the castle, comforting those who'd lost family and friends, and ensuring the stablehands cared for the horses, Logan climbed the bailey stairs. He rubbed his tired neck and made his way to the great hall.

Wounded men and lads lay on tables and makeshift beds scattered throughout the room. Maria poured water in a bucket hanging from a swing bar in the massive hearth as Randall threw another log into the fire. The dry wood caught quickly and flames rose to heat the pot.

Logan skimmed the room for Lindsey. It didn't take long before he found her. She sat beside a man and dabbed a cloth on his sooty, sweat-streaked face. Burns scorched his cheeks and brow. Her hand pushed a stray lock from her forehead as she dipped the fabric in the bucket of water at her feet.

She had risked her life to get help for his clan. His princess was a special woman.

A lass, arms full of linens, hurried toward him, and he stepped to the side to let her pass. He maneuvered the throng of injured and dodged a young lad racing by with a soft pallet.

As Logan continued through the hall, Agnes, hunched over her husband lying on a mattress, caught his attention. Face in her gnarled hands, the old woman cried, her shoulders shaking. Her sorrow reached out to him, twisted his insides as if contorted by The Tower's turning screw devices.

He stepped over to her and slid his arm around her ample frame. She turned her tear streaked face toward him. Her white braid had unraveled. Anguish and despair etched deep lines into her skin, and her mouth was stretched taut.

"I'm sorry for yer loss." His words would do little to comfort her, but he had to try.

She leaned her head against his chest, and he embraced her. "He was a guid man," she whispered as sobs racked her body.

Rage mixed with sorrow filled Logan. More than ever, he wanted to make Collins pay. He should not have postponed his pursuit for vengeance. Damn it! He'd never fail his clan again.

Githa hurried toward them, her arms full of linens. Logan motioned to her with his head. She placed the cloths on a table to his right and stepped up behind Agnes, her hand running down the woman's back. "Yer Roy was a wonderful man. He will be sorely missed."

Agnes straightened and turned to Githa. The maid pulled Agnes into her embrace and looked over the woman's shoulder at Logan. A stilted smile touched her lips. "I'll stay with her."

"Thank ye." Logan nodded, then left the women to check on Adam.

Colyne and Thom stood beside his friend who was stretched out on a table against the back wall. Logan made his way to the men and looked down at Adam. He laid still, his chest barely lifting. Blood stained the bandage that surrounded his head and the left side of his face.

Adam and Logan had been friends for many years. They grew up together, fought in the rebellion together, and suffered Collins's brutality together. His chest clenched, and he prayed Adam pulled through this injury.

"Has he awoken?" Logan asked.

Thom shook his head. "Maria says it might take a while before he comes around."

The men stood in silence.

MacAndrew leaned over a table across the hall and shook an injured man's hand. He patted his shoulder and straightened, then strode over to Lindsey. She glanced up and smiled at him.

Logan's eyes narrowed. "Did ye find anything on him?"

Colyne turned and followed Logan's gaze. He exhaled. "Nothing other than his clan seems to worship him, and he's ruthless to his enemies."

The information didn't surprise Logan. From what he'd witnessed of MacAndrew, his actions appeared nothing but honorable.

"Ross?"

He turned and faced Taylor.

"I'm escorting Field Commander Collins and his men to London in the morning." Taylor looked Logan in the eye. "I don't know what will become of him, but I promise to do my utmost to hold him accountable."

Could Logan trust Sassenachs to punish one of their own for crimes committed against their common enemy? Resentment over the lost opportunity to kill Collins gushed through him, and he hoped he had not made a mistake.

"And will ye stop at his stronghold in Northumberland?" Logan asked. "Many innocent men rounded up for questioning rot in his dungeon."

"Yes, it's part of my territory. I will personally see to it."

"I guess that's all I can ask."

Taylor fished a parchment from his tunic and held it out. "I realize there are soldiers who will not honor my decree, but for what it's worth…"

Logan looked at the thick papyrus. He hesitated, then accepted the document.

Taylor extended his hand. "My sincere apologies."

~~~

Glencara was quiet, the residents subdued. Lindsey sat at one of the worn oak tables in the great hall with a mug of spiced cider warming her hands.

They had received a severe blow.

She closed her eyes. Images of lifeless bodies scattered about the bailey, and bloodied and bruised men and women clutching fearful children tumbled through her mind. Loved ones' wails as they grasped the bodies of husbands, sons, and brothers rang in her ears, and the acrid stench of smoke still filled her nostrils.

The resilient clan vowed to rebuild. Commander Taylor ordered his soldiers to clear the inner yard and bury the dead. Lindsey had worked alongside Maria, Ainslee, and Skena. They bandaged and treated numerous cuts and broken bones. By midnight, order had been restored, but the atmosphere remained understandably somber.

A gurgling sound interrupted her thoughts. On the bench to her right, Skena snuggled beside Commander Taylor, who held their daughter. The wee one cooed, and her small fists waved in the air. When she latched onto her da's finger, the man chuckled and Skena beamed.

Lindsey's heart tugged. The little lass resembled her mum with wavy, honey-colored hair and big brown eyes.

How she would cherish a babe of her own.

Ainslee clutched Blake's arm as he hobbled into the room, his pale face pinched. His left side sported a thick bandage, and his leg had been secured to a wooden splint.

Lindsey hurried to them. "Let me help ye."

Blake threw his other arm around her shoulders. "Are ye all right?"

"Just a little shook up."

He took a step and grunted. "We worried when we couldn't find ye."

Sheepishly, she responded, "I was hiding in the barn."

She and Ainslee helped him limp across the hall and onto a bench, his stiff leg stretched out.

Alec's sister slid beside him. "Thank the Lord Blake was near Da's room when the attack started." She intertwined her fingers through his and gazed at him, her eyes adoring. "He carried Da into the secret room off the solar while I gathered Maria, Skena and her bairn."

She turned back to Lindsey. "We were so frightened, but Blake told us to stay put and he'd come for us."

Lindsey leaned over and clutched Ainslee's arm. "I'm so relieved none of ye were hurt."

"As I am." Mangus stepped beside her and addressed Blake. "What ye did was verrae brave."

Her friend shrugged. "'Twas nothing."

Ainslee rubbed his arm. "Ye saved my da. If the soldiers had found him…"

Thoughts of what would have happened to the old laird caused Lindsey's stomach to clench. She bowed her head.

Mangus sat on the edge of the bench beside her, his thumb stroking her shoulder.

Lindsey turned to him. "The past few days have been trying."

"I understand." He tilted his head, and his eyes narrowed slightly. "I had hoped to have yer decision tonight, but given the circumstances, perhaps it would be best if we spoke in the morning."

Lindsey

Relief swept through her. She'd been granted a
reprieve—one more restless night to ponder her decision.

~~~

The hearth's comforting warmth caressed Lindsey's
face. Mesmerizing flames waved between charred logs, and
red coals flickered in a chilly draft. Long shadows danced
across her bedchamber walls, the silence broken by the
fire's crackle.

The most important decision of her life loomed
before her. Mangus would make an excellent husband.

A perfect gentleman.

Kind.

Considerate.

He would provide for her, give her children. She
pictured his handsome face as he talked about his young
sister, the love apparent in his soft eyes. But, he could also
be ruthless and would protect Lindsey without question.
When he thrust his sword at Collins's men, fabric covering
his upper arms bunched with bulging muscles. Sparks flew
from the powerful swing of his blade as he secured Logan's
back.

Although girlish dithers didn't careen through her at
his touch, nor did his kiss invoke passion, she would grow
to care for him.

A knock on the door broke through her thoughts.

Who would be here at this time of night?

The door opened and closed with a click. She
straightened and turned in her chair.

Logan stood just inside her room. Hands clasped
before him, he clutched her woolen cap. Thick brown hair
brushed his broad shoulders, and wisps of the same color
peeked through his tunic's opening.

A slight smile played at his lips, but his eyes
captured her. The intense stare caused flutters deep within

her belly. He pushed away from the wall and advanced toward her. "I'm glad ye're still awake."

"I couldn't sleep."

He held up her cap. "Found it on the trail."

Her chin rose. "Ah, I wondered what had happened to it."

Logan tossed the cap on the table before the hearth and stood watching her.

Every nerve ached for his touch, but she refrained from throwing herself into his arms and burying her head in his chest…breathing in his scent.

"May I join ye?"

What could he have to say at this hour? She nodded while indicating the seat to her left. "Please do."

He dropped onto the chair and stared at the hearth's fire. Neither of them spoke and tension hung heavy between them.

Finally, he looked at her. "I can't tell ye the terror that struck my heart when I saw Collins chasing ye." He seemed to search her face. "I don't know what I would've done if something had happened to ye."

Her body trembled, but she willed herself to remain strong. She pulled her gaze from his and focused on the golden flames.

"Princess?" His deep voice rumbled in his chest. "Look at me."

Eyes narrowing, she turned to face him.

"This is one of the hardest things I've ever done." He exhaled a deep breath. "Lass, I want ye to marry MacAndrew."

Pain slashed through her chest, the breath knocked from her lungs. She struggled to remain composed.

"He's an honorable man, one who will protect and care for ye."

Her pulse pounded in her ears, building to a fevered pitch.

"We both knew the time would come when a titled laird would claim ye as his wife. I believe MacAndrew is that man." He stroked her hand. "At first I didn't care for him, but after witnessing his character and his genuine concern for ye, I believe he will make ye happy."

"Is that supposed to make me feel better?" she snapped. "Knowing ye're fine with me marrying another man?"

Logan's body stiffened. "I hoped to reassure ye."

"Well, thank ye verrae much, but I don't need yer reassurance." Her chest heaved from a torrent of emotion. "I asked ye to fight traditions that no longer make sense. To be with me. I don't give a fig about yer status, but ye've made yer wishes perfectly clear. Ye'd rather wallow in pity of yer bastard birth."

Something akin to pain drifted across his eyes. He straightened and looked down at her. Abruptly, he turned and strode across the room. When he reached the door, he paused.

She wanted to yell she loved him and beg him to reconsider. Together they could fight the status of his birth, expose the unjust tradition for what it was.

He faced her, and his eyes reflected unyielding aloofness. He bowed slightly. "Goodbye."

Chapter Twenty

Glencara Castle

Drowsy from a sleepless night of tossing and turning with Logan's words ringing through her ears, Lindsey folded a mussed up blanket and laid it across the top of the worn chest against her bedchamber wall.

Heart heavy, her gaze skimmed the room. Warm furs covered the comfortable bed. The small table and chairs before the hearth stood empty and charred wood smoldered in the fireplace. Ainslee's little vase of herbs still emitted a spicy fragrance.

Lindsey picked up her satchel and slid her wrap from the bedside table. With mixed emotions, she squared her shoulders and padded across the room to the door. Her hand grasped the knob. She turned and cast a last glimpse around the dim bedchamber.

She would miss this place.

Taking a deep breath, she strode from the room and continued down the corridor to Grant's chamber. How could she say goodbye? He had become a close ally, a ray of sunshine she looked forward to each day. She knocked on the heavy oak door, and a prayer ran through her head that he would understand.

"Enter," Grant called.

She slipped inside the room. As so many times before, Logan's uncle sat before the hearth, a carving knife in his hand and wood shavings stuck to the red woolen blanket that draped his legs.

He turned toward her, and his face lit. "Good morning, lass. Come in."

His cheerful countenance caused her to smile, but her insides roiled with a sadness that pierced her core. She slid into the chair beside him. Wooden figures surrounded him. "Ah, ye are adding to yer collection I see."

He leaned forward, grasped a black wooden horse and handed it to her. "I made this for ye."

Her breath caught at the carved detail. Lunging forward, the muscular horse stood on hind legs, his front hooves in the air. A thick mane flowed from the crest of his neck down to his withers, and a matching tail fanned out behind him. She turned the statue around. Grant had painted a white blaze down the horse's face. Her throat clogged, and tears clouded her eyes.

"Oh, Grant. He's beautiful." She clutched his forearm. "I will treasure it always."

His expression turned wistful, and his shoulders sagged. He took her hand in his warm palm. "Ye're leaving."

A tear trickled down her cheek. She nodded.

Silence hung between them.

"When?" he asked.

"Mangus awaits my decision. He is ready to return home today."

His head snapped up, and his grey eyes widened, frantic. "Today? But why so soon? Can't ye wait for a few more days?"

"Nay, Mangus has been most patient. It wouldn't be fair to him."

"But given the situation ye just endured, surely the man would be willing to stay a while, give ye time to recover."

"Whether I leave today or three days from now won't change anything."

He straightened in the chair. "I need to see Adam."

"Adam?" Her brow scrunched.

"I must see him now."

His agitated posture struck her as most peculiar. "He was injured, and I don't know if he has regained consciousness."

"Shite!" He looked to the ceiling as his wrinkled hand grabbed his forehead.

Lindsey reared back, never having witnessed his acting this way. "What's wrong?"

His hand dropped. He turned to her, his grey eyes worried. "Before ye leave, ask Kirk to come to my chambers straight away."

She patted his hand. "I will."

"Go now," he insisted and pushed her arm.

She gathered her wrap and the wooden horse as she stood. Furrows dug into Grant's leathery skin, and greying whiskers dotted his wrinkled cheeks and chin. His pleading eyes concerned her, his actions confusing.

Hugging the statue against her waist, she hurried across the room and down the hall. Why would Grant need to speak to Adam so suddenly? What could've caused the urgency?

Lindsey dashed down the stairs and out the back entrance to the stables. A lad raked hay into a pile before her, and another barreled from a pen, his arms loaded with straw. She weaved around them and ran down the main aisle, searching the stalls on either side. Where was Kirk? When she reached the front of the building, she stepped around the corner and into the empty storage room.

A noise sounded behind her, and she turned as a lad tossed a coiled rope into the bin to the left of the door.

"Do ye know where Kirk is?" she asked.

He scratched his shoulder as he looked at her. "He rode out this morning to the north pasture."

Damn. Her teeth raked her bottom lip as she stepped forward. "Will ye fetch him?"

"Aye, mistress." The boy's red hair bounced with his rapid nods.

"Please hurry." When he moved to leave, she caught his arm. "Tell Kirk Grant needs to see him right away."

The lad ran from the room. She followed and watched him leap onto a horse's back and gallop from the barn.

With that taken care of, her gaze traveled across the magnificent animals housed in the pens, filling paddocks and the exercise area. She strolled back down the barn's central pathway and stopped beside Pegasus's stall. The massive chestnut stallion tossed his head, his long black mane falling over muscular withers. Logan had wanted her advice on breeding her mares with this beautiful horse. How she would have loved to train his offspring.

A large hand clutched her shoulder, and she turned. Mangus stood before her.

With a boulder wedged in her stomach, she tried to smile. Tousled black hair swept his forehead and brushed his wide shoulders. His deep blue eyes focused on her as he took her hand in his. "I would have your answer now, lass."

~~~

The cold ramparts matched the bleakness filling Logan's soul. Wind whipped hair into his face as he watched the group gathered in the bailey.

MacAndrew lifted Lindsey onto Blaze's back. The late afternoon sun reflected fiery strands in her soft hair. A dark cloak covered her slender frame and draped the horse's hindquarters. She grasped the reins with gloved hands.

A lad led two horses carrying wrapped bundles—most likely Lindsey's belongings. One of MacAndrew's men accepted the reins and tugged the animals in line behind the others. The dozen MacDougall horses Lindsey had selected to travel to the Highlands were harnessed together and readied for the long trek.

MacAndrew leapt unto his horse's back, turned, and inspected the departing group. He held up a hand and motioned for the party to head out.

Logan's inquiries about the laird had come back clean. No ill will against the man could be dredged up. His clan admired him, and his enemies feared him. He had bounded into the fray and fought at Logan's back. As much as Logan desired, he couldn't find fault with the man. The laird would provide well for Lindsey, and Logan couldn't have chosen a more reputable man for her.

Feet planted firmly on the hard stones, he watched until he could no longer see her. Eventually, he would accept she was gone, but at this moment, his chest cleaved in two.

Taking a deep breath, he strode down the tower steps and across the bailey.

Blake, leaning on a wooden crutch, hobbled toward him. "Randall just rode in. Says he spotted soldiers off the north pasture."

"They weren't Taylor's men?"

"Can't say for sure, but he seemed to think they were stragglers." Blake shrugged. "There were only three of them. The lot appeared dirty and disheveled. Randall found remains of a fire still smoldering in one of the sheep shearer's huts."

Logan rubbed the back of his neck. Before Taylor left this morning, he swore Collins and his men would be held accountable for their actions. It's possible a few slipped from the commander's clutches.

Horse's hooves clattered on the wooden bridge. Kirk galloped into the yard with a stablehand close behind. He dismounted and bolted up the bailey stairs.

Logan frowned. If Kirk had encountered a problem while out, he would have stopped and informed him, but the man raced past Logan as if he didn't see him.

"Tell the men to stay alert. Report anything ye hear to me."

Blake nodded and shuffled toward the stable.

The trespassing Sassenachs fueled Logan's already foul mood. They'd best pray he did not discover them. Dusk fell as he climbed the keep's steps. Servants cleared from his unwavering path as he stormed through the hall.

Maria straightened and wiped her hands on a cloth as she stepped toward him. Her worried eyes studied him. "Logan?"

He held up a hand to stop her, then scaled the stairs two at a time to his chamber. He shoved the door and it banged shut as he marched over to the side table. Grabbing the flask of mead, images of Lindsey's departing straight back played on his mind.

Logan dropped onto one of the dark wooden chairs before the fireplace and swigged the drink. The burn that coursed to his gut matched the fire that spread through his chest. A pain, unlike any he'd known, dug deep into his core like sharp talons slicing his heart to shreds.

He sat in disbelief.

His princess was gone.

Perhaps she had been right. He should've fought against the injustice of his station, or simply ignored it.

Candles flickered in candelabras positioned against the laird's bedchamber walls. Two swords crossed over the mantel with the Campbell emblem carved in pewter displayed above the apex. How many times as a lad had he polished Grant's crest while dreaming of what it would be like as a family member? Not a nephew from a distant sister, but a real member.

Someone who belonged.

Memories of his childhood surfaced. Although he had grown accustom to boys' taunts of his lowly bastard status, their ridicule had hit a nerve.

They were right.

And here he sat, ensconced in the laird's chambers with the responsibilities of managing the clan hoisted upon his shoulders without the benefit of the title. And worst yet, because of his bastard birth, he had lost Lindsey.

He didn't know how long he sat, staring at the flames, consuming the numbing mead, but darkness had filled the chamber when a knock sounded at the door.

"Enter," he shouted a bit louder than necessary.

The door opened. Maria slipped inside the room and shut the door.

Logan sighed. Although she meant well, he didn't want her sympathy. As a young lad, she'd comforted him, told him she loved him as her own. And she did. In her caring embrace, he had cried upon her shoulder. But he was no longer a young lad.

She padded across the room and sat in the chair next to him. Neither of them spoke. Surely she must sense his need for privacy.

Logan leaned forward and grabbed the metal poker propped against the hearth. He jabbed the logs. The golden flames stirred to life and beckoned warmth into the room. Elbows on his thighs, he stared at the fire.

Maria clutched his upper arm. "I know ye're hurting, but yer uncle needs to see ye."

"Now? Can it not wait until the morning?"

She shook her head. "It's important."

"This is not the best time."

"I understand."

Shite.

He'd best find out what his uncle needed or Logan would not get the solitude he desired. Sighing loudly, he stood. "I'll go to him."

He jerked the door open and tread down the corridor to his uncle's chambers with Maria trailing behind. Light from the bedroom spilled into the hallway. He walked into the room and froze.

Alec sat next to Grant. What was he doing here?

Grant occupied his usual chair before the hearth. He turned to Logan. "Thank ye for coming at this hour."

His cousin stood, extended his hand. "And I thank ye for escorting Taylor. I'm happy to see ye weren't injured in the attack."

Logan shook Alec's hand. "What's this about?"

Alec shrugged and looked back at Grant. "I've been wondering the same. Adam said ye needed to see me straight away."

"Aye, please sit."

Logan didn't want to sit, but he did.

Maria shut the door, ambled across the room, and perched on the other side of Grant.

Logan hoped to God they did not intend to *comfort* him. His gaze swung from Maria to Grant.

His uncle cleared his throat and glared at Alec. "I had planned to speak with both of ye earlier. Adam carried a message from me, requesting ye travel to Glencara posthaste."

Alec folded his arms. "I received yer message and told Adam I'd come as quickly as I could."

"Well, he was injured on the trip back, and I didn't receive yer reply until Kirk saw him this afternoon."

What the hell was Grant babbling about? What did it matter whether Alec arrived last night or this evening?

His uncle turned and addressed Logan. "I have not always done things properly. Yer sweet lass, Lindsey…"

"She's not my lass."

Grant paused. "In the short time she was here, she taught me things, made me think. She showed me how to live again, cherish every day."

What was his uncle trying to do, rip Logan's heart out?

"I'm ashamed to say I've not always done the right thing. But I plan to from this day going forward." He hesitated, and his eyes displayed pain.

Silence stretched.

Maria's hand eased to Grant's shoulder.

Alec, sitting beside Logan, noticeably stiffened.

"Logan, ye are my first born son."

The air whooshed from Logan's lungs.

What? He leapt from the chair, his eyes wide. Grant's son? Sterling's kick to his head could not have stunned him more.

Alec's mouth dropped open as he stood.

Grant held up a hand. "Please, hear me out."

Logan's nostrils flared. "What the hell are ye talking about? Yer sister died birthing me."

"It is true my wayward sister died in childbirth. But her son never breathed air. The abbey's healer said the mother's cord had wrapped around the babe's neck long before he entered the world." Grant shook his head. "They couldn't stop her bleeding, and she passed along with her bairn."

What? Logan's mind raced, fists clenching at his sides.

Grant took Maria's hand in his. "Right before I wed Margaret, I met yer mother."

Oh, God.

"Maria and I fell in love instantly and before we knew it, she was pregnant. To form an allegiance with a border laird, I had no choice but to go through with my marriage to Margaret. With generous donations and support, the abbess agreed to care for Maria and ye until I could come for ye. When able, I brought ye home as my nephew so I could care for ye, keep ye close."

"God damn it," Alec hissed. "I always suspected ye cared more for yer sister's maid than Mum."

"We did our best to remain discrete, to not hurt yer mother. She didn't know about Maria."

"I hope yer conscience is cleansed." Fury coursed through Logan's veins. "Do ye know what kind of life I've lived because of what ye did? Labeled a bastard, never worthy. I grew accustomed to the scorn, the ridicule, but I never got past not belonging, always on the outside looking in."

"If I could change the past, I would."

"How do ye think your revelation makes me feel?" Alec asked, his voice strained, harsh. "Knowing I was the chosen one, depriving my...*brother* of his rightful position?"

"It is not my rightful position. I am still a bastard." Logan wanted to throttle the man sitting before him. Never had he felt such anger or betrayal. Chest heaving, he glared at Grant and Maria.

His parents.

Shite!

He turned to leave.

"Wait," Maria called and hurried to him. She grasped his arm.

He couldn't look at her. Instead, he stared straight ahead.

"I have always loved ye, son. So many times I wanted to tell ye." Her voice choked from tears. "It was so hard for me to hold ye, comfort ye about the mother ye never knew."

He held his body rigid. "Is that all?"

"Nay," Grant said.

Logan whirled and glared at him. "What else do ye have to say?"

Grant looked at Alec. "As Laird of Glencara, ye can right the wrongs I've committed. Ye hold the lairdship of the clan MacDougall. Will ye relinquish yer role as Laird here and bestow the title onto yer brother?"

The final blow.

All his life Logan had dreamed of becoming laird and in the recent months, never had it been more important, but it was not fair to Alec. Logan would not depose his *brother*. "Ye can't ask him to forgo his rightful place."

Alec faced Logan, his countenance dark. "I have no problem relinquishing the role that never should've been mine. I regret all ye've endured. The title won't amend the wrongs done to ye, but I hope it helps ye heal."

"Will ye accept it?" Grant, *his father*, asked.

"It's a bit late, wouldn't ye say?" Logan forced the words out. "The lass I love is now in the arms of Laird MacAndrew."

Pain shot through his chest, and he stormed from the room.

"Logan?" Maria cried and trailed him to the stairs. "Where are ye going?"

He ignored her and marched down the steps, across the great hall, and into the bailey. Lightning lit the night sky, and thunder rumbled in the distance. Wind-whipped torch flames shot into the sky. Glencara and Scotland flags fluttered and slapped their staffs. Several lads ran past as he strode into the barn.

Grant's words flooded Logan's mind. Sterling tossed his head as Logan jerked the saddle from the wooden stand next to the pen and hoisted it onto the horse's back. Logan's lip curled while he cinched the straps under the animal's girth. He grabbed his leather satchel and rolled blanket from the makeshift worktable.

"Is something amiss?"

Logan swung onto the saddle and looked down at Kirk. He nudged Sterling from the barn, galloped past the guardhouses, and across the wooden bridge. The horse's hooves pounded the ground as they sped down the dirt road and onto a pasture of winter grasses.

Wind whistled past his face. He ducked low against Sterling and urged him faster. When they crested the top of the knoll, memories of Lindsey's impish smile as she tossed her challenge to race, surfaced. How he loved her carefree spirit.

Sterling shot down the meadow to the loch. Logan tugged the reins and the horse slowed, his sides heaving. Lightning flashed, and the scent of rain hung heavy in the air. They trotted alongside the water to the empty shearer's thatched huts. He eased Sterling under a stone overhang. Covered in vines and ivy, the outcropping provided shelter. He tethered the horse, grabbed his satchel, and made his way to one of the simple shacks.

He ducked into the triangular shaped hut, and his gaze darted around the empty room. Darkness filled the space. As he crept farther into the shack, he felt along the wall for the small hearth. His foot bumped a log, and he stooped. Someone had stacked dry kindling next to the fireplace. Blake's words about the soldiers spotted in the area drifted through his mind.

Logan tossed the sticks into the hearth and rummaged through his satchel for the flint stones. His fingers closed around them. Striking them against each other, sparks flew into the tinder. Before long, a puff of smoke wafted up. Logan blew on the tentative flames and coaxed them to life.

He stood and turned to inspect the hut he had spent so many nights in as a young lad. Funny how he rode here without thought.

The old bed still hugged the wall before the hearth. A broken table and two rickety wooden chairs completed the cozy cabin. Logan brushed aside cobwebs and stepped to the bed. He jerked the lumpy mattress off and shoved it through the single door. Shaking the old cushion, dust and debris fell to the ground. He beat it against the thick oak logs forming the hut's structure. Satisfied nothing lived within the mattress, he tugged it back into the shack and tossed it on the bed's frame.

Logan grabbed his satchel and dropped onto the bedding while extracting his wineskin. Events of the past days bore down on him. He guzzled the mead, desperately wanting to numb his mind, dull the pain tearing through him.

How ironic he would discover the truth of his birth and be awarded the lairdship mere hours after MacAndrew whisked Lindsey away. Perhaps he should run after her, chase her to the Highlands, and beg her to reconsider.

He took another swig of mead.

She had made the decision to marry MacAndrew. He would make her happy, protect her, and give her children.

Logan leaned his head against the wall. A loud pop sounded, and several red sparks shot into the room.

How had he let her walk away? She held his heart, always had and always would.

Sterling whinnied, and Logan stilled. The English stragglers would rue the evening if they crossed him. He'd like nothing better than to beat them with his bare fists.

The clop of horse's hooves grew close.

Logan sprang from the bed and jerked the dagger from his belt. He peered through a gap in the wooden slats and stared into pitch black darkness. Plastering himself against the wall on the other side of the door, he waited.

Listening.

Lightning lit the sky, and a crash of thunder rent the air.

His ears strained. Did he hear a voice? He anxiously waited to pummel the trespassers.

Someone grasped the door.

A gloved hand pushed it open.

Logan grasped the person's arm and wrenched the intruder into the room. With his dagger poised at the churl's neck, he sneered. "Ye've got five seconds before I slit yer throat."

Chapter Twenty One

The tip of Logan's knife pressed into the intruder's neck.

Lightning flashed. Lindsey's alarmed eyes widened. "Damn it, Logan. If ye don't want me here, ye can just tell me."

"Lindsey!" He gasped and jerked the blade away from her. "I didn't realize it was ye."

She shook her head and held up a hand. "I should've announced myself."

Heart pounding, he scrubbed a palm over his face and backed away. Shite! He could've killed her. The thought almost knocked the wind from him.

A deep breath helped quell the fear that coursed through his body, but his ire rose. What was she doing here? He shoved his dagger into the sheath on his belt and jammed his hands on his hips.

Arms folded, she stepped to the middle of the hut. With the cloak's dark hood pushed from her head, firelight flickered across her auburn tresses. Her teeth worried her bottom lip.

He wanted to grab her, hold her next to him and bury his face in her beautiful hair. "What are ye doing here?"

"I couldn't do it."

His chest clenched, but his feet remained rooted to the spot.

"After Collins's attack, I realized how short life was, how easily it was snuffed out. I want to live every day to the fullest." Lindsey stepped toward him. "I've preached to change traditions that don't make sense. It occurred to me, I could start those changes by remaining at Glencara, working in the stables and…being near ye."

His throat clogged with emotion. "What about bairns?"

Her head tilted. "I *would* like children of my own, but I will spoil my sisters' wee ones."

Lightning lit the room again, and a deafening clap resounded. She jumped and rubbed her arms. He stepped within inches of her. She raised her face, and her blue eyes peered up at him, drawing him in like a mythological Siren.

He ran his knuckles across her soft cheek. "What of MacAndrew?"

Her fingers twisted before her waist, and she shrugged. "By the time we'd reached Glencara's northern border, I knew I couldn't continue. It wouldn't be fair to Mangus…or to me." She paused. "He was most gracious and told me he understood. Two of his men escorted me and my horses back to the castle. I arrived shortly after ye left."

He studied her expression and wondered if she had been told his…*news*. "I'm surprised ye found me."

"When I returned, Maria met me at the top of the keep's stairs. She told me ye were upset and had ridden out in a great hurry. She said as a lad ye frequented these cabins when ye were troubled." Her lids lowered. "Since I caused yer hardship, I hurried here as fast as I could."

He tipped her chin up. Sorrow had filled her eyes. "I didn't mean to hurt ye," she whispered.

He pulled her into his embrace, and she slid her arms around his back. Breathing in her fresh scent, he nuzzled her neck. "Ye are sure about yer decision?"

"I couldn't be surer."

He straightened and gazed at her. Rain pelted the roof and thunder rumbled in the distance. A spark of hope flickered deep inside his soul. He intertwined his fingers through hers and swung an arm toward the busted furniture and bed. "Not the best accommodations, but I have mead, and I believe a chunk of hard bread is in the bottom of my satchel."

The smile she bestowed caused the fellow between his legs to awaken. She unpinned the cloak at her neck. He took the garment from her slender shoulders and draped it across the wobbly table as she sat on the bed's edge, facing the hearth.

"Where's that mead?"

~~~

Logan tossed her his wineskin. She caught it and tugged out the cork. A strong smell wafted up as she took a gulp. The fiery liquid burned a path into her stomach, but after the past few days, she needed another swig…or two.

Logan squatted beside the hearth and threw a log onto the grate. When he straightened, a grin spread across his rugged face, and excited jitters whorled through her. He always could flip her heart upside down with one look.

He dropped onto the bed, took the wineskin from her, and leaned against the wall. "I spent many nights here as a lad."

"We're ye often troubled?"

He stared into the flames, then turned the wineskin up and gulped a mouthful.

She scooted next to him and placed her back against the wall too.

He glanced sideways at her. "Nothing I couldn't handle."

"I used to stay in the barn." She took the mead from him and drank a couple of swallows. Warmth spread through her and for the first time in weeks, she relaxed. "Whenever something bothered me, I found solace with my horses."

Logan chuckled. "I did the same. But, mostly I ran the poor devils until their sides heaved and lather coated their fur."

She threw him a grin. "Aye, there's nothing better for working out yer troubles than a fast ride."

Rain pelted the shack, but the cabin remained surprisingly warm and dry. A log rolled in the hearth, and the wind drew flames up the chimney. Red sparks shot into the room and disappeared in mid air.

Lindsey stole a glance at Logan. Light brown whiskers covered his cheeks and jaw. The hair swept above his upper lip and surrounded his firm chin. Thick neck muscles worked as he swallowed more mead.

How she had missed him.

She snuggled up to his side. He placed an arm around her, and she laid her head on his chest. Love for him washed over her. His fingers traced circles on her upper arm. She closed her eyes and relished being beside him. Her soul felt at peace. She had made the right decision.

Logan kissed the top of her head.

When she looked up at him, he drew a knuckle over her cheek, his eyes darkening. He seemed to search her face before he bent and captured her lips. His mouth's feathered caress had her craving more, but when his tongue slid into her mouth, a hunger for him struck deep within her core.

His arm coiled around her as his hand clutched the back of her head and angled her mouth to his. She drank in the taste of mead on his breath and inhaled a whiff of smoke in his hair. He trailed his hot mouth across her cheek. "Ye don't know how hard it was to watch ye leave."

"I'll never leave ye again," she whispered.

He eased her onto her back, and she clutched his muscular shoulders, then slid her hands down his arms. With his weight on an elbow, he watched her, his grey eyes almost black. He seemed hesitant, then finally spoke. "This evening I…"

He paused, his brow furrowing.

She tilted her head to the side. "Ye what?"

Sadness passed through his eyes. "I learned Grant and Maria are my parents."

"Yer parents?" Shock filled her. "Grant and Maria?"

"Aye."

"I don't understand. I assumed they were on *familiar terms*, but I thought their attraction had cropped up recently."

His finger wrapped around one of her springy curls. "They met before Grant married Alec's mum. A convenient story emerged upon his sister's death, and through donations to the church, no one was the wiser."

Rain pelted the roof. Lightning flashed through the room, and a strong wind howled, shaking the cabin. Thunder rumbled and vibrated the ground. Shadows from the hearth danced across his features. She couldn't discern his thoughts. "What does all this mean?"

His calloused finger traced her lips. When his gaze lifted to hers, passion had filled his eyes. "From this night forth, ye're mine."

How long had she dreamed of hearing him utter those words?

Elation soared through her as he lowered his mouth to hers in a gentle kiss. She slid her hands around his strong neck and into his thick hair.

"I've loved ye since the first time I saw ye in yer da's stable."

Logan loves me. Emotion tightened her chest.

His hand eased to her breast, and her breath caught. He kissed the side of her face then trailed his mouth to her neck, while he inched her tunic from inside her trews. "And I've dreamed of taking your sweet body ever since."

A hard ridge nudged her thigh, and a naughty delight rippled through her insides. Muscles between her legs pulsed, tightened. "While I've dreamed ye would."

He pulled up her tunic. She held her arms over her head and he eased off the top, then dropped it on the foot of the bed. Hovering over her, he slid a finger from her throat to the valley between her breasts.

His nostrils flared. "Ye're so soft."

She ran her palms along his broad shoulders, muscles rippling beneath her touch. He bent and feathered kisses across the top of her bosom peaking from beneath the bodice. When his tongue traced a circle around a nipple protruding into the silky fabric, she sucked in air. Her grasp tightened on his shoulders, the sensation gripping her core.

A pink ribbon held the undergarment closed. He tugged the bow, and it unraveled. While he eased the lacing apart, his eyes grew darker. Delicious tentacles of desire coiled through her as he exposed one breast, then the other. His finger traced little bumps around her nipples, and they puckered. "Ye're so beautiful, princess."

Her body hummed with a burning need. He lowered his head, captured a sensitive bud between his lips and suckled. Wondrous sensations coiled through her, and she clutched his head to her. His tongue circled one tip, then the other. He eased lower and shoved the shift apart as his mouth trailed to her ribs, his teeth nipping and tugging her into oblivion.

"Take off yer shirt." Her voice sounded husky. "I want to feel ye naked against me."

He jerked the shirt over his head and tossed it behind her. Light brown hair feathered his brawny chest and red puckered scars crisscrossed his torso as if a branding iron had seared his flesh. Anguish for the pain he'd suffered nearly overwhelmed her. She splayed her hand over his skin and bands of muscle bulged underneath her palms.

He bent and slid his arms under her shoulders as he kissed her. Chest hair brushed her nipples, and she arched her back, anxious for his touch.

His large body eased over hers. "Spread yer legs," he murmured next to her ear.

Heart pounding, she eased her knees apart, and his hips nestled between them. His mouth returned to hers in a hunger that made her tremble. When he thrust his tongue, his stiff member prodded at her core.

She moaned and raised her mons to him, straining against her trews. His mouth left hers, and his tongue once again found her breasts. He dropped lower to her ribs. Her trews tugged on her waist as his strong fingers opened them. His lips trailed to her abdomen, and his hot breath caressed her tender skin.

Senses heightened, she didn't think she could stand much more. Then, his mouth traveled to the top of her most private area. He rose over her as he tugged her trews from her hips and exposed her. His gaze dropped to the apex of her legs, and the muscles surrounding her privates ached. After he tossed aside the fabric, he sat back on his heels.

"Oh, my God." His fingertip traced her naval, then slid lower and brushed her curls.

The heated perusal of his stare caused her body to strum with a need so strong it shook her. Moisture pooled between her thighs. She wet her lips.

"I want ye," he rasped, his eyes dark with desire. He untied his belt and pulled it from his waist. "And I'm going to take ye."

Her body trembled in anticipation. His fingers worked the opening of his breeks, and his swollen manhood jutted out. Her eyes widened, her breathing quickened. He opened the breeks farther, rose on his knees, and shoved the clothing from his narrow hips. His member sprang free and stood stiff against his stomach.

He moved over her, grabbed her hips, and nibbled her stomach. Her fingers wound in his thick hair. His warm mouth created delectable sensations as he eased farther down her quivering body. With hands on either side of her waist, his tongue laved a trail across her belly, teasing her skin with delightful kisses.

She ached for him. Her breathing, short fast bursts, sounded loud in her ears. Thunder rumbled, and the hut shook again. She clutched his shoulders, and he dropped lower still, his hot mouth drawing closer to the apex of her legs.

"Logan…" She tried to sit, scoot back, but he held her still.

"Shhh…let me love ye." His hot breath caressed her heated flesh, and her fists twisted the bedding. "I won't do anything ye don't want me to do." His finger slid across the seam of her nether lips. "If ye tell me to stop, I will."

He parted her. His lips teased, and his tongue laved her swollen bud. A finger eased into her and stroked her core as he suckled her privates. She gasped, and her head pressed into the mattress. Never had she felt such exquisite sensations. Wave after wave of ecstasy crashed over her. She cried out, clutching his arms, but his mouth continued to suckle.

Spent, breathless, and limbs weighty, she tugged under his arms and coaxed him to move up higher. He climbed over her body, and his heavy member rested on her stomach. She rubbed herself against his manhood and nibbled his ear. "I want to feel ye inside me."

~~~

Lindsey's words caused Logan's engorged cock to stiffen even more. How many times had he dreamed of making love to her? He wanted to take it slow and easy, but the lad between his legs had a mind of its own.

His knees pushed her legs farther apart. He reached between their bodies and positioned himself at her entrance. "Look at me."

Passion emanated from her blue eyes. The swollen head of his shaft slid between her slick folds. He watched her face as he pushed farther into her tight sheath. He touched her maidenhead, and her eyes widened, her hands clutching his shoulders.

He lightly kissed her luscious lips. "I want to make love to ye more than anything." He rocked back and forth slowly pushing the head in and out of her tight passage. His muscles strained as he held back from thrusting into her. "But, if ye ask me to stop, I will."

She canted her hips to him. "Nay, please…don't stop." She closed her eyes and pulled his mouth to her. "Please don't stop, Logan."

That was his undoing. He thrust into her heat.

Lindsey gasped and stiffened.

Heavenly warmth surrounded his cock, but he had hurt her. He stilled his hips. "I'm sorry it's painful, but it will only be at first. I promise."

He kissed her nose and eyes and held still until she grew accustomed to his size. He gritted his teeth, and sweat beaded on his brow. "Are ye all right?" he whispered against her mouth.

She nodded, and he slowly withdrew his member, then pushed back in. When she wrapped her legs around his waist, he sank into her fully. She ran her palms across his back and cupped his buttocks. The simple act almost caused him to lose his seed prematurely.

She lifted her hips to meet his thrusts. Her throaty moans fueled his ardor. He pumped faster, reached between them, and massaged her pearl. Her body stiffened and she cried out, her muscles tightening, milking his cock. He grasped her shoulders as he pushed into her once again and threw his head back. "Ah, Lindsey."

Thunder rumbled again, and the little hut shook as she lay beneath him, his shaft still nestled in her haven.

Reluctantly, he eased from her, rolled onto his back, and tugged her into his arms.

He tipped her chin up to capture her mouth. He loved the taste of her, the feel of her naked and nestled beside him. They lay in each other's arms and listened to the rain pouring on the thatched roof. Logan thought of how close Collins came to taking Lindsey from him, and the panic that surged through him when he realized the ruthless cur chased her. "I want ye to stay by my side and grow old with me."

Lindsey rose over him. Her soft tresses brushed his chest, and her eyes seemed to search his face.

"I want ye as my wife."

"Are ye sure?"

"There has never been any doubt I wanted to spend my life with ye. But with my lowly status, I couldn't provide for ye as ye deserved. Hell, I worried yer da would disown ye."

"Da would never do that."

"Regardless of what ye believe, traditions hold strong." He traced circles on the small of her back. "Alec has agreed to relinquish to me his role as Laird of Glencara while retaining his lairdship at MacDougall Castle. With the title, yer da will be more agreeable to our union." His hand slid lower and cupped her luscious bottom. "I planted my seed in ye, and I long to see yer belly swell with my bairn."

"Oh, Logan. I love ye." She leaned up and kissed him.

"Does that mean ye'll have me?"

"It's my most fervent desire to become yer wife."

He flipped her underneath him as he lowered his head and kissed her, slowly stirring her passion again. "And it's my most fervent desire to prove just how much I love ye."

While the storm raged outside, it paled in comparison to the powerful emotions that careened through his body. Never had he felt so strongly about a lass. She invaded his thoughts, plagued his dreams.

Logan would protect her with his life. He prayed that would be enough.

Chapter Twenty Two

Glencara Castle
January 1300

Today represented a fresh beginning with the clan's affirmation of their new leader. A cold afternoon rain buffeted the great hall's windows, but the hearth's blazing fire warmed the group gathered to witness Alec pass the laird's role to Logan. Lindsey sat at the dais, the empty chairs to her right reserved for the two men, and anxiously awaited the ceremony.

They had waited a week to give Lindsey's family time to travel to Glencara. Alec escorted Heather and Da. A short time later, Robert arrived with Cameron and their rambunctious toddler Douglas. The evening would have been complete if only their youngest sister could've joined them. Lindsey missed Elsbeth.

She sipped her spiced cider and glanced around the spacious chamber. Suspended from the high pitched roof, chandeliers cast flickering candlelight over tables readied for the celebration. Steam curled from platters of roasted boar, venison, and smoked fish. Dishes of braised carrots and boiled leeks, trays of bread, and pitchers of ale covered tables set out in rows with the dais positioned across the front of the room.

Crowds of men and women milled about. Laughter, conversations, and shouts of good cheer rang from the boisterous group. On a raised platform to Lindsey's right, Faye strummed a harp while two men stood beside her, plucking lutes. A lad stepped forward as he blew into a flute. The melody was light and added to the festive atmosphere.

Tomorrow, Lindsey would become Logan's wife, the lady of Glencara with these good people as her family. She couldn't believe how fast everything had happened.

Just a few short days ago, she had journeyed toward the Highlands at Mangus's side. Now she sat, dreaming of her wedding to Logan…and their night together.

A loud guffaw caught her attention. One of the clansmen, his ruddy face lit in laughter, bent at the waist. Another grasped his wide belly and clapped the man on the back. She grinned, their mirth contagious. Several young lads and lasses snaked through the growing throng to stand in front of the adults. Serving girls, carrying trays and platters, hurried into the room and wove through the crowd.

"Ah, he kicked."

Lindsey turned to Heather, seated at her left. Her sister clutched her stomach.

"*He* kicked?"

"Here, feel."

She held Lindsey's hand over her firm, rounded abdomen. A thump hit Lindsey's palm, and she inhaled sharply, her eyes wide. "I felt it."

"His punches are strong." Heather giggled. "He often lands one on Alec when he gets too close."

The sisters laughed. How Lindsey looked forward to the day when she and Logan would have a little one. Images of a lad with sandy brown hair and grey eyes drifted through her mind. *Humph, with my luck I'll have a redheaded lass with a temper to match.*

A squeal sounded behind them. Lindsey turned as Douglas squirmed in Cameron's arms, a thumb stuck in his mouth. He scrambled from her, over to Robert, and onto the bench beside Da. Her father's wrinkled hand patted the lad's chubby leg as the bairn climbed on his grandda's lap.

Ainslee and Blake, deep in conversation, sat beside her father. Grant, having agreed some traditions could be broken, gave permission for Blake to court Ainslee. Perhaps Lindsey could change the world's attitude. She smiled. Well, maybe only the attitudes of those around her.

Kirk and Thom carried Grant into the room and eased him onto a bench positioned on the other side of Alec's chair. Maria, dressed in a blue woolen gown, her white hair twisted on top of her head, stood behind Grant. Her face radiated warmth. The night they returned from the hut, Logan had made amends with his parents, and Ainslee had rejoiced over having two brothers.

Logan and Alec marched into the room. The clan grew quiet as the rugged men stepped around the back of the dais to their chairs. Logan sat beside Lindsey. He winked, and dimples pressed into his whiskered cheeks.

Her insides turned to mush. He reached out, and she clutched his calloused palm, his rough thumb stroking her skin.

Alec faced the crowd. "It's good to be home, and what an occasion we have to celebrate!"

Shouts resounded, and a number of men banged their hands on the tables while others clapped. The reception Logan received caused her heart to swell. She lifted his hand and kissed his knuckles.

A smile tugged at the corners of his mouth.

Alec turned to Logan. "Will ye join me?"

He rose. Feet braced apart and hands clasped before his waist, Logan stood still, his back straight. A lock of hair dipped over his forehead. A tan tunic covered his broad shoulders, a thick leather belt wrapped his narrow waist, and brown trews hugged his powerful thighs.

Alec held a dark blue linen cape. "It is with great pleasure I pass the role of Laird of Glencara to Grant Campbell's eldest son…my brother, Logan Campbell."

Logan stood straight and tall, his expression serious. Lindsey could only imagine the emotions roiling through him. She yearned for him to feel he belonged, to be accepted for who he was, not disfavored for something he couldn't control.

He faced the clan and paused while skimming their expectant faces. "I pledge to do my utmost to protect and provide for all of ye. Our clan has suffered a great loss at the hands of the English, but we are resilient and will rebuild even stronger than we were before."

The room roared with cheers and good wishes.

Alec draped the cloak over Logan and pinned it at his shoulder with a broach displaying the Campbell crest, a red lion emblazoned on a shield. He extended his hand, and Logan grasped it. When Alec pulled Logan to him and slapped his back, more shouts and hurrahs filled the air.

Logan turned to Grant and Maria. His father beamed, and his mother's teary eyes shone with adoration. He leaned down to Grant and patted his back. When he straightened, Grant reached for Alec. Lindsey held her breath as her brother-in-law hesitated. Finally, his expression softened, and he accepted his father's hand. After heated discussions and accusations were assuaged, the brothers had come to an understanding and accepted the circumstances of Grant's unfortunate transgression.

Logan held his arm out to Maria. The older woman hurried into his embrace, and he kissed his mum's cheek. He hugged her then straightened. A moment passed before Maria stepped back and he faced Lindsey.

Joy for him washed over her. She rose on her toes and pecked his mouth. "Congratulations, *Laird.*"

"Ye don't get off that easy." He wrapped his arms around her and bent her backward, his mouth pressed to hers.

His lips stirred her senses, and her head reeled. More shouting and clapping echoed through the room, encouraging Logan. He broke the kiss, but his smoldering gaze held hers. "We'll pick up where we left off a bit later."

Delightful dithers careened through her belly, and she nibbled his bottom lip. "I look forward to it."

~~~

Logan's body reacted to Lindsey's soft curves with a vengeance. He restrained the overwhelming urge to hoist her over his shoulder, march to his bedchamber, and spend the rest of the night making love to her.

Men and women rushed the table. He appreciated their encouragement, but the lad between his legs had other things in mind. Logan gritted his teeth and pasted a pleasant expression across his face.

"We're happy to have ye as laird," Harold said.

Lindsey stayed at Logan's side. He nodded and shook the man's hand. "I'm honored."

"The clan's behind ye, lad," Betha said, her wrinkled face and toothless grin heartwarming. She tossed her head toward Lindsey and winked. "And ye found yerself quite a lass."

He curled an arm around Lindsey's shoulders and pulled her to him. She grinned and hugged his waist. "Thank ye," he said. "I think so too."

Logan repeated his gratitude for the clan's support over and over again as a line of members paid their respects. His chest swelled. The confidence these people...*his clan* bestowed upon him overwhelmed him.

Heather and Cameron hurried to them as the line wore down. Lindsey chatted with her sisters about the wedding—what she'd wear, what dishes they'd serve. Uninterested in the details, Logan turned to the festivities.

Jolecia carried a tray of tankards and a pitcher of ale as she weaved through the crowd. She paused before the revelers and handed out the drink. The curvaceous blonde stepped over to him. "Laird, would ye care for some?"

"Aye, thank ye."

She sidled closer, and her breast brushed his arm as she filled his tankard. "If ye need anything else, ye've only to ask."

He shook his head and accepted the drink. "I'm well cared for, lass."

"If that should change, I'm available." Her lips pursed. "Anytime."

"Congratulations," Colyne called as he, Thom, and Adam sauntered over to Logan. Jolecia offered the men ale, then strolled away.

A bandage still wrapped Adam's head. His coloring appeared a bit pale, his cheeks sallow. "It's good to see ye up."

His friend smiled. "Aye, I'm weak as a bairn, but I'll be fighting with ye soon. The Sassenachs won't keep me down."

"Take care of yerself," Logan said. "I'll need ye beside me when the time comes."

Thom rubbed the back of his neck. "Brandon expects more trouble?"

Logan nodded. "Rumors of planned attacks have spread. Brandon works to discern which ones have merit."

Taking a swig of ale, he glanced over the tankard. Skena placed a basket of sweet cakes on the table across the room. She straightened and wiped her hands on a cloth.

Logan set the tankard on the dais and addressed his friends. "Excuse me."

He made his way along the wall to Skena. She leaned over a table, lifted an empty platter, and stacked several dirty trenchers on it.

He stepped behind her. "Skena?"

She turned, and her eyes widened. "Oh, Logan. Congratulations."

"Thank ye."

"Ye'll make a wonderful laird. The clan is lucky to have ye."

He ran his hand down her arm. "We haven't had a chance to talk."

Her shoulders shrugged. "Ye've been busy."

"I'm never too busy for ye." He held her hand. "I know the news we share the same mum came as a shock, but I've always thought of ye as a sister. This just makes it a bit more official."

She smiled. "I'm proud to call ye brother."

"And ye sister." He paused, then grabbed a red apple from a basket on the table. "After the wedding, I want ye and yer bairn to move into Lindsey's chamber. We'll have someone take over yer duties in the kitchen."

"But what would I do all day? I enjoy working and staying busy."

He rubbed the fruit on his tunic. "I'm hoping when Lindsey has our bairn, ye'll help her."

Her face lit. "I'll be her nursemaid, and my Mary will grow up with yer wee ones."

He thought for a moment as he bit into the apple. Sweet and tart juices filled his mouth. "I guess that means I need to get used to the idea of having an English commander as a brother-in-law."

"Ye will grow to like Barclay. He's a fair and honorable man."

"I have to admit he surprised me with his swift actions in dealing with Collins." Logan sighed. "It'll take time to trust him…but I'll try."

Skena rose on her toes and kissed his cheek. "Thank ye, Brother."

Shouts interrupted them, and they turned to the noise. David and Travis blew into their bagpipes as Edward beat the drums, signaling the start of a lively reel. Thom, Colyne, and Randall shoved tables out of the way as women and men ran to take part.

Several groups of eight gathered and held hands. Lindsey and Ainslee joined, and sidestepping, the circles rotated. Logan's gaze followed Lindsey. Her head leaned back, and he longed to kiss the slender column of her neck. Coppery tresses swung as she slid across the floor. The ring broke in two as she, Iohne, Ainslee, and Blake joined hands.

The tempo quickened. The four twirled around faster and faster. The two couples turned from each other. Once again paired, they skipped in a figure eight weaving between the others. Logan's gut clenched as Iohne placed his hand on Lindsey's lower back. For God's sake, it was simply a dance. Feeling like a fool, he averted his attention to Frederick and Betsy, and laughed as they bumped into another couple. They quickly recovered, slid back into a ring, and the group glided around again.

The dancers repeated the sequence with Edward beating the drums faster, urging them to hasten their pace. Whoops and claps encouraged the participants until finally, the music slowed and the reel stopped.

Lindsey stepped back, her hand clutching her chest as she caught her breath.

This was his chance. Logan patted Skena's shoulder and weaved between the celebrating throng to Lindsey. "May I have this dance?"

She turned, her cheeks pinkened, and her luscious lips begged for his kiss. He twirled her into his arms. Her laughter washed over him like a soothing balm. He bent and nipped her ear. "On second thought, let's skip the rest of the celebration and go upstairs."

"Hmmm, that sounds good." She ran her hands around his neck and pressed her soft breasts into his chest.

A groan escaped his throat as he captured her lips. All of a sudden, someone grabbed his back. Alec and Robert gripped his arms and wrenched him away.

What the hell?

He looked at Lindsey.

She helplessly shrugged as Heather and Cameron giggled and tugged her from him calling, "None of that until tomorrow!"

Lindsey

~~~

The next day, Lindsey shoved her arms into the sleeves of her blue woolen cloak and wrapped them around her waist as she descended the keep's stairs and into the bailey. She breathed in crisp air, relishing the early morning hours before the clan awoke. Frost crunched beneath her leather shoes, the icy crystals causing chill bumps to pebble her skin. She shivered and hurried down the gravel path.

Flames from torches lining the interior yard shimmered in the winter breeze and cast light on Logan's warriors, who patrolled the ramparts. With swords strapped to their sides and bows at their backs, the formidable guards focused on the grounds beyond the thick castle walls.

Light spilled from the stable's entrance as two lads with buckets in each hand ran inside to milk the goats for the clan's morning meal. Lindsey passed the barn and turned left toward the old chapel. Logan and his men had finished the repairs in time for their wedding. Never having visited the sanctuary, she was anxious to see it.

Various sizes of grey and brown stones surrounded by thick mortar fortified the building. The single wooden door stood ajar. She jogged up the weathered steps and strolled through the entrance. The smell of smoke and charred wood filled the room, but new beams crisscrossed the ceiling and shored up the structure. She wandered down the main aisle, worn benches on either side. Dawn's light filtered through the stained glass above the altar and seeped into the chamber.

Her breath caught.

A white dove, its wings spread, hovered at the top of the window. Gold and blue rays shined around the bird, sunlight displaying the color's brilliance.

Doves represent love and gentleness.

Mum's voice wafted through Lindsey's mind. Her mother had loved the graceful birds and often told stories of how the creatures symbolized the Holy Spirit and gave hope to unfortunate weary souls.

Lindsey slid onto a bench, and a sense of peace enveloped her as if she sank into Mum's embrace. Not only had her mother squelched Da's rants about Lindsey's inappropriate attire, she had encouraged Lindsey's desire to work with the horses. The spirited woman instilled spunk in her daughters and because of her, Lindsey led the life of her choice. Tears misted her eyes. "I miss ye," she whispered. "Thank ye for believing in me, for giving me the freedom to follow my dream."

Wood creaked, and she turned to the noise.

Logan stood inside the chapel door, his hands clasped behind his back. "I didn't mean to interrupt."

She shook her head and wiped her watery eyes. "Ye didn't."

Brown hair brushed his broad shoulders. His cream-colored shirt lay open at the neck, displaying bronzed skin and dark wisps of hair. He stepped away from the door. Grey woolen trews hugged his lean hips and long muscular legs as he strode down the aisle. He dropped onto the bench next to her.

"Ye know we're not supposed to see each other before the wedding ceremony," she admonished. "'Tis considered bad luck."

His brow rose as he lifted her hand and kissed her knuckles. "I can't believe I just heard that from a lass bent on changing silly traditions."

She grinned. "I guess ye have me there."

His arm slid around her, and he tugged her closer, nestling her into his side. "I just wanted a few minutes. With overseeing repairs and yer family filling the keep, we never have time alone. I've missed ye."

He was right. Since her father and sisters arrived, they'd had little opportunity to themselves, and she had missed him as well. They sat in silence, enjoying the peacefulness of the quaint chapel.

A short while later she patted his thigh. "I'd best get back and help with the preparations for this evening."

Logan nodded and holding her hand, escorted her from the church and into the bailey. As she turned toward the keep, he tugged her into the alleyway behind the stables. Where was he taking her?

"Just a minute more," he whispered and backed her next to the outer castle wall. His lips captured hers in a gentle caress. Her body molded to him. She eased her hand on his chest and inhaled a fresh hint of soap. His hand cupped her bottom, his tongue sliding into her mouth with his moan. The familiar ache between her legs gripped her, and she squirmed.

"I can hardly wait until this evening," she breathed out and pushed on his shoulders. Her body screamed in protest. "But we must."

When he raised his gaze to hers, his eyes had darkened. His finger outlined her bottom lip, then trailed down the column of her neck to her breast and traced the sensitive tip.

Her heart slammed against her chest.

"Until tonight, princess."

Chapter Twenty Three

Later that morning while Lindsey visited with her sisters, Logan worked alongside his men to finish repairing damages suffered from Collins's attack. He and Blake rode draft horses into the bailey, transporting massive logs to replace burnt timbers. Logan dismounted and wiped his forehead as Colyne, Randall, and David unchained the trunks and wrestled the heavy wood to the smithy.

Masons clanged massive hammers against chisels and shaped slabs of stone into solid bases for the immense timbers. Travis and Iohne wrapped thick rope around the structure to hold the heavy foundation in place while others nailed iron spikes into the wood.

Alec strode across the yard with Robert. "Looks like ye're making headway."

"Aye, thankfully the damage wasn't significant." Logan untied the leather wineskin from his belt and swigged a mouthful of ale. "Fire destroyed the old storeroom so we cleared the debris and expanded the smithy's shop for better ventilation. We finished the smokehouse this morning and should have the barracks completed by late afternoon."

A lone rider trotted past the guard houses and into the bailey. Logan shaded the midday sun from his eyes. Hamish reined in his horse and dismounted. As McLeod's messenger strode toward them, he tugged off his gloves while eyeing Logan. "Gentlemen."

"Hamish." Logan extended his hand. The last time he saw McLeod's man, Logan wanted to kill him…or at least beat him senseless.

The messenger's assessing look dissipated, and he shook Logan's hand, then grasped Alec's and Robert's.

"What brings ye to Glencara?" Logan asked.

"Brandon's contacts have verified Edward's plan, and he requests ye remain on alert."

Robert folded his arms. "He suspects the Sassenachs will come this way?"

"There's a possibility."

Logan nodded. "Come inside and tell us what ye know."

He dodged the horses dragging logs and marched across the bailey with Alec, Hamish, and Robert following. They climbed the stairs and made their way down the long corridor to the solar.

Logan grabbed a flask of wine and several mugs from the side table and placed them on the desk. "Help yerself."

The men poured ale as Logan rifled through a cabinet next to the back wall. He extracted a map of Scotland and the surrounding areas. Spreading it across the large desk, he grasped the flask and set it on a furled corner to hold down the parchment. The men hovered over the drawing.

Hamish pointed at the small town of Kirkcudbright. "McLeod thinks they'll come across here or somewhere near the River Dee." He ran his finger across the map. "They'll make their way to Dumfries and travel north through the heart of Scotland to Edinburgh. That course takes them east of here, but Brandon asks ye to be watchful. I just returned from McIntosh Castle. They received word the soldiers will split into two groups. If that happens, there's a chance that route will bring them close to yer property, while other soldiers will continue north through Perth."

Logan exhaled loudly. "If that's true, the Sassenachs will march right through the area where Lindsey's younger sister resides."

Robert, who sat on one of the chairs before the desk, leaned back, mug balanced on his thigh. "Cameron says Elsbeth lives at an abbey just outside Scone, mere miles from Perth."

Hamish straightened. "There have been reports of Edward's soldiers stealing what little the houses of worship have then laying waste to the parishes."

"Will ye get word to Brandon so he can have supporters in the area watch for her?" Logan asked.

Hamish nodded. "I'll pass the information along and let ye know if we hear anything."

~~~

Lindsey visited with her sisters and Ainslee in the great hall. After the activities over the past couple of days had settled, the women finally had time to sit and catch up.

"Being with child becomes ye." Lindsey clutched a mug of hot, spiced honey water between her cold hands. "How do ye feel?"

Heather quirked a blonde eyebrow as she rubbed her swollen abdomen. "Like a fat cow."

"Och, and what's wrong with that?" Lindsey tried to keep a straight face, but failed miserably. "Don't ye remember Brother Michael expounding on The Goddess of Fertility? Hathor was a heavenly cow representing motherhood and love."

Cameron straightened. Her green eyes sparkled. She deepened her voice saying, "*The stars show milk flowing from her udders.*"

"Keep this up, and I'll be sure to remind ye of lovely Hathor when yer bellies are near to bursting," Heather threatened and laughed with the women.

Douglas squealed and wiggled from Cameron's lap. Chubby arms waving, he waddled across the room to Da.

"Well, there's my laddie." Da scooped him up and hobbled toward Cameron. "I was just going to the stables. May I take him with me?"

"That would be wonderful. I know he'd enjoy seeing the horses."

Lindsey watched her father stroll from the hall with the lad in his arms. "How is Da? Does he still get confused?"

"I'm afraid so," Heather answered. "Some days are better than others. He seems to remember things from a long time ago, but if ye ask about something that happened last week…or even earlier in the day, he can't seem to recall."

Sorrow for the once sharp, stalwart man filled Lindsey's heart.

"He loves caring for little Douglas," Heather added. "The lad lightens Da's spirit."

"And my wee one loves being with Da." Cameron grinned. "We visit home often, and it gives me a nice reprieve."

Heather leaned back in her chair. "He's a sweet bairn, but I don't know how ye keep up with him. I stay so tired I worry how I'll manage once this babe is born."

"One isn't too bad but I'm not sure how I'll keep up with two of them."

Lindsey sat forward. "*Two* of them?"

Cameron nodded. "I suspect we'll have another little one by fall."

"Oh, that's wonderful, Cammie," Heather said.

"I'll have three bairns to spoil." Lindsey grinned. "Maybe someday Logan and I will add to the family."

"In a few years, the hall will be filled with babes," Ainslee said. "And ye have another sister as well?"

Stilted silence fell over the women.

Ainslee looked from Lindsey to Cameron then Heather. "I hope I didn't speak out of turn."

Lindsey shook her head. "Ye didn't. We're just worried about Elsbeth."

"Have ye heard anything?" Ainslee asked Heather.

"Not since her message last summer." A wistful expression crossed Heather's face. "At that time she sounded happy."

Ainslee placed her mug on the table. "Tell me about her."

An image of her dark-haired sister with violet eyes materialized before Lindsey's eyes. "She has always surrounded herself with children."

"For years she helped Mum deliver goods and medicinal herbs to the abbey in Cunningham," Cameron said. "She often stayed for several days to help care for the abandoned or orphaned children."

"Then over two years ago, she moved with the sisters to Scone where they established a new church." Heather paused. "Da begged her not to go. He worried so, knowing he couldn't protect her. But, she was determined to devote her life to caring for innocent children and victims of the rebellion."

Ainslee patted Heather's hand. "I'm sure she's fine."

Men's voices drifted from down the corridor. Logan appeared with Alec, Robert, and Hamish trailing behind. Why was Hamish here? Knowing the man most likely didn't pay a social call, nervous jitters started in Lindsey's belly. Her sisters must've felt the same as silence fell over them.

The men shook the messenger's hand. Hamish tipped his head toward the women then marched from the room.

Logan turned to her. Worry lines etched his forehead, and concern showed in his eyes. Fear welled up inside Lindsey over what Hamish wanted, what news he delivered.

Logan, Alec, and Robert strode across the hall. Logan eased next to Lindsey and placed his arm around her shoulders with her brothers-in-law doing the same with her sisters. The stilted silence stretched thin.

Lindsey leaned up and peered at Logan. "Well?"

His eyes narrowed, and his thumb stroked her upper arm. "Sassenachs are expected to march through Perth."

Lindsey gasped and clutched her chest. "What?"

Cameron slid to the edge of her chair and looked at Logan. "When? What about Elsbeth?"

He held up a hand. "Hamish is going to get word to Brandon's contacts in the area to be on the lookout for her."

"Is there nothing else we can do?" Lindsey asked.

"I'm sending men to the abbey first thing in the morning," Logan said. "We'll do our best to bring her home before the English soldiers reach her."

The trip to Perth could take weeks with the winter weather bearing down. Once again, silence fell over the somber group. Images of Elsbeth, surrounded by children, telling stories and taking the wee ones on her *adventures*, flashed through Lindsey's mind. Although her compassionate sister had set out to save the orphans, Edward didn't give a whit whether she or the children lived or died. He and his army would plough through the country, leaving devastation and destruction in their path.

Bands squeezed Lindsey's chest. She prayed Logan's men would get to Elsbeth in time.

Chapter Twenty Four

The sun dipped low in the sky, sending long shadows across Lindsey's bedchamber.

It was almost time.

Her nerves jangled more now than when she ran missives for Hamish. Why, she had no idea. She was marrying Logan. She loved him and having already sampled what awaited beneath the blankets, she knew she'd be content in his arms. Giggles burst forth at her delightful thoughts.

Sinking lower into the tub's warm water, she closed her eyes. Images of his muscular body covering hers flashed through her mind. She relived the feel of his brawny chest and sculpted abdomen under her palms, his stiff manhood nudging her mons. Naughty tingles wound through her belly with memories of him pushing into her.

A knock sounded on the door, and she jumped.

Heather stuck her head inside the room. "Ye aren't out of the bath yet?"

Caught daydreaming wanton thoughts, heat crept up Lindsey's neck and spread over her face. She stood and grabbed the drying cloth from the three legged stool beside her. "I'm finished."

Heather swung the door wide and strolled into the room with Cameron, Ainslee, and Skena trailing behind. A cream-colored gown layered in silk draped Heather's arm. "I brought Mum's dress for ye."

Tiny lace flowers adorned with little white beads trimmed the bodice, and the skirt flared under a gold belt at the hips. An intricate design embroidered with matching gold thread circled the hem and long flowing sleeves.

How Lindsey wished Mum could be here. She held the drying cloth next to her. Tears filled her eyes. "Thank ye."

Lindsey

"Let's get ye into it," Ainslee suggested. "The clan awaits ye."

~~~

With her skirt bunched in one hand and clutching Da's arm with the other, Lindsey stepped through the chapel door.

Logan.

Draped in the Campbell blue and brown plaid, he waited at the altar beside Father Thomas, his strong hands clasped before his waist, powerful legs braced apart. Shaggy brown hair brushed his broad shoulders, and his intense look caused the rapid beat of her pulse. Nerves wound tight, tremors shook her body.

Da patted her hand and ushered her inside the sanctuary. The clan filled benches set out in rows on either side of the main aisle. Colyne and Thom stood next to the back wall and nodded encouragement.

Twinkling lights flickered from tallow candles arranged in the windows. Wrought iron candelabras positioned around the room sported thick yellowed candles and bathed the clan in muted shades of gold. Black smoke wafted off the flames and shining reflections twinkled like stars across the crowded pews. Perched on a bench to the right of Logan, Faye clutched a wooden harp. Her nimble fingers plucked the strings and cast a mellow sound through the small chamber.

She and Da started down the main aisle. The clan stood and turned to them. Lindsey smiled at the men's and women's cheerful faces.

Kirk tipped his head toward her. "M'lady."

To her left, Glenda reached out, and her fingertips brushed Lindsey's arm, her warm expression welcoming. Travis and David sat beside Glenda, grins plastering their faces. To her right, Skena, with her daughter propped on her hip, waved the bairn's wee hand. Several lads next to them also waved.

Lindsey grinned and continued down the aisle. Heather, Alec, Cameron, and Robert sat closer to the altar with Grant and Maria.

Da guided Lindsey to Logan and kissed her cheek. "I love ye, daughter."

Emotion welled in her chest as he placed her hand in Logan's warm palm.

Logan's fingers wrapped around hers. Dimples pressed into his bearded cheeks, and he winked. "Ye're beautiful, princess."

Joyous tears stung the backs of her eyes. "Ye don't look so bad yerself."

Father Thomas chuckled and cleared his throat.

Happiness burst through her as she faced the priest. Her fervent desire to marry the man she had dreamt of for so long was finally coming true.

~~~

Father Thomas closed the bible and held it before his waist. "May God bless and unite ye."

Logan turned Lindsey toward him.

She was his.

Now and forever.

He pulled her to him and captured her lips. Her fingers splayed over his chest. Luscious curves pressed into him, and he yearned to devour her sweetness.

The crowd rushed them, tugging them apart with congratulations and well wishes. "Get that look out yer eye, lad," an older man shouted. "Ye still have hours to go!"

Don't remind me.

"Come here, Lindsey," Grant called, motioning.

She hurried to him. He held his arms wide, and she bent and embraced him. His eyes closed, and he patted her back. Logan couldn't hear what his father said in her ear, but she kissed his cheek. She then reached for Maria's hand. Logan's mum had tears in her eyes as she beamed and nodded.

Heather and Cameron waited beside the altar with their father. When Lindsey turned, the sisters hurried to her and the three hugged.

The old laird nudged Logan's arm. "See what it'll be like to have a pack of daughters?"

Daughters? Logan swallowed hard.

"Son?" Grant called.

Logan stepped to his da and patted his shoulder.

"I'm so happy for ye and Lindsey," his mother said as she wrapped her arms around Logan's waist.

He hugged Mum to his side. "As I am."

"Let's celebrate," Colyne yelled. "Everyone to the hall."

More cheers bellowed from the uproarious clan. Lindsey held Logan's hand, and they made their way to the awaiting banquet.

Servants scurried around the room, their arms laden with trays from the kitchen. Tables lined the great hall, overflowing with another feast of roasted boar, smoked fish, and poultry. Breads, pastries, and wild berries crowded baskets beside platters of stewed kale and beans. Several men had already dipped into the barrels of ale. Musicians played, and a young lad chased another between dancers while Lindsey's father settled at the hearth with Logan's parents.

Alec stepped beside Logan and clasped his shoulder. "I hope ye know what ye've gotten yerself into." He shook Logan, his playful scrutiny on Lindsey. "That little spitfire about drove me daft!"

"Spitfire indeed," Lindsey scoffed.

Logan kissed her temple as Alec laughed and tugged Heather to his side.

"'Tis a good thing to have a spirited lass around to keep things interesting," Cameron said as she walked up with Robert. Douglas toddled along beside them with a firm grasp on his father's finger.

Logan couldn't agree more. As a matter of fact, he planned to explore a host of *interesting things* with his spirited lass tonight.

~~~

Logan twirled Lindsey into his arms and swept her onto the dance floor. He held one hand, and she placed the other on his shoulder as they glided amidst the revelers.

"Are ye happy?" he asked.

She toyed with his soft hair brushing her fingers. "I couldn't be happier."

He watched her, his gaze assessing. "I still need yer help peddling the horses."

Her heart flipped over. "Ye've got it."

His eyes narrowed. "But when ye become heavy with my bairn, ye will stay clear of the stables."

Aye, while with child it wouldn't be safe around the large animals. "Of course."

He pulled her close. "I'm anxious to see yer stomach rounding."

Naughty sensations bubbled up inside her. She pressed herself fully against him, and her lips grazed his ear. "Ye'd best get busy then."

He groaned and ran his hands down her back, molding her curves to his hard member. He bent her backward, and her arms eased around his neck as he slid his tongue against hers. She moaned, and heat shot straight to his cock.

The clan clapped and cheered.

He straightened while nuzzling her neck. A faint whiff of flowers filled his nostrils. "I'm hard with wanting ye, wife."

She canted her hips against his stiff member and nibbled his cheek. "I can't wait for ye to show me just how much ye want me."

Shite! Her words caused his shaft to pulse.

Several throats cleared. "Excuse us, Logan, but it's time to get Lindsey ready for bed."

Lindsey straightened and Logan turned.

Heather, Cameron, and Ainslee had emerged from the crowd, and with smirks slinking across their faces, waited behind Logan.

Excited jitters pinged through Lindsey's belly. Her wedding night had finally arrived. When she started toward the women, Logan stopped her. Before she knew what he was about, he scooped her up. She squeaked, and threw her arms around his neck.

He winked and a devilish grin grew across his face. "Just what I had in mind, lass."

Her sisters' mouths dropped open. Ainslee gasped, and her brown eyes widened. "Logan! 'Tis unseemly."

He chuckled and strode across the great hall. Excitement at his bold action mounted inside Lindsey and ribbons of wanton desire coiled through her. Cradling her in his arms, Logan took the stairs two at a time. Whistles shrieked and shouts rebounded with the clan's rowdy encouragement.

She nuzzled his neck and brushed her lips across his whiskered cheek. His face turned to hers, and he captured her mouth while he marched down the corridor and into his chamber. He pushed the door closed with his foot and carried her across the room before the blazing hearth.

Her body eased down the length of him. As her toes touched the floor, he buried his face in her hair. His hands roamed down her back and clutched her bottom, lifting her into the hard ridge pressing her stomach. "God, ye feel good, wife."

Wife.

The simple word enveloped her in bliss. Her dream had come true.

She was his.

"And ye, husband." Aching to feel his naked skin next to her, she grasped the hem of his tunic and tugged it up.

He stepped back and pulled it over his head. Brown shaggy hair fell to his broad shoulders as he dropped the clothing on a chair before the hearth. Firelight bathed his sculpted body in dancing shadows. Dark hair feathered his brawny chest and flat abdomen then disappeared into his tan trews.

She skimmed her fingertips over his muscular chest then splayed her palms across his ribs. Her touch brushed scars crisscrossing his rippled torso. She leaned into him, inhaling a scent of soap as her lips trailed over his warm skin. Grasping his lean hips, she knelt before him, and her mouth followed the soft hair down to his flat abdomen. At eye level, a thick bulge pressed against the front of his trews. His hunger heightened her desire, causing heat to pool between her thighs.

He grasped her shoulders. "If ye keep looking at me like that, I won't be able to control myself."

She straightened and feathered kisses on his lips as his fingers slid through her hair. "Exactly."

A hint of wine wafted off his breath. His tongue eased into her mouth while her hands explored the contours of his chiseled back and lower to his tight rear end. He broke the kiss, and the passion in his eyes struck her core.

She ached for him.

"I want to see ye." His fingers worked the ties of her gown.

Her breathing quickened, and her breasts' sensitive tips craved his touch. With her arms held over her head, he eased off the dress. Clad in a lacy chemise, she laid her mum's gown on the table between the chairs and smoothed the skirt.

He stepped behind her and pushed her hair to the side. She closed her eyes as his lips trailed kisses along her shoulder. A hand snaked underneath her chemise, and a warm palm covered her breast as he pressed himself into her back. She leaned back, her hand clutching his to her bosom. With each stroke of his thumb, tingles shot to the apex of her legs.

His other hand slid inside her drawers, across her bare stomach, then lower. She gasped, her quivering flesh anxious for his touch. He cupped her womanhood. Delicious bands of desire surged, and a sigh escaped her lips as she pressed herself into his palm.

He tweaked her nipple while a thick finger eased between her heated folds. He dipped into her entrance then circled her swollen pearl. "Ahh, lass, yer sweet body weeps for me."

"I want ye," she whispered, caught in the haze of passion.

His stiff manhood slid up the crease of her clothed bottom. He nuzzled her neck while his finger swirled her nub. "Easy, we're just getting started. I want to savor ye."

Passion strummed through her blood. Her legs grew weak. His hands left her heated flesh and soft kisses feathered her lower back. He pulled her drawers, and they slid over her bottom and pooled around her feet. When he turned her to face him, her breath caught at his intense stare.

He lifted her chemise over her head and cast the garment aside. She stood nude before him. Although cool air wafted around them, his gaze's heated caress warmed her, and she yearned for their bodies' joining.

~~~

Firelight highlighted Lindsey's lush curves, the puckered tips of her heavy breasts, and the auburn curls covering her woman's haven. Logan's mouth watered, and his manhood engorged.

She knelt before him and unbuckled his belt. Her fingers untied his trews, and his shaft jutted from the top. She hesitated, her eyes studying the head of his cock. God, he throbbed with need. When she inched the clothing down his hips, his member sprang free, standing stiff against his belly. Her finger brushed the sensitive head, and he hissed.

"Did I do something wrong?" she whispered.

"Nay, I want ye to touch me."

Her teeth caught her bottom lip. One hand encircled him, stroking him up and down while the other cupped his ballocks. He gritted his teeth, and threw his head back, the pleasure exquisite. Beads of sweat broke across his forehead. Unable to stand much more, he grasped her hand and tugged her up before him.

"Come." Fingers interlaced with hers, he led her to the bed. His hands splayed over her trim waist, and he lifted her onto the edge of the mattress. She scooted back, but he caught her ankles, and she fell back on her elbows, her luscious breasts bobbing.

"Not so fast." He placed her feet on either side of him. Starting with her lower leg, he nibbled her silky skin. He eased between her knees and pushed them farther apart.

Her eyes widened, and her body tensed. "Logan?"

"Aye?" His tongue traced circles on the inside of her thigh. "Just relax, and let me pleasure ye."

She hesitated, then laid back. He eased higher, taking his time, relishing every inch of her delectable body. A hint of lavender wafted from her hidden treasure as he blew over her curls. He feathered kisses on her soft mound, and she gasped. His tongue slid between her nether lips.

Parting her, he suckled her swollen bud and slipped a finger into her honeyed sheath.

She moaned, writhed beneath him, and her breathing became pants. He swirled his tongue around her delicate flesh, and she sharply inhaled. Her body stiffened, and she cried out as her sheath tightened around his finger in spasms, her warm juices flowing. After massaging her slowly, he slipped his hand from between her legs and climbed higher on her sated body.

Her luscious breasts filled his palms, and his tongue flicked the pebbled tips. Her fingers laced through his hair, encouraging him. The bottoms of her feet slid over his arse, and she arched beneath him. "I want to feel ye inside me."

Heat shot straight to his throbbing cock. He captured her kiss swollen mouth as his shaft glided up her slick folds. She wrapped her legs around his waist and canted her hips toward him. Leaning on his forearms, he looked into her passion filled eyes. His cock pulsed at her entrance.

"Ye're mine." He eased the head of his shaft into her tight sheath. "And ye always will be."

He thrust into her warmth.

Oh, God. Pure pleasure washed over him.

She moaned and moved her hips. He slid out of her haven, eased back in, and basked in the feel of her surrounding him. Wrapping his arms around her, he pulled her to him as he rose on his knees. She straddled his thighs, and he grasped her bottom, lifting her then settling her back on him. She clutched his shoulders, and her breasts bounced in his face.

When he reached between them and massaged her swollen jewel, her breath caught, and her sheath clutched. His finger swirled as he thrust, a building pressure mounting. She cried out and once again her muscles gripped him, this time milking his shaft. Waves of ecstasy washed through him as he held her tight and spewed his seed into her womb.

Her sated body collapsed against him, and he eased his spent member in and out of her honeyed sheath. He slid from her body and rolled onto his back. Wrapping his arm around her, he tucked her against his chest. Her soft breasts snuggled next to him, and he ran his fingers down her side.

A peaceful contentment flowed through his soul. His most ardent desires had come true. He had married the lass of his dreams, and as laird he could provide for her as a laird's daughter deserved. She would give him children, grow old by his side.

He smiled considering her wild, carefree nature. Aye, her fiery temperament oftentimes flared, but her intense passion matched the spirit of the lass defying traditions, riding on the back of a horse sprinting over the wild Scottish moors.

He was one lucky man, and he looked forward to many nights ahead with his princess wrapped in his arms.

~~~

Later that night, Lindsey snuggled beside Logan's heated body. After their love making, his rapid heartbeat steadied, and his breathing slowed. He traced little circles on her hip as she splayed her palm through the dark hair covering his chest. With the exception of worry over Elsbeth, the pieces of her life had finally come together, and she was happier than she had ever thought possible.

Continuing to stomp out ridiculous customs, she would work alongside Logan in the stables. He had requested her help; wanted her opinion. He treated her as a partner, not as an inferior woman. Together they would breed horses and add to the already magnificent herd. Having agreed to curtail her direct involvement in the rebellion, she'd consider how to use her animals to benefit the cause.

Lads just like their father and feisty lasses to keep everyone in line would fill their home. She smiled. Perhaps she carried his bairn now. The hearth's fire popped, and a shower of sparks sprayed into the quiet room. A comforting aroma of peat surrounded her, and she sighed.

Thank ye, Lord, for blessing me with a husband who loves me and gives me the freedom to be me.

Serenity washed over her as she lay nestled in the arms of the man who had always held her heart. And always would.

What's Next and Favorite Authors' New Releases

Thank you for reading *Lindsey*! I hope you enjoyed her story. Please visit my website to learn more about my books and let me hear from you. Email me at mcfarland.lane@gmail.com.

Check out Cameron's and Heather's stories, *The Daughters of Alastair MacDougall* ~ Book I and II. And look for *Elsbeth ~ The Daughters of Alastair MacDougall* ~ Book IV to be released Spring 2015. You can find my books at Lane McFarland at Amazon.

Cameron

Determined to band Scots together against English tyranny, Laird Robert Graham seals a truce with his feuding neighbor, the MacDougalls. But after his brother is nearly killed in a treacherous attack, Graham kidnaps the laird's daughter in an act of revenge.

Cameron MacDougall has devoted her life to the healing arts. She's long rebelled against her father's feuding ways, but when Robert Graham abducts her, she's finds herself at the center of the dispute between their families. She expects the anger she feels, not the simmering attraction to the powerful warrior, or the love she develops for his clan.

Can she stop further violence between the clans with her escape? Or will she find her surrender leads to a lasting peace and her own heart's desire?

Heather

Bent on overcoming the belief he's failed his aging father, Laird Alec Campbell concentrates on proving his worth to his people. He provides for them and leads men into battle, vowing never again to disappoint his clan or lose his heart.

Bound by a promise to her dying mother, Heather MacDougall secretly leads rebel warriors in her quest to keep her clan intact and hold off those who plot to overtake her father's land. She fights to keep her secrets safe, while resisting the lure of the handsome young laird who challenges her defenses.

They can't deny their passionate attraction, but can their love survive their secrets?

Next is a peek at Tess St. John's book *LAST CHANCE*
(Chances Are Series ~ Book 3)

Mr. Silas Green will never erase the memories of what he's
done to rescue the helpless, but he plans to relinquish his
post with the Royal Navy and live a quiet life making
compasses instead of saving lives. However, first he must
fulfill his father's dying wish by escorting his sisters to
their mother's Scottish homeland.

A bit in awe of Mr. Green, the man who rescued her from
nearly being sold into slavery, Miss Celeste Young also
senses his soul-deep pain. When he asks her to become a
companion to his blind sister and accompany his family on
a trip, Celeste seizes the opportunity to escape London and
the men eagerly seeking to become her protector.

The undeniable attraction between Silas and Celeste
develops into a tender friendship. The more time they
spend together, the more his torturous memories ease and
his pain lessens. But dangerous secrets await them in
Scotland. When Celeste is threatened, will Silas be able to
save her or lose his last chance at love?

LAST CHANCE

Ipswich, England ~ Summer 1826

Chapter One

Hell was not for the dead, but for the living.

Silas Green had witnessed the degradation of society,
the torture of slavery, and mankind at its worst. To him,
Hell didn't exist in some other realm, rather it surrounded
him every day.

And right now, in this carriage jostling down a grassy trail, he sat in a different kind of Hell.

Hell was mayhap a bit extreme, but at present he definitely resided in Purgatory. Atoning for his sins, for all the times he'd spent bedding women, for acts he'd knowingly committed and admittedly reveled in.

Miss Celeste Young, the reason for his discomfort, sat across from him. She personified temptation. And after being cooped up in this carriage with her for six hours, he'd sell his soul to Lucifer just to touch her, to confirm her skin felt as soft as it appeared, to feel the silkiness of her brunette hair, to learn if her lips against his would take his dead soul to Heaven.

Silas shook his head, trying to clear it. He wasn't this deprived. He'd only been at sea for two months. He should get out of the carriage and ride Zeus. However, his uncomfortable arousal would be more painful in a saddle. Over the last couple of hours he'd even contemplated the idea of learning to ride side-saddle to alleviate his problems. That ridiculous thought proved too emasculating, though, and also proved he was going mad.

He'd mostly listened to Miss Young and his sister, Brianna, during the ride, joining the conversation only when directly spoken to.

"Do you believe so, Silas?" Brianna asked.

He nodded. "I think you are right. It is safe for you to return to Coleman's."

She'd resided at Coleman's School for the Blind the last fourteen years, until a few months ago when one of the students was kidnapped. Silas rode hide for leather to get to Brianna and remove her from the school so she, too, would not be abducted.

"Oh, how wonderful." His sister seemed most eager. At times it was almost eerie how her sightless green eyes showed expressiveness. "After we visit Father, will you see me back?"

Damn. Their father had other plans for her, yet Silas refused to be the bearer of that news. "Whatever you wish."

Brianna turned toward Miss Young. "What will you do when I go back to school, dear? Where will you find work?"

Work? Would she prefer to work rather than find another protector?

Hiring Miss Young as Brianna's companion might seem unorthodox to most people considering she'd once been Sir Roderick's mistress. But after Miss Young's rescue from nearly being sold into slavery, Malcolm Westbourne, Silas's captain, implored him to hire her. And since Silas's return yesterday, Brianna had not stopped singing the companion's praises.

"Do not worry over me," Miss Young insisted.

"Perhaps you can find employ at Coleman's," Brianna said brightly.

Silas scowled. "Don't they have mostly blind employees?"

"That is true. I plan to work there next year." Brianna gingerly reached out, and when she found Miss Young's shoulder she patted it. "We will find you something."

How could his sister sound so certain? If Miss Young truly understood how the world worked, she would use her unparalleled beauty to secure her safety. Many men would offer their estates to have her as a mistress.

Silas never kept a paramour, not when there were willing females in every port and town. Yet after spending time with Miss Young, he might actually have considered asking her to sign a contract if she and Brianna had not formed such a close friendship. Plus, and he hated to admit it, he was unsure if he possessed the funds to support a mistress. For years he'd been in the Royal Navy. He often returned to London and Ipswich to check on his family, but had no idea the condition of the estate's finances. He'd paid Miss Young out of his personal accounts since hiring her, and he could live comfortably on his saved earnings until he joined a business venture with his friends Malcolm Westbourne and Zachery Derby.

Miss Young peered out the window and sighed. Her bodice tightened the slightest bit around her...

He shifted in his seat.

Yes, this carriage grew hotter each moment, resembling Hell more and more.

He should have visited Mrs. Vick's elite establishment prior to climbing into this godforsaken carriage. Then at least his body would be relaxed and sated.

Silas glanced at Miss Young's profile. Who did he think he was hoodwinking? He would still want her. As if sensing his gaze, Miss Young turned his way. Her sherry-colored eyes met his and a smile touched her lips.

He felt a jolt low in his abdomen.

"I cannot thank you enough for allowing me the opportunity to become Miss Brianna's companion these last months. I do hope to find another position as a companion, or possibly a governess." So she did intend to find employ instead of searching for a protector.

"It is I who must thank you. I never once worried about her welfare while gone."

"Silas, you must write her a glowing reference letter," Brianna urged.

"I will have it ready before we leave Ipswich."

The sun stabbed between the clouds and rained in through the window, catching streaks of blonde in Miss Young's brunette hair. How he wanted to reach out and capture the loose tendril hanging next to her cheek.

Returning focus to his sister, Silas switched the conversation back to her. "Brie, did you have many visitors while staying at the London townhouse?"

Brianna laughed. "I daresay we both did. Most were interested in learning more about Celeste and her reasons for becoming my companion. Tell him about the men, dear. About the flowers."

A hint of a blush colored the companion's cheeks. "It was nothing, really."

Her expression appeared shy and introverted, not the confident look of a courtesan. Being Sir Roderick's mistress should have infused her backbone with stiff solitude. She must have had propositions from half the men in London, yet she shied just now. Her actions did not make sense.

"Nothing? You are calling love sick men stumbling over themselves nothing?" Brianna folded her hands together in her lap. "After we attended Lady Drake's ball, we were inundated with callers. So much so, we moved to Celeste's townhouse to escape them. There we were still visited by many, but not hounded so badly."

"Unless you consider Mr. James," Miss Young added.

Ah, Mr. James. Silas wondered when the man's name would come up. Mr. James made no secret of his interest in pursuing a relationship with Brianna. Five years older than Brie, he taught at Coleman's. James's sister was blind, and he claimed to always want to work with others with the same affliction. However, the man clearly wanted to do more than work with Brie.

"And what did Mr. James want?" he asked.

"He seemed extremely curious as to when Miss Brianna would return to Coleman's," Miss Young playfully said. "I believe his comment was that the days proved endless without her about."

Brie's neck and face blazed red.

Silas grinned, enjoying the fact Brie had someone to tease and talk with.

Miss Young made a dramatic gasp. "He seemed forlorn to leave the premises each day."

"Each day?" Silas punctuated both words.

"Oh, yes." Humor ran in Miss Young's voice.

Brie inhaled. "Each blasted day." That caused her and her companion to laugh.

He smiled at their easy interaction and ignored the way Miss Young's laughter reached inside of him, making his chest feel lighter. He'd bedded many women hoping and praying one might deliver him from the darkness he'd experienced. Deliver him from his tainted sinner's soul. None had. Could this woman?

"Please do not misunderstand. I am fond of Mr. James." Brie bit her thumb. "But his visits seemed rather excessive."

The carriage stopped, and Silas peeked out the window to see his father's grey-bricked home. He flung the carriage door open and jumped down. After helping Brie descend the steps, he reached out to Miss Young. Her gloved hand smoothly slid into his, and she raised her foot over the carriage doorway.

Suddenly, her body plummeted toward the ground. She squealed.

Silas quickly stepped forward, wrapped his arms around her waist, and pulled her body against his. Her frantic breaths struck his neck.

He was back in Hell. And if this be what it entailed, he wished the devil would take him now. With her body pressed to his and her face buried in his neck, he never wanted to be anywhere else. He breathed deeply, catching the same scent that plagued him in the carriage. It wasn't overpowering, but subtle, exotic, and alluring—different than any perfume he'd ever smelled.

"What happened?" Brie frowned.

Miss Young held on to him for another three heartbeats and finally looked up. Their gazes locked. For seconds they stared at each other. Finally, her light brown eyes blinked and she released him. Obligated to do the same, he stepped back.

"My shoe caught on the carriage doorway and I toppled out headed straight for the drive. Your brother caught me and saved me from making an arse of myself." She straightened her dress, the shoulders having slipped down her arms. Some of her hair had fallen and curls now framed her face.

"Where are you when I need you, Silas?" Brie giggled.

"Dear, you make an arse out of yourself too often for me to save you every time."

Brianna slapped his arm. She had good aim for a blind person.

Miss Young smiled. "Thank you for your assistance, Mr. Green."

He opened his mouth to answer when Eric approached from the side of the house. The long-time stable master was almost completely grey-haired now. "Lieutenant Green. Miss Brianna. Ye are finally here."

"Eric, it is good to see you." He shook the man's hand. Silas tilted his head to one side, then the other, trying to stretch out the tension held there. "I am no longer a lieut—"

The front door flew open and his father's most trusted servant rushed out. Well, Hamilton was more than a servant, he—

"Come, Silas. Brianna." Dressed in black from head to foot, urgency had replaced Hamilton's normally staid countenance. "You must come quickly. It is your father."

Silas reached for Brianna's arm.

"Go ahead. I will bring her," Miss Young said.

He nodded and followed Hamilton, having to run to keep up. Hamilton uttered, "I only hope it's not too late." They scaled the stairs as if rabid hounds chased them.

Hamilton stopped at the top of the stairwell and pointed down the hallway. Father's bedchamber door stood open. Silas entered to find his sisters, Jean and Lorna, each on a side of the bed, both crying into handkerchiefs. Father lay on the mattress motionless. Lifeless.

The girls looked up and ran to Silas. He held them, each crying on a shoulder. Dr. Montgomery picked up his black bag, bowed his head as he passed them, and left the room.

Silas's focus returned to his father. He'd been expecting this day, yet…he swallowed hard. He loved and respected his father, even though they'd not agreed on many things.

He kissed his sisters' heads before leaving them to approach the bed.

His heart pounded in his chest and ears. It wasn't as if he'd never seen a dead person. Suddenly images of lifeless faces and bodies bombarded him.

To distract himself, he took inventory of the room. This bedchamber had not changed since he could remember. Decorated in rich colors of green, it housed a mahogany four poster bed, a huge mirrored dresser, and a single nightstand. Two wingback chairs flanked the fireplace in the corner.

Once at the bedside, he closed his eyes and took a fortifying breath, then peered down. His father's almost bald head looked dull, his skin white, and his cracked lips were blue.

Words eluded him. What did one say to a dead man?

Whispering at the door caught his attention. Lorna and Jean were in front of Brianna and Miss Young, stroking Brianna's hair and murmuring. Brianna's coloring had paled, and she still clutched Miss Young's arm. He cleared his throat as he advanced toward the women. "Brianna, would you like to say goodbye?"

"I would." She held out her hand. He gently placed it on his arm and escorted her toward the bed. "I may be spoiled from living with Celeste and her love of fresh air, but this room is sweltering. And it smells of laudanum, Silas. Heavily."

"I am sure they administered it for pain. We would not have wanted him to suffer."

"You are right," she agreed. When he stopped, she let go of him. "Can you direct me toward his hand?"

Silas reached over and grasped his father's still warm hand and placed it in Brianna's. She leaned over and raised it to her face, kissing the back. "May you rest well, Father." Such a sweet gesture, yet somehow cold. Not cold exactly; more detached. Brianna had lived at Coleman's for so long Father was more of a figurehead to her. Lorna and Jean, on the other hand, considered him a papa in every way.

"I wish I'd spent more time with him." Brie straightened, tears hovering on her lids.

He studied his father one last time. When he turned, his other two sisters were at the foot of the bed, both staring at Father.

"Shall we?" He motioned to the doorway and his sisters led him and Brianna out of the room and down the stairs. Miss Young was nowhere to be found.

And why in Hades was he looking for her anyway?

Silas helped Brie into the study and settled her on the settee. While his other sisters found places to sit, he walked to the door and shut it. This study remained his domain whenever he visited Ipswich. Since becoming an adult, he'd felt more contented here than anywhere else in the house. Maybe the feeling came from the familiar paintings on the walls or the various nautical items his father had accumulated while he served in the Royal Navy. Or perhaps the masculinity of the room, the dark red walls and dim lighting, made Silas relax.

"How was he before he passed?" he asked.

Jean's tears began anew. "Extremely anxious to speak to you."

It felt as if he'd received a fist to the gut. His father was supposed to tell the girls of their commitment in Scotland. Had he? Or had he left the task to Silas?

"He wrote you two letters. They are on the desk." Jean turned toward Brie and spoke as if addressing a child. "He also left one for you, Brianna."

Brie stiffened. "Thank you. I will have Miss Young read it to me later. Speaking of Miss Young, where is she?"

"When you entered Papa's room, she mentioned something about wanting to see to your things and hurried off." Lorna wiped her nose with a handkerchief. "I am sure she is giving us time as a family."

"What of services, Silas?" Jean rubbed her arms like she was cold.

"After I read Father's letters, I will know if he had any special wishes. However, I assume he would like to be buried quietly with a funeral feast like we did for Mum."

"When?" Lorna questioned.

"Soon as possible." Silas glanced at the side table. The brandy called to him, but he ignored the beckoning. He needed to read his father's letters with a clear head.

"I would like to freshen up." Brianna stood.

"Let me help you to your room." Lorna got to her feet and grasped Brie's hand.

"Lorna, have you ever noticed how Silas leads me around? I hold on to him, not the other way about. That is easiest for me and the person assisting me."

"Oh. As you wish."

"It is not a wish. It is a routine, one that helps me feel comfortable. If you and Jean would have visited Coleman's you might have learned that technique. It is one of the first things taught to those who are close to sightless people."

Silas could not fault Brie for finally bringing up the fact neither sister visited Coleman's, although this did not seem like the appropriate time.

Brie exhaled in a huff. "Is my letter from Father here in the study?"

"How did you know we were in the study?" Jean stood, retrieved the note, and put it in Brianna's hand.

"Three clues." Brianna's voice rose as she spoke. "One, I did live here and visited over the years, so I do know which way the study is from the stairs. Two, it smells of Father's tobacco. And three, you mentioned Silas's letters were on the desk. See how I did that using the powers of deduction. Do you not think a blind person can—"

"Brianna," Silas quietly reprimanded.

She threw her hands up. "Well, they think I'm an idiot."

"We do not!" both sisters quickly argued.

"Fine. A simpleton, then."

Lorna and Jean looked at each other.

Brie's voice returned to normal. "I have wants, needs, and dreams, the same as you. I have lived away so long, I do not expect to have a close relationship with either of you, but I am not to be feared or pitied." She let go of Lorna, walked around the desk, behind the settee, and pulled the bell pull. "I do remember some things around here."

The girls stood a bit dumfounded. Obviously, Lorna and Jean were surprised at their sister's words and actions. Brianna appeared both angry and astonished, the latter undoubtedly from finally confronting this issue.

Hamilton entered the room. "Yes?"

"Please ask Miss Young to come to the study." Brianna's words were short and clipped. "I am in need of her assistance."

"Right away." Hamilton left.

None of the staff was equipped to help Brianna. Indeed, their parents had been mistaken not to employ a person to assist her. Not even when she was a young girl.

Stilted silence hung heavy in the air.

Minutes later, Miss Young arrived at the door in the same lilac gown she'd worn on their trip, having freshened her hair. "May I be of assistance?" she offered.

Brie nodded. "I wish to freshen up."

Miss Young looked at Silas as she neared Brianna. He gave her an unhelpful shrug. Her eyes widened the slightest bit, yet she kept her face impassive. She reached Brianna, turned toward the door, and placed Brie's hand on her arm. "This way, dear."

What a gentle spirit the woman had. He'd witnessed it on their trip.

Brianna tugged Miss Young to a stop at the door and spun around. "Lorna, Jean, how many seasons have you had?"

"Three," Jean said.

"For three seasons you traveled to London and never once visited me?"

Silas folded his arms over his chest. He refused to get involved in his sisters' disagreements. He'd already interfered when Brianna lost her temper. It was not his place to make peace between his siblings.

Lorna frowned. "Papa didn't think it wise."

"Did he give any reasons why?"

"He only said you would be jealous and didn't want to upset you."

"Every season I expected you to at least call on me at Coleman's."

Jean stood. "I believe Papa's intentions were good."

"And what of your intentions? We are no longer children. Did either of you ever think to visit me?"

Lorna let out a heavy sigh. "We might turn that question back on you, Brianna. You stopped visiting Ipswich four years ago."

"True. I did not belong here."

"Perhaps we did not belong at Coleman's."

"Touché." Brie turned, grasped Miss Young's arm, and they left the room.

"Someone should get that bee out of her arse." Jean walked to the side table and poured herself a glass of brandy.

"Maybe Papa was wrong and we should have visited her." Lorna took Jean's glass and sipped.

These two sisters were close, like sisters should be, like twins. But they were not twins, they were triplets. He was unsure if Lorna and Jean would ever simply be friends with Brianna.

He glanced at one for a second, then the other. "Please, try to make her comfortable while she is with us."

"Of course we will," Jean pledged.

"Do you think we will not?" Lorna glared at him.

"Oh, no. Do not bring me into this. This is between you three. I'm loved by all of you and plan to keep it that way."

"We do love you." Jean smiled. "I must inform the staff Brianna brought a guest."

"Is she really a guest?" Lorna asked.

Silas looked at her pointedly.

"We have seen Miss Young before. We know she…" Lorna appeared uncomfortable and uncertain what to say.

"Has an association with Sir Roderick," Jean finished for her.

"Gossip does not become either of you," Silas admonished.

"It is hardly gossip if it is the truth," Jean defended.

"It is unfavorable toward Miss Young, and I won't have it mentioned again. Her association with Sir Roderick is over. As I wrote to you, she has been Brianna's companion since I last left London. In that time, Brianna and Miss Young have become good friends, and we will treat her as such. Please have the room across the hall from Brianna's readied for her."

"I will see to it." Jean hurried from the room.

Father's letters stared at him from the desk. He needed to read the bloody things.

Lorna set her empty glass on the side table. "How are you, Silas?"

"Weary. I only docked yesterday and have been traveling the whole of this day."

"Your voyage was successful?"

He thought of the freed slaves and rescued English children. "Extremely. Tell me, Lorna, how do you fare?"

"I am tired of the country. I believe I would much prefer to live in London. Papa claimed proper young ladies must retire to the country and live quiet lives." She scowled. "Why did he not just say boring, uneventful lives?"

Silas held back a laugh. Clearly his sisters were getting to an age where they felt free to air their complaints.

"Jean and I should have husbands by now."

"It's not for lack of suitors." Silas had been in Town for a few weeks during both their first and second seasons and witnessed the flock of young bucks around his sisters. "How many proposals have you received?"

"Four. Jean's had six. Each time Papa refused the betrothal and insisted we wait."

"Did he explain why?"

She shook her head.

Damn his father. He'd made some deal with the devil and his daughters would pay the price.

Well, not if Silas had anything to say about it.

~

Learn more about Tess at her books at tessstjohn.com.

Check Out the New Releases by Màiri Norris!

Available Now:

Rose of Hope - Ballads of the Roses, Book 1

"And did you ever daydream of a knight who would steal away your heart?"

Fallard blinked at his own question, startled all over again that he would think such, much less speak it. He was no poet, nor was sentiment high in his view of life. Yet, his rose was inspiration for many new thoughts and frivolous ideas such as the more romance-minded of his men betimes espoused around the fires at night. Never had he indulged in fatuous fantasies, nor could he think why 'twas happening now.

He was not unaware females enjoyed such nonsense. 'Twas rather he had never met one he deemed worth the effort of wooing. 'Twas far more convenient to find a willing wench and when both of them were satisfied, kiss her farewell and be on his way. But with Ysane, he would promise aught to gain from her a smile.

"'Tis possible knights might have figured in my dreams, now and anon." Ysane blushed crimson and ducked her head. "But if they did, none compared with…reality."

My rose deems me of more value than her dream knights!

He suddenly felt taller than the hills in the far distance, as mighty and invincible as the warrior-gods of the ancient lays. 'Twas too bad there were no more dragons, for he would slay them all with a single thrust of his sword, impervious to their fire, and lay their heads before her feet. 'Twas all he could do not to kiss her until she surrendered to him, body, mind and heart.

Ah, I do want her love, fool that I am!

She drew a sharp breath as if she sensed the change in him. "We are to be wed on the day after the morrow." She sounded winded, as if she had run some distance. Her next words were spoken so quietly he barely heard them above the falls. "Would you think it shameless, my brave knight, or too brazen of me did I ask for but one kiss?"

His heart slammed in his chest. He shut his eyes, fearing she might flee in terror. He knew raw passion blazed within his look.

She placed her palm against his chest. "You are so warm, and your heart thunders. It calls to me."

He needed no more encouragement. He swooped, and she flowed into his embrace. In that moment, he knew himself for what he was, a cynical warrior with hard, unrefined edges, and he saw her as his wounded, hurting lady. But he vowed, despite his ignorance, to do his best to care for her.

Lost with her in the magic, he wandered for timeless ages—or mayhap, 'twas only moments—in a world of shared glory.

Amazon

http://www.amazon.com/Rose-Hope-Ballads-The-Roses-ebook/dp/B00JG8LVJ6/ref=sr_1_1?ie=UTF8&qid=1401442329&sr=8-

1&keywords=mairi+norris+rose+of+hope

Barnes & Noble

http://www.barnesandnoble.com/w/rose-of-hope-mairi-norris/1119076059?ean=9781497526099

Coming in Autumn, 2014:

Viking Sword - A Fall of Yellow Fire

Kingdom of Wessex, southern England, 882.

Golden-haired Saxon, Lissa of Yriclea, is the sole survivor of a brutal attack against her village. Taken as thrall by a *vikingr* with the disconcerting ability to slip past all the defenses of her heart, she must bear the loss of home, friends and freedom while coping with the deprivations of travel across England in the company of the powerful Viking she both fears, and cannot resist.

A bizarre turn of events strands *vikingr* Brandr Ottarrson in hostile Saxon territory during a raid gone very wrong. Getting back home to the town of Ljotness on England's eastern coast will take all his courage, strength and wits. Complicating the journey is the lovely woman he desires, but cannot have, some troublesome, unexpected companions and a love-struck Saxon hearth companion relentless in his determination to rescue the lady he sees as his.

In this ancient time of darkness - and mystical beauty - when adversity, hardship and sudden death are the norm, a courageous woman and a single-minded warrior struggle to overcome perils, cultural taboo and the ambivalence of their own hearts to win a coveted prize: enduring love.

Another New Release by Beppie Harrison!

The Broken Heart

On an Irish hilltop, gazing out from the centuries-old stone mansion in which she'd been born, Lady Caroline Hawthorne looks past the brilliantly green lawns surrounding Kendall House. Beyond them all she can see are flower-bedecked and candle-lit ballrooms of London where she will glide among the dancers, as beautifully dressed as any. She will attend the glittering London theaters, to see and be seen; she will step out of a launch at the Vauxhall Pleasure Gardens and drink champagne, eat strawberries and dance, laugh, and fall in love.

It is 1811, the wondrous year when Caroline will at last leave provincial Ireland and make her way to the elegance and excitement of London—the center of her dreams for years past. Indeed, Caroline sails across the Irish Sea to make her debut in all the splendor of the Season, and it seems all of her dreams are coming true. She falls in love with the Earl of Linnell, the heir to his father, the Duke of Apthorp, and he is enchanted by her. They marry that summer, and happily ever after begins.

But happily ever after is transformed into aching heartbreak, and Caroline stumbles from the heights of romance to the emptiness of despair. Forced into starting again by the unexpected cruelty of events spinning out of her control, Caroline must find the path back to an endurable pattern of life, trying not to hope, learning to deal with life as it is. And, should love come again, will she dare open her heart again to meet it?

The Broken Heart

Suffolk, England – 1811

Chapter 1

She had never been this happy.

Lady Caroline Robinson, Countess of Linnel, pressed her heels lightly against her horse's side. Admittedly Caroline was no fearless rider, but the obliging mare her husband had insisted she ride today would have been more suitable for a child or a delicate old lady. The horse lacked a single competitive bone in her body. This was the third time Caroline had made an attempt to catch up to Henry, riding swiftly ahead. Her husband—how she liked the sound of those words.

How long had they been married? Not yet six months. His blond hair flew loose, just as it looked when she ran her fingers through it in their great bed. That would be at night, of course. This was the morning of a sunny autumn day, the only clouds white puffy ones that floated far away toward the horizon. The tall grasses and dry leaves added some fragrance to the air as the three of them rode across the field, Henry in front as always. Behind him came his brother, Lord Eustace, and a great deal to the rear, Caroline.

Henry was laughing back at her. "Caroline! My love!" he shouted over his shoulder. "You're such a slow coach!"

"It's this horse—stupid old Bluebell," she called to him. "She's the slowest in the stables, and you know it."

He was still laughing. "Better safe than

sorry. She must have a bit more speed than that, dear heart."

She shook her head at him, blushing a little. Her heart tightened with pleasure. It was so like Henry to share his endearments for her with anyone who happened to be around. He loved her as completely as she loved him and far more openly. But for him to talk about safety was not quite fair: his hair was blowing in the wind. What *had* he done with his riding hat? Caroline must remember to look for it when they took the horses back. His mother, the Duchess, would be displeased to find her son had been riding bare-headed.

Still well ahead, Henry turned his horse to wait for her. The great bay, Sylvester, was as eager to keep speeding forward as his master was, and clearly unhappy at being held back. Henry laughed, both at the horse and at Caroline. She gradually approached at the much slower pace that Bluebell maintained.

"Come *on*, Caroline," he called to her, shaking his head, his broad smile still on his face. "A sheep crosses the road faster than you do. Sylvester is losing whatever patience he had."

"So go on!" Caroline waved her hand. "I'll catch up."

He hesitated, but only for a moment and then, Eustace now close behind him, raced off toward the distant end of the meadow, marked by a stone wall. Caroline settled back in her saddle, no longer trying to match his pace. Bluebell was clearly bumping along as fast as she intended to move.

They trundled along, Caroline enjoying the lovely morning and the delightful picture the two men ahead of her made, almost like a portrait of horsemen at play. They were side by side until abruptly Henry veered off to the right, toward the closer wall running down the edge of the field.

"I'll bet I can take this one!" Henry's voice floated back to her.

Eustace yelled something, just as the horse and rider lifted up in the air and over the wall, graceful in their unity. Caroline looked to see them land on the other side, but instead of sight there was a hideous sound. It was wild as a shriek, horse and man blended together, until the sound cut off as abruptly as it had started.

Eustace was still shouting as Caroline vaguely realized he had been doing all along. "My God!" His words drifted back to her on the wind. "The new ditch! Great God, he must have forgotten the new ditch!"

Unbelievably, she saw Eustace jerk his own horse to a halt and slide out of his saddle, running to the wall and climbing awkwardly over it.

Caroline dug her heels into Bluebell's side—surely the stupid horse could go faster if she had to—but instead of bending over the horse's back to encourage more speed, Caroline could no more stop staring ahead in horror than she could stop breathing.

Panting, more accurately. It seemed forever—the seconds inflated themselves to minutes—until she was close enough to pull Bluebell to a stop, just as Eustace came back in sight over the wall. Before Bluebell had stopped enough for Caroline to get down to the ground unaided, Eustace had run to her, grabbing at the reins.

"We have to get help," he said, his hands around her waist as he pulled her out of her saddle and down to the ground. He seized one of her hands and dragged her to his own horse.

"What happened? Where's Henry?" Caroline demanded, trying to make her feet keep up with Eustace's pace.

"We have to get back," Eustace insisted. They had reached his horse; he almost threw Caroline up on the horse's back, and scrambled into the saddle behind her, wrapping one arm around her. They were in motion almost instantly, Eustace leaning forward, almost pressing her down under him.

She tried to wriggle herself free, grabbing at the long skirt of her riding habit lest it blow loose and frighten the horse. "What happened? Is Henry all right?" she demanded, repeating it over and over when Eustace said nothing but rode like a madman.

How long had to taken them to reach the meadow? The world whirled around Caroline. She needed to get back there, now! Where was Henry? Had she heard that sound or imagined it? And most of all, why was she being carried away from him as rapidly as the horse would go?

"Where's Henry?" she shrieked again. She grabbed at Eustace blindly. "I want to go back!" she wailed. "Take me back to Henry!"

Eustace didn't answer. His gaze was fixed,

straight ahead, past her.

"Eustace!" Her hands clutched at his riding habit and he pushed them aside.

"Help," he ground out. "We must get help."

She looked at his face, and realized suddenly that his lips were trembling and his skin was bleached of color. What did all this mean? Was this real or some horrible nightmare?

Where was Henry?

"Almost home," Eustace muttered.

When was the nightmare to end?

Somewhere along the way Caroline realized tears had started, rolling down her cheeks. What good were tears? A stupid woman's weakness. If she were not a woman she could have challenged Eustace, pulled away from him to get to the wall, and see for herself what had happened. But she was a woman, and when a man took command, she crumbled into obedience. Eustace had been free to climb over the wall to look, and he was only Henry's brother. She was Henry's wife!

Now the tears came so thickly she could not see properly. Eustace, when she glanced back at him, was only a blur. Impatiently she scrubbed her hand across her face, but her leather gloves could not mop up the wetness. They simply spread it across her cheeks.

How far from the house had they been? Time and distance lost all meaning. Only gradually through the blur could she make out the bulky shape that must be Apthorp Manor. Oddly misnamed, it was old and more like a castle, added on to over the centuries and now spread over the landscape like a lazy cat.

Apthorp Manor. The house that Henry would inherit when he became duke. Like a sabre knife the memory of her arrival pierced through her.

"It's peculiar, but it's home," Henry had said, more proud than he would allow himself to show.

Caroline had stared at the odd-shaped roofs and walls jutting into one another and wings flung off in peculiar directions and wondered how anybody could make such a miscellaneous structure into a home. How she would manage it.

The sudden shock of pain swept through her. No. This was not happening. How could it be? She could not be riding back to Apthorp Manor alone with Eustace. Henry! Where was Henry?

As soon as they came close to the drive, Eustace pulled his horse to a halt and more or less shoved Caroline down to the ground.

"Go to the house! Tell my mother!"

"Tell her what?" Caroline shouted back, clutching at her trailing habit.

Eustace was already riding away toward the stables, shouting. Men came running, and Eustace ordered them—what did he say? Why could he not speak louder? The men scrambled back into the stables again, almost tumbling over each other, and before it seemed possible they returned, each of them mounted. Riding like mad men, they rushed off, dodging around her, standing as she was in the middle of the drive. Eustace headed off with them.

"Eustace!" Caroline shrieked at him as he sped past her.

"Tell the Duchess!" He yelled it over his shoulder, and then he was gone.

Tell the Duchess what? What she knew of her own knowledge? Nothing. What she was afraid of? Or was all this still part of her nightmare? Why could she not wake up?

Caroline twisted around, watching Eustace's back as he rode wildly, catching up the grooms and flying past them. The thunder of their hooves drowned out all other sound at first, and then it was quiet except for the chirp of birds as they raced out of hearing.

Caroline stood in the drive, left alone. She turned her attention to the problem of walking as normally as possible to the house. Her shaky legs were forced to support her, and she kept her eyes looking straight ahead and her back rigidly erect. Her tears had stopped, but doubtless her face was still smeared. She did not touch it to find out.

Against all reason the sun was still shining. She could feel the faint warmth on her back as she paused to take a deep breath. The air still smelled of autumn. She closed her eyes for a moment. When she opened them she was still there in the drive. Still alone.

She walked up the steps to the imposing front door.

~~~